The animals made their way quickly toward the gathered settlement. They had to be warned to look away from the winged monster, or they would be destroyed. The hovering figure of the flying beast dipped once, spiraled away upward for a moment, then hurled itself straight toward them, great talons bared, drooling jaws opened on the terrible, dull yellow teeth.

Just as Borim raised himself to call out a warning to the others, the beast struck with a suddenness and fury that scattered trees and filled the air with harsh screams and the cries of the dying or wounded.

Borim did not remember doing it, but all at once the Horn of Bruinthor was at his lips, and the ancient instrument called out in a terrible voice, and the wind died away, followed by a shrieking sound of mountains tearing. Then the great war cry of his father's house flooded the wood. . . .

Books by
NIEL HANCOCK

THE CIRCLE OF LIGHT SERIES

THE WILDERNESS OF FOUR SERIES

Published by
WARNER BOOKS

The Wilderness of Four—1

Across
The Far Mountain

by Niel Hancock

WARNER BOOKS

A Warner Communications Company

In Viet Nam 1967–68, there were good compadres in Company "C," 716th MP Battalion, 18th MP Brigade. This book is for all of them, especially Sergeant Major Fredrick J. Shunk, Artie Newingham, Ivan Holmesly, Danny LaSeur, and Carey Anderson, who were disappeared in and by the war.

Adios, Mai Lyn.

God rest.

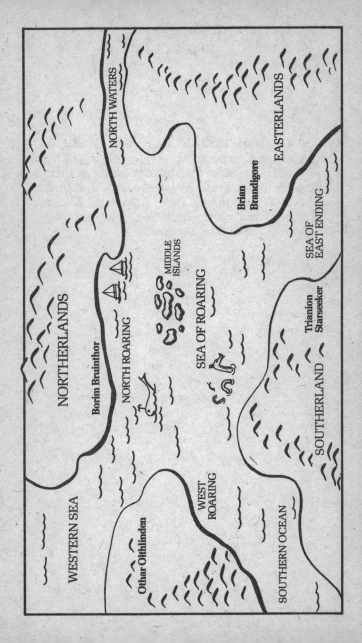

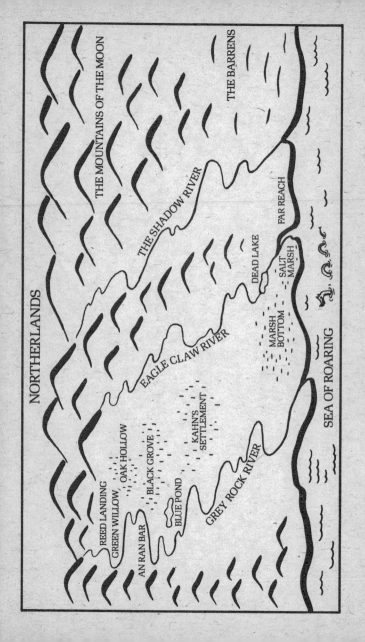

The Prelude

In the deep silence of the snowy passes of the great Wilderness of Four, there moved abroad the beginnings of the hordes of the Dark One, the sister of the Lady Lorini of Windameir. Throughout the vast regions of the Lower Meadows her shadow began to be felt, blocking out the light and life of those places, and striking an icy splinter of fear into the hearts of those who yet dwelled on Atlanton.

And as the Darkness began, so began the call to arms for all those who felt the Flame of Windameir in their hearts. In a simple cave in a winter wood, there was born to the bear Alena the cub that would one day become the Guardian of the Light called Borim Bruinthor.

These tales take place in the years shortly after the Golden Age, and are ancient stories that occur many lifetimes before the beginning of Circle of Light.

THE DEEP WOOD

The Cub Borim

In his youth, the stout cub known as Borim hunted the deep wood, and ran beside his sow, the bear Alena, who had lived longer than twenty turnings of the seasons, and had borne sixteen stout cubs before Borim.

The many brothers and sisters were flung far and wide throughout the wood, and they would sometimes cross the path of Borim and his sow, and when they did, it was a long evening of visits and exchanging of news, of one part of the forest or another, of the fishing or hunting, or of a particular good area to find berries.

Borim, being the youngest, was always indulged in romps and frolics, and his many brothers and sisters were always especially kind to him, and made sure he had the biggest grubs, or freshest berries, or that he was having a good time with one game or other. Sometimes it was the bear seriousness of stalk and find, or perhaps the sillier up-tails he loved to play, where you ran as fast as you were able, then ducked your muzzle between your forepaws and turned a long, rolling somersault on the edge of a grass-heavy meadow, letting yourself roll on forever in the warm sun, smelling the fresh spring earth, until at last you stopped at the bottom of the gentle rise to catch your breath and start the game anew. This was Borim's favorite game, and he loved to play it with as many as could get on the slope at the same time.

In the winter, in the gleaming white snow that creaked beneath his paws, he liked it better still, and he loved the soft smell of the white flakes, and to watch their dust falling gently off his mother's back as she loped along ahead of him, on her way to their winter cave, warm and snug, where he would nap most of the cold season away. It was hard to find anyone to play with in the winter, and he was told that he must stay in until the spring came and warmed the earth again, but Borim found it hard to stay quiet all that time, and he would often creep out of the cave on snow-frozen nights and watch the moon as she gleamed on the starched white blanket, shining on as far away as he could see, until the edges of the wood changed forms, and there began what his mother told him was the upper valley. Beyond were the mountains, and he could never get more out of her than that.

Bern, the next oldest of his brothers, said the Mountains of the Moon was where their father, Dralin, lived, a great shaggy brown giant who never came below the snow line, except to make his yearly visits to his mate Alena. No one knew much to tell of Dralin, except that he stood as tall as an oak sapling, and had lived to see so many seasons turning that there was no one left alive older than he was. Bern said their father's great age was because he lived in the mountains, and time could not easily climb that high.

Borim tried to question his mother about Dralin, but the grizzled old sow would only grunt and cuff him, and say that he didn't need to know more than he was a second Dralin, in looks and size.

"If that's anything to please him, I'll be surprised," she snorted. "I just hope you prove to have a bit more common sense than that oak head."

"Why?" asked Borim, always hungry for any knowledge of his absent father.

"He's never been one to follow reason," she went on. "Always curious about things that are none of his business, and always trying to see things he has no business seeing."

Borim remembered that Bern told him once that his father had actually seen the sea!

"But what's wrong with that?" persisted Borim.

"Wrong? Nothing wrong with that if you're a fish, or some animal that lives by the sea. But a bear?"

She snorted so disdainfully that Borim dared not question her further.

Later he would ask Bern, who didn't know.

"I don't know. I guess we're supposed to live right where we are."

"But he lives on the mountain," insisted Borim. "And *he's* a bear."

Bern shook his head.

"If you keep this up you're going to displease Mother, and you know how she is when she's upset."

Borim didn't have any further chance to question his brother that year, for the summer had drifted into fall, and the wind had a distinct edge to it, and all the other members of his family had begun looking to their winter quarters, laying in pine branches to soften their beds and sweeten their sleep. As the cold weather drew on, Borim realized he wasn't in the least sleepy, and that he certainly didn't want to waste his time lying around the woods all season long, not when he had so many unanswered questions spinning around in his head.

His mother constantly scolded him, and warned him repeatedly about laying in a proper store of bedding, but he didn't seem to hear, and went on long, rambling walks by himself, feeling the chill in the bright sun coat that the day wore, and looking for someone to talk to that might know what it was like in the mountains, or what it was like to stay up all winter long.

He might even find someone who knew of his father.

Borim didn't think anything more about it than that, but somewhere deep inside him, he'd already made his plans, unknown even to himself. There was a longing inside him that began pulling him from the comfort and warmth of his mother's side to the mysterious heights of the mountains. He could find no words to explain it, so in the end, just as his mother was preparing to seal off the cave against the first snows, Borim made his decision, and instead of returning from his long rambles as was his habit, he simply disappeared from that part of the woods, determined in his heart to find his father.

He felt saddened at leaving his mother, but then remembered that she was already making plans for him to have his own cave next winter. And too, he knew that he was merely

13

making a winter outing, and that he would see his mother and brothers and sisters again as soon as the spring came, and they were all abroad again.

Borim little realized that the journey he was now beginning would last for the rest of his life, and carry him far beyond his old horizons, and family, and friends.

A great white cloud rolled and turned on the mountain as Borim began his trek through the familiar wood, and as the afternoon wore on, it looked as if golden giants had crowned the clouds with a soft, shimmering light. A distant rumbling was heard, although he could not make out from where, and he quickly passed it from his mind, thinking perhaps it was merely another snowslide somewhere in those strange mountains, or a waterfall almost clogged with winter ice.

Borim had begun climbing in earnest as the pale sun started to sink, and weary of the long steady pace, he lay down for a quick nap, now beyond his own hearth, and alone in the wide forest. He thought of his mother for a moment, but grew so sleepy his eyes closed, and before he knew what had happened, he was dreaming of high mountain peaks, crowned with golden halos, and there was the great giant of a bear, beckoning him on with a huge paw, raised and motioning him toward the setting sun.

A Long Climb

Higher and higher Borim found himself climbing, until at last when he turned, he could see the faint edges of the forest spread out behind him, the green curve of the wood arching away into the distance, until it was finally covered in a gray cloak of clouds that hung dimly on the horizon. Looking ahead, he saw above him the stark white of the snow on the peaks, and on the lower slopes there were wind-beaten trees, leafless and dead, stuck up through the hard ground like bony fingers of frost.

Borim had slept little, and his hunger grew as he went on, but still the burning light inside him drew him on farther, yet higher, into those hostile and forbidding mountains where he knew his father to be. He had no fear of finding him, for every time he shut his eyes, he saw the figure of the great bear motioning him onward.

To keep his mind from his hunger and weariness, Borim

14

thought of his life as a cub, safe in the valley far below, learning to fish the cold streams beside his mother, or which berries to pick in the dense thickets of the berry patches in the late spring or early summer.

As he loped slowly on, there was a sound he wasn't able to place, and it grew louder by the moment. Borim searched the barren wastes above him, trying to catch sight of where the noise could be coming from, but there was nothing but the wind and the jagged outcroppings of huge gray boulders that reared their heads above the mountainside in such dangerous fashion it seemed to Borim that they would most surely topple and fall.

Some part of him shuddered, and he slowly began to recognize the sound as an avalanche or great walls of earth and snow hurtling down the sides of a mountain not too far from where he stood. He nervously tried to climb to one side of the bigger rockfalls that lay above him, and kept turning his head first left, then right, trying to pick out the less dangerous way through the boulder fields.

He had not gone far before a huge cloud caught his eye, and he saw the great cloak of it hung suspended over what looked to him to be the entire mountainside in the valley to his left, sliding down across the face of a cliff, and completely covering the edge of the forest, snapping huge trees as if they were tiny branches caught in the swift current of a flooding river.

Borim had no time to stop for long, and he could feel the quaking and trembling of the earth, and hurried on, hoping to go beyond the slides and safely on to the top of the high pass before dark. It was there he might find some clue as to his sire's whereabouts, and perhaps find a cave to nap safely to get over the cold numbness that was beginning to chill him as he left the warm valley and climbed ever higher toward the snow kingdoms.

He took a long detour to avoid a wall of rocks that tilted their great heads down to him, and made instead toward what looked to be a huge hole, its dark mouth plainly outlined against the bleached gray rocks. Great walls of stone and earth were now moving all about Borim, and he began to see that his one hope for safety on this treacherous slope was to reach the cavern mouth and perhaps take shelter there.

A gigantic granite boulder came rumbling toward him from higher up, bounding and leaping as if it were alive, followed by a whole train of smaller rocks, rolling and tumbling wildly behind. Borim quickly dodged aside, and put his paws to his head, and crept as low as he could behind a small outcropping, hoping the disturbance wouldn't loosen his hiding place as well, to tumble them all back into the distant, still green slash of the valley.

His mother had showed him gashes in the woods, filled with gray boulders just like these.

"These came from where your father dwells," she told him, as he carefully studied the rocks. "And they are likely all I'll ever get from him. Whenever he is restless, and wants me to come to him, he sends these huge stones down to tell me."

Borim, being only a small cub at the time, had believed Alena, and only when he repeated it to Bern did he get the truth.

"Alena is teasing you," said Bern. "There is no way a bear could toss these about as if they were no more than pebbles."

"Our father could," insisted Borim stubbornly. "And Alena says so."

Bern laughed.

"Perhaps he lives there on the tops of those mountains, but if he does, he must be hungry a lot, and I guess if you got bored enough of looking at all that snow, you might find yourself capable of throwing around a few stones like this."

"I shall go there someday and ask him," said Borim.

"Be careful, small brother, that you don't wander too near his playground, if he tosses such things as this around."

All the others had laughed as well when he told them of his plans.

Alena only cuffed him and told him to forget the bear who was his father.

"He is no good to be following after. That would make him very angry. He has many important things to attend to there, and he has no time for sassy cubs."

Borim could remember the feelings of frustration and anger when they laughed at him, and the desire only grew stronger within him.

Of all the brothers and sisters, Bern had come the closest to going with him.

"You sound as if you really mean to do this," he'd said, only a few days before Borim had gone.

"I do. I've waited long enough for him to come down to the valley. There will soon be no more time before winter falls."

"And if we find him? What do we do then? He'll most likely only chase us away."

That thought had occurred to Borim, and although it was a possibility, he put it out of his mind.

"He won't. And even if he did, we would just go on."

"On! To where?"

"To see what there is to the other side," replied Borim sternly.

He wasn't entirely sure there was an "other side," but then he knew he would never know unless he looked for himself.

That moment Borim finally reached the safety of the cavern he had seen and hoped to reach, and not a second too soon, for the entire upper slope above him gave way, and came rumbling its way down toward him, pushing great geysers of huge rocks before it, like a dark white-edged wave rising upward to meet the waiting shore. Borim hastened into the cavern, and barely had time to crawl to safety before a louder noise than even the mountain falling rang out, and he suddenly found himself staring around into pitch blackness, and outside, or where outside had been but a moment before, there was only an unbroken silence that filled his heart with dread.

Avalanche

Slowly the fear left Borim, to be replaced with the realization that he would never be able to dig his way free of the tons of earth and snow that covered the cave opening, but it was not the utter defeat he felt at being trapped this way, as it was the knowledge that he still could see the great bear inside his head beckoning him every time he shut his eyes.

Borim did so again, and there before him was the figure of his father, moving to and fro on a wide, windswept plain, the paw outstretched and motioning him onward. Borim could stand it no longer, and his eyes shot open. There, where there had been utter darkness and silence before, was a thin blade of light, shining brightly far ahead. It seemed to beam directly at him, and a faraway sound of high reed pipes began to make itself heard, until Borim found himself swaying gently to the faint melody.

Without questioning, he raised himself and started to follow the light ray, threading his way through the unknown cave as if he knew every rock and cranny, and he didn't hesitate or slow his pace until he was far underground. He began to hear the very heart of the earth beating, and the noisy tinkle of water splashing, and it seemed to him the light had gone from a narrow beam to a wider, glowing halo.

Stopping to rest for a few moments, he became aware of his exhaustion, and it dawned on him he had been going ever downward, for a period of time he could not measure. He had just kept his eyes filled with the glittering jewel of the light, and listened to the music, and marched in time to it, one foot before the other, until all time merged with the slow, steady pumping of his heart, and on and on he went, no thought in his mind but to seek the source of the light, now brilliant white, now golden blue. It changed with the music, and seemed to float as a cloud might, softly expanding, then contracting.

As he rested, Borim tried to make out his surroundings by the pale glow, but could see nothing that would give him any hint as to what sort of place he was in, or where it might be leading him. Squinting, he could barely discern shadows all around him, but they turned out to be huge rocks that stood out from the smooth walls of the cavern, and in these rocks, brilliant eyes reflected the other light, until it looked as if the cave were filled with thousands of small stars.

The music and the sound of water falling had grown louder, and as tired as he was, Borim drew himself up to go on, his curiosity overcoming his fatigue. He moved on a little more slowly now, and watched the light grow larger still, and listened as the music took on the sound of other instruments.

Other lights began to blaze out of the darkness alongside the first, and he hesitated a moment, the old fear coming back. He had never been taught any of these things, and Alena had never told him of their existence. Borim knew the Law, and how to hunt for food, and where to find shelter, and all the everyday things a bear must know to live, but these were all far beyond his scope, although he secretly felt that they must have something to do with his father, and therefore he had nothing to fear.

He breathed deeply, and screwed his courage up, and went forward again, alert and wary, but also confident that any moment he would understand the meaning of all the strange things that had been happening to him.

As the light brightened into a dazzling sun, and the music grew louder still, Borim stumbled forward into a blazing whirlwind of sound and light that threatened to sweep him away. Then it was gone, just as quickly as it had come, and he

18

found himself blinking around in stunned amazement, for what he saw were trees, and a stream, and high mountains above, and blue sky with fleecy white clouds higher still. And although he knew it was almost the time of the end of leaf fall, the wind carried no chill message, and the trees were all of a deep, forest green.

Spinning around, trying to see the cave mouth he had come from, he was met with a solid wall of sheer granite that towered above bim, blending at last with the pale blue of the sky. Borim ran a paw over the surface of the rock, and moved this way and that, sure that he must be mistaken. Search as he might, there was no passageway through the rock, and he finally tired of the nagging question of where it could have gotten to, and simply sat down heavily for a quick nap.

Before he could settle himself down, however, he kept getting those feelings along the nape of his neck that he was being watched, so one eye sprang open, and he pulled himself alert. There was nothing to be seen, but he still had the feeling that stood his hackles on end, so he got up wearily, and plodded on toward the forest, in hopes of finding a nice spot of shade where he might lie down comfortably in a pine-scented bed to have a proper nap away from prying eyes.

Borim thought that since he was in strange country, he had come into some other animal's territory. Since he had no intention of staying any longer than was necessary for a nap, Borim did not worry himself overly much, and knew that any other animal would see he meant no challenge, and let him pass on in peace.

Bear lore was not so much different from any other lore, and often was much the same in the basic lessons. Of course, Alena had taught him well all those things that defined a bear from a badger or mole, or muskrat, or elk, or owl, and it was important to know exactly what you were, or you wouldn't be able to understand anything else.

Borim lumbered along wearily until he reached the fast-flowing stream, which was clear and cool, and felt wonderful on his paws as he stood hock deep to get a long drink. As he lifted his muzzle, he caught a brief glimpse of a figure reflected in the water, but it disappeared quickly, and he could sense nothing when he lifted his snout to test the air.

He finished his drink, and decided to explore a bit farther before his nap, just in case he might find this stranger and be able to find out where he had gotten to, and what sort of animals lived in the surrounding forest.

19

As hard as he tried, Borim could not pick up any spoor from the meadow that bordered the stream, nor could he find anything out of place that would have marked a trail an animal would have used going to or from the water. Not finding any trace at all of the stranger started to upset Borim somewhat, and an edge of uneasiness began to creep over him, bordering on alertness to any sudden danger that might appear.

He worked one side of the stream for quite some distance, and still finding nothing, decided it had merely been some mistake, and that after all the brilliant light after he came out of the tunnel, his eyes had merely seen something that was not there. And the stream had been fast and deep, and it could well have been a distortion of his own image he had seen.

Borim went farther up into the trees, looking for just the right place to rest, yet still alert for any unusual noise or smell, and found a perfect spot for a nap in the hollow of a giant oak.

Curling upon himself, and settling down, he listened for a while, eyes closed, nose testing every breath of wind, and then the visions began again, only this time the figure of the great bear was no longer beckoning, but stood fully upright, in what seemed to Borim to be a dense green wood exactly like the one he now lay in. He went on watching the bear, trying to discover the meaning of it, if there was one, and did not realize he had opened his eyes, or how long he had been staring into the deep brown eyes of the great animal before him.

The Strangers Speak

Without speaking, the huge bear turned abruptly and set off at a rapid trot, and had almost disappeared before Borim realized he was meant to follow. He hurriedly rose and loped after, his surprise and fear gone, and his desire to question overwhelming his shock at seeing another animal in the alien wood, especially after he had neither smelled nor seen any sign of living beings in the forest, or in the small meadow by the stream.

The stranger halted far ahead, and now waited for Borim to draw up to where he stood, but went on before Borim caught up. On and on they went, mile after mile, and Borim began to notice a subtle change in the countryside. The trees of the forest had grown thicker and taller, and the sun filtered more weakly through the high branches, and the stream, which had been very broad where he had gotten his drink earlier, was now no wider than the width of his own sturdy body. Borim was no longer able to see the higher mountains because of the dense wood, but he knew they must be traveling in the direction he had seen them, for the stream was smaller, which meant it was getting nearer to its source.

The stranger had not spoken a word, nor allowed Borim to question him, but continued at a terrible pace, ever away in the direction of the stream, into the deepening shadows of the innermost wood. Borim felt the absence of light, and knew the sun must have set, for the gloom grew greater in the stillness of the forest, and he listened with all his attention, but could pick up no sound from any other living thing, except the bear that lumbered on before him.

Growing weary and thirsty, Borim wished he could stop for a rest and a drink, but the dim figure ahead raced on, although he had slowed somewhat so Borim could keep him in sight in the fading dusk. At last, after Borim was sure he could go no farther, the stranger halted, and motioned Borim next to him. There was the stream, fast and deep, and he drank his fill, and slumped wearily to the ground beneath a giant oak tree, whose girth was more than twice the size of any tree Borim had ever seen.

He thought surely the bear must speak now, but the stranger merely nodded to Borim to sleep, and marched around to the other side of the tree, and fell to musing on something beyond the shadows of the woods.

Borim almost spoke, then felt that there was something in the presence of the other bear that would not allow it. And he even felt that if he made the slightest effort to question him, the stranger would leave him alone in this frightening wood, and Borim had no desire to be deserted here.

He had had no time to pay attention to the trails he had taken, and knew himself to be hopelessly lost without his silent guide, so he forced himself to remain silent, and to wait until such time as the other bear would see fit to explain things to him, or at least tell him where they were bound.

Borim's eyes grew heavy, and he kept slipping into a light, troubled slumber, only to jerk himself awake and stare uncertainly into the darkness where the other bear lay, and only after reassuring himself that the somewhat darker figure still sat there, would he allow himself another quick lapse into sleep.

Borim awakened in a patch of pale, silvery light that gleamed off the thin ribbon of water and turned the bark of the trees a ghostly gray, making the shadows more ominous, and creating the illusion that he had awakened at the bottom of some dark, quiet mountain lake. He turned his nose this way and that, and although he could not catch the scent of the other bear, he knew the shadow was still there, right where it had been. He couldn't remember how long he had slept, but knew it was now long past moonrise, and he somehow sensed it was very late, and that he had slept for a long time.

He was startled badly by a voice next to his ear, and he let out a small yelp of dismay.

"You are rested?"

Borim's ears rang with the noise of the voice, and for a moment he wasn't sure he would be able to reply, that he had remained silent so long he had lost the power of speech.

"Yes," he barely managed, and for the moment, was too disconcerted to remember to ask all the questions that had troubled him since their long ramble had begun.

Just as he screwed up his courage to ask the stranger where they were bound, and who he was, Borim was suddenly aware that the voice that had spoken to him wasn't coming from the same shadow that still remained in the darkness of the huge oak.

"Who are you?" blurted Borim, too upset to remember even his proper manners of identifying himself or his sires.

"A friend, Borim."

The voice came again from right next to his ear, and Borim turned to try to make out who it was that sat close beside him, yet gave no clue by either noise or smell. A light shone from two dark eyes, reflections of the moon through the trees, and Borim could see that the figure there was a bear, and an even larger bear than the stranger who had led him all this way into the deeper wood.

"We have been waiting for you for some time now. I see Alena has taken the usual time in weaning her cubs."

"When have you ever known her to do differently?" asked another voice, from beyond Borim's left side.

He whirled around, and there beside him on that flank sat another dim shadow figure, laughing gently.

"She is indeed most particular with her offspring, and well

22

she should be. Times are harder now, and not likely to change," said the first.

Borim stared wildly about, and found that there were a number of shadows all about now, some moving, some sitting, and he noticed for the first time that there was a small hubbub of voices going on, low and almost inaudible.

"Where am I?" Borim blustered, his feeling of confusion growing by the minute. "And who are you? How do you know my name, and that of my mother?"

"We know the name of your father, too, Borim, and those of your brothers and sisters, and the names you've been called in other lives as well. But no matter. To answer your first question, you are in the forest of An Ran Bar. My name is Frael, and my friends are Earling and Lan. There are others here too, but of no concern to you now."

As Frael introduced the other two bears, each in his turn stepped nearer Borim, and bowed low.

"But I've never seen you in the Lower Wood. And how did you get here? I came through a cave on the side of a hill, but it was blocked, and I couldn't get back."

"That was only the door through the mountain. It was closed to keep the others away."

"You mean you came that way, too?"

"Long ago, my little friend, so long ago we might sound ancient were we to tell you the seasons it has been since we left the Lower Wood and passed through that cavern you speak of."

"I don't understand," complained Borim. "And I'm hungry as well."

"We have something to take care of that, and a proper bed to ease your journey. Come with us."

Frael rose, and as he did so, a dozen or more bright yellow lights burst into flame, and the darkness which had hidden all the voices vanished, leaving Borim staring and blinking around in some dismay, until his eyes adjusted, and he was able to take in the scene which now unfolded itself to him.

Frael

Frael, who seemed to be the leader, stepped forward in the new light of the blazing lamps, which seemed to Borim to hang from the very air. Their light danced and flickered as if they might have been candles guttering, but the light was much too brilliant for that, and the very center of what would have been the flames was a silver globe, twinkling and turning, as though the bear had somehow captured a star from the heavens and enclosed it in a clear bubble of shimmering water.

Borim had trouble following all that Frael was saying, unable to take his eyes off the silver-gray giants, Earling, and Lan. Lan had been the bear he first met, and he had seemed overly huge then, but now he saw he was the smallest of the others, although of the same shaggy grayish coat, and his smaller size seemed to be because he was younger than the others, and therefore not grown into his paws yet, as the saying went. That phrase was Alena's, and she used it often about Bern, who although a season older than Borim, was smaller than even his sisters.

"He's just not grown into his paws yet," she would explain to any who might ask, and give Bern a good-natured reassuring cuff.

"But he's more clever than any of my others," she would quickly add. "He doesn't need great size to keep him safe."

And that had been true, or seemed so to Borim. Bern was the closest to him in age and size, and it was Bern who spent the most time with Borim, explaining things to him that his mother or the others had no time for. Bern would have been dwarfed by the strange creatures before him now, and even he, who had begun to show the prospects of being the largest of all Alena's cubs, was only barely able to stand even half so tall as Lan.

There was mention of his father, Dralin, and his ears perked up for a moment, but he had trouble keeping his attention from wandering, and he let his mind drift back to examining the small clearing where they stood, the amazing lights making a large circle around them, showing flashes of old bark-worn trees, taller than any Borim had ever seen, and grass so green it was almost black, and as soft as moss.

24

His paws crept back and forth in the coolness of that grass, and he started once more to lie down in it, to feel its goodness on his back.

"He will be here soon, Borim. We were expecting you, but not quite so soon. He has had to come all the way down from An Ran Bar."

"That is where you'll make your new home," went on Earling.

His muzzle was broader than either of the others, and fine streaks of deep russet red shot through the gray, and his huge paws were marked with distinctive rings of dark black fur.

"My new home?" shot Borin. "But I hadn't planned to come here to stay!"

The others exchanged glances.

"You have not listened to me, little brother," scolded Frael. "I have told you already that there is no chance for you to return to the place you came through. This is your new life here, now."

"But my father goes there. Alena says he comes every year."

"He does, in truth," agreed Earling. "But you have many things to learn, and lessons to complete before you will be able to do the things your father does."

"Then how long will I have to stay here?"

"There is no set time, Borim, as I have explained. It is like your mother, Alena, keeping you until she knew you would be able to move and live on your own. Only then did she decide to set you out upon your travels."

At the mention of his mother, Borim's heart contracted. He suddenly felt a great desire to be there in the warmth of the snug cave beside her, listening to her stories of the winter, or of other animals that he would meet in his forest world.

She had never said anything at all of these bears, or their huge size, or lamps that glowed out of the darkness like great fireflies, or of any of the strange places that Frael and Earling and Lan had spoken of. He was not even sure that Alena had been through with his lessons, as Frael had said.

"What if I am supposed to be with Alena still?" asked Borim quietly.

Frael laughed, a deep rumble growl.

"You would not be here, little brother, if you were still to be with your sow. There is no mistake."

25

"I came from near your old wood," added Lan. "I know this all seems a bit unsettling at first, but it will grow upon you."

"I doubt it," groaned Borim. "I thought I was just to come out to the mountains to see my father, and that I would be allowed to return home to my own wood."

Frael studied Borim silently for a long time, his dark eyes troubled.

"There is more in your life than that, little one. There are things, great things, that are for you."

He paused, and the frown was replaced by a gentle smile, which seemed awkward on his broad muzzle.

"But then it will be full of great things for us all. We shall be with you, as well."

That news was no great comfort to Borim, although he didn't say so. He would gladly have given over all of them to be once more with Bern.

"I wish my brother were here," he managed.

"Bern?" asked Frael, a painful look spreading across the handsome muzzle.

"Yes. Did I tell you his name?"

"No. I told you we knew everything of you and your sire and sow, as well as all your brothers and sisters."

Borim took no notice of the older bear's expression.

"Do you think he could come here, too?"

Earling spoke first, before Frael could answer.

"He quite possibly could, and there's no doubt you'll see each other again."

Lan, shuffling his paws, hurriedly added that they were sure to meet again, so that they could all have a nice time where they were now, and go on with the adventures at paw.

"What adventures?" asked Borim suspiciously.

"We have many ahead of us, little brother," said Frael. "We have your education to complete as well, and much to plan and prepare for."

"There will be great fun, once we get back to An Ran Bar. Your father has a great dwelling there, and there is always company, and new things to see or learn."

"An Ran Bar?" echoed Borim, trying to place in his mind what Alena had said about the strange-sounding place.

Or had it been Bern?

Or perhaps it had been Earling, or Lan, or Frael. So much had happened to him, and he felt so tired and hungry, that he was not sure exactly what had taken place, or even that he was not merely dreaming all this.

The strange lights gleamed brightly, and far above the towering trees, Borim could make out a splinter of a moon and bunches of stars that glimmered faintly, and there was the soft smell now of the grass he lay in, and a new wind. He still had not caught the scent of the other bears there, and that began to trouble him greatly.

"I can't smell you," he said simply, not knowing how else to put the question.

Frael laughed, a short barking noise.

"Of course! We have forgotten."

Suddenly the air was filled with the heavy, dark scent of all his kindred, of oak leaves, and roots under earth, and the rich smell of new spring, and old winter, and fine summers.

"How did you do that?" cried Borim.

"How, you shall learn later," replied Frael. "But we had been traveling without wishing our presence known. There are those who might like to know of our whereabouts and the names of those we see."

A smile played across Frael's muzzle, but it was grim, and confused Borim.

"Enemies?" he asked, lowering his voice.

Alena had only spoken to him of those that would harm him once, and in simple terms.

"There will be those who wish you ill," she had said, "and there may be those who may try to harm or slay you. It is the Law that that shall be. It is simply that, no more, no less. There are reasons for it."

But she never said more about it, or what the reasons might have been.

"I hear Dralin," cautioned Earling. "He's signaling us to be silent."

Borim tried with all his powers of concentration to hear anything other than the noises they made as they stood and talked, but could not. After a few more moments of utter silence, he thought he could barely detect what sounded like a night owl, calling out in its burring notes, twice, then three times, before falling into silence.

Without warning, the glimmering lights that had circled the clearing flared once, then went out, leaving them in darkness once more.

A Dangerous Meeting

The animals remained frozen where they were for what seemed hours to Borim, and all his tired muscles began to ache again. Some places hurt on his body that he had never been aware of before, and after another long wait, he was quite sure he had been turned to solid stone. Even the wind through the treetops had been silenced, or so it seemed to him, and he was not certain that it had resumed, until Frael spoke at his side, which frightened him badly, and he jumped, calling out.

"It's all right, Borim. The danger is past now. There were some of the Eastern Wood beasts which were stalking not far from here. But we have learned how to avoid confronting them when we wish to go unnoticed. You saw, or rather sensed, one of the tricks we have learned."

"You can't find something you can't smell," laughed Earling softly. "These things from the Eastern Woods have long forgotten the Law, and are not above slaying their own kind, if they are angry, or hungry."

"Who are they?" asked Borim, his voice barely above a whisper. "I've never heard of such animals."

Lan answered.

"They aren't animals, exactly. I guess they once were, but something has changed them."

"Some of them look just like you or me," explained Frael. "But somewhere inside, they have no respect for the Law, and they have fallen into the habit of eating their own kind."

"They'll eat anything they can catch," agreed Earling, shuddering.

"But is that not permissible?" asked Borim.

"Didn't Alena teach the History to you?" growled Frael.

"Well, I guess so," stammered Borim, although he could remember no such thing.

"Hurrumph!" went on the older bear. "I forget that there are few anymore who bother to teach their cubs the Law. Too much time to do it, they say, no need anymore. Things have changed."

Borim grew distinctly uncomfortable as he listened to Frael, who was becoming angrier as he spoke.

"Well, it can't be helped! We shall improve your education as we get the chance."

"He's only a cub yet," cautioned Earling gently, trying to calm the old bear.

Frael glowered, then softened.

"Of course. I have forgotten. And all this to-do doesn't improve my outlook. I've not quite been myself lately, since all the troubles started."

"What troubles?" shot Borim, more and more confused by all the strange bears were saying.

"You'll find all that out soon enough," replied Frael. "Your father will teach you all you need to know as quickly as we reach An Ran Bar safely. That's his permanent shelter and once we get there, between all of us, maybe we'll be able to teach you all the things you'll be needing to know."

Borim grew uneasy at the mention of more lessons, for those had been painful things, usually ending with cuffs from Alena, or being chased up a tree. He hoped with all his small heart that his father was a bit kinder in his lessons than his mother had been.

"Don't worry," Lan reassured him. "We'll have lots of fun. I just finished my own wardship there, and I'll be helping you with yours."

"Wardship?" asked Borim.

"It's merely a method of teaching young hole heads like yourself," replied Frael. "There would never be any progress made without some system."

Borim did not like the ring of Frael's voice.

Before he could ask his next question, the other animals grew still once more, and hushed him into silence with a quick motion of their paws. Far away, almost beyond his hearing, he heard a strange noise, shuffling and loud snorts, followed by a long, piercing cry of an animal mortally stricken.

"It's them!" growled Frael. "They have hunted here for the last time."

A dangerous battle fire glimmered grimly in the great bear's eyes, and he raised himself on his haunches and did the terrible war dance of the bear, unsheathing his claws and baring fangs that gleamed stark white in the darkness. Borim cowered and tried to make himself smaller, to escape the horrible vision of Frael.

Earling and Lan rose up and joined the dance with their

older friend, and before Borim could question them, or find out what had happened to anger them so, the three great animals were gone, so silently he had begun to question if he had ever really seen or talked to them at all. They had vanished on the dark wind, and he was alone in the clearing, heart hammering in his throat.

Borim, out of habit when there was danger about, crept into the shelter of a huge tree, and scrambled for the only haven his mother had taught him to use. As he swayed back and forth on the branches high above the forest floor, he listened intently for any hint of the whereabouts of his friends, or some clue as to the noises that had angered them. Borim wished with every fiber of his being that Bern were here now, or Alena. He strained to concentrate on the woods around him, and the wind, but these woods told him nothing, and the wind was a blank face that did not speak.

Time dragged on, and still the awful silence hung over the wood, and the vast emptiness of the trees began to terrify Borim. His thoughts grew more confused and frightening. What if Frael, and Lan, and Earling had been slain by the beasts they spoke of? What if they had even killed Dralin, his father? And now they would be coming for him, hanging in the tree like a ripe wild apple, ready to be plucked.

His eyes grew watery from trying to pierce the darkness, and his ears were beginning to hear all sorts of terrifying sounds. Yet the wind brought no message of anyone near.

Then Borim remembered that Frael and the others had somehow been able to make themselves invisible to the nose. A new wave of terror swept over Borim. He could be surrounded now by enemies, and not know, until they had attacked him.

Wild, tangled thoughts assailed him from all sides, and he greatly regretted his foolishness at having disobeyed Alena and come seeking his father. He would be there in her snug cave now if he had not been so headstrong, safe by her hearth, full of mulled tea, and settling down for a nap after his blueberry scones.

The wind caught its breath, leaving Borim swaying silently in his dark prison tree. A sound caught his ear, very faint at first, then it grew into recognition. Several animals were coming through the forest toward him, their walking careless and loud enough to say they were not afraid of anything the dark wood might hold.

Borim thought at first it might be his new friends returning, until he caught the sound of the guttural tongue. He could understand nothing these strange animals were saying, and worse, they growled with every other breath, and the noise they made as they came through the wood sounded as if they were huge.

Borim almost fell from his perch a moment later when the first of these strange beasts broke into the clearing, dragging behind it what appeared to be the remains of a half-eaten deer. The thing dropped the carcass and turned to the shadow wall between the trees. Soon another dark form appeared, and quickly crouched beside the slain victim. The two beasts fell on their grisly feast, jaws dripping, smacking, and drooling as they spoke.

Grating, harsh snorts and growls were all Borim could make out of the strange language, but he was suddenly aware of new movement below him, and before he could listen further to the gaunt beasts talking beneath his tree, three silver-gray shadows had erupted from the darkness, and before a single cry could escape the beasts, they had been slain where they sat, still gorging off the slaughtered deer.

It was over so quickly it took Borim a few more moments of terrified silence to realize that the figures below him were Earling, Frael, and Lan, and that they were calling to him to come down from his shelter.

"It's all right, little brother. There is no danger now," said Earling gently, the battle fire dying in his dark eyes.

His claws had been sheathed, and he spoke in the same quiet, reassuring voice he had used before.

Borim eased himself down, and gingerly made his way around the slain beasts to stand beside Frael, whose great muzzle was lowered and eyes were closed. When he opened them, he looked directly into Borim's frightened gaze, and reached a paw out to pat him.

"This is the worst of this business, Borim. This is the thing your father has been trying to battle since coming to these mountains long ago. It seems to be growing yet worse, and from the stories we hear beyond our borders, there are other troubles spreading, too."

"What are these things? What tribe do they come from?"

asked Borim, forcing himself to look at the still forms of the two dead beasts.

"They are the echoes of animals that have somehow gone wrong, Borim. They have begun to come from the lower Eastern Wood in great numbers these last years. Some say there is an evil there that makes them come this way. But none can say for sure. We only see what comes to us, and these are the beasts we see."

Borim studied the slain creatures carefully.

"Why, they still look almost like animals," he cried.

"Almost," agreed Lan. "I have seen others that are like nothing in animaldom. They had smooth bodies, with no fur, and walked about on two legs."

Borim had turned to Frael.

"Does my father know where they come from?"

"He has his own thoughts on that matter. Yet we do know that the lower Eastern Wood is where they grow. There may be other places."

"But why would they go bad there? What could make them turn against the Law?"

Frael shook his head.

"I don't know, Borim. There are reasons that perhaps we might not understand for a long time. Perhaps it is like a fever, or a sickness. Who knows?"

"We'd best get on to meet Dralin," said Earling, looking up at the failing moon.

"There may be more of these fellows out tonight," said Frael. "Take my paw, Borim. I'll see if I can't rid you of any spoor you might leave to guide any of their friends."

Borim grasped the bear's paw, and felt a quick tingling through his body.

"Now we should be able to go on unannounced."

The low, burring notes of an owl reached their ears, from far away to their right."

"He's waiting for us. We must go."

Borim took one last look at the slain beasts and shuddered, then hurried on to keep up with his new friends, who were disappearing into the dark shadows of the deeper wood before him.

He took a great breath, sighed, and told himself resolutely that at least he would finally get to meet the great bear Dralin, his father. He tried not to think too much on all the other disturbing news he had heard, or of the slaying of the beasts from below the Eastern borders. Whatever he had thought this outing would be, it was certainly not meeting his expectations, and rapidly falling into downright unpleasantness.

Another call from the night owl reached him, closer now, and Borim realized that his mouth was dry and his stomach tight, his heart drumming loudly in his ears.

He would soon be face to face with his father.

AN RAN BAR

A Long-Awaited Reunion

Whatever Borim had expected to happen when he met his father, he was disappointed.

In the hushed glade where the three bears stopped, Borim had waited impatiently, trying to discover one sound from another, his heart beating so rapidly he felt short of breath. All that Alena had ever told him of Dralin came back to him, and he tried to picture how he would look, and what he would say, and how he would behave. Borim had dreamed secretly that his father would take him between his two huge forepaws, and give him a strong hug, or perhaps praise him for being such a handsome cub.

Bern had laughed when he told him of that hope, and said that Dralin's hug was death, and that no living creature had ever had anything like praise from his lips.

"Dralin is the head of the clan, Borim. He has no time to do as others would perhaps like him to do. All is on his shoulders. Food and shelter and the welfare of all the tribes are laid at his feet, sooner or later. He is not a bear of his own decisions."

"But doesn't he like to have a good time, or games with his friends?" asked Borim.

"His friends are warrior chieftains. Their games decide whether or not the clans live in peace, with food to eat, and shelter for the cubs. If they are not successful, then it would be exile, and starvation for us all."

"Why would that be?"

"Because we live in times that are hard, little brother. There has been trouble for a long while now, and if it weren't for the strong alliance the clans have formed, bears would have been driven out of the woods long ago, and starved. There are those, you must know, who have been trying to take over the woods as their own. They have great numbers now, and they grow stronger each season."

Borim had never paid much attention to those parts of Bern's story, because he had never really seen anything that would lead him to believe there was any danger in his small part of the wood, and Alena only snorted and dismissed his questions with a cuff.

"If Bern would tend to his berry picking, he'd be of more good use than spreading silly tales about these things that don't concern him."

"Then you don't think it's true?"

"It may be true, well enough, but what's needed is not spreading it around and disturbing all the rest of us. There are things being done to take care of the problems, and we'll leave it at that. You tell Bern the next time you see him that he is to stop filling your head with these wild tales of his."

Waiting in the clearing, Borim realized he wouldn't be able to tell Bern, and he had seen enough to decide for himself that there was something to the stories, after all. The slain beasts lingered on in his memory, and the fear he had felt as he hung desperately to the safety of his shelter at the top of the tree.

There was no imagining what would have happened to him had he not been in the company of Frael and the others. Perhaps, he, too, would have been slain and eaten, along with the unfortunate deer.

He was large for his age, but untrained in the real bear lore of fighting and self-defense, and knew only what his mother had taught him, which was only good for cubs, and he was past that point now, and could not depend always on his friends to fight his battles for him. He remembered the swiftness of the three bears' attack, and the savage blows that had felled the beasts from below the Eastern borders, and shuddered. And there was the gleaming fire that blazed in Frael's eyes, and the strange dance they had done.

Borim knew somewhere deep inside that he was to learn all these things from his father, but there was a part of him that wanted to go on being a cub, and to be protected, and to let the others do the killing and fighting, and to leave him to the berry fields and up-tails games on winter mornings, when he would feel the good crisp hardness of new snow beneath his paws, and know that he had the whole day to do with as he wished, to ramble the low meadows to fish the half-frozen streams or to wander farther up the hills into the higher forests, looking for bee trees and the spicy sweetness they made in the golden combs.

Borim saw the scars beneath Lan's fur, and could see that he had already gone through his cubhood, and was now a bear. Lan's eyes had burned with the same grim fire as Frael's and Lan had attacked just as swiftly as the two older bears, and had carried his weight of the fight.

Borim thought back bitterly on all the time he had wasted talking to Bern and making his grand plans to run away from his mother's cave, for here he was, just where he'd said he wanted to be, waiting for his father, and all alone, except for the three strangers, who frightened him.

He sat beneath the spreading boughs of the evergreen, trembling slightly, and unaware of the new shadow that had come under the tree and stood beside him. Borim started, and cried out softly. A bear of huge stature stood before him, gray coat shaggy and long for the winter.

"You are my cub?" boomed the voice, deep and cold.

Borim was speechless.

Dralin turned to Frael.

"Is he the cub?"

"He is."

"Not much to him."

"Perhaps after a stay at An Ran Bar. Our good Lan here was not much more to look at than this, in the beginning."

Borim sensed the bear Lan standing and bowing.

"Thanks to you, Frael, I've overcome most of the worst of my bad traits."

"There are still enough to work on, youngster," replied Frael firmly.

"Will you take the training of him, Frael? If anyone could do anything with this one, it would have to be you."

"Lan and Earling will help me. Perhaps between the three of us, we may build him into something acceptable."

"If it takes three, then by all means, do so. I fear we may not have as much time as we would like, but we shall have to do the best we can."

Frael scowled.

"We found two of the outland raiders not far from here."

"I tried to warn you. There is a large pack of them. They crossed into our borders yesterday. I have had reports from all our scouts now but Char. His post was the most distant, so it may only be he hasn't had time to reach An Ran Bar yet."

Lan's voice was tight as he spoke.

"He is one of the fastest runners in these woods. He would never take so long to reach home unless something had happened to hold him up."

"We'll find the answer when we reach An Ran Bar," said Dralin flatly, his voice becoming softer. "I hope Char has proven us wrong with his safe arrival."

Borim, shuffling his forepaws uneasily, tried to make himself as small as possible.

His father's attention was something less than kind or loving, and the confusion he felt turned into a deep longing to be back safely in his old woods with Bern.

"You, youngster! Are you ready to begin your training with Frael?"

Borim's mouth went dry.

"Well, speak out! If you have second thoughts, it's too late now. There's no way back over the mountain to your mother's side."

Borim's heart fell, and he resigned himself to the unpleasant task he imagined ahead of him.

"Alena is a good sow," said Earling. "She raises strong cubs."

"She has in the past," agreed Dralin. "Until Bern, I thought she raised stout, strong cubs every time. He was the first runt she's ever dropped. But then it was not all her doing."

"He's no runt," began Borim, raising his voice.

Dralin's cold look froze the rest of his words.

"Bern's birth is a circumstance we shall all live to regret, I fear," said Dralin.

"Does he know?" asked Earling, nodding toward Borim.

"Obviously not. Alena is not one of too many words, so I'm sure he never heard the story from her."

"And Bern would not be rushing to spread it about, either," added Earling.

"To spread what about?" asked Borim, overcoming his shyness and fear.

Bern had been the only one of his brothers and sisters to show him any attention more than a cuffing, or to be willing to spend any time with him. He felt a fierce loyalty toward his brother, and even the fear of displeasing Dralin could not hold back his defense of Bern.

Dralin studied his cub intently.

"Have you been taught the order of things, the Law?"

"Alena spoke of it to me," answered Borim.

"Did she tell you of all the orders and kinds?"

Borim grew confused.

"I don't know," he muttered.

"Then you will find this information of no use to you. Perhaps when you've completed your studies."

"He may as well know, Dralin. It will serve no purpose to keep him any longer in the dark."

Borim's bewilderment grew.

"Your father is not the sire of Bern," said Frael simply. "Alena was just up from her winter sleep, and had moved into a new area in search of food. It was beyond her old territory, but there was more foraging there, so she went. And it was there she was attacked and captured by a band of raiders from below the Eastern Mountains. One of them, the leader, took her to mate, and she stayed with that band until Bern was older, and then escaped, taking Bern with her."

Borim could hardly believe his ears.

"You mean that Bern's father was one of those beasts like the ones you killed?"

"One like them."

"Not all the beasts look the same, Borim. There are still some who look almost as we do."

Earling paused.

"And then there are the others."

His huge frame shook uncontrollably.

"No need to mention them," cautioned Dralin. "We shall have our time of reckoning soon enough."

"What are they?" insisted Borim.

"You shall learn all about them at An Ran Bar. But now we must make our start. There is a long way between us and our food and sleep."

Dralin rose and stretched, and the others followed.

Borim's next question was cut short by a curt nod, and the huge bear who was his father set off at a furious pace, skirting the trees in the darkness, keeping ever to the faint path that wound through the shadows, on and on, until Borim's head was full of his aching muscles and rumbling hunger.

At dawn, they paused to rest on the top of a long, rolling, tree-covered hill, and between pants and grunts, Earling pointed away to the west with his forepaw.

"An Ran Bar is over the next rise. We are almost home."

The name had a strange melody to it, and Borim spent the rest period trying to envision what this new place called home would look like, but his breath was taken away completely when he finally crossed the next peak and saw the sight that greeted him in the early gold of the dawning day.

Dralin

An Ran Bar was nestled in a long valley, with the thick forest growing right up to the river's edge, which ran fast and deep and provided protection for the gates to the settlement. Behind, on three sides, running almost straight up, were solid granite cliffs, overhanging the dwellings in An Ran Bar and making the large settlement almost invisible to the casual observer.

Borim could have passed right by the place, and never have known it was there, for not only was it difficult to see with an untrained eye, but he was sure these strangers had made it so no spoor was left to give them away.

Dralin stood at the edge of the great wood, looking about. Frael, Lan, and Earling had all disappeared a moment before, and Borim was searching for their whereabouts when a great outcry rose up across the river.

"Dralin, Dralin!" chorused a number of voices, and it was picked up and carried on the wind, until the entire settlement rang out, booming out the great gray bear's name.

"Dralin, Dralin, Dralin!" they roared, over and over, and then there came a silence so eerie and complete that Borim was sure these animals were somehow able to control all sounds as well.

He strained, trying to pick up any noise at all, and was relieved to find that he still heard the deep gurgling roar of the swift river. After the noise of the voices raised in unison, it seemed almost to be total silence, until his ears stopped ringing from the furor of the loud, chanting cry of his father's name. His hackles tingled, and he felt a chill creep over him, from the tips of his paws to his great head, and his heart hammered within his chest.

The voices now called out once more, and the roaring grew greater than the river, and a low, rumbling thunder, of great bear war cries booming in countless throats, began to fill the air. Numbed and confused, Borim heard them calling out his own name.

"Borim, Borim, Borim!" the voices boomed, deeper and louder still.

"Dralin Bruinthor, Borim Bruinthor!"

Borim had never felt the way he felt at that moment. His eyes swam, and his head reeled, and he found himself standing on his hind paws, stretched out with his muzzle pointed to the sky, falling into his own war dance, the secret rumbling sounds of the ancient lore low in his throat.

Then as quickly as it had begun, it was over, and Borim turned to find Dralin beside him, an almost smile flickering across the great silver-gray muzzle.

"We must go on now," he said at last, pointing to a great wall of stone that lay stretched out to the water's edge.

"How will we cross?" asked Borim, for although he was a good swimmer, and had spent a large part of his life in the fast streams and rivers with Alena, he knew that he would not be able to ford this river.

Great caldrons of white water roared and leapt high in the air, and a fine white mist of spray covered his fur, and made the air at the river's edge seem to be made of gleaming drops of reflected sunlight.

"We cross the way Frael and the others did. Move those stones, and you'll see," replied Dralin.

Borim touched a place on the stone face as he was instructed, and right at the bank of the river, a small slit of a cavern began to open, and slowly widened until a bear the size of Dralin would just be able to slip into it. Cold streams of the icy river ran down into the dark hole, and Borim shrank back until he saw his father disappear into the strange door.

With no choice left to him, Borim followed behind quickly, almost stumbling in the near darkness, and catching his breath as a torrent of freezing water soaked him. He had expected the cavern to be completely dark, and was surprised to find that once he was through the narrow slit, the walls soon began to give way into a broader passage, which was lighted by rush lamps, flickering dimly along the sides of the tunnel.

On they went, until Borim could no longer hear the water rushing above him, and he knew they must be beneath the settlement, although his father did not slow his pace, nor offer any explanations of the wondrous things Borim saw all about him. They were in a wide passage, which looked to have been an old underground bed of the river at some time in the past, and from the doors Borim had seen constructed at some of the tunnel mouths, he was certain that the stout frames held the water out, and guessed that they could be opened somehow, to flood this tunnel, should they ever need to close it off to an enemy.

The rush lamps grew farther and farther apart, until at one point, he felt the passageway must be very broad, for he could barely make out the edges of the walls in the shadows of the dim light the flickering fires put off.

Dralin led on still deeper, turning aside now into what appeared to be a side shaft.

"We're almost home," he said finally. "These are the riverdigs. Sometimes they can be very handy."

Borim waited for more, but his father lapsed back into a thoughtful silence.

"You will be living with Frael until you've completed your lessons. Listen well, and heed what Earling and Lan say."

"I thought I would be living with you," Borim blurted, trying to conceal his disappointment.

"Not yet, Borim. There are many things that must be done first, and many journeys that I shall be away on, so you would not see much of me even if you were in my hall."

"Where will you be going? May I go, too?"

Dralin laughed, and stopped long enough to look over his shoulder at the cub.

"You will be making these journeys someday, in my place. I think we can spare you a few."

Borim wanted to question Dralin further, but the older bear turned again into a smaller shaft still, and seemed to pause before a solid wall of stone. Borim peered closer at the glistening rock, seemingly impassable, and stared in amazement as an archway appeared, revealing a blinding light and the smell of pines on a fresh autumn wind.

As they stepped through the opening, Borim realized the brilliant light was the sun, and he found himself in a cool glade, carpeted in thick grass, which led down to a small, circular pool, rippling slightly in the soft breeze.

Dralin had closed the archway, and stood smiling faintly at his cub.

"This is the Garden of the Roe. You will find it to your liking, I hope."

Borim had never seen anything like the glade, and wandered about, looking at the strange flowers that grew there, and stopped before the pool, glistening and sending silvery reflections onto the low-hanging boughs of the evergreens.

"That is the Eye of the River Falling. It can tell you many things, if you listen. It knows of the mountains, and the Far Crossing Sea."

Borim's mind reeled. Then his father had seen the sea, as had been said about him.

The waters of the pool darkened as Borim bent nearer to look, blotting out the sun. He saw his image there for a moment, a handsome bear cub, broad muzzle, and dark brown, thoughtful eyes.

A great wreath of clouds crossed over the pool, and Borim was on the point of looking away when a faint, lone star blazed into life in the stillness of the water, and its burning flames seemed to draw Borim closer and closer into the spiraling white fire. When the flames turned into the blossoms of a large flower, it opened and revealed to him his father, Dralin, bending over the smaller figure of another bear, and dressed in a colored cloak that was a bright scarlet, edged in gold.

Alena had never spoken to him of any of these things, yet he seemed dimly to remember them, from somewhere, although he could not quite touch on where.

The figure of the other bear with Dralin turned toward him in the reflecting mirror of the pool, and Borim saw it was himself.

These images were followed by others, even more disturbing. A great cloaked form sat astride a huge war pony, solid white, and as tall as the tallest saplings. Beofre the mounted rider, a vast horizon of blue ran on until there was nothing but sea and sky and sun.

Borim tried to pull his eyes away from the scene, but could not.

His father spoke at his side, his voice gentle and far away.

"Do these things remind you of something, Borim?"

"Yes, but I can't remember something," answered Borim dreamily. "Is my name Bruinthor?"

"Bruinthor, of olden," replied Dralin. "We are here together again, as it was spoken of by the Old One."

"Who is he?"

"You have him in your heart, Borim."

"What does all this mean? It frightens me."

"The Eye of the River Falling says many things, to whoever is watching."

Dralin stood before the pool, and a clear, high sound began, pleasant to hear, yet terrible at once, and Borim saw the image of a bright figure, dressed all in what looked to be heavy metal armor, astride another war pony, and behind him, the sight of thousands of others, also dressed the same, reached on beyond the rim of the pool. Borim stared long at the fierce forms, and was startled into jumping by another voice at his side.

Frael reached out a paw to reassure him.

"I see you've already gotten to your lessons," he said, nodding to Dralin.

"I thought it just as well."

"Will you be leaving soon?" asked Frael.

Dralin fell silent, gazing into the still troubled water.

"Soon enough to start Borim's lessons right away. The sooner that is seen to, the better for all of us."

"I think then that we must have a tour of the settlement for our pupil, and try to clear up all these mysteries for him."

"Why did you disappear back there Frael?"

"Because, my young friend, we slipped on ahead to let everyone know you were on your way."

"Why should that matter?"

"It matters more than you might imagine, Borim. You'll see why after we have completed more of our lessons and finished up your histories for you."

"They were all shouting my name," went on Borim proudly. "And they said Bruinthor."

"It is what they said, right enough. But you won't be able to carry the load of all that implies until you have finished your wardship, and learned a lot more than merely how to fish and hunt with your sow."

At the mention of his mother, Borim grew saddened.

"Will I never see Alena again? She must be worried about me by now."

"She knows you are with your father."

"How can she know that?"

"She was told."

"Nobody could reach her. The cave I came through was sealed off by the rockslide."

"There are other ways," replied Frael simply, standing nearer the pool.

In the rippling surface, Borim suddenly saw Alena, looking directly up at him, the warm brown eyes full of love.

"Alena!" he cried, and tried to touch a paw to her, but the flat surface of the water clouded and grew disturbed, and her image disappeared.

Borim called out in dismay, and tried to stir the pool into bringing back his mother's face. He reluctantly left the pool at his father's order, and followed Frael.

"I shall see you soon, Borim," said Dralin, lifting a paw in farewell.

After a short march that carried the two through a garden of yellow and red flowers, trimmed into the shapes of different animals of the forests, Frael led Borim into a low, comfortable dwelling, half above, half below the ground. There by the hearth was a fresh pot of mulled tea and a large heavily bound book, opened to the beginning, and while Borim poured, Frael began to read aloud in a firm voice that seemed to paint pictures of words for the young cub to see and marvel over.

An Ancient Hall

As Frael read, Borim's mind drifted with the wondrous stories, the histories of all his kind on back to the first beginnings, and distinct visions began to appear to him, first in short, unordered bursts, then in longer moments that cleared within his thoughts, as if they were old memories brought forth from long disuse.

The large book that Frael held seemed full of an unending source of awe for Borim, and every time the older bear tried to stop, the cub urged him to read yet another page, or another. In these histories Borim learned the unnameable name of the Old One, which was never spoken aloud, but always said in silent prayer, and that the spirit never ceased to live, but went on and on.

He had never heard Alena or any of the others talk of

these things, yet he accepted them simply when Frael read them, as if he'd known all along they were the truth, and he was merely waiting to remember them.

The Golden Age that Frael described as he read aloud pulled Borim under its spell, and he longed for it to come again. He said as much to Frael.

"But you were there, Borim. We were all there."

"That's not so! I would have remembered."

"You shall, one day. It always takes hard work to reach the point of remembering things, but you will be there."

"I can remember all last winter, and Alena showing me how to eat snow when I was thirsty, and Bern showing me where to find the best berries."

Borim had begun to notice that whenever he mentioned Bern, Frael and the others cooled, and changed the subject. Even if Bern weren't the cub of Dralin, he still had the same mother, and Borim could not see that it would make all the difference that it seemed to make. Bern had always been the kindest to him, and had always been the one of all the brothers and sisters who had had time to listen to him, or play games with him, and Borim would not forget that easily.

As was true of all bears, he was slow to anger, and loyal beyond belief to friends. Once you had befriended Borim, there was never any question of any change of heart. He was therefore saddened when his new friends reacted oddly to the mention of Bern's name, for he thought that it would have been different, for he loved Bern as a brother and a friend.

"Why do you dislike Bern so?" asked Borim, as Frael took a rest from his reading.

Frael scowled, and looked down at the huge book in his paw.

"Hrumph," he snorted, and laid the thick volume aside, walking to the round window that looked onto the blooming garden in the rear of the dwelling. "I can't tell you something in words you don't feel, little brother. I know you have lived with and befriended Bern. He is clever, and he knows you well. He has made every effort to be your companion and guide, and I have it on good authority that he almost came with you when you left your old wood to come seeking your father."

Borim's eyes widened.

"Who told you that?"

He was sure no one knew of their plans but the two of them.

46

"It's no matter who told me, Borim, I know. That would have created a great deal of difficulty for us, I'm afraid. And I'm sure Bern knew that, or he wouldn't have suggested it."

"I know you don't like him, Frael, because he is not Dralin's cub, but that doesn't make him any less a bear. Alena is still his mother."

"Alena is very wise, and full of love. There is no fault to be found with her. She could not help what befell her."

"And neither can Bern," Borim insisted.

"Bern is a bear of another coat," said Frael patiently, deciding at that moment to try to explain to Borim the causes of concern that were sparked by the young bear Bern. "It's not that he was not born of Dralin, but that he is truly his father's cub."

"And that means what?"

"His father is a very ambitious fellow who has long wanted to fill the role of Elder at An Ran Bar in Dralin's place. He attacked Alena because he knew she was Dralin's mate."

"But Bern could not help that."

"Bern could not. There was nothing that said he would be any different than any of the rest of your brothers or sisters, until his own father took him from Alena, and raised him down below the Eastern Wood. He was there for four turnings, and then he was sent back to your forest. That's when he began to see you, and cultivate your friendship."

"Why does it make it bad that he has spent time in the Eastern Wood?"

"The Eastern Wood is on the border of the beast realms. They have been slowly eroded there, into falling away from the Law. It always happens this way. There is no sudden onslaught, no open attack. That puts the alarm up, and raises all the citizens against a common enemy. That was the early troubles, and it was always faced and defeated."

Frael paused, scowling down at the book on the table.

"And then, as you'll find when I go on, the idea began to occur to those who rebelled against the Law that the best way to fight a battle was not to let anyone know they were fighting. Intrigue and treachery began to take the place of attack and siege. Where you could not force one out with arms, you could cajole and trick them out with deceit."

"And that's exactly what has happened in the Eastern Wood, Borim," said Earling, who had come into the room while Frael was talking.

Earling went on.

47

"Your father has long kept an eye on that region, for it is in the mind of those Easterns that they would like to have An Ran Bar for their capital."

"An Ran Bar?" gasped Borim. "But it belongs to all bears. Anyone is free to come and go as he pleases. That's what Frael has just read, that this is an open settlement. All who wish to can travel here."

"Not all wish merely to travel here, Borim," said Earling. "There is a settlement in the Eastern Wood, named after An Ran Bar, but because it has not been built with love and wisdom, it is full of hate and corruption. There are those there, and Bern's father is one of them, that think that if they could capture our settlement, all the things that are here would be theirs."

"They think the place is what makes An Ran Bar what it is," went on Frael.

"But why are Bern's father and Dralin enemies? What has set them against each other?"

"That's a long story, Borim. It is easiest to understand if you know that they are both very powerful, and they both have been elders for a long time. But Kahn, who is Bern's sire, began to find the power very appealing, and he began to move from merely being a servant of the others to a tyrant who now controls the Eastern Wood with an iron paw."

"But no one has a right to do that!" blurted Borim. "All animals are free!"

"So says the Law," snorted Frael. "But the Law in the Eastern Wood reads a bit different from the version you and I might have here in An Ran Bar."

"I still don't see what all that has to do with Bern," said Borim, going back to his original thought. "Just because Kahn, or whoever he is, has broken the Law doesn't mean that Bern will follow after him."

Frael shook his head sadly.

"It is a noble thing to be true to a friend, Borim, and it can sometimes prove to be tragic as well. There is no explaining it, unless you understand how these things are crosswoven from many lifetimes, and they defy any reason, until you begin to see the pattern."

"We're not trying to turn you against Bern," said Earling softly. "We merely want you to be able to see things clearly. There will come a time when you must be able to use judgment that is not colored by your feelings."

"Then I hope I never have to see it," argued Borim, still

confused by all the words, and the ill will these two new friends seemed to feel for Bern.

"When we read on, we'll discuss this further, Borim. Now I think it would be good if we were to take you on a tour of our settlement, and to show you off to all those who have been waiting to see you."

"Me?"

"Yes, Borim. As I said, there is no reason to it, until you see the pattern. But don't frown, little one. You'll know all soon enough."

Borim wanted to question Frael longer, but he was led instead down the white rock path through the high, trimmed hedges, onto a broad street lined with huge trees. Behind these giants Borim could make out other dwellings like the one he had been moved into, and the bright green windows stood out against white walls, and the yards were all colored blooms of flowers of all sizes and shapes, which perfumed the air with a fragrance so thick it made Borim's head spin.

As the three walked down the broad lane, others began to gather along the hedgerows and in front of dwellings, waving merrily, or calling out to him as he passed. Others called to Frael and Earling, and he found his companions to be well known and liked, for all they met bowed low and touched a paw to their forelocks, or raised themselves on their haunches, making the sacred symbol of the lore of beardom.

Borim was amazed to find the settlement was even larger than he had been able to see at first, and what appeared to be merely deep forest was actually an umbrella for more dwellings and lanes, although if you had been looking down on the trees from the cliffs above, you would not have been able to see anything below the thick branches.

There were open-air verandas where many sat together over tea, and sheds where others worked at shaping stones for paving, or building new shelters.

In one street, all the doors were full of wonderful smells that made Borim's mouth water.

"The Bakery Street," explained Earling, although Borim already knew.

In the next lane down, they passed the vast storehouses, where food was kept from the bee harvest, and berries were brought in baskets to be poured into great oaken barrels. In another section of the settlement, the woodworkers built the tables and chairs and beds, and supplied all the needs of the community as to wooden implements.

At last they turned back onto the main lane, and approached the biggest dwelling Borim had seen in An Ran Bar. Its door was arched and stood many feet tall, and across the top, carved into solid stone, was the one word "Bruinthor."

"It is your home, Borim. Yours, and your father's, and all the Bruinthors on back to the beginning."

Borim's mouth was dry, and he could find no words to speak.

As he looked, the heavy oaken door swung slowly open, and Dralin himself stepped out to greet him.

In the House of Bruinthor

In the book-lined study of his father, Borim looked about sheepishly, and tried to make out all the titles of the strange, thick volumes.

Alena had read to him from the bear lore primer, which was enough to fill his young mind with a wealth of information to think on, and he had often read from it himself, on long afternoons by a lazy stream, with thoughts of a nap tickling his fancy, or a long, easy ramble through a meadow filled with tall, golden wild flowers. The stories there were easy to follow, and all had a bear moral, but Borim wasn't sure what lessons all these odd volumes might have.

Frael had read until he had grown confused, and unable to listen, and he hoped he wouldn't be expected to listen to or read all these books that surrounded him.

Dralin sat in a comfortable high-backed chair near the hearth, which ran from floor to ceiling, and studied Borim in silence.

Earling and Frael were telling their leader of their tour of An Ran Bar, and the eager reception of the young cub from the lower wood.

"Everyone is always quick to remember the best part of a story."

"Yet there is no rumor of any travelers from the Eastern Wood, Dralin. No more than the reports of the beasts we are always hearing. They have been raiding our keep for so long now, no one remembers when it was not so."

"That in itself is a bad sign, Frael. When one grows so used to living in a state of war, one might almost be said to have become fond of it."

Earling cleared his throat loudly.

"Beg pardon, sir, but I could gladly forget the whole business, and cheerfully go on about my own, if those troublemakers from the Eastern Lands were to find somewhere else to find their suppers or steal their shelters."

Dralin smiled, a grim determination edging into his voice.

"Yes, good Earling, I'm sure you would. They always say that the best soldier comes from the one most suited for a peaceful life."

"Earling is beginning to feel his years," laughed Frael, pouring himself another mug of the spicy mulled tea.

"I'd like to know who isn't?" growled his friend.

"Our young cub here hasn't reached a point where he dreads the coming of the cold season, I'd wager," argued Frael.

"I hadn't either, when I was his age."

"When you were his age, Earling, you were on the scouting parties that gathered the news from the most dangerous section of the Eastern Wood. You were hardly able to part with your sow when you were swept into all this."

"At least young Borim here had a few seasons with Alena, in the Lower Wood. Things haven't been so bad there yet, from all I've been able to gather."

"But that peace will be short-lived, it seems. There are the stories of the new beasts that have been spawned in that wilderness beyond the Salt Marsh."

Frael scowled, and muttered darkly.

"When did you have this news?" asked Earling, coming to stand nearer the warmth of the hearth.

The tiny tea mug was curled forgotten into his huge paw.

"While you and Frael and Lan were out gathering up the wanderer here. The party came in just after you had gone. They lost two of their number, and barely escaped to tell of it. These beasts are like nothing we've seen yet, and they are moving out of Dead Lake across the Salt Marsh in numbers that are growing daily."

Borim, eyes wide, listened intently to his father, and kept thinking that perhaps these were more tales from the lore book, but when he saw the stern frowns on the muzzles of the three friends, he knew these bits of news were indeed something of dire importance.

"What plan shall we make to counter these new attacks?" asked Frael.

"None," replied Dralin shortly. "There are no plans to

make. We must warn all the settlements that border the Salt Marsh, and have all who wish to do so move to An Ran Bar. We aren't beyond their reach completely here, but we shall be safe enough for the moment."

"Who is in charge of the party going to warn those left?" asked Earling.

"I'm going myself," answered Dralin, preparing to meet the protests of his friends.

"Impossible, Dralin. If there is truly as much danger there as you say, it would do no good for you to foolishly risk letting Kahn get his paws on you. He would love nothing more than to capture the Elder of An Ran Bar."

"Or to slay him!" added Earling sourly.

"You make too much of all this. It's time our kindred have a quick glimpse of me, so they'll know I'm not napping already, or losing my touch by being too long in the comforts of my hall."

Borim looked from one to the other, trying to get the attention of the older bears, and afraid to interrupt their serious talk. He felt that breaking in would be rude, yet he also wanted badly to ask his father if it would be permitted for him to go along with him. He did not quite understand the feeling that he had, but he was sure that Dralin intended to take him along on this outing, and that he was waiting for him to ask to be allowed along.

He caught Dralin's even gaze resting thoughtfully on him, and knew that the older bear was already aware of what he was about to say.

Borim became painfully conscious of the late afternoon sunlight pouring through the high windows, and the tiny specks of dust that danced about in that golden light. Time seemed suspended to him, and he was faintly reminded of a small tug of memory, which said he had gone through all this long before, and that the outcome had already been written.

He was even mindful of the stern Frael smiling slightly as he turned his gaze upon him, and Earling, looking into the depths of the fire, turned and blinked his approval to the words he was about to utter.

"I think it would be well if I were to go with you, sir," stammered Borim, realizing as he spoke that there was a great deal of fear behind those words, and the small cub in him shouted that he mustn't be allowed, and that he would prefer to stay there safe in his father's hall, watching the specks of dust dance in the sun.

"I could not ask you, Borim, for obvious reasons. It might be slightly risky, but not overly so. I will have to take you away from your book lore for a few days, I fear, but then you are also welcome to take Frael along, if you like, so that he may go on with your histories, if we're not too busy otherwise."

Frael saw Borim's face fall.

"Volunteering for the front won't keep me away from your mind, my young pup. It's not so simple a task to get away from your lore teacher."

"We may even get some firsthand lessons," snorted Earling. "Bear defense up trees is one thing, attacking quite another."

Borim flushed crimson beneath his thick fur.

He'd forgotten himself in the woods, and suddenly remembered that Frael, Earling, and Lan, had all seen him scrambling wildly up the tree when they had attacked the beasts from the Eastern Wood.

"Alena has taught him all the basics he need know for now," said Dralin evenly, without a hint of reproach. "It's a good thing to know when to make a smart retreat. I have known more than one hotheaded fellow who never learned that there were more than two ways to leave a battle, and those were victorious or slain."

Dralin stared straight into Earling's eyes, until the younger bear became uncomfortable and looked away.

"We get it as we are able," he said uneasily. "I was never given any other choice."

"We are making other choices now, my young quick paw. There are tides of change that are coming about which shall make us alter course from the actions we have taken in the past to protect An Ran Bar."

"What changes are those, Dralin?" asked Frael. "Is not our first duty to kin?"

"Our first and last, my friend. But the picture deepens, and we have a broader front to look to. And there are other animals that are joining with us to help defend themselves against the beast hordes from the Eastern Wood. They have come against these new brutes from Dead Lake, and think they would perhaps even be allied with our kind, rather than face the likes of them."

"What others?" asked Earling suspiciously.

"They are our brothers from the river and the hedgerow,

and the entire clans of all those across Back Meadow have sworn to aid us in any way they can."

"What? A lot of flat-tailed busybodies? Fine lot of help they'd be, if it comes to a fight."

"You will be glad of their aid when the time comes, Earling. Don't forget Boomer, and our friends in Oak Hollow."

Dralin's voice was strict and cold.

"You will be wise to loosen up your views a bit, and to lift your eyes above your own nose."

It was Earling's turn to blush, and he was badly flustered.

Frael broke the uncomfortable silence that had fallen.

"I respect and like Boomer and his clan, but how can the dam builders hope to help us contain the likes of the beasts we're dealing with?"

"They are small in size, brother, but they are very clever in their work. I wouldn't count them short, just on the face of things."

"Are they many?" asked Borim.

"A great many, and they are very handy with their crafts. They helped us fashion these halls in the old days, before they decided to make the river their home, and to give up the deep forest."

"I will read you the tales of those times, Borim, and of the other waterfolk, who sometimes travel down our river. They are a strange lot, these others, and we seldom see them in one place for long. No one knows much of them, or if they can be counted on to keep company for more than a few weeks at a time."

"They are to be trusted," said Dralin. "Their Elder is a very wise graymuzzle who dwells at the end of the River Falling. I have been to his court on more than one occasion."

"You were at their table?" asked Borim in an awed voice.

"It was no odd thing, then. Getting to be less odd now."

Borim thought back on the small volume of bear lore Alena had read to him from, and of all the brief passages that pertained to all the other citizens of his world, of the book of foes, and the strange nature of birds, and the flighty butterflies, and all the others that there were.

Looking around the book-laden walls again, he thought perhaps each of those books might be the lore of each other kind there was. He asked, and Dralin nodded.

"But don't worry," teased Frael. "We'll have time after our trip to make a good dent in these."

Borim's hopes fell.

"These are all things you'll need to know," said Dralin. "And if you are to come with me, then that is the cost of the trip. Our time is short now, and because you must travel with me doesn't mean that we can neglect the things that Frael is charged to teach you."

Borim's mind tumbled about with all the new information he had picked up since he came into the darkness of the cavern on the slopes of the high mountains, and his heart beat faster as he remembered the cheers and calls from all his kindred he had met on the broad lanes and byways of An Ran Bar.

Yet there was a deeper note that urged its voice to be heard above all the excitement and thrill of being Dralin's cub, and widely acclaimed, and that voice seemed to be full of sorrow, and weighed down by the fate of many hanging on shoulders that seemed not so broad as to be able to carry so great a load.

Borim found himself looking once more into the dark eyes and inner thoughts of his father, standing before the tall hearth in the hall of Bruinthor.

An Introduction to the Warrior's Craft

Lan, being the youngest of Dralin's circle, was given the task of certain of Borim's lessons. He was nearer the age of the cub, and Borim seemed more at ease with him than with Frael or Earling, so Dralin decided to use him as guide for some of the outings that they would have to make before they set off toward the outer colonies, and nearer to Kahn's outposts.

No one spoke at length of the pressing danger that daily crept closer to them in the fastness of An Ran Bar, but the thoughts of the beasts from Dead Lake were never out of mind long.

Lan blustered and flourished his great claws and fangs, and went into a mock battle dance, showing Borim how little he counted the threat. Borim, as young and inexperienced as he was, knew that Lan kept from feeling fear this way, and somehow was able to deal with the thought of the beasts from the Eastern Wood more easily by going through all the motions of combat.

Those terrible brutes kept coming into Borim's memory, as they lay slain in the clearing by Frael, Earling, and Lan, but he shuddered again to think what would have happened to him had he not had the protection of three seasoned warriors.

Part of the chore that faced Lan was to intstruct Borim in the ways of ancient combat, according to the lore of all beardom.

"You will have to forget all Alena taught you," warned Lan. "There is no more time for you to be running up the nearest tree. Bruinthors have never run from anything, ever! It is expected of them to stand, no matter what. Everyone looks to Dralin for their courage, just as they will look to you, in time."

Even though Lan was the older, and more experienced, and given charge of Borim's education, there was still a hint of deference to the young cub that crept into his tone. If he were being particularly harsh in driving home a lesson, he would soften his approach, and go to great lengths to explain why, or why not, a Bruinthor would do this, or not do that.

Lan spoke of Dralin as a friend, but also more than that.

"Dralin is the Elder. He has seen all things, and has all knowledge. He is the living Law, to all our kind."

"How did that happen, Lan?" asked Borim, curious as to how his father was the chosen leader among all the great numbers of others in An Ran Bar.

"It is a long story, little brother. But your father started out just as you or I. There were Elders then, as now, and they were responsible for the teaching of your father, as I am responsible for helping to teach you."

"And Frael, and Earling?"

"We all have the same task. Now there is more to learn, and not much time, so it calls for three teachers. It is simply quicker that way. When your father was but a cub, things were not like they are now. There was leisure time, and long years to spend in the lessons. He came at the end of the Great Kingdom."

"What was that?" asked Borim, trying to remember if Alena had ever mentioned anything of the sort in her lore reading.

"That is more Frael's line of history," replied Lan. "He will have to explain all that to you. But for the most part, all it was is that there were no brutes from Dead Lake to worry with, and Kahn was but a small cub, growing up in the same settlement as your father."

"He grew up with my father?"

"Yes, Borim. They were taught by the same Elder."

"Then how can Kahn be Dralin's enemy?"

"They weren't, in the beginning. Dralin and Kahn were taught all the mysteries and rituals of the hunt together, and thanksgiving, and all the other things that make up our lives. They played together as cubs, and grew up into brave young bears together, and the Elders then thought how lucky, to have such promising young leaders to take over their tasks when they were too old to go on, and had to give over their mantle of leadership to others."

"But if they were friends then, whatever happened to make them hate each other so much?"

"Kahn hates your father, Borim. Dralin does not hate Kahn."

Borim's brow clouded, and Lan continued.

"Kahn was the bigger of the two, and he was stronger in some ways. He was more clever in the hunt and kill, and cunning. He was forever off in the woods, or on the mountain, improving his skill as the taker of life."

Lan paused, frowning down at his own huge paws, thinking aloud.

"Kahn became the best at the hunt and kill, and he began to spend all his time gone from the settlement, even when there was no need for the hunt. All the other sources of food that we learn of as cubs were forgotten to him, and after a long while, the hunt was not for the food's sake, or to feed the settlement, but merely for the thrill of it, and the kill an end in itself."

"Didn't Dralin hunt, too?"

"Yes, as we all do. But within the Law. Not for the sake of taking life."

"What did they do with Kahn?"

"The Elders talked to him, but to no avail. By then, his eyes were turned from the Law, and he had become a renegade, and he had been cultivating friendships with many others who had taken to following him on his long hunts. There was a split in the settlement where Dralin was raised. There were those who favored your father's ways, and those who adhered to Kahn's. Frael will read you the histories of those times, but the end of it came when the two camps split, Kahn and his followers to the Eastern Wood, where they were able to do as they pleased without interference, and your father and his Elder and their camp to An Ran Bar."

"And now Kahn wants to rule here as well?"

"Exactly! Time has dimmed his pleasures, and he has begun to think perhaps Dralin's home might have more to offer him than the wilderness of the Eastern Wood. And the animals there have mated between themselves, and with even their own sires or sows, and that has produced the sort of brutes that you got a look at the day you met us."

"Can't anyone talk to Kahn?"

"Dralin has tried."

Borim gasped.

"He has gone to the Eastern Wood?"

"To Dead Lake, to sit at the table of Kahn, to talk of a truce, and to try to draw the two camps back together once more."

"What happened?"

"Kahn tried to kill your father, and had it not been for Frael and Earling, Dralin would never have lived to come back across the Salt Marsh.

Borim's anger flared.

"He tried to kill my father?"

His voice was tight, and he could hardly get the words out.

"He tried, but failed. Kahn has become almost as wild as the other beasts in that wood. He has forgotten the Law, and all the things he was taught, and his unhappiness has driven him to the point of madness. There is no reason left in him. The one thing that drives Kahn now is the idea that if he can capture An Ran Bar, he will find what he is looking for at last."

Lan fell silent and looked away into the fading afternoon, and his voice changed.

"Your father still speaks of Kahn as a brother, but I cannot."

Lan shook his head sadly.

"I can't call him brother either," said Borim fiercely.

"We must learn, Borim. Dralin says so. So does Earling, and Frael."

"Then they don't love my father!"

Lan smiled, his eyes full of a dark light.

"Frael has been with Dralin longer than I have been alive, and Earling almost as long. They growl and quarrel with each other, and to hear them, you'd think they were mortal enemies, but you don't have to look far beneath that rough surface to see the true love they hold in their hearts."

"I wish I could find Kahn, and slay him," growled Borim, blustering, and imitating the war dance that Lan had just shown him.

Lan's smile vanished.

"That is exactly the way Kahn would talk, Borim. To solve

the problem by slaying your enemy is no solution at all. That's what Frael says. He says then you have your problems, and the enemy's, too! I think perhaps he's right about that."

"Did you feel bad when you killed those beasts?"

"Not at first," answered Lan slowly, trying to touch how he really felt deep inside. "But it's always empty. In the end, there's a hole there."

His voice trailed off.

"I can't really tell you, Borim. These are things you shall have to find for yourself."

"Well said," nodded Frael, stepping forth to greet the two. Borim had not seen him approach, and snorted in alarm.

"You must teach him to be on the alert, Lan. I keep jolting him awake with my appearances."

"I don't think we're that far along with our lessons," answered Lan. "I'm now trying to teach him a thing or two that is more in your way of chores."

"What have you been discussing that's so weighty, then? The rain? The wind?"

"Kahn!" replied Lan. "And I haven't explained very well, I'm afraid."

"No one ever has, so don't feel bad, my young friend. If Kahn were to be explained, we would have had the problem solved long ago."

"He tried to kill my father," snarled Borim noisily, his hackles rising again, and the cold wave of anger flooding his mind.

"Exactly! That is all Kahn knows. When he should have been learning to live, all he studied was death, and the taking of life. I have known his teacher for many seasons, and know the agony he has endured, because he feels he has failed, and that Kahn is his responsibility."

"Hollen lives in An Ran Bar," explained Lan.

"It was not his fault," went on Frael. "Kahn always tended toward the physical tests, and in feats of strength, he always excelled. But the other, more difficult studies he felt no need to learn. If a thing took more than a day to learn, he would find excuses to disappear into the wood. He wanted immediate results."

"Do you see Hollen?" asked Borim. "I mean still?"

"Every day, Borim. We are close friends and have always been."

"Does my father know he lives here?"

"Of course. He is a friend of your father's, too."

"I don't understand," said Borim. "Kahn has tried to kill my father, yet Lan says he expects us all to call him brother. I can't do that, for I feel anger in my heart. Yet Lan says we must not."

"It is one thing to feel anger and give in to it, my little one, and quite another thing to feel it, and overcome it. And the way you do that is by understanding what you are angry at."

"I am angry at Kahn," shot Borim.

"And I, too, have been angry, and ready to slay him, should the chance have ever arisen. But in the end, I have discovered something very valuable. My anger gave it to me."

"What?" demanded Borim.

"Surrender," said the older bear quietly. "Simple surrender to the fact that it is not my lot to change Kahn, or slay him, or anything else."

Borim's brow knitted, and he tried to puzzle out what Frael had said.

"You will find that, too, Borim, if you have the luck, and if you are true to yourself and your father."

"I will have to ask Dralin," said Borim, his confusion growing.

"By all means. He is quite the talker when you are asking the right questions. I should think you've hit on a few that will probably open his mouth."

Lan looked at the older bear a moment, then spoke.

"When are we to leave on this outing of his? Has he said?"

"Only that it will be soon. I think he has been waiting on you to teach our youngster a thing or two about taking care of himself in ways other than finding the nearest tree."

"If that's the case, we may well all die here of old age, without ever leaving the settlement."

Borim flushed hotly, and looked down at his paws, the rejection stinging him deeply.

"Come, he's not so bad as all that! I have been watching you two for some time, and I have to admit that he is a bit awkward, but there is hope that with hard work we'll have him able to stand on his own before too much longer."

"Against a flat tail, perhaps," growled Lan. "But to stand against one of those brutes from the Eastern Wood is another thing."

"Come, don't worry, little brother. He shall have us to contend with all his enemies. Between us all, he will perhaps be able to confront Kahn himself."

Frael's voice was lighthearted, but Borim detected a note of seriousness.

"Is that what we're going to do?" he asked.

"We may, little one, we well may do just that. If Lan gets on with his teaching, and I make myself scarce, then we'll all arrive there the sooner."

And without further word, Frael was gone as silently as he had come.

"Do you think he means it, Lan?" asked Borim eagerly.

"He never jests," was all Lan would say. "And we still have an outing to make to one of the outer settlements. Frael and Dralin think you should have some experience with some of our smaller kindred."

"Do we have to?" asked Borim, not sure he wanted to make the trip if it had to do with more lessons.

"They have been expecting to see your father for some time now. He won't be able to put off this trip much longer, whether you are instructed or not."

Borim could get nothing more from Lan, and they spent the remainder of the afternoon hard at the art of thrust and parry, leap and dart, over and again, until Borim had at last done it to Lan's satisfaction.

What Borim had thought at first to be a wonderful game had turned out to be nothing more than grueling hard work, and he was too exhausted that evening after his meal to stay up to question Dralin or Frael, or dread the journey on the morrow to the outer colony, where Dralin said dwelled the flat tails who long ago had helped build the very hall he slept in.

A Clan of Flat Tails

The clan of flat tails the host of Dralin traveled out to see lived far within the borders of a very dense part of the forest, and the trees there grew to great heights, and even a bear as large as Frael could not put his huge forepaws completely around the gnarled brown trunks.

High above the ground, right up under the umbrella of leaves, was a patchwork of green and golden, leaf and sunshine, and Borim almost tripped and fell several times, walking along with his head tilted up, not minding where his paws went. It was he who noticed the strange growths at the fork of one of the great trees first.

"What can that be, Lan?" he asked, pointing.

His friend halted and peered upward, not seeming to mind the endless questions that the cub directed at him. Borim felt somewhat more restrained around Frael, or Earling, or his father, but Lan seemed as good-natured as Bern, and always took his time to explain in detail, if he could, or to ponder and worry, and then ask Frael, if he didn't have a satisfactory answer.

This was a question Lan had to put to the older bear.

Frael, who was deep in conversation with Dralin, did not take so kindly to interruption.

Dralin had thought to be in the beaver settlement an hour before, and there was still no sign of any of the dam builders, or any trace of what might have happened to them, or have caused them to move on so unexpectedly.

"This might be an answer to that," insisted Lan, ignoring the dour glance Frael turned on him.

After quickly explaining what Borim had discovered, the entire party, Dralin, Frael, Earling, Lan, and Borim, and a few others from An Ran Bar, all settled down in the silence of the wood to ponder these strange nests in the very tops of the trees. They nodded and argued among themselves as to what the meaning of the odd growths could be, until finally Lan suggested that he go up and examine one closely, so they might know more about the nature of the things, or who, or what, might have put them there.

"I'll go too!" announced Borim eagerly, for he knew he was a good climber, and he might have a chance here to redeem his dignity in the eyes of Frael and Earling and Lan, by showing off his climbing skill to more advantage than the last time, when he had scurried up terrified, to get away from the beasts from below the Salt Marsh.

"Come on then," replied Lan. "We'll take a quick look, but stay close to me, and don't take all day."

Heeding his friend, Borim scrambled up quickly behind the larger bear, who climbed awkwardly, but amazingly well, and was soon at the object in question, sniffing and snorting about, and trying to ponder what its use could be.

"Well?" called Frael. "What have you found?"

"It's sturdy, and someone has taken a lot of time with it," answered Lan carefully. "And someone must plan on coming back. There's water stored here, and some soursap apples."

"How old is the scent?"

"Not more than an hour or two. And it's been carefully hidden."

Frael turned to Dralin.

"Do you think perhaps it might be our friends?"

Before he could answer, Earling snapped out a short bark of laughter. "In the treetops? The small gray clans, may be, but not the flat tails. They can hardly walk, out of water."

"There are a lot more of these things in the trees all around," said Borim, showing Lan the others he had discovered from his perch high above the ground.

Lan scratched his head.

"I wonder who would go to all this trouble, and then just disappear?"

"Maybe we scared them," suggested Borim, looking down at the large animals still sitting on their hindquarters in the wood below them.

"Dralin? Anyone who still follows the Law wouldn't be frightened of the Elder of An Ran Bar."

"Then maybe these were built by someone else, who doesn't follow the Law?"

Borim's hackles began to rise as he spoke, and the terrible figures of the slain beasts crept into his mind.

"I don't think so, Borim," continued Lan. "Too well built, and I don't think those beasts from the Eastern Wood would take time to do all this. They're more interested in killing someone off and just taking over the shelter that's already been built."

"Come on down, you two!" shouted Frael. "We'll go on ahead a bit farther, and see what else we may find."

Borim and Lan came down the tall trunk in a crash of bark and leaves.

"There are a lot of those," said Borim, getting his breath back. "Some of them you can't see unless you're up high."

"Are they the squirrel clan, Lan?" asked Frael.

"Too big for those fellows," replied his friend. "And they aren't really much for that kind of building. I don't think it was them, but I could be wrong."

Dralin had remained silent as his two companions talked. He was looking away into a deeper part of the wood, where the trunks of the trees bunched more closely together and traveling between them would be difficult.

Farther on, the way was barred completely, choked with thorn and hurryback bushes that formed a solid wall of green.

63

"Do you remember that from the last time we were here, Frael?" he asked, motioning with a paw.

Frael let out a low woof, and padded forward to examine the thicket more closely.

"That's not too old, and grown by choice, rather than wild, I'd say."

"I'd agree there, my friend. Someone is putting up a fence, right enough. But to keep something out, or in?"

"Who would go to all that trouble?" asked Earling. "All they'd have to do is move on to the upper thickets at Marsh Bottom, and they'd have all the thorn piles they could ever use."

"But that is still Marsh Bottom, Earling. Whoever put in these thickets must want to stay right where they are, so they've brought some thorn patches where there were none before."

"How will we ever get through?" asked Borim.

He was taught as a cub the secrets of traveling in the deep wood, and knew the way of thorn and tree, and all the ways to move so he would not get snagged, but these thickets were so dense and high that he knew he would not be able to move at all through them. No light or space showed through the long, wickedly curved thorns of chokecherry bushes, and the hurry-backs grew so densely he would have been unable even to wriggle a paw through, much less the rest of his bulky body. And his father and his friends were so huge, there would be no chance at all of them being able to move among the solid green wall.

The party went on forward, and began nosing up and down in front of the thorn barrier, first one way, then another.

Borim followed Frael and Earling a long way down, until they were almost out of sight of the others. Earling lowered his nose every few paces, and kept snuffling and snorting, and mumbling now and again.

"What?" Frael kept asking. "Stop muttering under your breath and say it right out."

Frael had risen to his hind paws and towered upward, lifting his muzzle to test the air and reaching out a tentative forepaw to test the thorn brake. He pulled it back quickly.

"Nothing like chokecherry for thorns," he agreed painfully. "They always grow the longest, and are always the hardest to get through."

"No spoor," mumbled Earling. "These thickets are new, and someone has planted them like this, just like we've done behind An Ran Bar, but I can't pick anything up."

"No one would be able to find any spoor behind our settlement, either," Frael reminded his friend.

"Then whoever has done this is an ally?"

"Perhaps," said Frael cautiously.

Borim had gone along behind the two, imitating their every move.

"Could it be the beavers?" he asked at last.

There had been something about the way the strange nests had been built that reminded Borim of the way a dam had looked, stretched out in the bright morning sun across a small creek near Alena's summer cave. When he looked at the green thorn wall, it reminded him also of that interwoven stick dam, plugged with mud, and constructed in such a way that it was incredibly strong.

Frael looked at the young cub sternly.

"This would be highly unlike our flat tails. They hardly have time to come out of the water long enough to mess about with anything like growing this sort of affair."

Earling was frowning as he spoke.

"I think Borim sees the beaver's paw in something about all this, and so do I. I don't know if it's the work of the beaver or not, but it certainly does remind you of their style."

Frael reluctantly agreed that the handiwork of the thicket had all the minute detailed planning and design of a beaver project.

A shout from Lan caught their attention, and took them away from the contemplation of the thorn barrier.

"Come on, quickly! Hurry!"

Frael's ears shot straight up, and his hackles danced.

"Come on!" urged Lan, his voice full of urgency.

Earling lowered himself to all fours, and the two older bears momentarily forgot their small charge, and were racing swiftly away toward the sound of Lan's calls.

Borim ran as hard as he could, but fell behind the larger, more powerful animals, and in another stride or two, he found himself completely alone in the falling shadows of the late afternoon. He sped on, thinking he would overtake his two friends at the next clearing of the dense thickets, but he soon realized that not only could he not see them, but as soon as he stopped, he could no longer even hear them.

He stood perfectly still for a long moment, holding his breath and trying to quieten his thundering heart, but there was nothing but silence in the wood. There was not even the ordinary sounds of the birds getting ready for their naps, or the thin rustle of the wind, whispering through the high branches of the trees overhead.

Borim forgot himself for a moment, and stumbled on ahead, then turned, forgetting the basic law of the wood that Alena had taught him, of always keeping himself aware of where he had been, and land marks to guide himself by. After a headlong dash in the opposite direction, Borim was brought up short by the same thorn barrier he had passed just a moment before.

A slow, dull thought began to fill him with dread, choking him momentarily, and taking away his breath.

He was lost!

And just as he sat down to cry out for Frael or Dralin, the other noises began, and he quickly silenced himself, and forgetting the long lessons he had practiced with Lan on the art of attacks, he ducked his head, and without blushing, scurried soundlessly up the tallest tree he could put his paw to. At the very top, he halted, and trying to catch his breath, looked wildly about below, straining to discover whom these new voices belonged to, and if they were friends, or worse, from below Dead Lake, in the Eastern Wood.

Two Warring Settlements

"It's too big for a squirrel," agreed one of the voices, and it was followed by a murmur of agreement from at least a dozen others.

"Too noisy for one of the fluff tails," said another, so matter-of-factly, they might have been discussing the weather.

"Is it that pack of filth from below the borders?" asked the first voice.

"Too clean-smelling," snapped the answer.

Borim, high above all this talk, could not clearly make out where the voices were coming from, or the nature of their owners. He twisted this way and that, but still could not detect the speakers.

Hoping that the noise would attract Dralin and Frael and the others, he clung to his perch silently, trying to clear his racing thoughts, and to decide what his next course of action would be.

As Lan had told him over and over during his lessons the day before, the limitation of taking to a tree is the fact you have no further choice, and if the enemy can climb too, you're at the end of your rope. Remembering the high nests that he and Lan had just been exploring, Borim began to regret his decision to climb the tree instead of staying on the ground and either finding a hiding place there or confronting these newcomers, to see what their intentions were, and if they were friend or foeman.

"Bears!" snorted a voice so close beneath Borim that he was almost frightened into loosening his hold on the tree limb.

"Big, big bears," went on another voice. "All gray and silver, and from An Ran Bar!"

"That's good news, then," said the first.

"We have been looking to see Dralin or Frael these past weeks. It's been long since they've come to us."

"And what's this?" cried someone, directly under Borim's hiding place.

"Here's one here!"

Borim's heart stopped, and he went completely blank, freezing where he was.

"A bear!" shouted two others in unison.

"In a tree!" called a third gleefully.

There was a good deal of rustling of underbrush, and a great commotion below Borim now, and out of the thick wall of thorns came a fleeting vision of many small, powerful bodies, crawling and running to stand beneath his hideout. Upturned muzzles revealed to him very prominent front teeth and earnest brown eyes, all squinting in smiles.

"Good day to you, brother," called the voice of the leader, which Borim had been hearing as the smaller animals stood talking out of his sight.

"A lovely day for a climb, if you've a mind for it," added a second animal, who stood with his two forepaws on the trunk of Borim's tree.

"Go on up and fetch him, Tolly! He may have lost his way."

"I think I will, Boomer. I could use a little practice at this business."

Before Borim could straighten himself, or prepare to descend the tree, a pair of deep brown eyes peered over the top of a branch at him, blinking slowly.

"Hello. My name is Tolly."

"I'm Borim," said the cub, taken slightly aback by the sight of a beaver in a tree.

"His name is Borim," called Tolly, turning to the others who waited below.

67

"Borim! Are you sure?" asked Boomer. "Ask him again."

The beaver turned back to the cub.

"He wants to know if you're sure you're Borim?"

"My father is Dralin," replied Borim, blowing himself up a small bit, and hoping they wouldn't ask him what he was doing up a tree.

"He says his father is Lord Dralin," called Tolly, whistling out his cheeks.

"It's the sign!" concluded Boomer.

There was a short silence, then the beaver on the ground called up to Borim.

"We are expecting your father, Lord Borim. Did he come with you on this trip?"

Borim's mind raced.

"He came," he mumbled, turning his backside to the beaver in the tree and beginning to slide to the ground. "But I seem to have lost them somewhere near here. We couldn't figure out the wall of thorns."

Boomer, the leader of the group of beavers, laughed.

"They liked our new addition, then? We have been tending it now almost since the last time your father was among us. These Marsh Bottom chokecherrys grow quickly, and if you plant them close enough together, no one but a snake can get through."

Borim had begun to regain his composure, and trying to act more like Lan or Earling, sat down casually on his haunches.

All the beaver clan immediately did likewise.

"How come you to be traveling out here, Borim? These are dangerous times to be getting yourself lost from your party."

"I didn't mean to get lost," blustered Borim. "It just sort of happened."

Boomer gave some orders to two of his party standing nearby, and they moved rapidly away, one in each direction, going out along the outer wall of thorns.

"I've sent to see if we can't find Lord Dralin. In the meantime, I think we should find our way back to the safety of our barrier. I don't like to stay outside here too long. We've seen many of the beasts from Dead Lake passing through in the last weeks. They seem to be moving in force now."

At the mention of the beasts from Dead Lake, Borim's blood ran cold in his veins.

"We saw nothing," he said, trying to keep his voice even.

"You wouldn't," said Boomer. "They would never dare risk

68

showing themselves to the likes of Dralin. They don't fear for their safety against us, unless we're in great numbers."

Boomer extended a paw, indicating the large party that traveled with him.

Borim had not seen all the beavers until Boomer spoke, and then they came from everywhere, it seemed. Under the shadows of trees, from behind trunks, and out of the dense wall of the thorn brake, they showed themselves. Their bodies were small, but powerful, and Borim knew from Alena's reading of the lore that they were amazingly graceful in the water, and that they were clever builders, and had much craft in their paws.

Looking at the army of them around him, Borim was glad he was not an enemy, for the large size of their party, and the knowledge that their protruding front teeth could fell the stoutest oak in a matter of minutes, told him that any enemy would be made short work of.

As the cub sat studying the beavers, one of the animals who had been sent to look for Dralin returned, whispering hurriedly into Boomer's ear. The beaver then turned to Borim, his face anxious and drawn into a tight frown, pulling his muzzle whiskers down.

"My runner has spotted where your father's party came across the trail of a beast raiding party. They are pursuing them, from the signs, toward the lower swamps of Marsh Bottom."

Boomer paused.

"And from the looks of their tracks, no one has realized yet that you're not with them."

"I couldn't keep up," admitted Borim, hanging his head.

"You are but a cub," said Boomer, trying to make Borim feel more at ease. "These are full-grown bears. No one would expect you to keep up, and if it weren't such an emergency as a beast raiding party, I'm sure they would have realized they had you with them, and would have to pace themselves slower."

Tolly spoke up, his voice tight.

"We can't stay outside the wall much longer. If there was one beast pack running here, there must be a second not far behind. And Lord Dralin didn't bring enough in his party to clear out this end of the wood."

"He obviously wasn't expecting much in the way of excitement, or he would not have dared risk putting his cub into danger."

"I can take care of myself," grumbled Borim lamely.

"In a tree?" Boomer laughed, which crushed Borim. "Oh no, my young lordship, you won't keep away from those beasts from Dead Lake that way. They'll snap it in two, or wait you out, or fling rocks until they've bagged you up as nicely as anything."

He laughed grimly.

"No indeed, that lot is not stopped by such as trees, or hiding, unless you've mastered the art of concealing your spoor and can vanish into thin air, as we do. We tried moving into the trees. Good advice for squirrels, but not for our likes. We had to give it up. Now we're using something else."

Boomer pointed to the solid wall of thorns.

"These do nicely, too, and slow our friends up considerably, but I'm afraid they have learned new tricks, which means these thicket fences won't keep them at bay much longer."

"How could they get through those thorns?"

"Not through, my good fellow, over!" said Boomer. "I've heard a tale or two recently about how they will break saplings, lay them against the thorn brake, and climb right up and drop over on the other side, all of a piece, and not any worse for their effort, except a bit hungrier."

Borim looked up at the seemingly impassable thorn brake, and realized what the beaver said was true. If he had thought of it, he would have been able to breach the wall easily, if he could have found a sapling he could have broken, and that would have supported his weight.

After seeing the way the beavers came and went, he knew the bottom of the thorn patch must be thin enough that a small animal could move through it without harm.

"We're going to have to move on, Borim. We've been out here too long. Sometimes those beasts have watchers out, who don't attack, but who scout out any new victims for their masters. I fear we've been in the open too long. They are always watching this part of the barrier."

Suddenly Borim felt as if there were eyes staring into the back of his head, and his hackles began to crawl.

"Then if they are watching, they know where my father is, and the others," he said.

"Exactly! And they know Lord Dralin isn't in this neighborhood, and it may make them feel safe enough to try to attack, if they have enough numbers with them. They are overly brave when they outweigh you a dozen to one."

"Where should we make for?" asked Borim, staring about at the dark eaves of the wood all around him.

"Most of my party is going home," said Boomer. "Tolly and I, and a few others, are going to see you reach Lord Dralin safely. And if we can't do that, then we shall skirt this thorn brake down below the first swamp at Marsh Bottom, and make for the settlement at Blue Pond."

"Where is that? And how far?" asked Borim, the thought of reaching his father again drumming urgently through him.

"Don't worry, Borim. Blue Pond is just downriver from An Ran Bar. That is our closest settlement to you. We have begun moving all our mates and pups there, to guard against the chance of being cut off from help, should those filth from Dead Lake decide to attack in force."

"But wouldn't I be better off to stay here and wait? They'll be missing me soon, and be back to look for me."

"I'd never sleep another wink if I left you here, Borim, in these woods, in these times. And I know Lord Dralin would expect me to watch after you like you were my own."

The thought struck Borim of how high he towered over the small animal, and he almost laughed to himself, thinking of Boomer as his sire.

But the smile quickly faded when the other scout Boomer had sent out returned, out of breath, and eyes wild with fear. Between gasps and groans Borim made out the words "beasts are coming" and "attacked Green Willow."

Almost at the same instant, Borim heard the great voice of Dralin Bruinthor, lifted up in an angry battle cry, and the answering guttural bellows from the harsh throats of the beasts from across the borders that split the once peaceful lands into the two warring settlements.

The Cub Becomes a Bear

Green Willow was one of a dozen or more boundary camps, situated along the swift Gray Rock River, which separated the world of Dralin from Kahn's fastness. The change was not immediately evident to the casual observer, for the forest beyond the Gray Rock was still quite green, and there were even adventurous sorts who settled the far side of the river, although a sturdy bridge was close to paw, should the need arise to cross the quick flowing water, and of late, the need

71

had arisen so often, the settlements on Kahn's side had been abandoned.

There were many kinds who dwelled in Green Willow, and the other camps like it. One would meet bear and badger, rabbit and squirrel alike, as well as skunks, porcupines, hedgehogs, moles, an occasional fox family or two, many kinds and colors of birds, and in one or two of the camps, a wolverine, and even perhaps a small company of otters, although they never seemed to settle in any one place for long.

Deer were to be seen as they migrated through, looking for forage, and the elk and moose herds often came to the river for water, staying for a day or a week, then moving on in search of their next feeding ground or water hole. Those of elk, deer, or moose nature seemed always friendly enough, but preferred to keep to their own, and all the good common sense of banding together in one of the settlements for safety was lost on the restless animals, and almost as the argument was being pressed home, they were excusing themselves, and on their way once more, ever seeking the perfect water or more lush meadowland.

And always, it seemed, the beasts from across the Gray Rock hunted down and killed great numbers of the elk, deer, and moose, but no word of caution or warning ever convinced the tall, graceful animals of their great danger, and they went on beyond the safety of the settlement boundaries again, passing off the concern of the camp dwellers with a slight click of their tongue, saying, "Oh, it may happen to some, but never to us. We're always very careful, and we have a very brave and clever leader."

And without fail, there would come the news back to the settlement of a great slaughter of the animals by the beasts, and if there were any survivors of the herd, they would sometimes stay a season or two within the confines of a camp, only to join another group later who might be moving through. The fear vanished in that short period of time, and the elk, deer, and moose seemed only comfortable in the company of their own kind, and even to take a sort of satisfaction in the knowledge that they were to be slaughtered.

As it turned out, it was a great herd of elk who were grazing on the outskirts of the camp at Green Willow that had been attacked, which was most unusual in itself, for the beasts from across the Gray Rock did not normally carry out their raids so close to the large communities.

72

Borim raced along beside his new companions, trying to detect his father's war cry again, but the air was confused with the shrill cries of the dying elk and the vicious snarls and growls of the beast horde that was attacking. It appeared to Borim, whose heart was pounding in his throat, that every beast from Kahn's settlement must be here in these woods, bent upon slaying every living soul who followed his father.

Tolly and Boomer, and the other small members of their party, were amazingly quick for their size, and they often moved away into the underbrush, causing Borim to think they had left him, which sent him speeding ever more quickly forward, for the last thing he wished at the moment was to be left to himself in this hostile wood, without a single friend to help him protect himself or show him the way to safety.

When he looked around again, his small companions were back, calling out to reassure him, although he didn't feel any too much more comfortable because of their efforts, for he had seen these beasts from beyond the borders, and knew that his tiny companions would be no match for them.

"See to the next traps!" shouted Boomer, and two of the beavers scrambled into the undergrowth again, off on a mission unknown to Borim.

As they neared a break in the thorn wall the beavers had planted to protect themselves, a huge animal, with burning red eyes and a long, drooling snout filled with ugly yellow fangs, crouched to attack Borim and his new friends. The beast's coat was a muddy brownish color, mottled and bald in places, and it ran on huge, misshapen paws.

This brute was much larger than the others Borim had seen Frael and Earling and Lan slay, and for a moment, he was frozen with fear, his thoughts wildly racing through his confused brain. At once, he moved to go up the nearest tree, but something held him back.

He looked down at the tiny animal beside him, staunchly baring the huge front teeth, and preparing to defend himself the best he could. Tolly stood next to him, a shrill war cry coming between stutters of fear.

Borim's hindpaws froze, and before he realized what he was doing, he had risen into the fighting bear stance that Lan had struggled so hard to show him, and from somewhere inside him, there was beginning to boom the terrible war cry of Borim, cub of Dralin Bruinthor. It frightened him, until he realized that it was he who was making such a dreadful din.

The great forepaws flashed out, and a cold, white fire

gleamed dangerously off the extended claws, and Borim danced back and forth on his hindquarters, the battle fire beginning to build within him. This was a new sensation to Borim, and he emitted a long rumble of warning to the enemy, who had slowed his attack, seeing that Borim was going to defend himself, and had started to circle, hesitating to get nearer his almost equal adversary.

The beast knew he could easily slay the two small animals, but he had had close calls battling the tall one, and remembered well the terrible blows he had received from those deadly claws. He circled warily, waiting for the bear to make the first move.

Boomer, who had taken shelter behind Borim's upright form, shouted out to an invisible animal in the wood behind the snarling beast.

Almost unnoticed, a great wall of thorn bush and vines seemed to appear as if rained from the sky, and Borim watched in amazement as the dreadful enemy disappeared under the crushing force of the trap.

Boomer leapt forward, and began to haul the vines tight, and Tolly helped, and soon the terrible roars of the beast ceased altogether.

"He'll be safe enough there," gasped Tolly.

Borim stood beside the sprung trap.

His father's words came back to him, about the usefulness of the small animals.

"You were ready to make a stand, Borim. I knew you'd not forget what I had shown you, if the time came."

Borim spun. "Lan!" he shouted, and pointed to the now still form beneath the thorn vine trap.

"Boomer has trapped one of the beasts!" he said proudly.

"So he has," agreed his friend.

"As he has done often for quite some time now," went on Frael, who had also appeared out of the shadows of the forest.

The beaver bowed low to the new arrivals.

"Lord Lan and Lord Frael, my greetings. May your muzzles grow grayer."

"May you never hunger, little brother," growled Frael cheerfully. "Come, Tolly, my wee river fish, and let's find Dralin. This attack may make it more important than ever that we visit the rest of the settlements to make sure all are ready to defend themselves. It seems Kahn grows anxious across the river."

"He has been anxious for some time now," replied Boomer.

"We've built as many traps and snares as we can, and they are always full, yet there always seem to be more of these beasts to fill up the ranks. And these!" he said, indicating the trapped beast. "These are larger than any of the others. And there are some that have begun to appear, I've heard, that look like snakes with legs."

Lan looked to Frael, who scowled, and studied the earth carefully, as if searching for an answer.

"That is the same news we have heard, but I haven't seen anything of that sort to prove it so. These are big enough fellows, by all rights, but hardly anything like a snake with claws."

"Tolly's brother's great-aunt has seen one, and lived to tell about it. She was badly injured, and no one thought she would survive, but she's a tough old soldier. She said the thing crossed the Gray Rock River up near Ash Hollow, and carried off half the settlement before they could drive it away."

"Ash Hollow," echoed Frael. "That's been one of the more peaceful settlements, hasn't it?"

"Until that happened. We've sent all the animals we can spare to help them rebuild their defenses, but we may have to have them all come back down here, before it's all said and done."

Borim sensed another latecomer enter the group, and spotted the great figure of his father, now standing beside Frael.

"How long past was this, Boomer?" asked Dralin, reaching out to exchange paw holds with his small friend.

"Greetings, Lord Dralin. We shall feel much better now that we know you've taken an interest in these matters."

"I told you to come to me if anything unusual were to happen, Boomer. I should have thought to see you long before now, if what you say has happened at Ash Hollow rings half as bad as you say."

"We didn't want to bother you until we were sure, and it's hard to make heads or tails of some of the reports. Some of the elk herds who have been through Green Willow spoke of these snakes that went about on legs, but I'm always inclined to believe only half of that they say. It's not that they mean any harm, it's just that they have a habit of not always saying things the way they really are. Why, it wasn't too long before the attack on Ash Hollow that some of those silly animals had come through saying you were gone to the mountain for good, and that all the rest of An Ran Bar was deserted."

Boomer laughed as he finished speaking, but fell quickly silent as he saw the concern on Dralin's great muzzle.

"Who but Kahn would be spreading rumors like that?" he asked aloud, although no one could be sure whom he addressed.

"It is Kahn's way, to be sure," answered Frael grimly. "To undermine the faith the animals have in you, then to send some new beast hunting across the river."

Borim stood silently beside his father, looking from one animal to the other, trying to understand what was happening. He was bitterly disappointed that Dralin had not mentioned his battle stand, even though he had not had to prove himself by combat with the snared beast.

"I think we should take a party from An Ran Bar up the Gray Rock, as far as Reed Landing, and perhaps even across, to see what my good brother is up to with all this talk of his about our deserting for the mountain, and snakes that walk."

Dralin looked from Boomer to Tolly.

"You, my good friends, spread the word among your settlement that we shall be back inside a few days, to begin our scouting party. We'll need at least a few of your animals, who are familiar enough with your wood, so we won't constantly be ending up like this nasty fellow."

Dralin nodded to the snared beast.

"I'll come with you myself," volunteered Boomer.

"You'll be needed here, my faithful Boomer. Tolly can come. And I think Borim has seen enough to know your worth, to boot. Thank you for taking such good care of him."

"He was prepared to take care of us, Lord Dralin. I have no doubt but that he would have defended us well, had we not had the advantage of this little surprise to discourage our friend here."

Borim's ears burned red, and he felt a great compulsion to flee, although but a moment before he had been hoping for the very praise that Boomer gave.

Lan dashed his spirit with a snort.

"That show looked well enough, but the forepaws were held too high, and you'd be a sure goner, dancing to the left like that. These beasts all attack to the left, for the most part, and that's a weak spot you have to cover."

Before Borim's head fell too far, his father turned to him, and placed a great paw on his shoulder.

"It was well done, Borim. Not perfect, but for your first

time, well done. Lan only has your own protection at heart. Heed him well on his lessons. He is the best there is in battle."

Borim shuffled his forepaws and stared painfully at a small clump of pine needles on the forest floor.

A great outcry away toward the river caught the companions' attention. Listening carefully, they could make out the shrill cries of the elk, and another, deeper, harsh roar of an enraged beast.

"They're still at it," called Dralin over his back, already at a dead run. "Quickly, we must drive them back, and show these river folk we are all not quite gone yet. Come, Borim, come beside me! They will see the new strength of the Bruinthor strike fear into the hearts of those who live in the shadows across the Gray Rock."

His heart dancing, the young cub took his place beside his father, and followed by Frael, Lan, and the small animals, Boomer and Tolly, they swiftly broke free of the forest's confines and onto the leveler ground of the meadow that ran down to the river's boiling edge. Ahead in the distance, they could see the terrified elk dashing frantically about, chased by the remnants of the raiders.

Seeing these new defenders, and the battle fire that gleamed in their terrible eyes, the beasts from across the boundaries turned and fled, throwing themselves into the quick-running current of the river.

"Those that don't drown will have a story or two for Kahn," said Dralin, as they came to a halt at the waterside.

"It won't make Kahn happy knowing Borim is with you in An Ran Bar," agreed Frael.

"And I'm sure he will come up with some new mischief when he finds out," added Lan gloomily.

"Never mind, we will go on to Green Willow with Boomer and Tolly, and gather what news we can there, and show off Borim. Then we shall have our hands full. You and Frael will go, Lan, and Borim and I will visit here until you return with the others."

Borim's ears picked up.

"We have a few more lessons for him, and Boomer is just the beaver to do it. It's time he had some lore learning of our other brothers."

Borim turned to his father, and caught the broad smile on Frael's muzzle.

"There's no getting around the lessons, Borim. Even the hero has them to learn."

Borim had no more time to think, for he was following the rapid-trotting Boomer and Tolly, who ran ahead of his father, toward the barely visible rooftops of the settlement of Green Willow.

"Well," he thought to himself, "I've always wanted to know why a beaver's tail was flat."

And cheering with that thought, he loped on, enjoying the memory of the new way his father had looked at him, and even the thought of the teasing of Lan did not hurt.

He knew that Alena would be proud of him, too. Her cub was no longer a cub, and the tree-climbing days of Borim were over forever. The day had arrived that he was a bear.

GREEN WILLOW

News of Black Grove

Beneath the dense green overhang of the inner forest, right where the thorn wall ran to the river's edge, there was a large clearing that had been constructed by the industrious clan of Boomer and Tolly. The beavers had felled all the trees on this one side of the Gray Rock River and constructed intricate dams that formed deep pools throughout the settlement, and made the wild water of the river a tame stream to flow down the main street of the camp. In fashioning the dams, the beavers had also provided a series of floodgates that would wash away any attackers, should they be opened.

Against the dew-heavy grass, the lodgings and holes themselves were compact and snug, built somewhat similar to the ones in An Ran Bar, but with less fancy outside work. They were sturdy and well built, covered over in part by sod that had been used to chink in the ceilings, and it gave all the dwellings the added beauty of a deep green lawn for a roof. There were rows of these dwelling places stretched away in all directions, and Borim even saw a rude huddle of shelters built across the river, although at the moment, they appeared deserted.

Borim turned this way and that as they entered the camp, nodding and speaking politely to all who addressed him and his father. Evidently these folk knew and deeply respected Dralin, for all called him Lord Dralin, and bowed low before his gray shaggy form. They called him Lord Borim, and he felt uneasy and embarrassed at their bows, but spoke up and called to them as best he knew how, trying to imitate his father's every move.

Lining the main part of the settlement a great number of woodland animals of every kind, from the small, sturdy beavers, to hedgehogs and moles, a large party of porcupines, quite a few skunks, squirrels, rabbits, and birds, a separate company of moles that were deep in discussion with a single, powerful-looking badger, and in the near background, close to the water, Borim saw a large herd of elk milling about, dodging this way and that, and calling loudly for this or that missing animal.

"They are trying to find who they have lost to the beasts," explained Tolly. "They do this every time. You'd think they'd listen to reason after these tragic affairs, but they never do. Next thing you know, they'll all be off again, right back out there. It's no wonder those louts from across the river have such a fancy for them. Supper on the hoof, ready and willing!"

The beaver snorted in disgust.

"They can't help it," said Boomer. "They elect this leader or that, and they are so many, they think they're perfectly safe, with all those numbers. Whoever they've chosen to be their herd master keeps on assuring them no one would dare attack so large a herd, and of course, the beasts love it. More food, more beasts. They come in greater numbers every spring."

"Why doesn't someone tell the elk, and those others, to graze farther down along the river, out of danger?" asked Borim.

"That's a good question, my Lord Borim. But who would be able to carry any weight with the silly things? They hardly even listen to themselves."

"My father might talk to them," went on Borim.

"I've tried," answered Dralin. "But I think they're more frightened of me than of the beasts. They shift their eyes back in their heads, and can barely stand still long enough to hear me out."

"It's true," nodded Boomer. "I was there when he tried to warn that large herd of moose two winters ago. They almost stampeded right over us when he crawled up on that rock to address them, and I'd wager they're still running yet, if they haven't all been eaten down to the last one of them."

"What's wrong with them?" asked Borim, astounded that anyone would dare risk angering his father, especially by being impolite enough not to listen to him.

"Wrong? Nothing, really," said Tolly, waving a paw in the elk's direction. "They don't seem to be overly accustomed to using what's under their antlers, that's all. I've seen some animals a bit denser, but then they don't go about much aboveground."

"You just don't like moles, Tolly," teased Boomer. "Ever since you had that run-in with that mole family about your hole on the lower pond."

"Long-headed, that's what they are," insisted Tolly. "Long-headed, and not above common tricks to get their own way."

"Well, it was a nice spot to build on, you have to admit. And Clark Mole has a big family, and needs the room."

"He could have built somewhere else just as easily as I could," said Tolly firmly.

Boomer laughed suddenly, and clapped his friend on the back.

"You're lucky, Tolly. At least you don't have all those hungry mouths to feed. Look at the bright side."

Tolly brightened a bit.

"There is that," he conceded at last. "He may have my spot for his shelter, but I do have my peace and quiet."

Dralin had taken Borim aside, and pointed out the various kinds who made their dwellings in the settlement of Green Willow.

"There are the moles, Borim. Good fellows in a siege. Fast tunnel makers, and no matter how Tolly feels about them, very good thinkers. Not quick in their decisions, but they'll always come to the right answer, one way or another."

"Good planners," offered Boomer, voicing his approval.

"Alena told me a little of them," said Borim, "but I never saw them up this close."

"You weren't likely to, there," laughed Dralin. "They haven't made much progress yet, and they are all still fearful. Probably lucky to have seen any there at all."

"Where do you speak of, Dralin? The Lower Wood?" asked Boomer.

"The same."

"I don't suppose you would see much of this sort of thing there."

Boomer indicated the thriving, busy settlement, with its hubbub of activity going on all around them.

Borim turned a puzzled look at his father.

"You mean these settlements are only here?"

"Here, and farther on in the high country," replied Dralin. He went on with his lesson.

"There are the squirrels, which you know of. And the rabbits, as well."

"I know all these animals," said Borim proudly, for he was familiar with all the kinds that had made their homes in Green Willow.

"Good. Then that's one thing out of the way. Do you think you can speak to all of them?"

"I think so," said Borim.

"You're able to make good sense to me," agreed Boomer firmly. "I can understand every word."

"Frael has already had hold of him," laughed Dralin. "Whatever else he is, he also makes a good teacher."

"You're afraid not to pay attention to him," agreed Boomer. "He is not a bear to be taken lightly."

"Are the other settlements like this one?" asked Borim, delighted by the beaver ponds and grass-roofed shelters.

It wasn't like An Ran Bar, but then that settlement was all bears, which made something of a difference in the size and style of the dwellings.

"Like Green Willow?" asked Boomer. "Well," he began thoughtfully, "in a way, yes, and in another, no."

"What he means is that here there are mostly the small animals," said Dralin. "So here you find the beaver lodge and mole digs, along with all manner of other small shelters."

"Even a sprinkling of otters here," put in Tolly grudgingly. "Not that they're ever about much, but they do build a good holt, when they put their mind to staying anyplace longer than a week or so."

"Blue Pond is mostly beaver, except for the hedgehogs. There are a lot of birds there, too, but then you know how birds are as neighbors. Flighty bunch, and not really interested in much that's going on outside their own nests."

"Don't forget Black Water. It's almost as large as Oak Hollow," threw in Tolly.

"Who lives in Black Water?" asked Borim.

"All sorts of odd characters. Quite a large bunch of water

rats and moles, and more than a dozen families of porcupine. Rather a standoffish lot. Never did understand those quill heads."

"You're not very kind to your brothers today, Tolly," laughed Boomer.

"No need to be," grumped Tolly.

"And the rest?" asked Borim. "Are there any other bear settlements?"

"One other, this side of the Gray Rock," answered Dralin, his voice going oddly flat.

Boomer looked uneasily at the young cub.

"He means the lost clan of Bramweld, in the Black Grove."

Borim's ears shot up.

"I never heard that story," he managed, waiting for his father to explain.

Dralin took a long time, and seemed to stare off into space, until at last he appeared to come to himself, and remembering where he was, began the tale.

"Black Grove is the last bear settlement between the boundaries of Kahn and An Ran Bar. Bramweld grew up with me, in my old home, along with Kahn, before the split came that marks us as enemies now."

"I never heard of Bramweld," complained Borim.

"I'm surprised," answered his father. "But then, I guess there was never any need to mention him until now. Frael would be able to tell this better, but I can't wait for him."

"Does Frael know Bramweld?"

"He is the cub of Bramweld," replied Dralin. "His lot has not been easy, as things have fallen out."

After another silence, Dralin continued.

"Bramweld moved a large colony of bears to Black Grove quite some time ago, even before Kahn went his own way, and crossed the Gray Rock. The beasts he's spawned in these later seasons were no threat then, and we had had no hint of trouble on the border, as with Kahn.

"Bramweld had grown as large as myself, a husky fellow, looking for his own territory to rule, and his own wood to roam. He chose Black Grove, which had good water and food, so his band left An Ran Bar to settle into their new home. Kahn was often a visitor at Black Grove, and they spent more and more time to themselves."

"Bramweld still hasn't been seen till this day," put in Boomer. "Except for a few folks who said they had heard news of him, or said that someone they knew had heard from a friend of his whereabouts."

"No, Bramweld might find it distasteful to have to deal with his two warring brothers. He was always the strict one. A thing is one way or another, or it isn't at all."

"Did he go over to Kahn, and the beasts?" asked Borim.

Dralin shook his great head sadly.

"No, he went with Bramweld. They have hidden themselves in Black Grove, and keep the settlement to their own members. If they are even still there. No one knows for sure."

"Are we going there?"

"Yes, Borim. This trip we must go to see if Bramweld is anywhere about. There were rumors that he had crossed the Gray Rock and gone into Kahn's country, but I can hardly believe that. I think his own inner code would take him perhaps elsewhere, if he has moved at all."

"Bramweld is a strange one, by all accounts. We have tales now and then, brought in by an odd late winter visitor or two, about the goings-on in Black Grove. They'll find signs of a camp here and there, or stumble across a shelter, but never anyone at all! Not a single living soul!"

"Grandad Greenspar said he came on a camp there once, with tea still simmering in the pot, and the cups laid out, and some blueberry scones waiting on a plate, but just nobody to be seen or found anywhere."

Tolly broke into a small titter.

"He said the scones were good, but the tea was a bit strong."

"Are you going to try to find Bramweld this time?" asked Borim.

"Indeed we are. You see, this time we have a sign he can't ignore. You!"

"Me?" gasped the cub.

"Yes, you, Borim. It is said in all the ancient tales that there will come a time when the brothers of animalkind are divided, and they shall be brought back together again by the coming of a cub."

"But how can you know which cub?" asked Borim. "It might have been anyone at all."

"It is said in the stories, Borim. Frael can give you the fuller account, but it was to be this way. The next cub of the she-bear Alena, after she gave birth to a cub of Kahn, would be the chosen one to bring the animal clans together again."

"Don't forget the part about the cub of Kahn," grunted Tolly.

"That's the part we'd all be better never to have heard," added Boomer, looking sternly at his friend.

"What about that cub?" asked Borim. "Is that Bern?"

Dralin nodded slowly.

"But that is a matter we won't have to deal with for quite some time to come."

"Bern is a good bear," insisted Borim fiercely.

"Indeed he is, Borim. There is no doubt of that. And he has his own part to play out, as well as the rest of us."

Borim could get nothing further from his father, or the two beavers, except other news of the settlements along the Gray Rock, and odd bits of happenings from the few settlements that were scattered farther into the woods away beyond Blue Pond or Black Grove. Those bits of information nagged Borim for answers, and his mind worked in many directions, always coming back to the mysterious ways they all talked about Bern; and then there was the other bear, Bramweld, who seemed to want nothing to do with any of them, except that now he would be forced to, because Dralin brought the cub with him that was spoken of in the old stories, that had been a part of bear lore since the first of their kind had come to live in the deep woods and mountains of their present world.

Borim at last gave up the endless line of questions that had no answers, and allowed himself to be seated at a long, outdoor table, and amid great celebration, all the animals of the settlement were gathered together, and a day-long feast was held in his father's honor, and there was dancing later, wonderful lumbering tunes, and quick beaver jigs, and skunk strolls, as well as trots for the porcupines, and great galloping side steps for the moles. Borim enjoyed himself immensely, and by the end of the long evening, he was worn out by all the doings of the settlement, and was quite content to find a cozy sleeping hammock in the great hall where the meetings for the camp were held, and unable to keep his eyes open any longer, even to listen to the low talk of Dralin and Boomer, earnestly nodding now and again, he fell into a light sleep, dozing fitfully off and on until the sun awakened him just past first light.

All the camp was quiet, and Borim saw the huge figure of his father curled into a hammock near the door.

Above the loud snores and snorts of the animals asleep in the meeting hall, Borim detected another noise, coming from somewhere outside, and he crept from his bed, stealing carefully to the window, trying not to wake any of the sleepers. Peering into the golden light of the early dawn, he was not sure he was fully awake yet, and he blinked rapidly, trying to clear away the visions that danced before him, near the dying remnants of the fire of the night before. There in the settlement clearing were two enormous silver-gray bears, with broad white streaks all down their fronts and paws upraised to the reddish gold orb of the sun.

He turned around to call out to his father, but was held enthralled by the handsome bears, and as he stared out the window, one of the two faced him suddenly. Borim was transfixed by the startling blue eyes of the bear, and he could neither move nor breathe as the huge animal held his gaze. In the look he could find nothing to give away the other's identity, and as he watched, the second bear caught his gaze. This bear's eyes were a darker gray-green, and a dim light smoldered there, almost threatening, had it not been in such a handsome animal. Borim forced himself to look away, and hurried to wake his father.

Alarm Bells in An Ran Bar

"It must have been a dream, Borim. Sometimes we dream things so real that it's hard to tell if they happened or not."

"They were there," insisted the confused cub. "I saw them."

"Could it be Frael and Earling are already returned?" asked Boomer.

"Perhaps. But they would not have disappeared without coming to tell me the news."

Dralin paced to the spot where Borim had said he'd seen the strange animals, and leaning close to the earth, he examined the ground carefully. Frowning, he bent even nearer, and then raised himself onto his haunches, testing the air first one way, then another. His ears were laid back flat on his massive head, and he began a low rumbling growl deep in his throat.

Boomer and Tolly scurried for cover, and Borim, not knowing what else to do, rose on his own hindquarters, trying to imitate his father.

Dralin's fangs gleamed a fiery white, and he turned to face a certain place at the edge of the wood, where two huge trees overhung the clearing, shading the shelters built below them and creating odd patterns of shadows out of the early morning sunlight. In a thundering voice that left Borim trembling, Dralin called out.

"By the Sacred Tree, you may come out now. There's no need to skulk about in the presence of friends."

He was answered with only silence, which seemed to anger the huge bear. He stalked grimly toward the deeper shadows, his growl menacing.

"Come out and let us see you! There's none here who would harm you."

Borim's heart stood still, but there was no reply from the concealing underbrush.

With an abrupt leap forward, Dralin had torn away the bushes that grew close under the two trees, and lashed out this way and that. After a furious few minutes of storming around in the thick brush, he lowered himself and came back to sit calmly beside Borim.

"Who could it have been?" asked Boomer, returning to Dralin's side. Tolly joined him, moving cautiously, in case the big animal decided to strike out again.

"Bramweld, and another. Probably one of his clan from Black Grove."

"Bramweld! But what could he want here in Green Willow?" asked Boomer.

"Me," replied Dralin tiredly. "I think perhaps he may have heard some news that might have interested him enough to come out of exile."

"You mean Borim's arrival?"

"Exactly, Boomer. Perhaps he wanted to see for himself if it were true."

"But wouldn't he just come in openly? There's no need for him to lurk about like one of the beasts from Dead Lake."

"No, but you must remember he has been living apart and hidden for a long time now. It's not easy to overcome old habits. He won't find it easy to trust anyone, after all these seasons that he and his clan have lived alone."

"Do you think he's gone?" asked Borim.

"Not far. He may come to talk, or he may not."

"Aren't you going to find him?" asked the cub, looking nervously about at the dark eaves of the wood.

"No, Bramweld may be a grouchy sort given to being a hermit, but I don't think he's dangerous."

87

"He was as big as you," went on Borim, turning to his father.

"Yes, he is. And Kahn is even bigger."

Dralin smiled at the graveness of the cub.

"But one's size is not always measured in tallness or weight."

Borim tilted his head, looking puzzled, and waiting for his father to explain further.

"Look at our friends here," said Dralin, pointing to Boomer and Tolly. "They aren't mountains, as animals go, yet they are brave and loyal. Those are the things that make an animal big, Borim. You must never forget that."

"I won't," said the cub, so seriously his father had to laugh.

"Those two in the woods may come in if we go on with our breakfast. Let's have something to eat, and see if we can lure them in."

Boomer signaled on a small horn carved of a dark-colored wood, and before Borim could blink twice, the clearing was filled with busy animals, tending the fire and laying out small neat cloths on the ground, and soon the teapot was singing and loaves of brown bread were spread around, filling the air with a mouth-watering secret smell that seemed to pull the entire settlement into sitting around the clearing and joining in the noisy task of breakfast.

Boomer sat next to Tolly and Borim, and the two small animals kept the cub amazed with their stories of life on the Gray Rock, and the strange things they had seen on their travels above Oak Hollow.

"These beasts from across the river haven't always been so bold," explained Boomer. "In the old days, you hardly ever heard of them attacking anyone on this side of the river. There were a few rumors, of course, but it was always, or almost always, in the denser part of the wood, or far away from any of the settlements. Of course, the camps weren't near so many, or as big as now, because mostly everyone was living wherever he wished, since the danger was not so great."

"We didn't begin banding together until your father suggested it," went on Tolly. "There were more attacks here and there, but we never realized the extent of the threat until we began to see Dralin in Green Willow, and Oak Hollow, and Blue Pond, and Reed Landing. He and Frael had traveled back and forth across the Gray Rock many times, and up- and downriver, and knew that there was something going on below Salt Marsh and Dead Lake."

Dralin listened in silence, nodding now and then, and keeping his thoughts to himself. Boomer looked at him from time to time, as if to ask if he were leaving anything out.

"Go on, my friend. You are doing a good job of all this past history. I've forgotten a lot of it myself. It has been a long time."

"We were just pups when we first started seeing Dralin," said Tolly, widening his eyes. "It was some scare to get sight of something so big back then. My mother thought it was the ending when she first saw him coming to Oak Hollow. There were only a few families there then, and mostly all beavers. No one had seen a bear in so long I guess everyone had almost forgotten what one looked like."

"And I don't think anybody had seen one *this* size!" added Boomer.

Dralin snorted.

"Go on with your story, and leave my size out of it."

"No one was to eager to have a run-in with him at first," continued Tolly. "It was hard to believe that he and the other one were actually friends of the other animals in our wood, and that they were trying to help everyone overcome the threat of attack from across the Gray Rock."

"Kahn was just beginning to spawn the beasts there," said Dralin. "His clan was mating without regard to the Law, and the cubs that came as a result were often malformed, and then the other animals began showing themselves, until they eventually came down to the beasts you see today."

"Don't forget the snakes with legs they're talking about," said Tolly. "We may not have seen them yet, but we have it on good word from those I know, who wouldn't tell of something that wasn't there."

"Do you think there's truth to that, Dralin?" asked Boomer. "And if so, should we do something more to protect ourselves here in Green Willow?"

"We shall know more as soon as Frael and I take our little exploration across the Gray Rock."

Boomer's fur turned a shade lighter.

"You're not going across there, now?"

"Of course," replied Dralin. "And young Borim shall have a firsthand look at all these things we've been filling his ears with."

"What will we do meanwhile?" asked Boomer. "I don't like the thought of having to hang about here with you gone."

"And what about those two Borim saw? If it is Bramweld,

89

and he's picked now to start coming out, maybe he's in the mood for trouble. It doesn't sit well that he would be lurking about out there in the trees even after you called out to him."

"You may get to meet him sooner than you thought, Tolly," said Dralin, nodding toward the edge of the wood behind the council hall.

There in the green darkness beneath the trees stood the huge silver bear Borim had seen, but there was no sign of the other animal.

"Welcome, Bramweld," boomed Dralin. "It's been a season or two since we've had a bite together beside a friendly hearth."

The bear moved closer, still without speaking.

As he came beside the fire, Boomer and Tolly edged closer to Borim, their hackles raised, and small whines racking their powerful forms.

"Is that the one?" asked Bramweld abruptly, his voice deep and harsh, as if he were unused to speaking.

Dralin turned to Borim.

"This is Borim."

"He's not as I would have thought," said Bramweld.

"Would you have thought of him as otherwise, brother? How would you have had him?"

Bramweld reached out a huge paw and poured himself a hot mug of tea. Slurping noisily, and gobbling down a thick slice of bread, he went on.

"We have moved from Black Grove."

Dralin showed some surprise at the statement, but covered it, and waited for the other bear to go on.

Bramweld chewed and swallowed, then washed down his meal with another cup of the mulled tea.

"Kahn has new tricks," he said. "Big animals, not like anything I've ever seen before."

Tolly could not keep quiet.

"Are they snakes with legs?" he blurted.

Bramweld turned a cold look on the beaver.

"Not snakes, small one, but they are bigger than bears, and have snouts as long as my arm. I have lost many of my band to these beasts. I thought Kahn was satisfied with his part of the country across the Gray Rock, but he is not. He has broken his word to me."

Dralin had gotten up, and paced restlessly about the clearing.

"You say your settlement has been attacked in Black Grove?"

"So often we have moved. We have a temporary camp now, not far from the burned valley."

"Have you seen these new beasts? Are they many?" went on Dralin.

"Their number is large enough to make us seek shelter elsewhere," replied Bramweld. "And we are not known to be frightened easily."

Dralin studied the other bear in silence, then nodded.

"It must be a great threat indeed. We may not need to make our trip, Borim. If Bramweld has moved his settlement from Black Grove because of these beasts from Kahn's territory, then there is truth to the stories that they are dangerous, and many."

"Will you be staying here, to help us?" asked Boomer, overcoming his fear of Bramweld and standing nearer the large animal.

"I must return to An Ran Bar. We shall have to see to our defenses more quickly than I thought."

"What of Blue Pond, and Oak Hollow, and Reed Landing, and all the other settlements? They shall have to be warned," said Tolly, enjoying the feeling of having been proved right about the new beasts from across the Gray Rock.

"We shall have to gather everyone into one settlement," decided Dralin. "If this new threat from Kahn is as serious as it seems, our best hope is to band everyone together, until we can make other plans."

"I will not move my settlement again," said Bramweld coldly. "We have always lived in Black Grove, and I don't intend to go too far from there. Kahn will tire of his new game. We will outwait him."

Dralin looked sternly at Bramweld.

"You may bargain on a wait longer than you think, brother. Kahn has been at this business for many long seasons now, and I don't think he is going to tire of it."

"You have your own thoughts, Dralin. You always have. You and Kahn are alike in that manner, for he is as sure that you won't tire of your game either."

A dangerous flame ignited in Dralin's eyes, and an icy edge of danger crept into his voice.

"We have shared our first food in many seasons, Bramweld. I have no desire to count you as an enemy, but I shall warn you now that you will do yourself no good by courting my disfavor."

Boomer and Tolly had leapt for cover behind Borim, and

91

the cub, terrified at the sudden chill that had come over his father, involuntarily took a step backward, almost falling over the two cowering beavers.

"I neither court your disfavor nor your pleasure, Dralin. I came to see if it were true about the cub. You may take my words as you wish. I will return to my settlement, and we shall keep to our own business, as we always have. I might urge others to do so as well."

The huge bear bowed curtly, and lumbering heavily away, was soon gone into the strained silence that had fallen over the animals gathered in the clearing.

Dralin was the first to speak, and he acted as if nothing out of the ordinary had taken place.

"Finish your food, Borim. We shall have to make a start for home, and we won't have time to eat on the way."

"But," blurted the cub, "are you going to let him go?"

Dralin finished his tea.

"He has chosen his way, and I mine. And Kähn has made his own choice, long ago."

"Will we see you again soon?" asked Boomer.

"As quickly as you warn the other settlements. Pay no attention to what Bramweld said. It bodes good that he feels it not necessary to join with us. The beasts of Kahn may well decide to hunt below the Gray Rock after all, and leave us in peace."

"And if they don't?" asked Tolly, trying to mask his unease.

"Then we shall see what's to be done," replied Dralin, and before the others could get anything further from him, the two bears, father and cub, had set off at a grueling pace for the settlement of An Ran Bar.

As they neared An Ran Bar, Borim's heart raced, for there high and clear was the alarm bell, pealing wildly above the noise of the afternoon wind through the trees.

Jar Ben

In the main square of An Ran Bar, a great crowd had gathered, and Dralin had to force a way through for his cub that followed along behind him. A great uproar greeted the huge bear as he neared the cause of the excitement.

Borim, dazed by all the noise and confusion, tried to keep up with his father, and to keep from getting lost in the shuffling animals in the crowd. Above the voices of the others, the cub heard Frael call out.

"Here, Dralin! We're glad you've come. You can settle this once for all."

"Kill them! Kill them! They have slain, and they must be killed now!" roared the crowd in unison.

Frael's voice boomed out over the noise.

"Silence! Lord Dralin will decide."

In another moment, Borim found himself beside his father, greeting Frael, Lan, and Earling, who stood before the angry crowd.

Behind the three huge animals, there cowered a pair of the beasts from the Eastern Wood, although Borim could see that there was nothing terrible about these brutes, and they whined and rolled their eyes in fear.

"What's happened here?" asked Dralin, addressing Frael and turning a dark scowl on the crowd, to quieten their outbursts.

When the noise subsided enough for him to be heard, Frael answered.

"These two came across the Gray Rock, not long before you arrived. They said they had news for you, and wanted to bring you greetings from Kahn."

Dralin's ears shot back in surprise, then he turned to the two.

"Is this true? Or are you trying to lie yourselves out of a quick death? What have you been up to here? Speak up!"

The largest of the two deformed animals whined, then bowed low before Dralin. He spoke in a halting, guttural tone, but the words were clear, and Borim could understand everything he said.

"Greetings, Lord Dralin. We have come in peace. We have harmed no one."

He whined, and bowed even lower, and the second beast did the same.

"We have done nothing. We never hunt across the boundary."

"Then you will not be harmed, unless I learn otherwise," said Dralin in a firm voice, but he never took his eyes off the two, and they had difficulty in meeting his glance.

"They have killed!" shouted an animal from the front of the crowd.

"Have you seen it?" asked Dralin, turning to question the accuser.

93

An awkward silence fell, and the animal fell back a pace or two before replying.

"Well, I don't have to see it to know these beasts have killed. They even eat their own. And I know they mean no good to any of us here across the Gray Rock."

Dralin stepped in front of the animal who spoke.

"But have you seen these two slay anything since they have come here?"

"No," he mumbled, lowering his eyes. "Not yet, anyhow."

"Then we know how to deal with them when they do. In the meantime, we shall find out what business they have so far from their own hunting grounds."

"Thank you, Lord Dralin. We will leave here as soon as we have delivered you our message and receive our answer."

"What news do you speak of?" asked the huge gray bear. "Is it from my brother Kahn?"

"It is from Lord Kahn," replied the first beast, curling his lip in a cruel smile, although still clearly frightened.

"Cast them back across the river, if we can't kill them," called another bear, standing close enough to hear what was being said to Dralin.

Borim thought his father would silence the animal, but he never took his attention away from the two beasts.

"What does Kahn want of his brother?" Dralin asked quietly, his voice even and flat.

"He's tried to trick us like this before!" shouted a voice from the crowd. "Don't listen to them. They're up to something!"

Frael lifted himself onto his hind legs, glowering.

"This is enough. We will hear what is to be said, and then we'll decide as to what shall be done. Now hush your cackling, and quieten down so Dralin can hear what news these two have to bring."

Dralin nodded his thanks.

"You have my ear. Speak! If you have broken no part of the Law here, you have nothing to fear from us, and may return as you will."

"Lord Kahn sends his greetings," went on the first beast, relief showing clearly on his malformed muzzle. "We were sent to ask you to a meeting on the next fullness of the moon. Many things have happened that our Lord Kahn would wish to talk to you of."

"What are these things?"

"The beasts from Dead Lake!" answered the animal shortly, lowering his voice to a whisper as he did so.

"Are they not followers of his? Why should he need to speak to me about things of his own making, and in his own country?"

"These are not of Kahn's making. They belong to no clan of ours."

"Are they the snakes with legs?" asked Earling, breaking in at the lull of the conversation.

The misshapen animal looked at the bear in some surprise.

"Have these things been on your side of the river already?" Earling shook his head.

"Then there is some truth to those tales!" shot Frael.

"It must be serious if Kahn is asking for a meeting," said Dralin, frowning, and deep in thought.

"What could he want of us?" asked Lan. "He has a large number of settlements, and many followers."

The beast, who called himself Jar Ben, spoke up.

"Oh, we have numbers enough," he said, his fangs creeping past his lower lip. "And we are in no danger for ourselves. Lord Kahn thought it only brotherly to warn Lord Dralin, and to offer any aid we might be able to provide."

Frael snorted a short bark of laughter.

"And what aid would you fellows be likely to provide? Other than helping us out of this life into the next?"

Jar Ben assumed a hurt look.

"We may have been wrong in our effort to come and warn you, and offer you Lord Kahn's aid. Perhaps it would be as well to go on back, and leave you to your own defenses."

"Don't let them leave here," called Lan angrily. "They have come to scout our numbers, and will only betray us to Kahn."

Dralin looked at the young bear evenly.

"Your point is well taken, Lan, yet we don't have to let ourselves get lathered up over it. We shall think it through."

"Let's call a meeting of the Elders," said Frael. "We shall have to decide this among all the settlement."

Jar Ben looked uneasily about him.

"We shall ask you only to escort us to the Gray Rock. We have a party that is to meet us not far from the crossing."

"I'll wager you do," shouted another voice from the crowd. "They'll be waiting for the word from you to come in and butcher us all."

"Don't leave them alive!" cried others, farther back.

"Call the Elders," said Dralin, and turning, ordered Jar Ben and the other beast to follow him into the huge meeting hall that occupied the very center of the settlement.

They reluctantly nodded, and took up a position behind the huge bear, and sat down to await the gathering of the Elders.

The beast used his best manners on Dralin.

"We know some of our less enlightened brothers have caused your settlements grief, Lord Dralin, but there has been a change in Lord Kahn's reckoning of you these last few seasons. He's always saying that the two of you should be brothers again, and share the same forest in peace."

"What has brought about this amazing change of heart?" asked Dralin, studying the two intently.

"No particular thing. Just the turning of the season."

"Then he will be anxious to end the killings, and to try to bring himself back to the Law again."

At the mention of the Law, Jar Ben winced, but forced himself to smile.

"Lord Kahn has had thoughts on the matter. Of course, nothing could be done about those concerns until the beasts from below Dead Lake have been dealt with."

"Why not invite them into our fold as well? Wouldn't they take easily to life in our settlements?"

"You must jest, Lord Dralin! Those beasts have no loyalty, no code, no Law! They even slay themselves, if the fancy hits them. We have talked to them, but all to no avail. Of course, they are afraid to attack any of Lord Kahn's settlements, for they know the great risks they would run by doing so, but we fear they may turn their raids toward you, below the Gray Rock."

Borim had followed the others into the council hall, and stood beside his father. He moved back closer to Dralin when Jar Ben directed a question at him.

"You're a fine-looking cub. What is your name?"

The beast's smile revealed a row of uneven yellow fangs.

Borim was too frightened to answer, and tried not to show his surprise when his father replied.

"Bern is the cub's name. He has just come over from the Lower Wood."

Jar Ben's eyes narrowed to slits.

"That is a name familiar to Lord Kahn. He will be interested in knowing of this."

"I'm sure he will find much to interest him, once we meet. We have much to talk over, he and I."

The conversation was interrupted for a few moments as the other bears filed in, along with a smattering of the other animal kinds that lived in the settlements in the vicinity of An Ran Bar.

Borim's eyes widened as he saw Boomer and Tolly come into the long hall. He waved shyly to them.

"I see our friends have already gotten word of all this," said Dralin, motioning for the two beavers to join him.

As they neared, Boomer raised a paw.

"You weren't even out of sight before my scouts said there was a party on its way to An Ran Bar. We thought we'd just tag along to see what the next move would be, and when we got here, we heard that you had some visitors from across the river asking you to meet with Kahn."

"There they are," replied Dralin. "They say they have come to warn us of the beasts from Dead Lake, and to offer us aid from Kahn, to help us protect our settlements."

Boomer's eyes widened.

"Now there's a real lot of help for you."

Jar Ben smiled weakly.

"We send greetings to you, flat tail, from Lord Kahn. He is willing to aid your settlement at Green Willow as well."

"How do you know we're from Green Willow?" asked Tolly suspiciously. "We've not said where we're from."

Jar Ben shuffled uncomfortably.

"I thought you said that's where you were from. Blue Pond, perhaps?"

Earling had come in with the two beavers, and now spoke.

"It seems you know our settlements well, friend, and know who belongs to each of them. It must be quite a chore to learn so much geography."

"Oh, we are familiar with all your settlements," replied Jar Ben. "Lord Kahn teaches us all about our brothers across the Gray Rock. He says we must learn to be closer."

"I'm sure he means it," said Lan. "The closer the better, especially if it's suppertime."

"That's enough," admonished Dralin. "We'll get nowhere accusing each other of ill will as to our reasons for this or that. We shall hear out what these two have to say, and then the Elders shall have their say."

"That's fair," said Frael. "We shall decide among the Elders, and then we shall probably have to cast votes as to what else is to be done."

"What about the other settlements?" asked Boomer. "Will we need to gather the other settlements?"

"Only after we find out what the real threat is," said

Dralin. "They say the beasts from below Dead Lake are even beyond Kahn's rule, so they will have no reason to stay away from us. We shall have that to decide upon. And they say Kahn wants to meet with me, himself."

"Surely you won't do that!" shot Tolly. "Why, it's probably a trap, set up to get you into his grasp once for all."

"There would hardly be a bear so dense that he wouldn't foresee that," laughed Dralin. "We don't know yet how, or where, we are to meet, if we are to do so at all."

He turned back to Jar Ben.

"What were you told to tell me? Where were we to meet?"

The beast lowered his gaze to the ground.

"Lord Kahn thought you might want to join him across the Gray Rock, at the old settlement of The Narrows."

"It is a long season since I've set foot there."

"Lord Kahn said that's where your last meeting took place."

"Under not such very good circumstances, I might venture," said Frael grimly. "I don't know if you were around to know of it, but I've remembered it right enough."

The great bear held out a forepaw, and pointed to a long, deep series of dark scar tissue that ran beneath the rich fur, from his heavy shoulders all the way across his massive chest.

"Those were trying times," said Jar Ben softly. "I know Lord Dralin and Lord Kahn have had their differences, but it seems the time is come to end all the ill feelings and bad blood that is between them."

Jar Ben hesitated a moment, as if unsure of himself, then went on, haltingly.

"Lord Kahn would very much like to see the new cub, Bern, too. If you choose to meet with him, I'm sure he'll want to see so handsome a fellow as this. It's not often you see a bear of such a nature."

Borim shuffled uneasily.

Tolly, snorting loudly, turned and clapped Borim a hearty pat.

"Our good cub Borim is not to be met often, nor the likes of him. Lord Dralin's cub is a rare bear."

Dralin had started to raise a paw to caution the beaver, but too late. Jar Ben showed great surprise at the beaver's revelation, then quickly covered it.

"Borim?" he asked warily. "I thought I had heard you say Bern, my Lord Dralin?"

"It is Bern, Jar Ben. My friend Tolly refers to a cub we have heard of, also from the Lower Wood."

Tolly, wrinkling his whiskers in embarrassed silence under the glaring eyes of Dralin, simply nodded and muttered, "Quite right, quite right! Bern is what I meant, anyhow."

The beaver was so upset, it was evident to all that his attempt to correct his mistake only made Jar Ben more suspicious. Borim, catching the eyes of the beast staring intently at him, moved away a step, and felt a cold chill of horror raising the hackles along the back of his neck.

Final Instructions

Around a late fire, a troubled council was held.

Drinking mugs of mulled tea, Dralin, Frael, Earling, Lan, Hollen, Borim, and a few others of the different bear clans sat talking with Boomer and Tolly, who represented the beaver tribes. And then there were various other animals, bringing news that there would be others present, as soon as they were able to reach An Ran Bar from the more remote settlements of the wood.

Dralin paced back and forth, gazing away into the fire, his brow deeply furrowed. Frael looked worriedly from the fire to Dralin, although he kept his thoughts to himself. At last, after a long silence, Dralin turned to the others, speaking in a slow, thoughtful voice.

"I have thought long on what Jar Ben has said to us of Kahn, and what possible motives he may have in wanting a meeting now, to offer us aid to defend ourselves against these new beasts that seem to be even beyond Kahn's control. I don't paint any rosy picture about a sudden change of heart on my brother's part, but I would be interested in finding out how dangerous a threat these new beasts are; and if they have frightened Kahn into a meeting with me, then there must be something to the rumor everyone has been spreading about so eagerly."

He paused, looking sternly at Tolly, who shuffled his forepaws uneasily and cast his glance away from the bear's.

"I wonder that Kahn should think we would have anything to do with him, after the treachery of the last meeting he arranged," said Earling.

"Then you would vote no to any new expedition?" asked Dralin.

"I would vote no to anything to do with Kahn or his affairs. It can mean no good to us."

"Even if we might find some news that would help us prepare a defense against these new beasts Jar Ben says are beginning to come forth out of Dead Lake?"

"You don't need a meeting with your brother to find out the truth of those tales. We'll simply send out a party on our own to see what's the lay of the land, and make our own decisions without risking getting tangled up with Kahn. He has never been anything but grief and trouble to us."

"You speak with earnest feelings, Earling, and I don't misdoubt but that you believe what you say. Yet we must think evenly where so much is at stake. And if there is even the slightest chance that Kahn has changed his ways, then we must not miss any opportunity because of past behavior. We all change from day to day, and I can't say with absolute certainty that something has not happened that may make Kahn look on things in a different light."

"Don't you think he might have come himself, if all that's true?" asked Boomer. "That might show a bit more goodwill than sending Jar Ben." The beaver shuddered. "I hate to think of meeting that nasty fellow in a dark wood."

"Kahn might have felt that he would have been slain before he reached me," replied Dralin. "There are those in this settlement, as well as the others, that would have no second thoughts at slaying one responsible for the deaths of so many kin."

Lan slammed his mug down on the arm of his chair.

"He would never have lived to see you again, had I had an opportunity to meet him on his way here!"

The young bear's voice was ice-hard and brittle.

"He is no green cub, Lan," admonished Dralin. "You might find yourself more than evenly matched."

"Then I would at least have the honor of a clean, swift death in battle."

"That's exactly what Kahn was always so fond of saying," said Hollen, an ancient silver-gray bear, who had great tufts of fur on either side of his muzzle, and darker gray rings around his paws. "And look where that hot blood got him."

"Hollen is right," agreed Frael. "We can often become as bad as a problem we are trying to overcome."

Unrepentant, Lan snorted.

"Then I would gladly become as bad, or worse, than this one. If there was even a chance that I might succeed, I would leave tomorrow in Dralin's place, to meet Kahn and end this business forever."

"You may forget that," said Dralin coldly.

There was a tone to the huge bear's voice that caused Lan to lower his hackles immediately and sit back quietly in his chair.

"Do you propose to go through with this, Dralin?" asked Frael.

"I am thinking of it," he answered, moving the cup back and forth in his paws, thinking deeply.

"I'll go with you," put in Boomer solidly. "You'll need a good craftsman along, someone who can get about quietly, and perhaps someone who might not be so obvious."

Dralin smiled at the small animal.

"You are a true friend, Boomer. I thank you for your support, but I really don't think any need go with me on this trip, except perhaps Bramweld and Frael."

"Bramweld!" cried Lan. "But he won't go. I can go as easily as he."

"But it will have to be Bramweld. Otherwise I don't think Kahn would find it in his interest to listen to our proposal."

"Will you be able to convince Bramweld?" asked Hollen. "He didn't seem any too anxious to have anything to do with matters outside his own settlement."

"I think we can talk him into going, if we can show him that it would be the best for all of us."

"Will I go?" asked Borim suddenly.

Dralin studied his cub a moment before he answered.

"I think you will stay with Hollen. You have things that will demand you be right here in An Ran Bar."

There was something in Dralin's voice that caused Borim's heart to skip a beat.

"I would like to go with you," he said.

"I don't think that will be possible this time, Borim. Bramweld is my more likely companion, simply because of a long-standing feud among the three of us—Kahn, Bramweld, and myself. We'll take Frael along to keep an eye on things, and to be the general second to all that might go on, and as a messenger to bring any news back here, should anything unexpected happen."

Frael's ears shot forward.

"What would happen of that nature, Dralin? You surely

don't intend to do anything foolish enough to place yourself in danger, do you?"

"Bramweld won't be a party to all this," said Lan, getting up angrily. "I know him, and I know he won't agree to any of it. I'm the one to go with you and Frael."

Earling joined in, coming to stand beside Dralin.

"If anyone goes, it should be me."

Dralin shook his head, but gave his friend a hearty clap on his broad back.

"What we need here is as few in numbers as may be advisable to travel across the Gray Rock. We're not looking for a fight with any of the beasts from Dead Lake, or combat with Kahn. What we are seeking here is a meeting with my brother, and for Bramweld to accompany me. Frael is my second elder here, and has the most experience in these matters, and if there is anyone who knows his way around these woods, it's him. We may be going into a part of the Eastern Wood no one else is familiar with. It's this knowledge we need, not muscle."

"I knew that wood as a cub, before it was taken over by the beasts of Kahn and this new filth from below Dead Lake."

"That's why it is you who must guide Bramweld and me to a meeting. We will take no one else with us."

"What about Jar Ben? What will we do with him and his friend?" asked Earling.

"We shall find some way to keep them occupied here in An Ran Bar," said Dralin. "I don't think it would be wise to let them go before we have met with Kahn. He seems to have some reason of his own for wanting to leave here in a hurry. And he knows Borim is here."

"Why would that matter?" asked the cub. "And why did you tell him my name was Bern?"

"Because Kahn has been waiting for a sign, just as everyone has," replied Dralin. "Bern is a name as familiar to his followers as Borim is to mine."

"What has my brother to do with those beasts, and Kahn?"

"More than I can tell you now, Borim. You must not worry yourself over these things as yet. There will be a place for these questions to be answered, and you will find them all revealed to you in good time."

"But why would Kahn want to know anything about me?"

"Because he knows that whenever you show yourself in An Ran Bar, Bern won't be far behind."

Borim jumped up from his chair.

"Bern! Is he to be coming here, too?"

Dralin nodded sadly.

"He is. And I don't expect he's too far behind."

"But that's wonderful," exclaimed Borim.

Frael and Earling looked strangely at him, and Lan turned away, snorting wearily.

"We will have much to catch up on," went on Borim, his spirit undampened by the cool reception the news of Bern's arrival brought out in the others. "And I shall be able to find out about Alena, and all the rest."

"You will have small talk to your heart's content, Borim," said his father.

"Will he come here?" persisted Borim. "Or will I have to go somewhere else to meet him?"

"He will be brought here, I'm sure. All the settlements are on watch for his crossing."

"But then I'll have someone to talk to while you are on this journey."

"Perhaps."

"Better if it were not so," said Earling. "I'd feel much easier if I knew you would be gone and back before Borim's brother shows up."

"That might be the case. We can't say for certain."

"I'd much rather it be so," agreed Frael. "Kahn may take the news in another light, and then there would be only trouble."

"We may meet with Kahn before he has word of any new arrivals in An Ran Bar."

"I hope so. But won't he suspect something if you travel to meet him with Bramweld?"

"Why should he be surprised to see his two brothers together?" asked Dralin. "Isn't that only as it should be?"

A faint, mocking smile played across the bear's large muzzle.

"It's as it should be, and exactly as it was said to be, at a certain time. Whether anyone tells Kahn or not of Borim's arrival, he'll suspect as much when he lays eyes on you and Bramweld traveling together."

"He may. Then again, he may not. Times have changed. Jar Ben has said there are things across the river that are different now."

"Not that different," growled Lan. "And he may still have it in his plans to rid himself of the Elder of An Ran Bar. If you were gone, it wouldn't take him long to try to take the settlement for his own."

"There is Borim," said Dralin evenly. "And with Borim here, it shall never fall to Kahn, or any of the others from across the river."

"Not in battle, at any rate," said Frael.

"And it need not fall under any circumstance," went on Dralin. "We must all do as we feel we must, and take the path that beckons us. There is nothing that says that things may not change, if you look for the best, and act as such."

"We shall see that day in with a loud hurrah or two," grumbled Hollen, looking about him wistfully.

"Indeed we shall," agreed Dralin.

A commotion at the back of the room interrupted the bear before he could go on, and two figures were seen forcing their way toward where the other Elders sat, now turning curious faces to the new activity.

"They've gone!" called a tall, gangly bear before he had reached Dralin. "They've wounded their guards, and gone!"

Dralin had risen, and went to stand before the flustered, winded bear.

"Now slow down a bit. Who has gone? Jar Ben?"

"Him, and his scum of a friend. They've wounded two of us badly, and before we knew it, they had taken the secret tunnels across the Gray Rock. No one thought to look for them there, and they've gotten away clean."

Frael leapt up.

"How did they know of the tunnels? Did someone speak aloud about them in front of the prisoners?"

"No one speaks aloud of the tunnels, Frael. We searched aboveground, and in the edges of the settlement, but when we found no trace of them there, someone suggested we look to the tunnels. We didn't really think we'd find anything, but that's exactly where they had gone."

Earling scowled.

"Someone has betrayed us. No one could possibly find the tunnels unless they knew where to look."

"It was no accident. No one could find that entrance by accident."

"Then how could they have found out?" cried Lan hotly. "Someone must have spoken of it."

"No one, Lan. They knew where to go, and what to look for."

"Do you think they have too big a start to catch?" asked

Frael. "If we sent out a party now, would we be too late to keep them from gaining the deep wood across the river?"

"There was a large party waiting for them," went on the guard. "We found the tracks all over the other bank. It looked as if they had been waiting there for a long while."

A grim silence fell over the animals as this news sank in, and they all turned to see what Dralin would have to say about these new and frightening events.

He hesitated only a moment before answering.

"We are leaving right now, Frael. We shall find Bramweld in Black Grove, or nearby, and travel on from there. Earling, you and Lan stay with Borim. Hollen, you are in charge here. Boomer, you and Tolly go and bring all the Green Willow animals into An Ran Bar, and send messengers to all the others to join us here."

"What are you going to do, Dralin? There's no point in trying to meet with Kahn now. Jar Ben will tell him everything. And if he knew how to get out the secret tunnels, then they have somehow found news about all the rest of our defenses. No one will be safe here any longer."

"We're not staying," replied Dralin. "I said gather everyone here, not that we were staying."

"But then what?"

"We're going on up the Gray Rock. Or rather Hollen, Earling, Lan and Borim will lead all the rest of you up there."

"That's madness, Dralin," cried Hollen. "The beasts are already there."

"We're crossing upriver, and moving on toward Kahn's settlement."

Dralin paused a moment.

"No one will expect to see us there."

"And what about Kahn?" asked Lan. "Won't he move to stop us?"

"He's long wanted An Ran Bar, so we'll leave it to him. But Kahn may find something else to hold his attention now, other than settlements."

Before the stunned animals could question him further, he had sent them all away, except for Borim, who sat down beside his father and tried to listen as Dralin began to give him his final instructions before departure.

The Wayward Brother Appears

If Borim ever spoke of that meeting with his father, no one ever heard of it, and even long ages later, Lan wondered at the mystery of it, and what could possibly have been said at such a late hour.

Borim went with Dralin into the ancient hall of Bruinthor, past the tall book-lined rooms and the feast rooms, farther on, until they reached a small study, done in simple wood and stone, that overlooked an inner courtyard which was built around a fountain that bubbled and sang in a cheerful fashion and changed from bright blue to clear silver ever so often, much to Borim's delight.

But what his father had to tell him had saddened him almost to the point of numbness, and it was a long space of time before he could answer Dralin. In that quiet room, which was his father's private study, and a room not many in An Ran Bar had ever seen, the great bear had told his cub his plan, and what must be done, and what was expected of him as the new Elder.

"But you're the Elder," insisted Borim stoutly, trying very hard to overcome his great tendency to surrender to the overwhelming grief he felt welling inside him.

"I have been so for a great many turnings, Borim. It is now time that I shall finish up the part I have been given to play."

"What about An Ran Bar? And Earling, and Lan, and Frael? You can't just leave!"

"Frael and the others have known that this time would come to pass. We have discussed it often enough."

"Then why can't we all go? Why not move the settlement across the Gray Rock? You said that was what we should do."

"That was before I had word to the contrary."

Dralin paused and studied his stout cub thoughtfully.

"Your half brother is here. He arrived not long after Jar Ben disappeared. It seems he was brought to An Ran Bar by the beast party, and came through the tunnels as the others left."

"Bern!" cried Borim. "Bern is here?"

For a moment he was elated, but lapsed back into a confused silence.

"It is the time that was given, Borim," went on Dralin

softly. "I have an idea that Kahn perhaps has thought this was a way to destroy me, and my settlement here, for he knew of the old lore, and that it was all put down into the Law. He read parts of it as a cub when we were coming into our bearhood, and I'm sure Hollen taught him well, as he always does. I'm afraid Kahn was not as astute a student of the Law as he was of the hunt, though, for he forgot or overlooked the fact that the time I have marked for my departure is the time for his own. You are to me what Bern is to Kahn. It is now time to turn over these matters to the next in line."

"I don't know anything," insisted Borim desperately. "I don't know the first thing about An Ran Bar, or anything that you do. I've hardly been here at all, and now I'm to become an Elder? It doesn't make any sense. There's Hollen, and Frael, and Earling. There are any number of bears to replace you, if you leave."

"None but you, Borim! It is already done, and has been, long before any of us ever walked these fields and woods."

"I won't do it. I'll just turn it all over to Hollen," said Borim defiantly.

He was badly frightened by Dralin's behavior, and terrified, and saddened at once, to think that after so short a stay with his father, it was to be ended.

"It won't be agreeable to any of them, Borim. They have all had their time, in one place or other. They will help guide you, and be at your side, but this is your responsibility. There is no other way."

"Well, I won't!" snapped Borim. "We'll see who will or won't do what. Anyone can see that Hollen is the next in line to rule An Ran Bar. He is the oldest."

"He has already served," answered Dralin simply.

"Then why are you leaving? You said we should have a long time together to learn all the things I'd need to know."

Dralin shrugged, and looked away from the perplexed cub.

"There are things that even the wisest cannot know in advance."

"But you promised," insisted Borim, a wild panic beginning to grow deep inside him.

The older bear's voice hardened, and for a moment Dralin looked as he often did to those subjects at An Ran Bar that might need a rebuke or correction in some aspect of their behavior. An icy chill ran down Borim's back to see this side of Dralin, the Elder of An Ran Bar.

"You are not to argue further with me, Borim. I feel I have been as patient with you as I have been able, and we are wasting valuable time arguing the point. I have reasons of my own for not wanting to see Bern, but not what you might suspect. He is, after all, the cub of Alena, and no matter what else, there is that to be considered."

Borim suddenly remembered Bern.

"Will he stay here with me?"

A new interest took his mind off the fear he felt at being abandoned.

"Yes, he will be here with you for a time."

"Then it won't be all bad," said Borim. "I shall at least have a friend to talk to and have games with."

He suddenly recalled that there were to be no more games for him. His cubhood had been cut short since his arrival within the confines of An Ran Bar.

"You have many friends you may talk to, Borim. Do not neglect Hollen, and Frael, and Lan. And Earling has always taken a great interest in your doings, even before you came to us. We have kept up with you, although you may not have known."

"None of them can replace Bern. I like them well enough, but he knows me better than any of them ever could, and has taken time in the past to be a friend, when no one else would."

"There's no doubt of that, my good cub. I have no mistaken ideas of that. And I know it will be as it shall be, yet I caution you to heed Frael and Earling in their words of advice to you."

"I shall, if they don't ask me to do something like give up my friendship with Bern. I know how they feel about my brother."

"Then we shall leave it at that. There is no point in going over what cannot be changed."

A soft rap at the dark carved door broke the silence that fell after Dralin stopped speaking. Borim's hackles were half raised, as they always were whenever anyone challenged his loyalty to Bern, but he quickly calmed down upon the entry of Boomer and Tolly, who acted as though they were in the habit of often visiting Dralin in his very private quarters.

Borim had seen that behind the other door was a snug sleeping hammock, hung in a simply furnished room, whitewashed, that held only a plain wooden stool before a small desk. Upon it were two large books and a tall candle, housed in a beautifully shaped glass globe, which Lan had told him had been fashioned by an ancient clan of folk that lived beneath the earth, almost like animals, but more upright in stature, and with peculiar habits of thought and dress. All these were new tales to Borim, and he enjoyed listening to Frael reading to him from the lore books. Except now it would all be different, and he would not be able simply to enjoy them as quaint stories to fill his mind. Borim tried to make himself believe that his father was really leaving, but could not force himself to accept that fact as truth. And with Boomer and Tolly there with him now, in the quiet stillness of the warm room, it was impossible to understand the things Dralin was saying, or to take too seriously the idea that his father might, indeed, go suddenly and forever out of his life, even though he himself had only shortly before arrived in An Ran Bar.

All these ideas confused Borim, and he tried to concentrate on what the beaver Boomer was saying.

"We've brought you good news. The Gray Rock is clear on beyond Blue Pond, and Reed Landing hasn't had a sniff of any trouble in so long they thought my scouts had lost their senses, even suggesting such a thing. They finally did agree to posting an outguard, after much argument, and they've sent two animals along here to study the situation and report back."

"You've done your work quickly, Boomer. I had hardly hoped to hear back from Reed Landing so soon."

Borim frowned, then turned a questioning look to Dralin.

"Are you going to Reed Landing?" he asked.

"Perhaps. I was interested in knowing if the countryside up that way was troubled by the onset of some new beasts from across the river."

"If you're going to be gone, what difference does that make?"

"It is for you the information comes," replied Dralin.

It was Tolly's turn to look confused.

"Are you off on another outing, Lord Dralin? Do you need our service?"

The huge bear smiled at his tiny comrade.

"My thanks, Tolly, but this is a trip that only Bramweld shall accompany me on."

"Bramweld? Isn't he in Black Grove still? I wouldn't think he'd be any too eager to go with you anywhere, after all that to-do here."

"He's waiting for me at this moment," replied Dralin. "We have agreed to this trip, and its importance. He is never one to waste a trip that can be better left undone."

"No offense, but he seems a bit crabby to my way of thinking. I'd much rather have someone a little more cheerful about."

"Oh, he has his cheerful side," said Dralin, laughing a short bark of amusement. "I have seen him plenty enough times enjoying himself, although that's been a long time ago, now."

"Maybe there's not too much in Black Grove to be happy about," suggested Boomer.

"There's little enough anywhere to be laughed at," agreed Tolly. "Still, it's a sorry animal that can never find anything of a lighthearted nature to share with his neighbors."

"Beaver talk," smiled Dralin. "All you fellows are the same, always trying to look at the light side of things."

Boomer's brow knit slowly, and he studied Dralin a moment before he replied.

"I wouldn't say we were as light-headed as the otters or squirrels, but then I guess we might be a bit more taken with a sense of humor than a mole or a badger."

"You see?" laughed Dralin. "Always so serious. It is one reason I have come to trust your views on certain things, and one of the main things I'd like for you to try to teach this thick-headed cub of mine."

"Bears don't do dam mending well at all," began Tolly, but Dralin cut him short.

"You have known these woods for a good long while, and you know a part about them that no others know. If you will teach that to Borim, I think he will come to find that knowledge to his advantage."

The beavers frowned, thinking.

"I don't know that we have anything of interest to a bear, or anyone else, for that matter," mumbled Boomer. "We do a fair job of work with our river, but I can't see how that would be of any interest to any but other beavers."

"I'm speaking of something else, Boomer. Something I told you of many turnings ago, when we had first met."

Boomer turned a puzzled look to Dralin.

"Whatever could that have been? I mean, we've discussed a lot of news in our friendship, but I don't remember anything out of the way of what might be called ordinary."

Dralin's face changed, and suddenly he looked very old.

"There is a place we spoke of, you and I. And there was to be a chore you were to do for me."

Boomer's jaw fell open, and his eyes turned dark brown.

"That was only your way of teasing me," he began, but saw that the bear was in earnest, and awaiting his reply.

Boomer swallowed twice in succession without being able to speak.

"What chore was that?" asked Borim, beginning to be afraid of the answer.

The small animal shuddered and turned to Dralin for help.

"We won't have to weight anyone else down with our little secrets, Boomer. It is enough for us to know, and no one else. It's merely a matter of each of us having a certain job to do, and no more."

"Why can Boomer know, and not me?" asked Borim, beginning to feel hurt at being excluded.

And after all, a beaver was a beaver, and a bear was a bear, to say nothing at all of the fact that Dralin was his own sire.

"Boomer has a need to know, for he is the one for the job," replied Dralin. "And it was decided long ago, when he and I were no more than pups ourselves."

"I never dreamed it would really come to pass," stammered Boomer. "It all sounded grown-up and exciting when we talked about it then. And it seemed so unreal that it could never happen."

"These things are no more than passing moments, my friend. And we must carry out our parts as best we are able. There's no need shirking in hopes something will change."

"Will someone please let me know what we're talking about?" shot Tolly, finding his voice at last.

"A mere matter of dams and tunnels," said Dralin easily. "Nothing more than that. Boomer has the task of helping me find a certain place, and then of making sure it is hidden again."

"Where on earth could there be that Boomer would know of that you wouldn't?" continued Tolly. "Especially in An Ran Bar?"

"This isn't in An Ran Bar, or anywhere near here," replied Dralin. "It is to be known only to myself and one other. Boomer was told then what the task was, and where it was to be."

"Is Bern here, then?" asked Boomer, his voice tight.

Dralin nodded.

At this, Borim's hopes rose again, for he had forgotten the news of his brother's arrival.

"If he is here, then where can I find him?"

"He'll be with you soon enough, Borim. Now I have a word

111

or two for Boomer, so I'd like you to take Tolly back to the library. You may wait for us there."

Boomer looked drawn and upset, but forced a smile.

"We'll be along before you know it. You two run on."

Dralin was bent close to the small animal's ear as the friends left the room, and Borim could not mistake the obvious discomfort of Boomer, although his father had been trying very hard to make light of the matter, whatever it was.

"What do you suppose they're up to?" asked Tolly, looking back over his shoulder as they left. "You'd think they had a good deal to hide, from the way they're carrying on. Regular conspirators."

"I don't know, but I'm worried. Boomer doesn't look like he wants to do whatever it is."

"Boomer can sometimes be rather slow to take up things," agreed Tolly. "But once he gets into the swing, he's a fair good one to have along."

The small animal spoke with considerable pride.

"My father may have trouble talking him into this, by the looks of it."

"Oh, Boomer warms up to an idea easily enough, once you've got him on to it. And there's no arguing with Lord Dralin."

"On some items," agreed Borim. "Although I think they've treated my brother rather unfairly."

Tolly didn't answer right away.

"There's always been a bit of a rumor about that, although I can't say I hold too much by stories of that nature."

"What sort of rumors?" asked Borim, drawing to a halt at the tall oaken door that led to the library.

Tolly shifted his gaze to the floor.

"Oh, you know, this and that, but nothing you can ever remember."

"Are these stories about Kahn?"

"Some of them," replied the beaver. "I've never been able to find out who started them, although you hear them everywhere, even in settlements a long way from An Ran Bar."

"I'd like to find out who starts them," said Borim hotly. "I'd soon put an end to their tongue wagging."

He had thrown open the door as he spoke, and gotten halfway into the room before he saw the seated figure at the long table before the book-strewn wall.

Bruinthor's Ancient Horn

Bern sat with his back to Borim, facing the row of books before him. He held a thick volume in his paw, and snapped it shut with a loud noise as his brother entered the room, and called out.

"Well met, little brother!" exclaimed the older bear. Bern was aged, and looked much different, especially about the eyes.

Borim forgot himself for the moment, and despite his brother's loud protests, he fell on with a series of strong hugs and low growling nips such as they had shared as cubs in Alena's cave. After another bout of hugs and nips, Borim held the smaller bear out to inspect him carefully, his mind spinning with questions he wanted to ask, so that nothing but various woofs and snorts and barks were heard.

Tolly, embarrassed by the outburst of Dralin's cub, excused himself noisily, leaving the two bears alone.

"Easy, brother! You'll be the death of me, if you're not careful."

Bern slipped from Borim's grasp, and retreated to stand by the table where he had been reading. A strange look passed over his pinched muzzle, and he leaned over to paw the book he had placed there.

"I'm sorry if I'm so edgy, Borim. I have had a bad time of it these past weeks trying to find you."

Borim crossed the room to stir up the fire.

"Can I get you something, brother? There's mulberry tea here. We can go back to the kitchens if you're hungry."

"No, nothing right now. I'll be all right as soon as I get my breath. The excitement of finally seeing you again is too much, I guess."

Borim started forward to grasp Bern in another hug, but the smaller bear kept the table between them.

"No, I'm fine now. I've been sitting here waiting since they brought me. They said you were with Lord Dralin, and that I could wait for you here."

"How did you ever come to find me? Did you come over the mountain behind me? In the dead of winter?"

"I guess I followed along the same path you took. There

113

were a few animals about that told me they had seen you. It was a bit of bother, with all the snow, but I've seen worse."

"Did you come through the cave?"

"There was a cave," went on Bern. "Or a cave of sorts. There were a lot of lights and noises, and then I ended up not far from here. It was all very strange. It wasn't winter anymore here."

"Were there some other bears there to guide you? A big bear named Frael, and another called Earling?"

Bern's eyes clouded over, and he looked away from Borim.

"No, I don't think those were their names. They found me, though, as you say, and brought me along here. I don't recall them saying their names. An odd sort. Very silent."

"That was what happened to me at first, when I first saw Frael. But he finally told me who he was, and then Dralin was there. That really frightened me. I'd come all that way, and then there he was, as easy as that."

"Was he glad to see you?" asked Bern cautiously. "Or was he disappointed?"

Borim frowned.

"I don't know what to think. He seemed very cold at first, but now that I know him better, I can see that's the way he has to be, since he's Elder of An Ran Bar. We've had some nice talks since then, though."

"Did he mention me?"

Again Borim gave a troubled snort.

"He has mentioned you. In truth, he was the one who just now told me you were here. Or would be here."

It was Bern who frowned next.

"Lord Dralin told you?"

"Just a few minutes ago. We left him with Boomer, and came along here, and then I saw you."

"I wonder if I could see him?" asked Bern, shifting his gaze from Borim to the great wall of books.

It was hard for Borim to read the look, although for a moment he thought he saw fear there.

"I'm sure he wouldn't mind," said Borim, although deep inside he knew the opposite to be true.

Borim wasn't sure what had happened to change Bern, or what it was that had been changed, but he felt an odd uneasiness when he caught Bern's eyes studying him.

"I'm not so sure. He has spoken against me, hasn't he?"

Borim started to shake his head to deny it, but Bern cut him off with a wave of his paw.

"I know it well enough. And I know that the others here have all filled your head with nonsense about me, and all the trouble I shall be, and that I am Lord Kahn's cub, and not to be trusted."

Borim gave a relieved sigh.

"At least you know of all of it. I have had many arguments with Lan and Frael and Hollen about that. They told me you were not Dralin's cub, and that you would only be trouble wherever you went."

Bern looked frightened and defiant at once.

"Can I see him?"

"He is with Boomer now. I don't know if we should disturb them."

"Who is Boomer?"

"A beaver friend."

Bern's voice lowered once more.

"I wouldn't want to pry or snoop into your affairs, Borim, but I have had it on good authority that those beaver clans have something planned that won't be very well suited to any but themselves."

Borim, shocked at these words, looked puzzled.

Bern went on to explain.

"It is to everyone's advantage now to be allied as we are, one clan with another, in our common defense. An Ran Bar has spread its protection to all the other settlements in these woods for a long time now. But there is talk about that the other clans are getting more than our own."

Borim, somewhat disappointed to be talking about affairs that did not interest him, and hoping they would soon get down to other matters, tried to change the subject.

"That may be so, but Lord Dralin can handle that sort of thing. He knows who to see and what to do."

"You see how it starts? First I see you with the beaver Tolly, then I find out that there is another with Lord Dralin at the very moment I try to warn you. These small clans are very clever."

"Boomer and Tolly are friends!" snapped Borim, looking hard at his brother.

There was not much of the old Bern that Borim had known so well that was still evident in the other bear. And Borim felt that he himself was not quite the same cub that had insisted on taking an outing in the dead of late fall to find his father in the high mountains.

"Boomer and Tolly have saved my life, when a beast from across the river attacked us."

"Very convenient for them, I should imagine. It is always good to have someone indebted to you."

"What do you mean, Bern? Speak what you mean."

"I mean nothing, except that things aren't always what they seem to be on the surface."

"Everyone here has said that Kahn and his followers are the ones responsible for that," snapped Borim.

"I am Lord Kahn's cub, of Alena, who is your own sow. I am not ashamed of the fact."

"That's exactly what I told Frael," blurted Borim, sorry at his anger showing. "I told them that just because Kahn has gone bad doesn't mean that his cub will."

Bern paused a moment before he answered, a curious look crossing his muzzle.

"Then they have even told you all those lies about Kahn. I should have guessed as much."

"Everyone says it is Kahn who has created all the trouble," said Borim. "He wants An Ran Bar. And now we hear that some other beasts that even he can't control have come into his settlements, and he wants to meet with Lord Dralin to talk of a truce."

"You were always too quick to believe anything anyone told you," scolded Bern. "Do you remember our sister telling you how much fun it would be to jump out of the top of that tall oak tree into the pond?"

Borim coughed nervously.

"You almost drowned that day. All because you believed what she said. And what she wanted was for you to go away and leave her alone. If I hadn't happened along just when I did, I daresay we wouldn't be having out little chat now."

"She didn't mean any harm," defended Borim stoutly.

"No, I don't think she thought you'd be silly enough to take her at her word. Yet how were you to know? It seemed a good idea then."

"That's different."

"How? You see, you've done the same thing here. All these animals are giving you their version of a story, and you've accepted it all without question, or waiting to hear the other side."

"Bramweld said it, too," said Borim, more confused than ever.

He saw the brother he remembered from when he was a small cub, talking in that same logical manner, endlessly explaining things to him, except that now it seemed odd, and didn't feel exactly right.

Bramweld was a bear that Borim knew wouldn't lie, or attempt to deceive anyone. It was true that he had heard only Lord Dralin's side of the story, and that he had accepted everything as the truth, mainly on the force of having seen the slain beasts, and then Jar Ben and the other, who had just escaped from An Ran Bar. And they had said that Bern came with the group who had known where the tunnels were. His thoughts grew more disorganized, and he began to hate himself for his disloyalty to Bern, half brother or not, who had shown him all the patience and kindness, and who had, as he pointed out a few moments past, even been responsible on at least one occasion for actually saving his life.

"Who is Bramweld?" asked Bern.

"Dralin and Kahn's brother. He lives at Black Grove."

"The renegade? I've heard tales of Black Grove."

"Bramweld was in a camp not far from here. He's strange, but I don't think he's a renegade."

"Has he helped defend An Ran Bar, or any of the other settlements? Or offered to come to anyone's aid?"

Borim was shaking his head.

"He said he didn't want any part of anyone's feud, and that he was simply going to live out his time in peace."

Bern snorted.

"More sensible than some I know. He might be an all right sort."

"But Dralin wants him to go along to see Kahn."

"Are they going to do that?" shot Bern, suddenly interested again in the talk.

"I don't know. I guess so. That's what Dralin says. And he says that Bramweld would go with him, once he knows you're here."

The other animal looked perplexed.

"Why would that make any difference? And how will he know I'm here?"

"Dralin said you'd be here when I first came."

"I wonder how he came to know that? I only knew a few nights ago."

Bern's voice had an uneasy ring, and he glanced nervously about.

Tolly came back at that moment, and the silent appearance of the small animal seemed to shake Bern.

"Here you are still," complained the beaver, "chattering like magpies when there's work to be done."

"What work is that?" asked Borim.

"Getting ready to move the settlement, that's what work. And that's no easy task, if you ask me. I don't see any sense to it, but there's no arguing with Lord Dralin once he's made up his mind. You know how stiff his neck can be once he's got it into his head how a thing is going to be."

Bern's eyes widened.

"Move the settlement? You don't mean An Ran Bar?"

Tolly looked steadily at Bern.

"That's the news as I have it. It seems that Jar Ben and his friends have somehow found out all the secret passages into the settlement, and Lord Dralin has it in his mind to just give over An Ran Bar to Kahn."

Bern's jaw dropped.

"Why on earth for?" he managed to blurt out at last.

"That's what I'd like to know," agreed Tolly, nodding vigorously. "Makes no sense at all. No need to do anything more than flood the tunnels, and that would be that."

"Can that be done?" asked Borim, finding a fleeting hope that perhaps if that could be done, then Dralin wouldn't have to leave, and the whole question of Bern wouldn't have to be dealt with.

Borim had odd emotions flashing through him, from elation at seeing his half brother again, to a disturbing note that lingered just below the surface that something was out of harmony, some small shadow he saw in Bern's eyes that had not been there before.

"Oh, the tunnels can be flooded anytime, and there would be no problem with anyone coming through that way. It's the other problem now that may be resting in Lord Dralin's craw."

"Would that be my arrival?" asked Bern quietly.

Tolly nodded twice.

"It would. There's no doubt you've caused a bit of a stir with your showing up just now."

"Be careful of your tongue, Tolly," warned Borim, but the small animal was not intimidated.

"There's no secret to any of these goings-on, Borim. If you study your lore books with a little more care, you'll see this repeated over and over."

"See what?" snapped Borim, angry that he had let a nagging little doubt enter his mind, and angry at his small friend for forcing him to face it.

118

"It's always the same," went on the beaver. "There's the loyal, good sort, who is faithful to the end, and it is his very loyalty that blinds him to all the deceit and treachery. Read your histories of any of the lores, and you'll find that lesson in all of them."

"Is this the way you allow strangers to treat your brother?" asked Bern, his tone injured, although he was unable to meet Borim's glance.

"It's too much, Tolly. You make grave accusations here, and I think it would be better for you to leave your thoughts to yourself."

"They are not my thoughts alone, Borim," said Tolly evenly. "It's one thing to be a friend, and another to be a fool."

Borim had gathered a huge breath to speak, but Bern interrupted him.

"It's all right, Borim. I don't fear the tongue of any who speak ill of me."

"It's beyond good manners," blustered Borim. "And friend of my father's or not, I think an apology is due."

Tolly bowed gravely to Borim.

"I don't wish to offend anyone, Borim."

"Then keep your lore stories to yourself. They don't apply here."

"As you will," said Tolly, shrugging and falling silent.

"We might straighten this whole matter up if I speak to Dralin. He surely cannot refuse me equal time to answer all these ridiculous charges that seem to be leveled at me on all sides."

"I think that would be the wisest," said the beaver, ignoring Borim's icy glare.

"We shall decide on our own what is to be done," snapped Borim. "And I'm not sure my father is through talking to Boomer yet."

"Then Frael might be able to help," suggested Tolly.

"Frael is one of the worst to talk to," glowered Borim. "He's one of the first who tried to turn me against Bern."

Bern smiled thinly.

"You won't find many in this camp who will be willing to give me a fair hearing."

"Then we'll find some way," insisted Borim grimly. "I'm supposed to be learning how to be the Elder of An Ran Bar, and one thing I know Dralin does in a case like this is to give an animal every chance of a fair and just hearing. He made all the others in the settlement listen to what Jar Ben had to say, and would not let the crowd kill the beasts."

"And they tricked us all, by slipping away through the tunnels," reminded Tolly. "What I'd like to know is how they knew where to go?"

"They may have feared for their lives," said Bern. "If they were only messengers, and found that the settlement was going to slay them, they may have felt that they should escape as best they could. Especially if they thought they had no chance of being heard."

"How do you know they were messengers?" asked Tolly. "All we said was that Lord Dralin was going to hear out what the beast Jar Ben had to say, since he came from Kahn."

"You told me they were messengers," said Bern smoothly. "You forget things in your anger."

The beaver glowered at the large animal, but said nothing.

"It doesn't matter," snapped Borim. "What's more important now is that we find out why Dralin must leave, instead of blocking the tunnels. That would stop any threat there, even if Jar Ben did know about the passages under the river."

"It may run deeper than that," said Tolly. "Boomer has been in there with him a long time, and it sounded as if they may be in there for a long time more."

"Let's go see. We may find out something new, and Bern will get a chance to see Dralin."

The older bear stared at Borim strangely, but did not speak. As the three started for the door that led out of the library, Borim turned to Bern.

"It is good you're here, brother. You've come at an odd time, and a proper welcome isn't possible now."

"It's enough to see you again, little brother. I always remember you as the wide-eyed cub, always full of questions and mischief, and Alena forever having to chase you into her cave to get you to sleep."

"That seems so long ago now," said Borim dreamily. "I can hardly remember that at all."

"It does seem a long while ago, but it hasn't been so long."

"It must have been coming through the cave that did it," mused Borim. "I don't remember much after that. I can hardly tell you what Alena looked like."

"Maybe the mountain does that," agreed Bern. "And you seem very much different too, little brother."

"So do you."

"I? In what way?"

"I can't put my paw to it," said Borim, shaking his head. "But there's something different."

"I guess it's being grown up," offered Bern.

The beaver glowered directly at the older bear.

"It's closer to being something you aren't, and pretending otherwise, to my way of thinking."

A dangerous smile flickered across Bern's muzzle.

"A role we all play at one time or another," he countered.

They had entered the long hallway that ran the outside length of the great house of Bruinthor, and in the passage before the anteroom of Dralin, a strange noise came, followed by an equally baffling silence.

"Whatever was that?" cried Borim, breaking into a rapid trot.

"The Horn of Bruinthor," replied Tolly, close on his tracks.

They had reached the small bedroom of Dralin, where they found the outer door bolted, although they could raise no one inside with their loud cries and calls to Dralin and Boomer. Only when he stopped to catch his breath did Borim notice that Bern stood back in the shadows of the hall, and had made no move to help rouse the occupants of the locked bedroom. And the unbroken silence only echoed their calls that fell on the cold stone and wood, sending an icy blade of fear into the very depths of Borim's heart.

After a time they succeeded in finding a spare key that Frael knew of, and the grim knot of friends finally opened the door to Lord Dralin's private study to find all deserted, and no clue as to what might have become of the Elder of An Ran Bar or his friend Boomer.

In his confusion, Borim stumbled over a small object half hidden by the chair that stood pushed beside the desk, and in his frustration, he kicked savagely at it, sending it clattering loudly into the center of the floor. Stooping to pick it up, his heart leapt to his throat, and he had a good deal of difficulty breathing.

Frael, standing next to him, nodded grimly.

"The Horn of Bruinthor," he said simply. "It has passed into the hands of the next Elder of An Ran Bar."

A Fading of the Past

It took some time for the shock to wear off and he could speak again.

The snug room was just as he had left it not long before, and the small signs of his father were scattered everywhere about. A large lore book was folded open on the table, next to the flickering candle, and the chair where Dralin had sat was still warm. Of Boomer, nothing remained as a clue to his disappearance, and Tolly went about wringing his paws and making moaning noises low in his throat.

Frael and Lan were there, flanked by Earling and Hollen. None of the animals acknowledged Bern, or met his eyes, as he came to stand beside Borim.

"I can make a guess as to what has happened here," he said to the stunned Borim.

Without turning to look at his brother, the young cub merely grunted.

"It was as I told you earlier, but you were not so willing to listen then."

"What have you told the new Elder?" asked Frael harshly. "Are you to be his new adviser?"

Bern bowed low, and replied with a gentle tone.

"That is a job only worthy of one of great wisdom, sir. Perhaps you will fill that most delicate post."

Lan, barely able to conceal his hostility, stepped a pace forward, where he was held in check by Hollen.

"If it comes to a vote of this settlement, you'll be banished soon enough."

Borim regained his speech at the hard tones of his friend.

"There will be no banishment for Bern. This is his home as long as I have a say."

"You have all the say, youngster," reminded Hollen. "Your father has followed the signs, and the ritual is complete. You hold the Horn of the ancient Bruinthor there in your paw, and the mantle of power has been laid on you."

Borim forgot his confusion a moment, and drew himself up, glancing again at the sacred object he held.

It was heavy, and carved finely all around the thick throat of the instrument, and banded in simple mithra, and as he studied it, it seemed to Borim the scenes that were shown there took on a life of their own, and a dim light, first golden, then dark blue, glimmered from the surface of the horn, turning his paw a rainbow gray. His first feeling was fear, and from habit he tried to drop the live thing that glowed more fiercely as he watched, but it was as if it were grown to his body, and try as he might, he could not place the horn on the table.

"I'll help you," offered Bern, seeing what Borim was trying to do, and before anyone could move to stop him, he had reached out to grasp the instrument that his brother was struggling to put down.

Lan called out, but it went unheard in the flashing roar that followed, and the room filled with a dense white cloud, and a low rumbling note of a war horn erupted suddenly, then changed to a high reed pipe, blowing a note of warning that was at once painful and soothing to the ears.

"Who struck me?" cried Bern, looking about him vengefully as soon as the room had cleared of the thick white blanket of mist.

"No one laid a paw to you, Master Bern," said Hollen. "It was the horn. There is no one who can touch it but the rightful holder. Dralin has passed it to his cub, and until such time as he lays it to whoever follows, no one will be able to put a paw to it."

Bern's eyes blazed, and an ugly smile crossed his muzzle.

"Are you hurt?" asked Borim, still wide-eyed at the fireworks display, and amazed at the fact he could not put the horn down, and that it had kept itself from being touched by another.

Bern's tone was one of enduring forgiveness. "No, I'll be all right. I was simply trying to help you."

"I thank you," said Borim. "But it seems this is a load I shall have to carry on my own, if it is as Hollen says."

"There is the book on the table," replied the old bear. "Dralin left it out for you to study and learn, since he had no time to teach you himself."

Borim's confusion returned in a wave that threatened to engulf him.

"Why couldn't he wait? We were just talking, and Tolly said that the lower river tunnels could be flooded to keep anyone from crossing. He said An Ran Bar was safe, even if Jar Ben did know of the secret passages."

Frael shook his head sadly.

"That is not the worst thing we have to fear in the settlement, Borim. There is a danger far greater than that."

"Greater than Kahn?" asked the cub, staring wide-eyed at his friend.

"Much greater, by far. And now Kahn, Bramweld, and your father have no further roles to play here. I'm sure if we send scouting parties out tomorrow, they'll all find that there is no sign of Bramweld in Black Grove, or Kahn across the Gray Rock."

"What about those others? Jar Ben, and the other beasts? And the new ones they came to ask Dralin for help with?"

"Oh, those are there, right enough. The passing of the old order, I would imagine. Jar Ben would look well mannered compared to these things he came to complain of."

"Why do you think Kahn is gone?" asked Bern, making his voice sound uninterested.

"Because Dralin is," answered Hollen, looking at the newcomer almost sadly.

"They have nothing to do with each other," replied Bern.

"I am well aware of that. And I think Dralin felt it would come as somewhat of a surprise to Kahn, to find that a cleverly contrived plan would not work out as he would have liked it."

"What plan?" asked Borim. "Was there a plan I didn't know of?"

"It's all there in the book, my young friend. It will explain a lot of mysteries that might otherwise be baffling."

"What about Boomer?" chirped up Tolly. "All this business is among you bears, and doesn't have anything to do with the likes of us."

Bern, unnoticed by the others, turned and nudged Borim.

"You see? When it comes down to the truth of it, all this business about being allied closely to us goes out the window. His only concern is about his own clan."

"That's as it should be," replied Borim, but he looked a bit closer at the beaver, as if to see if he could read his innermost thoughts.

"And don't be surprised if there isn't something more to this than meets the eye."

Bern nodded toward the small animal before them.

"What more to it could there be?"

"We'll see when we find out some more about who was where," said Bern cryptically.

Before Borim could question him further, a large commotion outside drew their attention, and all else was forgotten for the moment. A great outcry went up from An Ran Bar, and the thriving settlement was filled with torchlight, and confused citizens, who raced about the streets, questioning their neighbors and turning worried looks on one another.

The quiet lane that ran through the courtyard was suddenly filled with anxious animals, clamoring for Dralin.

"What'll we tell them?" stammered Borim. "They won't believe he's gone."

"They'll believe it when they see you hold the Horn of Bruinthor," said Frael.

"But what will I tell them?"

"That you hold the Horn, and it is your duty to keep the settlement together, and to ensure the peace."

"But I don't want to," complained Borim bitterly. "I told Dralin so when I was with him. He's the Elder, and it's his job."

"He's gone, Borim," said Frael gently. "Like it or not, we must carry on, as he would have us."

Borim was near tears, and only an inner strength that he did not know he possessed kept him from surrendering to the feeling of despair and desertion that threatened to wash him into a great black pit with no bottom. There was Bern, it was true, but it was not the same any longer, and Bern told him such disturbing things, and created small slivers of doubt that began to erode his trust and belief that things were the way they seemed on the surface.

Borim had accepted as truth that Kahn and the beasts below the Gray Rock were guilty of forgetting the Law, and running unchecked, yet Bern presented the picture in a whole new light, and raised the question that perhaps Dralin was somehow at the bottom of the problem. Borim didn't really believe that, but it was hard to shake the nagging doubt that plagued him.

"Go on, little brother. You are the Elder now. You must reassure the settlement that nothing is wrong."

It was the way Bern phrased it that made Borim's stomach knot in fear.

"You tell them, Hollen. You are the oldest. My father said it was to be you who governed in his absence."

"I was his steward, Borim. I ran things while he was away on a journey. There was never a question of his not returning."

For the first time the finality of what he knew to be true flooded into his awareness.

"There cannot be two Elders," went on Frael, seeing the pain in Borim's eyes. "Your father was always thoughtful and considerate in matters that affected others. He knew long ago, as you will see when you get down to reading the book he left for you, that it would be painful in passing the cloak of Elder to you. When he discovered how it was to be done, he was very relieved that it would be quick and over with, and no great dragging it all out."

"Then it can be done just as easily by me handing you the Horn, Hollen. I'll pass it to you, until I know more about what is expected of me."

The old silver-tipped bear shook his head.

"It cannot be, Borim."

"It can!" he insisted, and tried to press the Horn into Hollen's paws.

Again the room filled with a dense white cloud, and the distant roaring of a great sea thundered and rolled until the animals had to cover their ears. Hearing all the noise and seeing the strange light inside the Hall of Bruinthor, the crowd outside renewed their chorus, calling louder for Dralin.

Borim felt a white-hot flame sear his paw as he thrust it at Hollen, but he could not release the dreadful object.

A deep voice suddenly boomed over the noise and confusion, causing Borim to stumble backward.

"The Elder of An Ran Bar is the only one who shall hold the Horn. It is written, and none but the rightful heir shall touch it."

"Dralin!" cried Borim, and whirled about, trying to find the source of the voice, for it was his father's, and hearing it meant that he would not have to carry the terrible burden that had been placed on him, after all.

"It's the Horn, Borim," explained Frael.

"It's Dralin! I heard him."

"It is the voice of the Horn. It may sound like your father, but it is the Horn."

"It's unusual to hear it speak," said Hollen. "I have only heard of one other time that the Horn spoke, and that was many turnings ago, when Dralin first came to be Elder."

"Now we must let the others know what has happened. There's been enough mystery about tonight, as it is."

"Are you going to tell them Dralin is gone?" asked Bern.

"Of course. They must know it for what it is. They are used to his disappearances by now. They have seen him come and go many times before this."

"What will they say when they hear he won't be coming back?"

"We don't know anything more than he has passed the

Horn of Bruinthor to his cub. That does not have to mean that he won't be back."

"He took the beaver with him. That was written! The beaver who knew how to seal the crossing place."

Frael frowned at Bern.

"And there is the appearance of the new order! That was to be the sign."

"Someone must speak to the others," said Earling, coming back from a window that overlooked the courtyard. "They're all frightened to death out there. It seems someone has put it in their heads that something has happened to Dralin."

Hollen looked straight at Bern, but said nothing.

"Come with me, Borim. We have to go now, before the rumors spread further."

"What about Boomer?" wailed Tolly.

"He'll be showing up shortly, my small friend," said Frael. "Boomer's job was perhaps the hardest of all."

"It's always hard for the traitor," said Bern quietly, the remark directed for Borim's ear only.

"There is no traitor's work that a beaver would touch," snapped Hollen, leading a reluctant Borim onto the veranda that gave onto the courtyard.

The lane was tightly jammed with animals now, and a constant stream of them filed from one street to another in An Ran Bar, some groups melting away, others forming, but the clamor grew louder and more confused, and the mobs seemed more restless.

Hollen raised a paw to quieten the uproar that was caused by his appearance. Four or five voices from the front of the throng called out loudly for Lord Dralin. After considerable difficulty, Hollen managed to make himself heard.

"I know you are upset, friends, and up in the air about the journey of Dralin."

Here a loud outcry was heard.

"Some journey! Why did we hear that he'd gone to Kahn's camp, and plan to leave An Ran Bar open to that filth from across the river?"

Hollen raised a paw, motioning for Earling and Frael to join him as he did so.

"Our plans are to evacuate the settlement and regroup on the other side of the Gray Rock, as had been arranged."

"The beasts are there," shouted a voice angrily. "We won't move a step across the river!"

"Things have changed, friend. We know now that Kahn

127

has gone, and that we must move our own settlement to avoid the new beasts that Jar Ben told us of."

"They lied!" cried the crowd. "They want An Ran Bar for themselves."

"They didn't lie," went on Hollen calmly. "They told the truth as far as they knew it. The beasts they spoke of are there, right enough, and they are more dreadful than anything Kahn ever spawned."

"Then we should stay and look to ourselves here!" called a tall brown bear in an angry voice. "Bring the other colonies to us, and let us stand at An Ran Bar. No beasts can break our defenses here."

"No beasts we know of," agreed Hollen. "But there is a new horror at work across the Northern Wood and Dead Lake. It is only written of in vague terms, but the threat is real enough."

"If that's true, then let Lord Dralin tell us himself. He must not think it much of a threat if he is off on one of his travels."

"Lord Borim is your new Elder," announced Hollen suddenly. "The passing of the Horn has been completed, and you know what that means."

A stunned silence fell as the crowd tried to comprehend this new information. Borim had frozen in his tracks at Hollen's words, then a lone voice called out from the back of the crowd.

"Let him sound the Horn of Bruinthor!"

And the chant was taken up, by one voice after another, until it had touched the tongue of every soul in An Ran Bar. Even those who were far from the Hall of Dralin heard the call, and took it up. The chant grew and multiplied until it sounded as if the wind had joined, and the mountains behind An Ran Bar trembled and echoed wildly.

Bern had come to stand beside Borim, and looked strangely at his half brother, his eyes guarded.

At that moment, the Horn called loud and clear over the noise and clamor of the gathered throngs in the streets of the settlement, and the hackles, as well as the deepest hopes, lifted in the animals' secret hearts. Twice more it rang out, its notes as sharp and fine as frozen crystals in the air. When the last echo had died away, a new chant began, and soon filled the darkness.

Borim shuddered as he heard his name carried by the voices on the wind, and the last part of him that remained a cub listened, then departed into the long-ago past of the warm cave of Alena, and the happiness of playing beneath the honey trees.

128

CROSSING
THE GRAY ROCK

Into the Realms of Kahn

After the crossing of the river that separated the realms of
Dralin and Kahn, the members of the settlement of An Ran
Bar made directly north, toward the very heart of the harsh
lands that spawned the beasts. There had been much debate
about the proposed journey, but in the end, it was finally
Frael and Hollen who pointed out that any who wished to
could stay in An Ran Bar, but there would be no safety in the
place any longer, and that the plan to move had been Dralin's
own.

Bern listened to everything with great interest, although
he never offered any suggestion of his own, and tried to keep
from being noticed as much as he could. Borim felt more at
ease talking to Bern than to any of the others, for the simple
reason he had known him the longest, and it seemed only
natural, in spite of all the dark glances he got from Lan,
Frael, and Earling.

Tolly, who had returned to Green Willow to gather his clan
there, had returned a short while later, accompanied by
Boomer, who was very grave and withdrawn, and who simply
nodded at Borim.

"Wherever have you been? And where did Dralin go?" asked Borim, faintly hoping that Boomer would have something to report that would perhaps mean that Dralin, after all, would be returning to claim the leadership of the settlement, and the heavy weight of the Horn of Bruinthor.

Tolly answered for his friend.

"I haven't had three words out of him. Found him wandering down near The Breaks, his coat full of thorns, and a wild look in his eyes that almost scared the wits out of me."

"The Breaks!" echoed Borim. "That's one of the most dangerous places of all. Frael read all about it to me, and as much as said that no animal in his right senses ever went near there."

"What sort of place is that?" asked Bern, addressing his brother rather than the beaver.

It was Frael, however, who answered him.

"The Breaks is a wild fall, so high that clouds cover the top part of it. Its sheer cliffs rise straight up, and its walls are solid rock, and slippery with the water that's always like a heavy mist there. The pool at the bottom is not large, but it has been written that it goes forever, and that there is no bottom. It's like a white storm there, and not many animals have lived to tell of seeing it, for those that dare go that close are swept off the banks by the wind that howls down through the canyon."

"It's an awful place," agreed Tolly, looking at Boomer. "One of our scouts came to me and said he'd seen Boomer there, but I didn't want to belive it. And I wasn't sure that even if we went looking, he would still be alive."

Boomer's eyes had turned darker, but he did not speak.

"Three of us went, and sent the rest of the settlement on here. There was no need putting everyone in danger."

Tolly turned to the other beaver as he spoke, and patted him gently.

"Poor old fellow, we caught him just at the edge of the Pit, wild-eyed and making groaning noises like he was going over."

"Dralin did," said Boomer so quietly that no one understood him at first.

"He talked!" shot Borim. "Maybe he'll tell us what happened now."

"Quickly, get a cup of mulled tea for him," ordered Frael, who was helping the small animal to sit beside the fire.

"What did he say?" asked Lan impatiently.

"He said Lord Dralin went into the Pit," said Bern.

A shocked silence followed, as each of the animals tried to comprehend the meaning of the dreadful news.

"The Pit," breathed Boomer. "It was there Lord Dralin disappeared. I was to go with him, to seal off his last cave, but he felt pity for me, and saved me that chore. But he didn't spare my grief."

Boomer's voice broke, and he was unable to go on.

"Are you sure, Boomer?" snapped Borim. "Was there anywhere he could have escaped to, a ledge, or outcropping?"

The beaver shook his head.

Tolly, his eyes glistening, worked hard at keeping his tone even.

"There's nothing there but the white mist of the water, where it comes over the top, and it's everywhere. There's no way you could hold to anything. Too slick! And where we found Boomer, the path, if you could call it a path, is barely wide enough for me, much less a bear the size of Lord Dralin."

Borim, refusing to believe that his father had allowed himself to perish in such a senseless fashion, went on.

"Then there must be a part of the area you didn't explore. You say yourself that the mist from the falls is so bad you can't see well! It could be there is an outcrop, or a wider path that you overlooked."

Tolly shook his head sadly.

"I wish it were so, Borim. We scoured the entire area, up and down the path both ways, until it was dark. There was nothing more to be seen, and in the dark the place is even more treacherous, so we brought Boomer away while there was still light enough to see."

Tolly frowned slightly.

"I don't think he would have ever come away at all, if we hadn't found him and made him come with us."

A queer look crossed Bern's muzzle.

"Maybe that's what he would like for you to think. It does seem odd, the whole business. If the place is as dangerous as you say, then what would they have been doing there to begin with?"

"Lord Dralin needed no permission to go anywhere, dangerous or not," snapped Tolly. "I'm sure if they were there, there was a good enough reason behind it."

Bern waited a moment before speaking, then nodded.

"As you say, Master Tolly, I'm sure there was a good reason behind it if they were in a place as dangerous as The Breaks."

"Bramweld had gone there before him," said Tolly, going on with his story and avoiding the ominous suggestions that Bern made.

Tolly did not like or trust the animal, and he was made uneasy by the acceptance that Borim showed toward him. The beaver noticed all the others around the campfire felt the same as he, and that none of the animals present looked at Bern if they could help it. Yet it was that fact that the bear used to force himself into the conversations, and it was that which seemed to make Borim overly defensive of him. It was as if Bern purposely invoked the scorn and rejection, in order to keep Borim on his side.

"Bramweld was out of Black Grove?" asked Lan. "Now there's news that's something. I never thought I'd hear the day that Lord Bramweld would give up his precious neck of the wood to go off somewhere as senseless as The Breaks."

"Bramweld left the signs," explained Tolly. "We saw them from the time we began to approach where we found Boomer. They were there, plain enough, and told Lord Dralin that he was waiting for him at the Pit."

"Then no one actually saw Bramweld at all," snorted Bern. "It could have been anyone who left the signs."

"Why would anyone want to do something like that, if it wasn't them?" asked Lan hotly. "It isn't done!"

"It's done, brother Lan, at times when you might want someone to think something other than the truth. Perhaps to throw them off guard."

"Off guard? About what? It was plain and simple, and I know it was Bramweld, for we saw his tracks as plain as day, in the mud on the lower trail. The only other bear that big would be Kahn himself."

A light glimmered in Bern's eyes, and a new thought seemed to occur to him.

"Oh? You saw the tracks, then?"

"We saw everything on that trail, in and back," insisted Tolly. "I had two of my best scouts with me. They've been at it a long turning or two, and I daresay they know signs and spoor as well as anyone in these woods."

"I'm quite sure they do," soothed Bern. "It just seems so out of place for Bramweld to be out of his own wood."

"It seems out of place for these bears to be out of An Ran Bar," shot Lan, his temper flaring. "I'm not sure yet what it is

132

we're about, or where exactly we're bound, but I'd welcome anyone with some solid answers to that."

"Hear, hear," said Frael. "The hotpaw has some sense of logic, after all."

"And a sense of disaster, too," the young bear snorted. "First we find news that Lord Dralin's gone over, then Bramweld, and we're now without a permanent shelter, across Kahn's river, walking around in the beasts' backyard, sitting down to tea, just like any afternoon gossip."

Hollen nodded, smiling slightly behind his gray muzzle.

"Well put, my young friend. I think that covers it all nicely."

Lan lowered his glance, and shrugged.

"We are, indeed, as you say, out like afternoon gossips, having tea in a hostile wood, wondering where the leaders have gone, and what we are about, and where we are bound. That's a fair enough question, and should be answered."

All the animals turned to Hollen expectantly.

In the clearing were Borim and the others of his party, as well as Boomer and Tolly, and a great number of various animals from the other settlements that had joined the exodus when they discovered that An Ran Bar was to be abandoned. Only the fact that Borim held the Horn of Bruinthor convinced the vast majority of them that the wisdom of leaving the old settlements might carry other weight beyond the whims of a green cub, only lately arrived, and without the added testimony of Hollen, Frael, and Earling, the animals would have likely stayed where they were, no matter how great the rumored danger was.

Tolly, leading the still grieving Boomer, had had no trouble in getting the settlement of Green Willow to join with An Ran Bar, for the smaller animals of the wood felt if there was danger for the bear settlement, then there was danger indeed.

There had been tales of departure for a good number of turnings in all the settlements of the wood, but as time wore on and nothing happened, the stories of dangers that would perhaps arrive someday were slowly forgotten, and the more pressing tasks of everyday living took on greater meaning. At one time or another, the settlements had suffered losses in raids by the beasts from across the Gray Rock, and almost every family had a sad loss or two to relate, but then the beasts that ran across Kahn's realms went back beyond the boundaries, and an air of peace once more settled over the lives of those left, and they took great pains to forget the unpleasantness as quickly as they were able.

Hollen cleared his throat and began, as if he were addressing a following of cubs.

"I've lived to see many things," he began, "and some of them would explain why I've had gray in my muzzle even before I had earned it."

There were a few scattered laughs at the comment, for Hollen was by far the oldest member of the settlement of An Ran Bar, and it was said he had been a full-grown bear when the Community League had been founded, and the animals had begun to gather together for protection from their wilder counterparts who roamed the Northerlands, and who, even from the very beginning of the lore books, were a dangerous lot, and to be avoided at all costs. No one ever explained exactly why the Northerlands were so desolate and dangerous, but it was enough to know that no decent animal ever went there, and if so, then he never returned.

The Gray Rock was a later boundary, much below the cold, harsh climate of the Far North, but Kahn had settled within the wood there, and those of his following, and the split between Kahn and Dralin had widened over the years until no one dared cross the river. There were settlements in some places that were built, for one reason or another, on the far bank of the Gray Rock, but always because of an exceptional beauty, or a good fishing spot, or because it was not frequented by raiding parties of Kahn.

Hollen scratched his muzzle, deep in thought.

"It seems we've been given a hard chore to do, giving up our homes in An Ran Bar, but then they wouldn't have given us much further pleasure anyhow, with all the goings-on that have begun to happen all across the wood."

He shook his head.

"No, I don't believe any of us would have remained alive long, had we chosen not to stay with the big lot of the settlement. Dralin knew of the new threat that has begun to move, and it seemed to unsettle Kahn, too. And that is a strange thing to happen, since he has been behind most of the trouble between the two realms all these turnings."

"To hear you tell it!" interrupted Bern. "What of the other side?"

"The other side," went on Hollen patiently, "is that Kahn didn't mind all the renegades and rogues in his realm, and if they raided settlements on our side of the river, then more's the worry for us. He made no effort to keep those war parties in check. In fact, it was taken for encouragement, his tolerance of all that has gone on over the turnings."

"Lord Kahn's settlement was as peaceful as An Ran Bar," protested Bern. "You make it sound as if they were nothing but savages there."

"Oh, it is always calm at the eye of the storm. Kahn wanted no part of the others living next to him. But they served his purpose well enough when they were out of sight, killing and burning across the Gray Rock."

"That's the lore according to you, old bones," snapped Bern. "But I never saw anything like what you've described."

"That is quite possible, my young friend. It isn't always to our advantage to show one everything about ourselves, especially if it brings out a part of us that's flawed, or in a bad light."

Borim, who had been sitting silently beside Hollen, arose and directed a question at the old bear.

"You said Kahn allowed these others to live within his realm, and he used them to his own advantage. Then what about this new horde of beasts that caused Jar Ben to come seeking my father? Did Kahn think we would have helped them defend themselves against some mutual enemy?"

"It seems so," replied Hollen. "Jar Ben acted as though they were concerned about the safety of our settlements here, but the truth of the matter, if it be known, is that these snakes with legs had nothing to do with Kahn, and refused to give him their pledge of obedience. He couldn't control them, I think, and when they began to attack his own settlements, it stirred up the others into a series of revolts. He began to lose control of all the beasts he had given shelter to, and one by one, they all started to turn from following him, to following a new and powerful leader called the Purge, and who treated Kahn as no more than a minor problem to be overcome."

"Where did you find all this out?" asked Lan. "Did I miss something somewhere?"

"If you listened as well as you fight, we'd have a master diplomat," chided Hollen. "Never mind where I got my news, I got it. It comes from both sides of the Gray Rock, although the scouting party we met from the settlement of Black Grove filled me in on some late news that I had not heard."

"What was that?" pressed Lan.

"Just what I'm telling you. These snakes with legs, and

135

this one called the Purge, are from farther away north than any of the other beasts, and I don't know of anything that could live there, except something that could withstand the great ice and snow and bleak wilderness."

"Is that what you called Four?" asked Borim, questioning the old bear in turn.

"The same, my good cub. Those are the lands that are said to have been here when this creation began, so long ago that there is no telling how long it really was. But the first of all the settlements was started there, and flourished for a period of time."

"What happened?" asked Tolly, always curious about lore.

"It disappeared," said Hollen, looking down at the small animal. "No one knows how, or why, but it vanished off the face of the world, and there was nothing more there for so long no one knew of the history between. It is then, it is said, that the beasts, of all kinds, were spawned there, in the cold Northerlands."

"And then the second settlement came," offered Earling, quoting his old teacher.

"And then the third. It is now the fourth, and we see how matters stand. The Purge, or these snakes with legs, are claiming to follow a new leader."

"Who is the new leader? Who would that be?" asked Lan. "If Kahn is gone, too, then who would that leave?"

"The scouts didn't find out a name. No one seemed willing to talk about a name. The beast king that is said to lead the great snakes has let it be known that the name of power is not to be given out to any but those who follow their path."

"Do you think there's anything to all this?" asked Frael, who of all the animals there was closest to the age of Hollen, and as such, second in knowledge and wisdom.

The old bear frowned and seemed to ponder the fire.

"I've lived to see a lot of things, and I've never known any goings-on to top these that have happened in these past few weeks. Meetings with beasts, and raiding parties, then the disappearance of Lord Dralin, and Bramweld, and Kahn. Those are things that don't occur in many folk's lifetimes, and I'd wager not one family among all this brood, other than myself, has ever lived outside a settlement before this."

"Borim and I grew up with only our sow," said Bern proudly.

"But that was in the Lower Wood," corrected Hollen. "There is not much there in the way of settlements. Most everyone lives alone there."

"You still haven't gotten to where we are bound for," broke in Tolly. "Are we just to live from paw to mouth from now on?"

Hollen laughed, a deep, low rumble.

"No, my good beaver, that would never do. Just wandering from one camp to the next would not be much in the way of a solution to any of our problems."

"The reason I asked is because I'm called to account every evening, after the day's march, to give some explanation of where we're bound for, and what we are to do once we get there." The beaver knitted his muzzle whiskers. "Most of us are working folk, and don't take well to all this senseless business of just drifting from one end of the wood to the other."

Borim added his voice to the conversation.

"Where is it to be, Hollen? Did Dralin tell you?"

"He had talked of it to me many times, over a late fire. He said that one day it would most likely come to it, although he didn't know whether it would be in his time, or his cub's. As it turned out, he was right."

Borim stared stiffly ahead, seeing nothing.

"I can still hardly believe he's gone."

The older bear patted him gently on the paw.

"Not gone, Borim. Away on another of his journeys, just as always."

"He's at the bottom of the Pit," said Bern coldly. "There's no need in working around that fact any longer. We must deal with the reality of the matter. And as yet, we don't know the real truth of how he met his death, or at whose paw."

"The reality of the matter, my young upstart, is that we know exactly what has gone on, which was written long before. And now the answer to the question of where we are going is settled by the knowledge that we are making for the very edge of the wood, to the place where the mountains drown in the Sea of Roaring."

A long, stunned silence greeted this announcement of Hollen's, and it was some space of time before anyone found voice to reply.

The Lands Beyond Water's End

Borim had heard tales of the Sea of Roaring, mainly from Frael and Earling, after his arrival in An Ran Bar. Alena had only once referred to anything so remote, by saying that his father had once been there. And the cub Borim had wondered in awe at the brave father he had, who would have dared all the dangers there were in the world to set eyes on a land so terribly far away that it was highly doubtful one would ever be able to return, should he be foolish enough to go in the first place.

It was never mentioned in any of the lore that Alena had taught him, and even Frael, in giving him his lessons in the book-filled room in the settlement, never spoke of it at any length, other than mentioning that where the land ended, that was where the sea began, and there wasn't anything more to it. Fish lived in the water, and animals on the land, so there was no real point in discussing it at any length, although Borim found the idea intriguing, and he had tried to press Frael into more stories that concerned the mysterious place, and for some idea of who lived there and what they did. Frael had shaken his head time and again, and gone on with the history of their family, and where the first Bruinthor had come from, and his name, and all the deeds he had done.

Borim was not so much interested in a bear history as he should have been, and in the end, Frael had had to report his behavior to Dralin.

"What is this, my young one? Not interested in your forefathers?" scolded his father gently.

"Yes, sir, I am, but that's mainly bear lore. Alena told me practically all about that. I mean, she didn't say who the first was, or the names of his mates, but she did teach me all the things I needed to know of our rituals and doings. It hasn't changed so much since the first."

"That's a point, Borim. No, it hasn't. Lore is lore, and it's been passed down from generation to generation for all this time, and it looks as if it's still working yet."

"Why did you go to the sea?" asked Borim, persisting in the line of questioning that had caused Frael to bring him to his father for correction.

"Why?" mused Dralin. "Why not, I asked myself. Some-

138

thing had always intrigued me about a place that no one wanted to speak of. Just like you, I wanted more than a vague shrug or nonsense answer that decent bears never went there."

Frael was glowering in the background as Dralin went on, but said nothing.

"I set out when I wasn't much older than you. Hollen had given me instructions on how to reach there, and who I was to see."

"Hollen? What did Hollen know?"

"You'll find that out one day. It's not for me to say now. There is no need to get ahead of ourselves at this point. It is enough to know that he told me the way, and gave me a name."

"But who lives there? Are there bears, and other animals like here?"

"There are many kinds who live on the edge of the Roaring. It is a strange place with the woods and water that reaches on away until there is nothing more to see but a vast desert of blue, with white tips all through it."

"Were they friends?"

"Some are still," went on Dralin. "There were some I met who didn't care for our kind, and who would not find it disagreeable if they could slay us all."

Borim's hackles raised.

"Yet they didn't know that we had progressed just as they had, and were quite surprised to find that I was as mannerly as themselves, and was in no way a savage, as they all seemed to think, especially anyone who did not come from one of their settlements."

"What did you do to keep them from harming you?"

"I talked," said Dralin simply. "I had the name that Hollen had given me, and I asked for him everywhere. As soon as I spoke the name, I was made welcome, and given food and shelter, and helped along my way."

"You mean even the ones who had tried to hurt you?"

"They were quick to mend their ways, and I still count many of them as close friends." Dralin smiled a secret smile to himself. "I have news of them from time to time."

"But how? No one travels now that the beasts roam all over so freely. How could anyone get through safely? You have to cross Kahn's realms even to begin the journey, from what Frael says."

"I have ears in many places," laughed Dralin. "It would be

139

unwise to think I couldn't have allies across the Gray Rock. In the least likely places, you'll always find your most trusted friends. Remember that, and mark it well."

"You'll confuse his lessons if you keep filling his ears with all this tale of the sea, and all those folks who live there. I'm trying to do as you told me, and fill him in on the basic history of all our clans, and where they sprang from, and where all they'd been."

"He'll have time enough for all that dull routine later," said Dralin. "When he's old and unable to leave his cave, he can read to his heart's content all the tribes' names, and how many cubs they had, and where they dwelled. That is the worst of the lessons. It has nothing to do with the *real* bears that made up those histories."

"I'm only trying to follow your instructions," complained Frael, his feelings slightly hurt at the sharp retort from his friend.

Dralin clapped him mightily on the back.

"Great shakes, friend, remember how you hated the lessons when you'd much rather be out in the late night air, following a moonbeam through a mountain stream?"

Frael looked sideways at Borim, raising an eyebrow.

"There's no question as to what I'd rather be doing, but the fact remains I have a task set for me, to teach this young whelp a season's worth of history in a week's time, and I'm getting no help from his father in getting him to concentrate on the lesson at hand."

"He'll find his own time to study the lore that's written. Now what he's after is the feel of all his forefathers."

"Then you want me to drop the history for now, and go on to something else?"

"Not so much drop, just add somewhat. It's important that he learn when things began to change."

Borim's ears picked up.

"What sort of change?"

Frael fell into his teaching voice, and began to recite. "There came a time in the history of beardom that the Elders of the clans began to go beyond their separate boundaries and travel among the other kinds in the wood."

"Wasn't that always so?" interrupted Borim. "I didn't ever hear of a time when we all didn't live in a wood full of the others."

His instructor frowned him into silence, and continued.

"In the first beginnings, only the clans of beardom dwelled

140

in the Lower Wood, and had no cause to go beyond their own kind. As time drew on, and the world began to be populated with others, great conflicts grew up, and there was violence and bloodshed among many of the clans, until the arrival of the first of the Bruinthors, of the bear clans, and certain other Elders who led the various animals that also dwelled in those times.

"The first of the Bruinthors was Alon Rab, and he spoke to the first of the tribes, and they formed the first settlement in history that included animals of all kinds and clans. It went on peacefully for many turnings, but was finally abandoned for lack of mutual support. Everyone again went their separate ways, until your great-uncle Freylock once more joined the animals under a common settlement."

"I never heard that story," said Borim.

"Not likely. Freylock was but a season into the first season of the truce, when he mysteriously vanished, and was never heard from again. It was said he was slain by warring factions who wanted the truce broken, and others said he crossed over the Sea of Roaring on a mission of great import, but no one ever knew the truth of it, and I guess no one will, until someone else goes after him, and sees where he's been."

"There's nothing on the other side of the Sea of Roaring," snorted Borim. "There couldn't be."

"So said those who believed Freylock dead."

"After that," said Dralin, "a few of the clans decided to band together, and to let those who didn't wish to simply go their own way. That was the beginning of the wilderness, and the animals there that have long lived among themselves and fought with all who come near their borders. They were the worst of the troublemakers in Freylock's day, and it is a common idea that these forerunners of the beasts today were responsible for slaying Freylock.

"That was never proven, and even though I doubt the truth of the story, some say Freylock crossed the Shadow to soothe the rift between the beast clans, and to try to get them to form a truce with the other tribes. He was obviously unsuccessful. And now the rift has passed on down from sire to cub, over all these turnings, until Dralin, and you."

"And you are to do much more than Freylock ever dreamed," said Dralin, his voice lowering, and he grew very grave. "It has been my lot to divide the clan between Bramweld, myself, and Kahn, as well as the Elders of the other tribes. I have seen much confusion come of it, but there has been nothing more to do, until your turn at the job, Borim. You will have the chance to finally unite all the clans beyond the Gray Rock, and the Shadow, and even beyond the Roaring. And you are to be the one who shall find the others who will help you, and join all the lands once more together in harmony."

"I'll go with you, to help you, sir," blurted Borim, "but I know nothing of what I would have to do!"

"You'll have all your friends," comforted Dralin. "And there shall be one with you, from your cubhood."

Before Borim could question Dralin further as to what he meant, Frael had gone on with the lesson.

"You were asking about the Sea of Roaring, if I remember correctly, and what those beings who lived there did."

Borim started to protest, but the mood that had moved Dralin to speak at such lengths had passed, and he heeded his father's scowl and fell silent, trying to pay attention to what Frael was saying.

"In the Far Reach, there are fisherfolk who keep to their own, and are not known to be friendly with other animals. They are tall and strong, and have been in those regions for as long as anyone can remember. Dralin traveled there, and because he was able to speak with them in peace, he found that they have been waiting for the arrival of a powerful leader, who is to aid them in their struggle against the Northerlands. They have lost many, just as we all have, to the beasts."

"Then they are hunting Kahn, as well," said Borim.

"Not so much Kahn as the one behind the control of the beasts. Kahn simply has used what was already there to his advantage. But I don't think the beasts all owe their allegiance to him. For the most part, it seems as if Kahn runs the wood, but it is not really his realm. In numbers, he is strong, but Dralin and I both think there is something else there that has been building the strength of the beasts. We feel more so now, after Jar Ben's visit, and the news of these snakes that fly."

"Who else would be behind it?" asked Borim, curious about the puzzle of Kahn's power, or lack of it.

"Evidently someone knows, for there have been rumors that come out of the Northerlands every so often, from the clans that still border there."

"You mean someone still tries to live there?"

"Yes, Borim, they do. When your home is all you've known

142

for your entire life, it's not easy to simply give it up and leave, no matter how great the threat.

"We have a friend who lives near the last of the settlements before you reach the real wastes that mark the boundaries. He had told us all along that there's a real problem brewing, although he isn't certain what exactly it is, or how it is to come."

"We do know it's more than just the raiders," said Dralin. "They are nasty enough to deal with, but hardly the sort of danger that Ellin talks of."

"Is Ellin the friend whose name you knew, when you went to the Sea of Roaring?" asked Borim.

"No, although it is a good name to know, and will stand you in good stead in many a clan along the Northland borders."

"I'm really confused now," complained Borim. "Now I find out most of these beasts from over the Gray Rock are not really the true danger at all. And that Kahn has no real control over any of them, or has anything to do with this new threat that Ellin sent you warning of."

"And I'm worried now," said Dralin. "I've had no word from my friend in a long time. It's not like him to remain quiet for such a space."

All these conversations came back to Borim as he stood studying the rough terrain that spread out about him.

Dralin had not said so much that the answer was to be found somewhere on the Sea of Roaring, but he had mentioned friends there, although he no longer knew if they were still alive, or had disappeared into the vastness of those wild lands that made up the harsh North. He tried to remember if Dralin had said more about the name of the friend he had carried with him, or if he had left any hint that any of the party who remained in An Ran Bar might know. Evidently Hollen knew, for he had been the one who had decided the issue of where to go once they were away from An Ran Bar, and he was the one who knew the way to the mysterious sea, and he must know the names of those they went to seek.

Bern remained quiet, but listened carefully to every bit of news that came his way, and he tried hard to please Hollen, and Earling, and Frael, although he would have nothing to do with Lan, and would seldom go near the younger member of the inner party of Dralin's old settlement. The two half brothers, when they were together, which was almost always, were polite enough, and Borim did make an attempt to regain the old feelings he'd held for Bern when he'd been a

143

mere cub in Alena's cave, and he tried to gain acceptance for him in every corner of the now rootless settlement, but there remained a tiny spark of distrust deep inside him, and he felt a certain sureness that that must have been the way Dralin had felt about Kahn, and even Bramweld. He remembered the strange bear's visit to the settlement, and how frightened everyone had been of Bramweld, except his father, and how strained that visit had been. Yet underneath all the growls and threats, there had existed between Dralin and Bramweld a deep and affectionate respect.

Borim pondered his own relationship with Bern, and could not say if it were the same or not, but he knew he felt an odd combination of revulsion and horror on the one paw, and compassion and sorrow on the other. He supposed, in his own rather inexperienced way, that he had the latter confused with love.

As the days wore on, and the animals moved farther and farther away from An Ran Bar, a noticeable change took place in Borim that Frael remarked on to Earling, and that Hollen called to Lan's attention.

"He is growing into some likeness of his father, it seems," said Hollen proudly, remembering all the great pleasures he had had as the instructor of Dralin.

There had been Kahn then to reckon with and attend to, but Kahn had been the sort of animal who was always bent on his own amusements, and as he grew older, he spent less and less time in the company of any of the older members of the settlement, and in the last of those days, he had simply disappeared out of the settlement and gone into the wood to hunt and practice his art of killing.

Even Hollen, who had tried on several occasions to interest Kahn in other things from the lore, at last grew impatient with the then young cub, and called for his exile, hoping it might bring him to his senses, and back into the fold. That had been a dreadfully hard thing for him to do, for he had taught the cub from the time he had been weaned, and felt a great deal of concern for the arrogant black giant who grew more skillful and crafty in the dark side of the lore, and more strange and violent every season.

Hollen looked at Bern, and knew that Borim was feeling the same things. Torn by loyalty on the one hand, he had the safety of the entire settlement on his head now, and as much as he hated the idea, there seemed to be no escape.

The old bear sighed aloud.

He was getting on in seasons, and the grief he had seen in all his turnings grew as the days turned shorter, and he watched the same lessons being given and received over and over again. In the innermost recesses of his mind, he envisioned being able to wander off for a day's ramble along a good, deep trout stream, with enough berries for dessert, and a tall, cool oak to give him shelter for a short nap afterward. And no one to ask him for advice, or seek him out to settle some dispute that was none of his business.

It had been a long while, longer than he cared to remember, since he had been free of the heavy responsibilities he had borne since the old days of Dralin, before Kahn had taken the road he had taken, and before An Ran Bar had been split apart by the warring brothers. And then later had come Bramweld, who was just as reckless in his own way, taking the view that if he simply ignored it all, the problem would eventually solve itself.

Bramweld had been Hollen's least favorite of the three cubs, always reticent, and always ready with his answer of leave well enough alone, or to withdraw totally, if faced with a problem. He had taken his followers and gone to Black Grove in those old days, against everyone's wishes. Even Kahn had disliked him for his running away, and eventually gave up trying to convince him to join the colony beyond the Gray Rock.

Hollen shook his old silvered head, thinking of it all, and now seeing another turn played out between the cubs Borim and Bern. It would be a long trip to the Sea of Roaring, but Hollen knew that the friend they sought would put together another piece of the mystery that had now come to include the disappearance of the three older bears, Dralin, Kahn, and Bramweld, and brought forth the new players, Borim and Bern, half brothers, and the central figures in the next part of the drama that Hollen had been watching unfold for the better part of his extremely long life.

One thing that kept the old bear going was the promise he'd had that he would get to meet the great Elder from across the Roaring, and see the beautiful lands that spread out beyond the water's end. That, he thought wistfully, would be a proper finish to one part of his life, and a great way to begin another.

The Brothers Debate

In the gray morning light, before the sun had fully risen, Bern sought out his brother. The settlement members had camped in the protected hollow of a glen, and the dew was heavy and glistened on the grass, and on the bears' coats where they had touched the earth. A slight wind had begun, barely whispering through the quiet forest, and Borim was not sure which had awakened him, whether Bern's soft call, or the gentle breeze over his head.

"Are you awake, brother?" asked Bern, his voice hardly audible.

"Yes, Bern. What is it?"

"I thought we might use this time to talk."

"Without the others about, you mean?"

"I have enemies in your camp, Borim. You can't be so blind as not to see that."

The younger bear nodded.

"I can see you're not well received in all quarters."

"They hate me because I speak the truth, and don't try to put fancy names to plain facts, or avoid issues."

Borim sat up on his hindquarters and stretched.

"What issues do you think have been avoided, brother?"

"You know what issue. First your father is gone, then the beaver Boomer comes back, and then we hear a long tale about what happened. And not a very convincing tale, at that."

Borim studied the smaller animal.

"What do you think happened, Bern?"

"I think the truth, and go only by the facts. Number one, Boomer was with Dralin when he disappeared, and we have only his word that anything he says actually happened. Perhaps Bramweld was there at The Breaks, perhaps not. Maybe he told Dralin that Bramweld would be there, in order to get him to go with him to such a terrible place."

Borim shook his head firmly.

"I don't mistrust my friend Boomer, nor do I think it's any too wise of you to cast doubts on his loyalty. He has been the one most grieved at the whole business. He's hardly spoken a word since the day it happened."

"Some animals are natural actors," suggested Bern, "although Boomer may not be one of them. He may well feel grief, yet I suspect it might be a guilty conscience."

"You speak of things you know little of, brother. I have lived among Boomer's kind for some time before your arrival, and I never saw anything but kindness and good manners, and upright bravery in bad times."

"Oh, brave enough, Borim. I cast no doubt on their bravery. They have been known to do astounding things, for their size."

"We'll forget this line of talk. What else do you have on your mind?"

"The Sea of Roaring!"

"Yes?"

"Doesn't it occur to you that it's odd?"

"What's odd?"

"That you hold the Horn, yet Hollen and Frael have made all the decisions. They use your name, and make it sound as though you said it, but it all comes out the same."

"Hollen has been with my father since he was born. He knows all there is to know about Dralin, and all that has anything to do with him. And Frael was his best friend."

Borim's hackles had begun to rise, and although he couldn't say exactly why, he was suddenly growing very angry with Bern. For the entire talk, he had been defending his friends, and Bern had been subtly suggesting ulterior motives for everyone's behavior. He straightened himself, and barked a short woof of displeasure.

"I begin to grow tired of your forever attacking all these animals, Bern. It is very rude of you to treat your hosts that way. And I don't think you're giving them an even chance. You might try changing your own ways a bit. Going halfway would open a lot of hearts."

Bern snorted.

"That's easy enough for you to say. They are your friends, and from your settlement. I wonder what it would be like if the situation were reversed?"

Borim looked evenly at his brother.

"I wonder? What *would* it be like?"

Borim caught himself half thinking that it might indeed be unpleasant for him, were the situation changed. He wasn't sure what had happened to Bern in the space of time between his leaving Alena's cave, and their meeting again in An Ran Bar, but there was none of the old Bern left, no patient explaining, or long afternoon games, or even the quiet friendship they had sometimes shared, simply sitting under one of the honey trees, full of its warmth and glow, looking across the still meadows that reached beyond the Lower Wood below Alena's summer digs. Something had happened to Bern, for he was forever full of gloom and doubt, and he was firmly convinced that there was a dark side to every picture.

Borim was not such a cub that he thought there weren't two sides to an issue, but he wondered at his brother's insistence that everyone from An Ran Bar was out to show him up in a bad light, or to try to run him out of the traveling settlement's confines.

"I would gladly alter my opinions if I had even the slightest reason," said Bern, taking on the hurt expression Borim had grown accustomed to seeing his brother wear. "It might help if I thought you would at least consider some of the things I say. You treat me no better than a stone."

"I consider the things you say, brother, but they don't make much sense."

"Not even about your father's disappearance?"

"No."

"It was very sudden, Borim. And why was it only Boomer who was there? We were all out in the library. We could have all been told, if Dralin was going out to meet Bramweld. The easiest way out was right through the hall where we stood."

Taking Borim's silence for approval, Bern continued, speaking more quickly.

"And where was the door they went out? Boomer never said exactly how they did get away without passing us."

"I'm sure he'll tell us everything when he feels up to it."

"I'm sure he'll find something to tell us. Whether it's the truth or not remains to be seen."

"There are a hundred secret passages in Dralin's hall in An Ran Bar. Frael told me so."

Borim suddenly felt sad, remembering that they would not likely see the beautiful settlement again. He dared to hope so, at the bottom of his secret heart, but Hollen would not answer him when he asked, and Frael simply looked grim, and stared away into the distance.

Lan had snorted.

"If we don't, then we'll have been in the fairest place we shall ever be."

Borim agreed, and thought it was unfair that he got to stay in the fair shelter only for so short a period of time before all was thrown into disarray and confusion, and he found himself in exactly the same situation he had been in when he had gone seeking Dralin. Except that he now had company, and his brother, which he had thought would have made him happy, but which had turned out to be frustrating and disappointing.

And worst of all, he now carried the Horn of Bruinthor, which had been forced upon him almost overnight. That was the heaviest burden, and he could not get used to being Borim the Elder, for he still felt he was a cub, and did not want the dreadful loneliness that was forced upon him with the title and position of leader. He saw how differently the others looked at him now that Dralin was gone, and he saw the distance between them.

Borim's disturbing thoughts were interrupted by the arrival of Frael.

"Good morning, Borim. Good morning, Bern."

The older bear's tone was guarded, and he nodded to them both.

"We are to reach the first of the wilderness settlements today, if we see to our march and don't drag along too slowly."

"Which settlement is that? I didn't know there were any but beast camps across the river."

"This is a border shelter, Borim. It has been here a number of turnings. Quite like Bramweld's Black Grove. They never lost too many animals to the raiders, and they had many in their number, so they stayed on. Rather a wild lot, in some ways of thinking, but I've always admired them. There was a great friend of your father's who was Elder the last time I was here. He may have some advice for us, and he'll be able to tell us how it's been since last we've met."

"Who is this?" asked Bern.

"He goes by many names, and some know him by no name at all. I think the one he prefers to be called by is Nob."

"I never heard of him," grunted Bern scornfully. "It must be some settlement to have an Elder named Nob."

"Oh, he has names enough, but I wouldn't fret myself over his settlement. Sometimes there's no one there at all, and at others you can't find room to stretch a paw. I've been there when there were so many animals I thought it must surely have been the Sign, when we are all to gather under the oak and begin the long migration back."

"What sort of animal is Nob?" asked Borim, always interested in friends of his father's. They had proven to be an interesting assortment, from beavers to squirrels and hedge-hogs, to great bears like Bramweld, Frael, and Hollen.

Frael laughed.

"He's not so easy to pin down, this Nob. I've heard him described as a rogue and killer, and also that he has been the salvation of many a poor starving animal that's wandered out of the woods and into his settlement."

"Does he fight the beasts, and Kahn?" persisted Borim, always hating it when Frael answered in such vague terms.

Borim's mind was very orderly, and he wanted all the information that he gathered to fit into a neat pattern, but it was very seldom that that was possible, and since living in An Ran Bar, and becoming involved with Frael, Earling, and Dralin, less and less fit into any orderly manner of thinking, and times grew more and more confused. It had been a long time since something had been either one way, or the other.

There were things, Borim thought, about cubhood that he liked, in its utter simplicity. As he grew older and more mature, he saw that it wasn't very often anything was very simple.

"Nob neither fights nor runs," went on Frael. "And some-times both. Tolly and Boomer have met this fellow. What do you two think? How would you describe him to Borim?"

The two beavers had joined their friends, looking for break-fast. Boomer started a small fire, and Borim began to help him gather their mugs and plates.

It was Tolly who spoke at last, after thinking to himself for a few moments.

"Nob is Nob," he said sagely. "I wouldn't know how to describe him, other than that."

Borim exploded angrily.

"Can't someone please just answer a simple question? What does he look like? How old is he? What does he do?"

Bern, seeing a chance to bait his brother, added in a mocking voice, "Well, you can't say exactly what he looks like, and no one could tell you how old he is."

"Nob is old enough," said Frael curtly. "And he's also one that has been among Kahn's settlement, and knows of some doings in that camp."

Bern fell strangely quiet, and soon was completely with-drawn into himself, his muzzle wearing a worried frown. Frael thought his behavior strange, but laid it off to mere sour humor, and let it go.

As suddenly as he had quit the conversation, Bern underwent an amazing transformation into the dedicated brother, whose only concern was Borim's welfare.

"If this Nob is as you say, don't you think it might be dangerous to seek him out? He sounds a bit wild to me. Perhaps even beyond the Law."

"Nob *is* the Law, in his end of the world. There's no one else who is able to enforce it, or to keep folks on the straight, or to help those in trouble."

"Is he an Elder?" asked Borim. "Like Dralin?"

"Yes, and no," replied Frael, driving Borim to the point of frenzy. "In the sense of his being the head of his settlement, he is; yet he's also much more."

"How can he be more than Elder?" asked Bern, smoothing the dislike in his voice.

"He can be many things, as I've said. He is one of the Old Ones."

"The Old Ones!" cried Borim. "You mean like those you read to me of?"

"The same," replied Frael. "It was to have been a surprise, but your father was planning on taking you to see Nob, on his next outing." He smiled gently at the cub. "Now we shall have to do it on our own."

"The last time we were there with Lord Dralin, there was a feast," broke in Tolly, beside himself in his excitement. "And Boomer recited a poem he wrote right at the table with Lord Dralin and Lord Nob, and then there was some music like I never in all my life heard before. It was so fine and sweet, it had us all dancing around the fire all night long, and at dawn nobody was tired, so we all went to the river, and Nob took us all sailing in his boat."

"A wonderful boat," added Boomer, speaking for the first time, the pleasure of the memory alive in his eyes.

"It was green and yellow, with white sails," went on Tolly. "And he said he had sailed all the way down the Eagle Claw, and even on to the Sea of Roaring."

"He said he'd crossed it," said Boomer, looking down at the fire, as if he'd suddenly remembered why he was sad. His voice was flat again, causing his friends to grow concerned once more.

"We went with him all afternoon. Remember, Boomer?"

"I remember. There were no decent dams on that entire stretch of water, and he said he'd welcome any of our clan who might be up that way to help him with some waterworks he had in mind."

"Nob is a fine sailor, among other things," agreed Frael. "I'd never actually done it before I met him, and only read of a few kinds who went about on water."

"It's an awful lot of fun," said Tolly, trying to find a subject that Boomer was willing to talk about.

No one had been able to draw him out of his brown study, and Earling noted that the small animal was beginning to lose weight, and he seemed interested in nothing at all. Tolly was glad of the topic of Nob, for he recalled how eager Boomer had been about the water there, and the boat that Nob sailed.

"Could you teach me how to do it?" asked Borim, more and more intrigued with the stories of the strange animal who had been a friend of his father's.

"Oh, anyone can do it," Tolly assured him. "It's the simplest thing in the world to do, once you catch on to the hang of it."

"Tolly almost ran a good-sized island down," snorted Boomer, almost laughing.

"I couldn't help it. Who was standing in front of me, blocking my view?"

"I wanted to be able to jump free in case you piled us up."

"I'm glad you saw fit not to damage Nob's boat. I don't think he's the kind you'd want to make angry," said Frael.

"Not in the least bit worried, though. He just sat there watching it all as calm as you please. He told me in a voice like he'd say good morning that I was about to put us aground, and that if he were I, he'd swing hard over."

"Which you did, and almost threw that fellow off the bow."

"It was that, or all of us swimming for our lives," replied Tolly.

Bern smiled oddly when the other scouts had come to report to Borim and Hollen that the first signs of Nob's boundary were in sight, and that they would be in the large animal's camp before supper.

"Well, brother," said Borim, "if nothing else, we may get a sail out of our meeting with Nob."

The smaller bear smiled through clenched teeth, but said nothing.

A mounting tension grew steadily as they neared the borders that marked Nob's settlement boundaries, and yet they were still not challenged by any sentry, and could detect nothing at all that might indicate any settlement being in the nearby vicinity, or that would give away the presence of any animals other than their own group of travelers. Nearer and nearer they went, yet they were greeted with nothing but the sun's afternoon warmth and the heavy stillness of the woods.

Arrival of the Purge

After a tense march through a bad stretch of thorn brake and gorse, Hollen and Frael called a halt for counsel, and to send out scouts even farther, to see if any clue could be found as to the strange absence of any of Nob's sentries.

The travelers from An Ran Bar, and all the other animals who had joined the journey, grew more restless and frightened as the afternoon wore on toward evening, and Hollen and Frael still lingered over a small tea fire, their muzzles drawn into deeply troubled frowns. Borim, sitting beside the old bear, could get nothing from him but grunts and snorts, and Hollen started up every time a scout returned. Frael could see Hollen's disappointment grow as one after another of the scouts returned with no news to report, or any answer as to the question of where the settlement of Nob was, or had been, or had moved to.

"Could we be in the wrong part of the wood, Hollen?" Lan forced himself to ask.

The old bear looked hurt, then perplexed.

"I don't know," he finally replied. "It's been a long turning since I have been this way. I may have led myself down a false path somewhere."

"We're lost," said Bern, "and a proper job of it, as well. There's no telling where we're stuck now, without any hope of friendly camps, or any direction to go to escape."

"I don't understand it," said Hollen, ignoring Bern's tirade. "I was sure I read the old signs right. You saw them, Earling. And you, Frael. They were plain enough."

"They were there, right as we saw them," agreed Frael, defending his old friend against attack.

"They may have been put there by someone else," sneered Bern. "Someone who wanted to trap us."

Although Borim disagreed aloud, in his heart a sliver of fear had begun to loom larger.

Supposing they had taken a wrong turning somewhere

back along the long trail that wound ever deeper into the dense wood? Surely the trail would not have led them into such a thicket as this, he thought to himself.

"I don't wonder that we're all nervous," said Earling. "But I'm sure there must be an explanation to satisfy every question that's been raised. Nob has always been a strange one, and what he sees fit to do out here is his own affair. He may have changed everything to throw off some enemy from his trail. And it's doubtful he knew we were going to be making this journey, so he wouldn't be looking for us, or be able to give us the location of his new camp."

Hollen brightened visibly.

"That must be it," he agreed hastily. "That has to be. Living here in these wild times must surely demand that you move about a lot."

"That wasn't the way you described the settlement before," argued Bern. "You made it sound as though it was large enough to withstand any attack from the beasts. A settlement like that would be hard to move on short notice, and we surely would have come onto some evidence of where it had been located. I can't imagine tearing down An Ran Bar to the point that no one would be able to tell where it had stood."

"We don't know that An Ran Bar is still there, my young friend," said Frael. "The beasts may have come in and destroyed it the moment they knew we were gone."

"They perhaps did, although I think not. Why would they destroy something they had been seeking for so long?"

Lan leveled a cold stare at Bern, who continued, "Where is this Nob? Does he think we're here to destroy his settlement, that he hides it from us?"

Bern was forgotten for a moment, as another scout came to make his report. This one was a stout beaver from Boomer's old settlement of Green Willow.

"There's been a big to-do not much farther on," he said, pointing away toward the edge of the thicket that was less dense. "There's the river there, right enough, and there has been an attempt made to conceal any signs, but I've found the bottom churned and trampled, and there's no hiding that. An animal who wasn't clever about water might never think to look there."

"Good lad," offered Tolly. "That was a smart piece of thinking."

"There was a large number that was there, and I can't tell how they did it, but they waded in a bit, and I guess they

154

swam. There's no more tracks, and no others across the river where they landed. I came back to get some others to help me, to see if we can't find the spot on the other side where they landed."

Hollen raised a paw.

"You found the Eagle Claw, then?"

The young beaver scout nodded eagerly.

"It's a big one, too."

"That's it. I don't think we need look for where they landed, my good fellow. They didn't swim away."

Hollen's eyes brightened as he went on, and the tiredness went out of his voice.

"That will be the river I remember. It's fast, and broad, and runs all the way into the Roaring Sea."

Borim's hackles shivered.

"Is this the water you sailed on, Tolly? You and Boomer and Nob?"

The beaver smiled a faint smile.

"Those days were somewhat happier," he replied. "I think I must have felt a little more excited then."

"What he means is that he couldn't wait to get home to build a boat," put in Boomer.

"Now we have no home to go to, and he never did figure out how you got a stack of trees to look like Nob's boat."

"He was going to show me, but you were in such a hurry to get back to Green Willow, he never got the chance."

"We may get the chance now," said Frael. "If we can but find our good friend who knows how to turn trees into boats, then we may have a need to learn that wondrous art, if we are to reach the Sea of Roaring safely. From the looks of these woods, the going may be tougher yet, farther on. It seems almost all this end of the world has been growing wild for some time."

"You actually hope to reach the Sea of Roaring in a boat?" asked Bern, taken aback. "No one here knows the first thing about how to go at building one, much less getting it to go anywhere we'd want to go."

"I can sail one," corrected Tolly. "The problem is finding one to sail."

"But there would never be a boat big enough to get everyone on," protested Bern. "Look at the size of this settlement! Why, it would take a hundred boats, or more, to take everyone. And I'm not so sure the rest of the animals would take so tamely to the idea of floating around on the river."

"They'll do whatever they think will get them safely through this part of the wood," said Hollen. "And boats aren't so alien to us. Our great forefathers knew of boats, and the workings of them. That's how Nob came by his knowledge. His family had been of a boating nature down all those turnings, so it was only natural for him to follow along in the way of his sires."

"Maybe natural enough for him," snorted Bern. "Yet I don't think the idea will be too well received by these folk that are with our party."

"Were there any signs of anything left behind?" asked Boomer, directing his question to the scout who still stood before Hollen.

"No, but I didn't really have time to search the other side, except for just at the river's edge."

"Some scout," spat Bern. "You made it sound as if you'd searched the river upstream and down for a day's march."

"He's done his job well, Bern, and come to get help to make a more thorough search. You would do well to save your strength for the tasks ahead, rather than finding fault with how others are carrying out their own."

"I'll have my share of strength when it's needed," replied Bern shortly.

"Go with him, Tolly, and find some more sharp eyes to help you. Maybe we can locate some trace of Nob, and some idea as to where they may have been heading."

Hollen then turned to Boomer.

"Are you up to going?"

"I've got nothing more to do here but lie about and mope. The exercise might cheer me up."

"Good! You can lead the party on the far side of the Eagle Claw, and Tolly will see what he can find on our side. Meanwhile, we'll start felling some suitable trees to construct our rafts with, and set ourselves to work at that."

"Rafts?" asked Borim. "Are you sure? I thought Nob had regular boats, with sails, from what Tolly said."

"But Nob is Nob," laughed Hollen. "We're simple woodfolk, and don't know the secrets of the water as he does. Still, I think we might lash together some of these floating logs that I have read of from time to time, so that we may take a short cut to the sea. Otherwise our path will be a long and dangerous one, and maybe one too hard for the entire settlement to make. We must remember we have many gray muzzles, as well as pups and cubs."

"We should never have started this business," complained Bern. "It's the sheerest folly. We should turn back to An Ran Bar while we still have the chance. There's no proof anyone has discovered it's undefended."

Frael studied the younger bear evenly.

"There will be a time for our return, Bern. But that is not for now. There are things that must be done before any of us may go home."

"What could we possibly have to do with the Sea of Roaring? Or this fellow Nob?"

"Those things you'll find out when we get to the sea, and when we find Nob."

"If, you mean. *If* we ever find this renegade, or *if* we ever reach this so-called Sea of Roaring."

"I think we've had enough of this discussion, Bern," scolded Frael. "We have our tasks, and we'll waste no more time bantering about here. We still aren't beyond danger, and the longer we delay, the worse chance for us to come through safely."

"What about the others?" asked Lan. "Shall we all help with the trees?"

Hollen nodded.

"Tolly's settlement can fell them, and you can haul them to the river, Lan. You have strong paws to help get that job done quickly."

"Will you come, Borim?" asked his friend.

"I'll go wherever needed, Lan. Wherever Hollen thinks I should go."

"You must be everywhere, to encourage and cheer," laughed the old bear. "That is the role you shall have to get used to playing."

"That will never fit easily," mumbled Borim. "I don't know that I shall ever feel that way."

"You will. You have changed already, only you are probably the last to notice."

"The only change I've seen is that I've grown a lot more confused since we left An Ran Bar. I didn't understand much then, but I feel I know even less here."

Hollen laughed, and clapped his young student on the back with a mighty swat.

"There's much to be said for the fellow who knows where he stands, even if it's in a place that's not too grand."

"There's nothing grand about this place, right enough,"

agreed Bern. "And I can't see that there's to be much improvement anytime soon."

"Oh, there'll be plenty of improvements, Master Bern, and some, I think, might even tickle your fancy."

Bern fell silent, and stood glaring at Frael.

Before the animals could move into action on the various tasks they had set for themselves, two more of the beaver scouts hurried into the center of the companions, out of breath, and their fur ruffled and matted with burrs, as if they had run carelessly through the heavy undergrowth.

"What is it?" cried Tolly in alarm, seeing the wild look in the eyes of his scouts.

"The beasts!" panted one, completely out of breath. He had to stop there and take a great gulp of air into his lungs before he could continue.

"What beasts? The raiders? Kahn's band? What beasts do you speak of?" asked Earling, helping to support one of the small animals, who had almost fallen from exhaustion.

"The snakes with legs!" blurted the beaver. "There's a whole party of them just beyond the river."

Hollen frowned, his eyes clouding.

"This may be the answer as to what's happened to Nob. I didn't think any of the ordinary beasts would cause him to go to such lengths to move his settlement."

"How far away are these things?" asked Frael. "Do they suspect we're near?"

"They're not far enough away for my liking," answered the beaver, shuddering. "But I don't think they know we're here yet."

"They're awful," added the other scout. "All covered with scales, and teeth as tall as me."

"I think we're going to have to have a look at these beasts, Hollen. So we'll know what we're up against. And to get over building them up in our minds until they're worse than they really are."

"They're bad enough, Master Frael," shot the first of the beavers. "I don't know if we'll be able to keep our settlement here, or not. They may fly, when they see these new beasts."

"There's more bone to a beaver's back than a simple beast can rob," said Hollen. "And we are many in our party. We can make a fair accounting of ourselves, if it comes to a fight."

"You haven't seen these beasts," snapped the second scout. "They're enough to turn you blind with fear."

"That may be a fault with the beaver tribes," put in Bern, "but I hardly think we need worry about it."

"These beasts would have no trouble with bears. They're big!" snapped the beaver. "I've never seen anything like them."

"Is this going to throw us off about the rafts, and the river?" asked Borim. "If we can't build the rafts, will we still use the river? Or if not that, how are we to get to the sea?"

Hollen was deep in thought, and did not reply immediately. When he spoke, his voice was hushed and urgent.

"We must warn the scouts that were to cross the Eagle Claw! No one is to go over the river now. We will move on as quickly as we can, until we find someplace downstream where we can get our trees in peace."

"They've already gone," cried the first scout. "We saw them crossing. We couldn't call out to warn them, and we thought they'd spot the beasts and hurry back here."

"Then let's hope that's so, and that they aren't the ones that get seen first. I hope they were as quiet about their business as good sense demanded."

"They were moving very quietly," agreed the first scout.

"Then with any luck at all, they'll soon be back to report what you've already told us," said Frael.

"We'd best get the rest of the settlement warned, and told of our plan," said Hollen. "We can't broadcast, so we'd best go in twos and threes, and spread the word."

"Let's get to it, then," said Lan, the battle fire glimmering dangerously in his eyes. "I don't like sidestepping a fight, but we have the rest of the settlement to think of. And it's not, unfortunately, a war party."

"You may be glad it's not, once we see what we're faced with," said Earling coolly.

"Beasts are all the same," snorted Lan indifferently.

"These aren't, Master Lan," protested the first beaver scout. "They're long, and tall, and have heads that are all full of big teeth. I don't know what they are, or where they came from, but they are more dangerous than anything we've ever seen."

"What's dangerous to a beaver need not be so frightening to a bear," snorted Lan, who had started to say something else when the very air about them grew leaden, and a cloud seemed to pass before the face of the sun.

A cold wind sprang up, and every single bristle of hair on the animals' backs stood out on end, and their hearts beat

159

wildly in their throats. Borim heard a dull humming noise that he could not make out, but it grew louder still, and seemed to fill every ear with dread. Bern, who stood beside him, had begun to whine a low note of warning, but it went ignored as the strange sound grew louder, and still louder.

A moan went up from the traveling settlement of animals that were gathered near the Eagle Claw, and even Borim felt a great desire to cry out. He turned to Hollen, and saw the old bear scanning the tops of the trees, standing upright, and in his fighting stance. It looked strange, and out of place to Borim, for the old graymuzzled animal to be taking on the pose of a warrior.

His attention was taken from Hollen by the sudden appearance of what at first he thought was a shadow, falling across the glade where they stood. Borim looked up, and his heart leapt to his mouth, and he was sure he would never be able to move a muscle from the spot.

Circling high above the wood was a long, winged beast, with the body of a snake, only huge, covered with barbed scales that glittered in the sun like dull metal. Borim saw the thing's head turning this way and that, and the huge beast seemed to be hanging still in one spot, its tough, leathery wings barely moving enough to keep it aloft. A row of teeth glimmered a dull yellow, and Borim saw that the beavers hadn't made up their tale of what they'd seen. If anything, the beast was worse than they'd described.

And Borim noticed a tendency welling up inside him to call out to the beast, to tell it where he was. Fighting down that impulse, he drew his gaze away, and found that the desire to call to the thing was somewhat weakened.

"Look away!" he hissed, his voice barely above a whisper. "Don't look at it!"

He saw Bern, eyes wide, and smiling, on the verge of raising a paw to wave, or call out. Borim tackled his half brother, and threw him roughly to the ground.

"Look away! There is a spell about these things that makes you want to call to them."

Bern struggled violently for a moment, and in that time, his bitterness and fear all came to the fore, and he landed a glancing blow to Borim's shoulder, which had it struck squarely would have left a deep wound. As quickly as it had hit Bern, the feeling passed, and he was quick to apologize, and began tending to his brother's injury.

"I'm sorry, little brother," he gushed. "I was so frightened, and when you tackled me, I thought one of those beasts had me."

"What's this?" asked Frael, under his breath. "Shut up, or that thing will hear us."

He noticed Borim's injury then, and hurried to his side, forgetting the rest of his scolding.

"How did this happen?" he whispered.

"An accident," replied Borim, not meeting his friend's eyes. "Bern thought he had been attacked by one of those things."

They were interrupted by a low, wavering call that began to grow louder.

"That's one of the beavers!" said Lan, taking his own eyes off the terrible flying figure.

"Quickly, quickly, we must have everyone look away," hissed Hollen. "These things have some strange power."

The animals had made toward the rest of the gathered settlement to warn them and have them look away, but too late, for the hovering figure of the flying beast dipped once, spiraled away upward for a moment, then hurled itself straight toward them, great talons bared and drooling jaws opened on the terrible dull yellow teeth. Just as Borim raised himself to call out a warning to the others, the beast struck with a suddenness and fury that scattered trees and filled the air with harsh screams, and the cries of the dying or wounded.

Borim did not remember doing it, but all at once the Horn of Bruinthor was at his lips, and the ancient instrument called out in a terrible voice, and the wind died away, followed by a shrieking sound of mountains tearing, and then the great war cry of his father's house flooded the wood. Without knowing what he had done, or even where he was, Borim leapt forward at the huge beast that rolled and coiled about its fallen victims. In the next instant, he was firmly attached to the scaly hide behind the thing's head, right below its ear.

Nob

In the lore books that followed long afterward, the story of Borim's slaying of the snake with legs was much embellished by hearsay, and enlarged by the heroic deeds that made Alena's cub the most well-known Elder that beardom had ever known.

That was many turnings after Borim had made his promise to return, and vanished in a sleek white ship that had carried him over the Sea of Roaring, and beyond the Sea of Silence, and to the Islands. Borim, telling the story himself, was short and modest, and saw nothing wonderful or worth relating about the afternoon of horror and death that had befallen them. Many of their number had been devoured in that first terrible onslaught of the dragon that belonged to the growing number of what was called the Purge, and a great many more animals were injured. Even the animals who had been accustomed to the war waged on their borders by the raiders of Kahn were not prepared for the brute which swept out of the sky that day, with a fury and savageness that numbed the mind with a black terror that stopped the blood cold in the veins and turned bones to water.

Boomer and Tolly had both been at Borim's side, along with a party of others of the smaller settlements, as well as Lan, Earling, Hollen, and Frael. Those had formed the line of defense that had finally held the giant enemy long enough for Borim to leap onto the thing's long neck and find a hold there, among the barbed spikes of the hardened hide.

It was in the time of Dralin yet, when there were no weapons other than what the animals naturally had, teeth and claws, and the contest would have been highly one-sided and fatal to all who were there that day had it not been for the mysterious power of the Horn Borim carried, which had been carefully handed down from paw to paw to each succeeding Elder, and which came into its own then, as Borim, tossed and flung about on the stalk of the neck of the dragon, finally found the gleaming instrument, by now a bright white flame attached to the end of his forepaw. Managing to put it to his mouth, he blew a note so high and clear it deafened the animals in the clearing, and the air was torn asunder by that blast, and a light more intense than the sun settled over the beast, its gleam dancing across the dull scales until it was afire with a pale, shimmering glow. The light circled Borim, and in another moment, the total silence was even more frightening than the wind and sound that had gone before, and there, unmoving and sprawled senseless on the empty floor of the clearing, was the new Elder, the Horn of Bruinthor pulsing softly at his side.

As the stunned animals came to their senses and rushed to Borim's aid, they suddenly realized that the beast had simply vanished into thin air. No trace could be found of the terrible thing, nor any of the victims it had slain.

Frael and Hollen wept openly as they cradled Borim's unmoving form, and soon they were surrounded by the remaining survivors of the attack. Calls and cries of those trying to find loved ones filled the clearing, as the battered members of the settlement searched the scorched and wrecked ground where the savage battle had taken place.

"Is he dead?" asked Lan, his voice choked with tears and the dying fire of the battle.

"He lives," said Hollen. "By the Great Lord, he lives!"

"Where's Bern? Has anyone seen Bern?" asked Frael, turning his attention elsewhere, once he knew Borim was alive.

The beaver Tolly shook his head sadly.

"He fled before the attack. I saw him for a moment, on the edge of the wood, then he was gone."

"Then he must be alive," replied Hollen. "I didn't think the play would end this way."

"What about your bunch, Boomer? Are you missing any?"

Hollen's voice was low and even, his great strength and wisdom coming to the fore, calming the other animals with his matter-of-fact tone. He might have been asking about the weather in An Ran Bar.

Collecting himself as best he could, the beaver set out to find who was missing, and to tend to any of the wounded that might need looking after. One by one, those left were accounted for, and the slow realization began to sink in about those that were gone.

"The miserable filth!" said Tolly, gnashing his teeth savagely. "It devoured the best of animals without a blink of an eye."

"Easy, old fellow, easy," soothed Hollen. "It may be the best way."

"It's not fair," went on Tolly.

Hollen nodded wearily.

"Fair or not, it's clean. We won't have the task of straightening up the mess this thing has made. And even *it* has given us the good fortune of disappearing."

"What happened?" asked Earling, bewildered.

"The Horn," replied the old bear. "The Horn of Bruinthor."

Breaking in wildly, Lan danced around the circle of friends.

"Did you see Borim? Great Lord, what a thing to do. I couldn't get to that thing, and he seemed to be everywhere!"

He paused a moment, his brow knitting. "And to think I taught him not long ago."

"And taught him well," said Frael, smiling grimly at his young companion. "Dralin chose his cub's mentors properly."

A low moan escaped Borim, and he struggled to sit upright.

"And speaking of him, here he is," went on Frael.

The young bear's eyes fluttered twice, then opened, and he struggled to focus on the circle of animals that surrounded him.

"Easy now, you've had a nasty knock," said Earling, helping Borim sit.

In a flash, Borim whirled about, and was on his hind legs, once more in a fighting stance.

"It's all over, Borim. It's gone," Hollen said, clapping the young Elder on his broad back. "The Horn has done its work well!"

Borim looked down, and still clenched tightly in his paw was the soft glowing instrument, pulsing as if in time to some hidden music within itself.

"It's done, then?" he asked at last, looking into the deep brown eyes of Hollen.

"When this Horn was carved in the Halls of the Great Lord, it had in it the end of this battle, all those turnings ago. It had other things, too, which other Elders have found. Your father held it safe for you, knowing it would be your lot to keep it, and fulfill its next calling. It sounded only twice at An Ran Bar, and that first time was when Dralin blew it when he became Elder, and the last was when it passed into your keeping."

"It seemed to blow all on its own," said Borim, shaking his head, trying to clear his thoughts.

"And now it has called for the first time in the heat of battle," went on Hollen.

"Where's my brother?" asked Borim, turning about, searching among those there for Bern.

Finding no one would meet his eye, he feared the worst. And then another voice came from some hidden place, and dared let him hope that Bern was gone, but he quickly stilled it. Bern was an emptiness in him that would require more than a death to fill.

"Dead?" he asked softly.

"If that were so, I would gladly tell you that the end had been written happily, Borim. But I think perhaps we shall not have such an easy lot."

"Then he lives?"

"Bern ran away," said Lan, his disgust thinly concealed.

"Ran away?" An odd pain welled up inside him, and hung heavily about his heart. "Are you sure?"

"Tolly saw him, before the fight."

"Is this true, Tolly?"

The beaver looked away, nodding.

"I'm sorry, Borim."

"Then perhaps we'll find him. We'll send out a search party. He probably hasn't gotten far."

"We have no time, Borim. This was only the first of these things. There were others. We'll have to make directly for the sea now."

"I can't leave him here without help," said Borim angrily. "I wouldn't leave you, Hollen."

"You would, if you felt the safety of the settlement depended upon it."

Borim's hackles lowered, and he looked around slowly.

"I don't like these decisions, Hollen. Why must I be forced to choose? My heart says one thing, and you say my duty is otherwise."

"I think at the bottom of it, you'll see they're both the same."

"Then we'll search as we go. That will do, won't it?"

"That will serve both ends, Borim. And we'll be that much nearer to Nob, if he's not already gone. This nest of those ugly louts may have caused the sudden removal of his settlement to somewhere nearer the Roaring."

"If he's still alive."

"Nob is not one to be caught unawares, as we were."

"These beasts don't need surprise. They have such a great power, it's lucky we've escaped at all."

"I wanted to call out to that horrible thing," agreed Tolly. "But I looked away just in time."

"Some of us didn't," said Lan. "Someone cried out, just before that filth attacked."

"We all felt it, Lan. I almost called out myself."

Hollen's voice was firm, and Lan started to speak again, but saw the warning in the older bear's eyes.

"What's done is done," said Boomer. "What we have to think of now is getting away from here. We'll gather up everyone who's left, and get on with this business. I can't stand being here much longer."

"The sooner we get on, the better, Borim. I think it might be best if you tell the rest what our plan is to be."

"What plan, Hollen? I have no plan."

"To go on to the Sea of Roaring, and to find Nob. Now is when we all need to hear a concrete plan of action. If we wait too much longer, we'll have a time of it getting anyone to move anywhere."

Borim studied the other animals in the clearing, nursing their wounds or talking among themselves in that numb voice of those who have barely managed to survive some great danger.

"Gather them up," said Borim, taking a long breath. "We'll see what we can do."

"They'll listen to you now, Borim. You have changed in their eyes this past hour."

Hollen spoke softly, and he patted the strong young cub affectionately.

"Why now? I'm still the same as when they first saw me. Except for this."

He held up the ancient Horn, which had now resumed its old color of polished ivory. The glow had gone, and the gentle music had lapsed into silence.

"You are the true Elder, Borim. They all see you differently after the battle with the beast. They will never again look on you as a cub. And I won't have to back up anything you say from here on in."

"I don't know why I did that, Hollen. It seemed I had no choice," Borim confessed. "I was terrified of that thing, and I almost called out to it."

"We all did, Borim."

"And it made Bern run away." The young bear shook his head sadly. "I feel bad about that. I was hoping that if he stayed with us, we could win him over and show him we were truly his friends."

"It seems that will have to wait, my young friend. There may be a time for that yet."

Their talk was interrupted by the others of the settlement, who had formed a large semicircle about the two. They were talking noisily among themselves, and more than a few arguments were under way.

"We've gone far enough, to my way of thinking. We've lost eight or more of our party, and I say this whole trip was madness from the start. Let's go back to An Ran Bar and hole up until these things find somewhere else to hunt!"

The voice belonged to a beaver known as Thistle. A hedgehog, right at the edge of the crowd, agreed loudly. There were murmurs from two smaller bears from An Ran Bar, although they quickly subsided when they felt Borim's glance on them.

"Let's go home," sang out a voice far to the rear. "We've had enough."

Hollen stepped forward and raised himself to his full height.

"We will hear each of you as always, but speak your name, and say your piece. Otherwise, hold your tongue."

Every paw in the crowd shot up, and a clamor of strident voices joined in at once.

Borim watched for a moment longer, then spoke, his tone calm, but full of a new authority.

"We will hear out any who wish to speak. We are all animals here, so let us remember our manners. Now, you there, Thistle! What have you to say?"

"I'm Thistle, from Green Willow. What I have to say is short and sweet. Let's go back to An Ran Bar. You'll be able to protect us with that Horn you carry. There are more of these things out there, and there's no need to go on to find them. They'd never discover us in the old settlement."

"What of those beasts that are already back there? They know where An Ran Bar is."

"We can deal with their likes," argued Thistle.

"Anyone else?" asked Borim, looking over the crowd of raised paws.

"Nester, from Reed Landing, sir. I'm for going back, too. I think all of us are. We didn't know we'd be faced with monsters like this one you killed. We have our pups and the she-folk to think of. If it was just a war party, it might be different, but it's not."

"Where's that brother of yours, who called that thing down on us?" shouted an unidentified animal from the rear.

Borim knew it was a bear, by the volume, and his heart contracted.

"Give us your name, friend," said Hollen sternly.

"I'm Greenleaf, from the fair settlement of An Ran Bar, where we all belong, instead of out here with these things that fly, and bears that betray their own."

Lan, great hackles bristling, had moved in a flash toward the bear Greenleaf.

"Hold, Lan. He says but what he knows of the truth."

Borim lowered his paw.

"I'll answer you, friend, the best way I know how. You've

seen the Horn of Bruinthor my father left me to hold, and you've seen its power today. I did not wish for this, nor to lead you from your home in An Ran Bar. I had dreams of staying on there forever, until I could sit by a fire and remember a long life in that place that is truly the fairest of settlements in that part of the world. But Hollen has told me the lore, and we must follow, willing or not, until it's done. My brother Bern may have called out to the beast, but he is either swallowed by that foul thing, or lost, so it is of no import to us here. I must claim fault if he has harmed any of you, and I shall try to make it up as best I can, by helping us all reach the safety of the Sea of Roaring, where Hollen says we will find aid and shelter."

"There's nothing there," cried Greenleaf. "No one lives there."

"Lord Dralin has friends there, and that is where we're bound. You may do as you wish, as may any of you. No one is forcing you to stay with us, or to follow us to the Roaring."

"You know we can't return safely to An Ran Bar without the Elder," shouted a large brownish gray bear, standing next to Greenleaf.

"Come back with us! It is your duty to the settlement," cried another.

Order was lost for a moment, and arguments broke out on all sides.

Above the din of voices, a short horn call, low and urgent, was heard. Borim spun about just in time to see the arrival of a new group of bears, who marched resolutely straight through the bewildered throng before them, and stepped smartly to bow low before the young Elder.

"Nob!" cried Hollen in delight, and he fell on a grizzled giant with growls and great claps on the other's broad back.

A stunned silence had fallen over the gathering with the new arrival, and Nob's appearance was enough to quieten even the most vocal dissenters. He stood as tall as Dralin, and was as large as Borim had imagined Kahn to be, with a swath of grayish whiskers at his muzzle, and paws that were big enough to hold Boomer and Tolly together, and a hedgehog or two, and it was a paw such as that that grasped him now, and pulled him to the smothering confines of a brawny chest.

"Bruinthor!" he growled, the rumble of it tickling Borim's ear. "Well met, cub of Dralin. I had suspected you might be

168

seeking old Nob one day, up here in the reaches of the beast hordes."

Borim was smashed into the grasp of the great bear again, then pushed away.

"Let me see this cub of the good Dralin," boomed Nob, casting a wary eye over the young bear, and turning at once to Hollen. "Well, old beard, I guess he does have the makings of a Dralin, given some time with a renegade like Nob. He's had the Law from you and your bunch, and now I guess he'll find out what it's like living on the edge."

Hollen laughed a long ripple of short barks.

"We were worried that we weren't going to find you," Borim said, when the laughter had subsided.

"And well you should be. Nobody finds Nob! Nob is a sly one, he is, and *he* does the finding." The great bear looked about the assembled animals. "I heard the fracas a while back. We were just beyond those groves there, but it was all over by the time we reached here. What happened? Did you drive that slime worm off?"

Hollen shook his head, and pointed to Borim.

"The Horn of Bruinthor! It lit up like another sun, and then the beast was just gone."

Nob looked again at Borim, his glance altered. His paw went up, and his band suddenly bowed low once, then raised themselves on their hindlegs, into the terrible war dance of their kind.

"Bruinthor!" they roared, then once more, yet louder.

"Dralin was right," Nob said, after the noise had died away. "He said his cub that was coming would be the leader that would one day cross the Sea of Roaring for the others."

Behind the new arrivals, a clamor of voices broke in.

"Who is this? Are we taken captive?"

Nob whirled on the members of the settlements Borim led.

"Captives of my hospitality, and prisoners of my wisdom, cousins!"

Nob produced the small, curved horn that had announced his arrival, and blew a soft call that was at once answered by a dozen others, all around the clearing. On this signal, the wood was filled in a moment's blink of an eye with a host of bears that all bore a striking resemblance to their leader.

"Follow, please," growled Nob, and without waiting to acknowledge any protest from Borim or the others, the

169

enlarged party struck off at a steady pace, away in the direction of the rapidly setting sun, which was still peeking over the snowcapped shoulders of the mountains, twinkling in that light like signal fires on the shadow of a sleeping sky.

A Mention of Dwarfs

After a long march that left them exhausted, Borim's group, along with the new arrivals, found themselves in a lush valley, bordered by soft hills that climbed away into the early evening darkness. Stars, just up from their naps, twinkled and shone, filling the sky with their dazzling light, and reflecting on the broad river that ran gurgling and calling in the darkness, singing its song of distant mountains and of its meeting with the sea.

All the animals of the settlements of An Ran Bar gathered around Borim, looking at the beauty of the place, and talking quietly among themselves. Nob's band had vanished, and only their leader remained.

"They've gone on downriver, to see what's been doing since we've been away."

"Will they bring the boats?" asked Tolly, standing beside the huge bear.

Nob laughed suddenly, and reached down to pat Tolly on the back. The beaver shuddered and withdrew, but the touch of the great paw was gentle and reassuring.

"My young sailor, is it? Old waterdogs like yourselves should well be asking about the boats, because that's the thing that's going to get us past those ugly louts that you had the pleasure of meeting today."

"Have you fought with one of them?" asked Boomer.

"Nob doesn't fight, my little bushlily. Nob hasn't lived as long as he has by fighting. Especially with the likes of these ruffians who've started appearing. I don't know where they spring from, or who their sows are, but I'd hate to meet one in a dark patch of wood some night."

Borim, who had withdrawn from the conversation, turned to Hollen.

"Do you think Bern escaped safely? Tolly said he saw him at the edge of the wood, I know, but then a lot of our number disappeared too, and we're not accusing them of having run away."

The old bear studied Borim a moment in silence.

"That's well spoken, Borim. Tolly did see Bern at the edge of the clearing a moment before the beast attacked, but there is no one to say that Bern ran away. No one had time to be looking about after it started, and when it was all over, the thing itself was gone, which was a surprise, or would be, if I didn't know a little something about the Horn of Bruinthor."

"Do you think he was taken by the beast?"

Hollen smiled faintly.

"It would be a tidy way to end the affair, I must say. Bern devoured by the beast, Kahn gone, but then so is Dralin, and Bramweld. Except that with Bern out of the way, the rest of the lore would all have to be rewritten."

"Why would that be?"

"Because, young friend, there is more to all this than something that can be ended by such a simple thing as a beast devouring Bern."

Borim put a paw on his friend's shoulder.

"Please tell me the truth, Hollen."

Their eyes met and held.

"Do you think Bern called out, and betrayed us?"

Hollen answered without a pause.

"He had no choice, Borim. You felt the strange power those beasts have. You want to tell them where you are, and surrender to them. I have read in the old books about things such as these. It was one reason the Horn was handed down from Elder to Elder, and kept safely all these turnings. Where there is a power given in the one direction, there is its opposite. The balance. It is the same with you and Bern. He has no choice but to follow the path he has been given, as you must follow your own."

"Do you hate him?"

The old bear looked away toward where the river shed its sparkling lights in the gloom.

"We have all been like Bern, my young friend. And we hate only the things we fear." He shook his head, suddenly feeling very tired. "If it were but hate, it would be so much easier to deal with. That always seems to be the case. Pity, it so happens, is the worst of the lot. But beyond that, with any luck at all, is an understanding."

Borim could not follow the old bear's words, and felt an

emptiness inside him since the disappearance of his half brother, who was at once irritating and pathetic.

"I know if we could only keep him with us long enough, we might reach him. He's lived so long thinking that we're all enemies, and going around acting as if everyone were out for his blood, that no matter what happened, he always proved himself right."

"I'm sure he blamed this as our doings," offered Lan. "And there is some truth to it. If we hadn't left An Ran Bar, I doubt we would have chanced across that nasty lump of hide we ran into this afternoon."

"Not for a while," agreed Frael. "They may have taken their time about moving too far abroad. Nob says they have only been here a short while, and they have their nests somewhere nearby."

"Does he think they've come from across the Roaring?" asked Hollen.

"No, from the Far North. Beyond the ice."

"Why have they settled here?" asked Lan. "There's more going on in the other woods."

"That's what Nob has been trying to find out. He's scouted up and down the river, and has gone as far back to the mountains as he could safely go, and been all the way to the sea, and up that coast. There's something afoot, and he knows it, but no one has any idea exactly what. He thinks the beasts like the one we saw today are gathering strength, so they may invade all the other lands."

Nob, at the mention of his name, broke off the small talk he was engaging in with Tolly, and ambled over, his great bulk moving easily. The gray of his coat caught and held the reflected starlight off the river, and that silvery glow made odd patterns on the muzzles of all the animals there.

"Who has said old Nob's handle here? Anyone wishing to speak up, let him. We keep everything over and by the board here. No skulking about like that pack that you met today."

"Frael says you think they're waiting for a sign, or for someone to show up," said Hollen.

Nob frowned, and his claws and fangs glistened a deadly white as he spoke.

"I've been hoping to run into whatever, or whoever. Those louts have destroyed two of my snuggest shelters, and sunk three of my boats just at the far delta. I've got some reckoning with them, right enough, but I need to know more of the picture. Not counting the one you blew to glory today, Borim,

172

I've crossed paths with a dozen more. They seem to hole up at an old cliff settlement, near where I grew up as a cub. They're not always out. Just certain times. I guess whenever they get hungry, or just start feeling mean."

"Where is this place, Nob?" asked Frael.

"You were almost to it when you were attacked. Another little walk, and you would have been right there with them."

All the animals shuddered.

"I think what saved you at all was the fact that all the beasts were out. They'd never suspect a tidy snack right at their front door."

Borim glanced around nervously.

"Don't you think we should be pushing on then, to get beyond their reach?"

Nob laughed, a harsh snort.

"There is nowhere beyond their reach, stout Borim. You could go for days at a good brisk bear trot, and they would have found you by dinner time, as easy as you please."

"Then what will we do?" asked a somewhat jumpy Boomer.

"Do? That, lad, is a good question that will keep us busy over a few campfires yet, if I don't mark my guess wrong. Borim here was able to destroy one of those louts with no trouble, but how it happened, I don't understand yet. Neither does he, from the looks of it."

Borim was dumbfounded.

"I don't know how it happened. The Horn just blew by itself, and then I woke up, and the beast was gone." He paused a moment. "But then there were a lot of others gone with it."

Nob raised a paw, as if to brush the memory of their lost friends away.

"They're beyond it all now, as they should be. It is for us here to ponder on this mystery, and to solve this puzzle as best we may."

"I can't really even say how I got close enough to that thing to blow the Horn at it."

"I can tell you that, Borim," said Lan, moving into the center of the animals, darting and whirling.

He whirled first one way, then another, and rose onto his hindlegs, his movements so fast now they could barely detect any sign of where he would strike out next. Back and forth he spun, and at last he stopped, breathless, and looked at the gathered animals.

"And then he was holding onto the thing's neck, which was just before we heard the Horn."

"Lan has taught me well," said Borim, bowing to his friend. "Yet it did not make me any less fearful, or any too glad to be there, instead of by a safe fire, reading the lore books, back in An Ran Bar."

"Tell me of that settlement again," said Nob, forgetting all else for the moment. "Dralin always spoke of it in such a way that it made me want to visit there."

"Perhaps one day you will," said Frael.

Nob looked long at the shimmering lights of the river, and the stars, and shook his head slowly.

"It would have been nice, once. But I'm too far from there now, and I don't feel that old Nob will be going back that way. Too far from the sea!"

A note of sadness in the great bear's voice caught Borim's ear.

"But you would like it. And I know my father would have wanted you to see it."

"Dralin had many good times over my campfires," laughed Nob, the sadness replaced now with a hushed tone, as if he were recalling them all at the moment. "He loved the stories of the Roaring, and meeting the folks who lived along the coast. It was a shame that I couldn't have taken him in my own boat, but that seems the way of it. One more thing to look forward to, after all this dust-up is over."

"That's a strange way to put it," said Frael, wondering at Nob's total disregard for the news that Dralin had disappeared—once and for all it was feared—and mainly at the fact that Borim now carried the Horn of Bruinthor.

"That's the only way to put it, my friend," laughed Nob, looking from Frael to Hollen. "You must spend more time at your teaching, good Hollen. You've left some gaps."

"Not as many as I would have liked," chuckled the old bear. "I've had my fill of lore, and teaching. Give me the simple life of action, that's my answer. Just let me be involved in something that'll keep my attention off wanting to know too many answers."

Nob's laugh boomed out over the quiet setting, startling the weary animals that lay all about nursing their wounds and talking quietly among themselves.

"Quiet up there!" came a fretful voice. "We've lost two of our party today. It's no time for your good spirits."

"You'd best go see to them, Borim," said Nob, lowering his

voice. His clear eyes had turned a sea gray as he spoke, and his features had softened.

"I don't know what to say," blurted the cub.

"They'll think it better coming from you. And you did lose your own half brother, although we don't know how, whether to that beast or to something worse. I'll go with you," said Nob. "I know how these things go. I've had it fall to my lot enough, living as I have all these turnings up on the borders."

"I'll come too," said Tolly. "That sounded like one of our settlement."

The animals wound their way among the survivors of the afternoon, giving encouragement or sympathy, and all the while Nob spoke hopefully of their trip on the morrow, and that it would be better once they got beyond the beasts' lair. He said nothing of his doubts about being able to get beyond the reach of the things, nor did he mention how far they would have to go to reach the Sea of Roaring, which Borim knew was a long and dangerous voyage by boat, down the Eagle Claw, which according to both Hollen and Nob ran through the wilder part of the border lands for a straight three- or four-day trip, and then on and beyond the terrible wastelands that separated the sea from the land behind.

The more Nob talked of the journey, the more Borim respected Dralin, and the trips he'd made there.

"Did you know Ellin, whom my father knew?" asked the cub, remembering the name as one his father had mentioned.

Nob stopped dead in his tracks.

"I know Ellin well. He is a good friend. Or was!"

"What happened?"

"He went on a scouting party when these beasts first began to appear. Nothing more has been heard of him."

"Did he live in your settlement?"

"Ellin? No, he lived with his own, in his own settlement. Didn't Dralin or any of the others tell you about Ellin?"

"Only that he was a friend. There was another name, but Dralin never told me. Hollen said he would, when the time was come that I should know it."

Nob sat down suddenly on his haunches.

"Whew, but that's a secretive bunch your father lived with. I always told Dralin that. Get it out in the open, let it all be seen, so that everyone knows what they're dealing with." Nob shook his head, smiling at the memory of it. " 'No, it's not time,' he'd say. 'It's good you live as you do, on the border,

175

out of the reach of almost everyone. If you lived in An Ran Bar, there'd be a major migration tomorrow.' "

The huge bear shook with stifled laughter.

"That's what he always told me, and I guess he was right. I've been too long here on these harsh borders to play with the truth or call a thing by one name when it's another. Yet I can see, after being with you only a short time, what he had to deal with there."

"In An Ran Bar? It was beautiful," argued Borim. "There were streets full of baking, and tea, and woodwork, and everything else you could ever want."

"Oh, no doubt, my young friend, no doubt. Dralin told me of the things that were there, and gave a good picture of the easy life, interrupted now and then by Kahn's raiders, or a stray beast or two from across the Gray Rock. Still, everyone wanted to stay, and would go back, from all I heard this afternoon. Even knowing that it won't be safe for long. Dralin knew that of the place, and it's why he and the others like him traveled a lot. It kept them aware of the pull of An Ran Bar. It calls out, just like the beasts call out, to tell them where you are hiding, so they may come and devour you."

Nob's great muzzle loomed above Borim in the darkness, and seeing the fierceness in his eyes, he grew afraid for a moment.

"I've changed my settlements a hundred times here. Before one can get attached to it being one way, I've gotten it off to someplace else, or there will be a whole new group living there. The drifters and wanderers of all the clans have lived at my hall at one time or other. Your father had long talks to me about that, and about Bramweld and Kahn."

"Did you ever meet Bramweld?"

"Once."

"Did he come here?"

"No, I went to Black Grove. Your father had talked to me of the settlement, so I went to see it for myself."

"Did you like Bramweld?"

"That's a strange choice of words, Borim. Liking is very much different than understanding. Pleasing, or not pleasing, fearing, or not fearing. It all comes back to the way we describe it." He stroked a great paw across his chest. "No, I don't think liking is a term I would use for Bramweld. He was cautious, and slow to move on matters, and had no interest in either Dralin or Kahn, only because he felt they should stop the bickering among themselves and let things lie."

"Was there anything wrong with that?"

"No, Borim, not in itself. But Bramweld refused to even acknowledge there was a problem to be dealt with, and I doubt very much that the settlement of Black Grove has moved an inch since its leader disappeared."

"There are some animals here that came from Bramweld's settlement," insisted Borim, growing more confused as Nob spoke.

"Then I'm glad to know there's still some sense left in the settlements below the river. But I'd wager not all are with you."

Borim shook his head.

"Only a few came with the messenger we sent to tell them we were leaving An Ran Bar."

Nob looked at the river awhile, then snorted.

"I've been called many things in my life, Borim, and I can't in truth deny too many of them, except the ones that might say I willfully hurt any living thing that had not provoked me. But I don't mind, for I've spent my time here on these wild borders for one reason, and one reason only, and it has finally come to pass: I shall at last be put to some real use, and not just run a foundling settlement to keep a herd of strays from starving to death, or falling prey to that pack of filth from the Northerlands."

"I hadn't gotten to that part yet, Nob," broke in Hollen, who had come in the darkness and stood silently beside his friend.

"Well, it's time enough you should," shot Nob, his mood changing, and his voice taking on the gruffness it had held when Borim first met him.

"I thought there would be time enough."

"No time, old beard. You are forever lagging along, dragging your paws. But now it's time we took some action and moved up the pace a bit. I've been enough turnings down here on these outlands, waiting for the signal."

"There's still the trick of getting us all safely to the sea," cautioned Hollen.

"We shall do that, come morning. We'll find just how many of your lot are to be counted on, once they get aboard a vessel like they're going to see come downriver by first light."

"We'll be all right," snapped Lan, also coming to stand beside Borim. "If it's a scrap you're looking for, there's enough in our settlement are no strangers to standing down to it."

Nob's great paw shot out, almost knocking Lan down.

"There's no offense to you, Lan. I know these folk are ready enough. I've been too long stuck out here, and had to watch too many turnings go by without lifting a paw. I'm just ready, that's all, and high time, I say." He snorted, turning to Hollen. "I've been saying that for a good long while now, but there was always one thing or another that kept coming up."

Borim addressed a question to Hollen.

"What was the other name my father knew? After Ellin, I mean."

"Have you seen Ellin?" asked Hollen. "We've had so much excitement, I can't get all the things we need to speak of straight."

"He said Ellin is gone," answered Borim, hoping Hollen would fill him in on the rest of the story that concerned the mysterious Ellin, and the other name that no one had told him.

Hollen's eyes opened wide.

"Ellin? I don't for a minute believe that."

"It's true enough. I talked to one of his party, after the first of these new beasts had been seen abroad. They had attacked one of Ellin's outposts, and he led a party to find where they nested. But that was all anyone saw or heard of him."

Hollen rubbed a paw across his muzzle, a worried frown creasing his old features.

"This is a bad stroke of luck, if indeed it's true. Ellin was to give us something that we would need, but Dralin didn't say what, though."

"Then one of the others might help."

"Will we be able to find them? And reach the Roaring, too?"

"It's on the way. I've kept their bunch up on where my camps will be."

Hollen nodded, as Nob went on.

"They have a new Elder, too, that's come to power about the same time as our good Borim."

"Who is this? A new Elder?"

"It caught me by surprise, too, but it was Ellin told me, not long before he disappeared. Said they had been waiting for him for a long time."

"What's the name of the new Elder?" asked Hollen.

"Brandigore. Brian Brandigore."

Borim could hold still no longer.

"Are these bears? Is it a clan I haven't met yet?"

Hollen's shaggy brow shot upward.

"Did Dralin tell you nothing at all?" He wrung his old paws together. "I can see I'm not through with my teaching chores yet."

"Dralin told me nothing. But who is Ellin? And this Brandigore?"

"Dwarfs!" snorted Nob. "Of the first water."

Ancient History Repeated

They had no fire that night, for fear of attracting the beasts, but the companions sat in a wide circle, sprawling wherever they found comfortable on the grass by the river, and the talk lasted far into the night, and into the early morning. Hollen and Nob took turns at relating the history of the dwarf clans that had come to live in their end of the wood, explaining the beginnings of the strange creatures, and how they had finally met, in ancient times, in the first of the years that animalkind had begun to become civilized, and then to fall from the high ideals of the First of All Things that had drawn life.

It was Hollen speaking now, his old voice creaking in places, although it still carried very strongly in the shroud of darkness that lay over the clearing on the banks of the water. The rippling chuckle of the current passing by seemed to grow quieter as Hollen began.

"It was in the time of Alon Rab, as the story goes, that a hunting party was out one late afternoon, in the very farthest reaches of that realm's woods. Alon Rab was leading the group, and there were Elders there from a dozen other clans, who had banded together with him to protect themselves from the invaders from the Northland, who had begun to grow in numbers and even then to raid across the lower boundaries. Charon Lin was there, who was the sire of the clans in the Western Wood, and many others who were important advisers, or friends."

Borim had begun to fall asleep, thinking the tale was taking on too many aspects of a history lesson. His ears perked up, however, at the next statement.

"They all fell victim to a cunning trap that had been laid there, just at the outskirts of the deep wood, where it met a wide, open clearing that bordered the Shadow."

"The Shadow is the last boundary before you reach The Barrens and the heart of the true North," broke in Nob.

As he spoke, the animals could almost see the white frost of his breath hanging before him.

"It was high summer, but there was snow on the ground across the Shadow, and that terrible river was swollen with ice. It was even snowing a few flakes on this side of the boundary, and that's what caused Alon Rab to be so careless as to allow what befell him to happen.

"There was no beast then that the Elders of those times did not know of, and it was a great shock to all of them to find themselves rolled as neat as you please into the tiny cage of earth, locked securely, and even the dreaded Alon Rab's great blows couldn't free them from the confines of the prison they found themselves in."

"Wasn't Alon Rab looking for trouble in going there?" asked Boomer, sure that had it been a beaver Elder, they would never have dared venture so close to a known danger.

"They patrolled those areas, just as I patrol my own," replied Nob. "But they had never before run across the likes of what had happened to them. The beasts across the Shadow weren't the clever sort, and the only trick they knew was to ambush you when you least expected it, when they outnumbered you a dozen to one."

Nob snorted his disgust before going on.

"The Elders weren't ready for what they found, which was a deep pit, so cunningly concealed and covered over with such real-looking trees and earth that it even smelled safe."

"A pit?" shot Tolly. "You mean like we used along the edge of our old settlement at Green Willow?"

"That's where the idea came from," explained Hollen. "It was handed down from the Elders of Alon Rab."

"Didn't they know about those then?" asked Boomer.

"Not until they fell into one first," laughed Hollen. "And it caused no small concern, for all the leaders of the settlements were there, trapped as neat as you could imagine, and they had no doubts but that it was the doings of the beasts across the river."

"They were prepared to fight for it," went on Nob, taking over the tale easily. "They knew it was a matter of no surrender, and not one among them was of a cowardly sort, so they prepared to make themselves as best a defense as they could. They were no helpless party, I can assure you."

"And then, right above them, there was a voice, speaking the High Tongue, but no one to be seen."

Hollen had taken up the narrative, and played all the parts vigorously.

" 'We've got another pack of those miserable filth,' it said, addressing some other unseen voice behind it.

" 'Put them out of their misery, poor blighters, no need to make them suffer any longer than they already have.'

" 'Let me see them first,' said another voice, and this one must have been one of the Elders of those voices, for no one said anything more, and soon Alon Rab saw the strangest sight he had ever seen in his extremely long life. It was so strange he went to great lengths to describe it in his book, which is one of the major lore texts now."

Borim nodded glumly, for he had picked up the huge volume that had had "Alon Rab" across the front of it in fine gilt print, but he had not been forced to read it, for which he was grateful at first, although he now saw that there was much he could have learned, had he taken the time to read a bit more before he had been forced to leave An Ran Bar.

Hollen's voice burred on, cloaked in darkness, and with the air of a skillful tale spinner.

"Alon Rab said at first he couldn't tell what sort of animal's head it was, except that whatever he saw had a bright green plume above skin so clean of fur it almost startled him out of his wits. Two piercing brown eyes studied him intently, and then the rest of the body came into sight, which was even stranger.

"Where the fur should have been, there was a strange-looking colored design of some sort, and the animal, if that's what it could be called, was only tall enough to reach the tops of the shoulders of the great bears when they were sitting on their hindquarters, which was a favorite way they had of resting when they wanted to think things over or to watch bees in a sweet gum tree."

"What was it?" urged Tolly. "What did Alon Rab see?"

"I'll get to that," said Hollen curtly, hating to have his story interrupted. He knew that the beavers were an impatient lot, and that they never took the proper time with their descriptions of things, always preferring to rush helter-skelter on until the finish, and the listener would have to put the puzzle together as best he could.

"What it was, was as baffling to Alon Rab and his friends as it is to you, Tolly. No one had ever heard tell of, much less seen, anything like the animal with the strange-colored fur, and the odd plume, and the striking brown eyes. And their paws had no claws, and their hindquarters were squared and rounded, and their hindpaws were more like hooves."

"And if Alon Rab thought that was strange, he was even more surprised when he saw another exactly like the first, then still another. In the end, there was a ring of these strange beings all around the deep pit where the companions were trapped," said Nob, his teeth shining in the dark as he smiled.

" 'Who are you?' one of them asked, and Alon Rab was so startled to hear the High Tongue spoken just as if he had spoken it himself that he was dumbfounded.

" 'There's no need to waste your time talking to the likes of those, friend. They're just more of those poor wild souls from across the Shadow. We might as well put them out of their suffering, and save a lot of pain for the other settlers farther on.'

" 'No, I think these can talk. I know I heard them talking there, just a moment ago.' "

Hollen was taking on all the parts, and changing his voice for each character he was describing.

" 'There's none of those beasts can speak,' sneered another.

" 'Come and see for yourself,' said the first, and he had never taken his eyes off Alon Rab.

" 'I can speak, as can all my friends,' boomed Alon Rab, finding his voice, and deeply curious about these strangers who had no fur, yet were not enemies that he would imagine coming from beyond the Shadow River.

" 'See! He can speak. These are not the beast hordes. I knew these were different.'

" 'Who are you?' asked Alon Rab. 'And where do you come from?'

" 'They can speak,' the strangers agreed, all becoming highly agitated, and talking among themselves.

" 'It's impossible, but true. We've never met any of your kind who had speech,' said the stranger. 'What are you called?'

" 'Alon Rab,' replied the bear, beginning to feel that they were no longer in danger, and lowering his hackles. The others did the same.

" 'My name is Co'in, and these are my followers. We have a settlement nearby. We thought you were more of that lot from across the river.'

" 'We guard these boundaries from them, as best we can,' said Alon Rab, 'but we can't always keep them all back.'

"The stranger, Co'in, looked to the others. 'They are at the same job as we are.'

" 'They lie,' grumped another of the short ones. 'They're trying to save themselves. You can see with your own two good peeps that they're beasts.' "

Hollen took another rest, for he had worked himself into each part, and talked much longer than his voice would allow, without a rest.

"Hollen here spins a good yarn," laughed Nob. "I can't tell it so well as that, but I remember from my lore book that Co'in finally convinced the others that the animals they had trapped weren't the same as the beasts from the Northerlands, beyond the Shadow, and that they must speak to them further, and find out all they could of these animals who spoke the High Tongue, and guarded the borders, the same as themselves."

"Why hadn't they met before?" asked Borim. "If they were trying to guard the same territory, it looks as if they would have had other meetings."

"The dwarf Co'in explained that by saying they had long dwelled underground, just as we did, in the Lower Wood, for a part of the year. They seemed to know a good deal about matters dealing with the earth and all that dealt with that way of life."

Hollen resumed, with his voice breaking at times.

"This dwarf, this Co'in, told Alon Rab that the clan he came from had been there for a great long time, after having spent many turnings in the Lower Wood. They were animals of a sort, but they went about on only two feet, and those were the odd hooves that Alon Rab had remarked on in his book. Yet they spoke the same High Tongue, and were obviously of the right sort, for they trapped beasts and tried to patrol the borders along the Northerlands, just as the bears and other animals were trying to do. Co'in gave Alon Rab a history of his forefathers, and how they had gotten to the Lower Wood, but it was all so similar to Alon Rab's that he didn't bother to write anything more about it, other than to say that during the Great Beginning, all kinds came forth from the Islands to dwell in, on, and above the Lower Wood, and that there would be all those kinds until the cycle would end to start anew."

"Did they become friends?" asked Lan, wondering at all this new lore that he had never heard before.

"Friends?" asked Nob. "Perhaps. I think it might be closer to say they shared a common interest, and were able to help one another in reaching a goal that would be helpful to them both."

"They became friends," snorted Hollen shortly. "At least it is written so in Alon Rab's lore. I don't know how the dwarf Co'in wrote of it, if he kept a lore book."

"Oh, he did," laughed Nob. "I've read parts of it."

"Where did you ever get to do that?" asked Borim.

"Ellin! Ellin has all the volumes of his clans. I hope they're safe, and that someone is taking care of them."

"You've read Ellin's lore books? How wonderful," said Hollen. "I would give a lot to be able to do that."

"You shall, if we can find our thick-necked dwarfish friend, and if he and his band haven't been swallowed up by that nest of long-tailed slime."

"I would like that," echoed Hollen. "I've never had the chance to read a dwarf's lore, right out of his own book. I'm sure it would be most interesting."

"When we get settled somewhere, Hollen, we'll bring you all the lore books, and just turn you loose before a nice fire, with a cup of mulberry tea, and nothing more to do. No trips like this one, or beasts to bother with, or any decisions to be made." Nob, half serious, clapped his friend on the back. "You're quite the bear, old beard. I would never have thought to see the day that this one has come to, with you out among the rest of us, with nothing for a bed but the grass beneath us, and no light but the stars on the river."

Hollen laughed in the dark, and for a moment it sounded to Borim that all age had been removed from the old bear. It also sounded to Borim that it was a voice a lot like his father's that spoke.

"I never thought of it this way either, Nob. My last trip was made many turnings ago, and I'd hoped to live out my time in my study at An Ran Bar, getting forgetful, and having someone bring me my tea in the afternoon."

"It may come to that yet, if you're not careful," warned Frael. "You keep on talking like that, and we may see to it that you never get to go on another of these little pleasure outings with us."

The humor was thin, and Frael's laugh nothing more than an effort to comfort the others.

184

"Oh, I'll hold you to that promise, don't worry."

"What about the dwarf Co'in?" asked Borim, getting the old bear's attention back to his story.

After a silence, as Hollen collected his thoughts, he went on.

"Co'in and Alon Rab formed a mutual clan there by the Shadow, and they became the true guardians of the border, and remained so for many turnings."

"And then what happened?" asked Tolly.

"And then what happened is this. There were those among both clans that distrusted the other, and it finally happened that a dwarf was slain by a beast that had slipped past their vigilance, and the dwarf who had wanted to slay Alon Rab spoke out against the bears, and said that it had been the friendly clan of Alon Rab that had murdered the dwarf."

Borim's bristles raised. "He was a traitor, then."

Hollen shook his head, but went on softly.

"Not a traitor, but very afraid, Borim. Afraid of Alon Rab, and the fellowship of the bears. And he was afraid, too, that the two clans would become so close that more secrets would begin to be shared, and that meant allowing animals into the lower delvings where the dwarfs lived, all up and down the edges of the wood and river. That is a very special thing to a dwarf, and they are very closemouthed about their digs."

"No different than me," offered a gruff old mole from Reed Landing who was sitting next to Tolly.

"No different than all of us, friend, but there comes a point where the fear has to be undone and gotten over, or it goes on growing, and the more it grows, the more dangerous it becomes. This fear caused Co'in and Alon Rab to rip asunder their mutual clan of border guards, and the two never had dealings with the other again. I've heard that Co'in still lives, but somewhere to the far west, and has never come aboveground since the whole affair. It was his cousin's mate who was murdered, it seems, and the one who carried the word had long been courting her, and it was on one of these secret meetings that the tragedy had occurred, when they had been surprised by the beast."

"That's a sad story, right enough," said Nob. "One of the saddest I've heard. Ellin has told me that on one or two outings we've been on together, and I never could figure out why it was that Co'in believed it was one of Alon Rab's clan that did it."

"You mean you went out with Ellin?" asked Frael.

185

"And have been to his digs, and seen the lower delvings."

"However did you manage to do that?" asked Boomer. "If all his sort were on the outs with you bears, why would he let you in?"

"Co'in was the one who was on the outs with bears," corrected Nob. "And still is, according to the stories that Ellin told me. Co'in is very old now, and doesn't move around much overground. He's built a huge settlement, up near the last of the boundaries, and keeps mostly to his own."

"Doesn't Ellin know about Alon Rab, and that it was all a lie?" asked Borim.

"Of course. Ellin was just a young spanner then, and knew the dwarf that caused the lie to spread, and who was responsible."

"Why didn't he tell Co'in?"

"Co'in knew. But you must understand that these dwarfs are a strange lot."

"They must be, to go furless, and to have to go on their hindpaws all the time," said Tolly.

Hollen continued, ignoring the beaver.

"Co'in had known of the beasts who were to follow, and that they would be unable to keep them from leaving whenever they wanted, and that it would cost a great many lives, both bear and dwarfish, to try to continue the border patrols that were keeping the two clans in contact. And Co'in also had in mind that it would take something more than either of the two clans had to deal with these new beasts who were said to be coming."

"Dwarfs are handy with all sorts of things that I never heard of," agreed Nob. "They can make many things out of ground-up dirt, and water, and fire. You never saw the end of all the smoke and noise down where they live. Always hammering away on this or that, and blowing up the fire until you'd think it was so hot you'd melt."

"They are known for their craft, such as it is, and I recall reading somewhere that it is to be the dwarf clan who will arm the heir of Bruinthor."

"Arm what?" asked Borim, his confusion getting the best of his patience at waiting for the end of the story. "I have two stout forepaws, what more could I need?"

"Arms such as these dwarfs forge," went on Hollen, "are cold as death, and as hard as the breath of a norther. And they are said to know where a heart lies, and how to slay it."

Boomer's eyes opened wide in the dark.

"I don't want anything to do with anyone like that!"

"These are things that are strange to all of us, Boomer," explained Hollen. "But it's a thing we shall have to overcome, in order to be able to keep from being defeated and destroyed by the likes of that thing that attacked us today."

"Borim handled it with the Horn," said Boomer. "There's no need for anything more. All Borim has to do is get close enough, and that's all there is. There wasn't even any carcass left of the beast, or anyone else."

"Borim won't be able to keep up with the numbers of these beasts, even if he were to blow from sunrise to sunset. These are another thing, and I don't think that Borim can help, except by leading all of us, with everyone doing his part."

Nob's eyes gleamed out of the darkness as he spoke. "We have all been waiting for our sign, and now it's come. Borim has the Horn of Bruinthor to rally the clans together, so that we may stand against the beasts, and to end the threat from the North once for all."

"If that's the case, I think I'll just mosey on home," said Tolly. "I was just coming along to find a new settlement where all this business won't keep me away from my supper, or ruin my dam building come spring."

"Not this spring, my little friend," said Hollen. "What Nob says of Ellin lets out any plans we all might have of settling into anyplace now. I wasn't sure how it would be once we got here, or what we would be called upon to do, but as our good companion has said, it seems Borim has the key to the question in the Horn, and we shall all be called upon to carry our share of the load to help him."

"But what'll we do, Hollen? Nob says Ellin is gone! There's no way to get any of these things like he's talking about without the dwarfs, and the other one, Co'in, is too old, and lives too far away for us to ever find, anyhow."

"We shall find him, Borim, if we have to. There's no going back now, and nothing to look forward to but more encounters with these things like we met today. I, for one, don't relish the thought of ever having to see another one of them, but if I do, then I'd like a little something that might deter him from having me up for a tea snack."

"Well spoken, Hollen, and I'm sure we will all come to feel that way sooner if we have to deal with another of the beasts anytime before we forget what it was like," said Frael.

"Who's going to break this cheery bit of news to the others?" asked Borim. "About all this battle and beasts, and trips to the Westerlands, to find something called a dwarf that no one of them has ever heard of before?"

"Why, you, Borim!" clucked Nob. "They'll listen to you."

"Why not you, Nob? You're in charge of this neck of the wood."

"Not old Nob. No one ever pays attention to me, unless it's the last breath. I'm just the guide here, and the one who makes all the proper noises when the arguments start taking a turn toward slowing down."

Borim, his attention suddenly drawn to another matter, asked the grizzled older bear a question in a lower tone of voice.

"Would your party that's gone for the boats be likely to come across any strays from our party? I mean, if they're out in that direction, they'd bring back anyone they found there, wouldn't they?"

"Anyone but a beast," laughed Nob. "They have their orders about guests and callers."

"I was wondering about Bern," said Borim. "I still can't believe he was taken by the beast."

"Oh, I'm sure he wasn't," comforted Nob, his voice cool and without feeling. "We had sight of him as we came through the last of the wood, just before we reached you."

"Why didn't you tell me?" shot Borim, his heart leaping.

"I was going to, but you would have found out soon enough, tomorrow."

"Why tomorrow? Is he coming back tomorrow?"

Nob's smile was undecipherable in the dim light, and Borim could get nothing further from the great form sprawled beside him, so he at last turned to the others, half of himself filled with an unbounded joy at the news of Bern's sighting, and the other half shrouded in dread.

The Crowning of the Horn

On the day recorded in ancient bearlore as the Crowning of the Horn, which was the day after Borim Bruinthor had slain and vanished the terrible snake that flew, it was said to have dawned fair and clean, and the earth seemed to have been swept down with new smells, as if by a glimmering rain of stars that had fallen all through the night.

A great meeting was held at the top of a high knoll that

overlooked a fair green valley, where the swift river curved and turned in the sunlight, and wound away into the distance, reaching on beyond gentle woods and broad clearings. And there, just at the end of it, where the blue of the sky touched the lips of the earth, there hung a faint white mist that Nob said was the beginning of the sea clouds, and that it was the Roaring.

All of the animals that had been in any of the various settlements of An Ran Bar were written down in the ledger of Hollen, and kept to be passed on as the beginning of the reign of the Elder Borim, the beast slayer, and all the names, and kinds, and clans were recorded, along with the name of Nob and all his clan. Nob had objected to this, but Frael had finally convinced him that it would be necessary for the proper keeping of the Book, so Nob had given in, grumbling to himself.

"There's more of a need here for some fancy marching, as I see it. Writing all the fal-tra-hoo down for some future lot of sassy cubs won't go near so far toward getting it down as just hoofing it now, and getting a bit closer to the boats. We're to meet them downriver, and we haven't made a step in the right direction since we stopped to rest for the night."

"Plenty of time, Nob," cajoled Hollen. "You are going to get your place in the lore books, even if we have to make up a story to tell about you that would be decent enough for a cub to hear."

Nob snorted.

"You'd have to go a far piece to find one you could tell a cub."

"No one told me anything about you, except for a hint here and there. I wasn't ready for what I finally saw, I'll admit," laughed Borim. "Tolly told me of sailing with you on the river, but he didn't tell me how you really were. Nobody would."

"That's the way I like it," said Nob. "No one can say one thing or another if they don't have anything to complain of. But I'd as soon be remembered as the strange bear on the borders, as made a fuss over."

"There'll be plenty of fuss made over you," said Frael. "The cubs won't be able to hear enough of the exploits of the bold Nob."

At this, the grizzled bear shot out a huge paw that almost bowled over Frael.

"You tend to your chores, and I'll look to my own, my

friend. And first of all, I'd say we need to find out how we stand this morning, and gather ourselves up for a march."

He paused, looking upward, studying the sky.

"And I'd say it would be a smart thing for us to get on with it, and get out of sight before the rest of those things discover one of their brood is missing and come out looking for it."

Borim called his clans together and gave them instructions as best he could about the trip to the Sea of Roaring in Nob's boats, and the dangers they faced, both from the sky and from the unknown woods that lay between them and the end of the trip. And even there, on the coast of the sea, there was no sure answer as to what they would find.

Borim left the dwarf tales to Nob, who did not paint a very bright picture of even finding the grumpy creatures, let alone enlisting their aid.

"Who is this Ellin?" asked Greenleaf, the most outspoken of all the bears from An Ran Bar, who never let an issue go by without questioning it.

"A dwarf, as I said," replied Nob.

"And this dwarf, this thing you describe, is to give us something to defend ourselves against these beasts that fly?"

"They are to forge new weapons for us, beyond our own natural claws and fangs," said Nob. "And Ellin has told me of a skin we can wear over our own, which would protect us from the bite of the snake creatures."

A wave of approval swept the throng of animals.

"Can we trust these dwarfs?" asked another. "Are they respecters of the Law?"

Nob nodded.

"As much as any of our own clans are."

At this, Borim thought of his brother, and grew saddened at the thought of what would ever become of them, and what had become of Kahn, and Bramweld, and his father.

"And how are we to reach this dwarf, and how long is it going to take to get these things he's going to give us?"

Hollen raised a paw.

"Hold, friend, we've jumped ahead of ourselves here. First we have to reach the boats Nob is bringing to carry us, and then there's the trip to the sea. Once we're out of the way of these beasts, we'll think on those other points you mention."

"We need to move on now," said Nob, looking skyward and glowering. "I have a strange feeling that we may just get a visit from that filth, if they come looking for their friend who didn't fly back to the nest. They're a close bunch, and from

190

what little I've been able to study them, they have clans just like we do. That one that didn't return will be missed."

"Brrr," shuddered Boomer. "I hate to think of an entire clan of those things. It's enough to stand your fur right on end."

"And worse, for that matter," agreed Nob. "Ellin told me that there's an Elder that rules them, and that he answers to an even higher Elder, somewhere in the great ice fields in the Far North."

"Dralin told me something to that effect," said Frael. "Before we knew for a fact about these things, he had hinted that there was more to the whole affair than just Kahn and his beasts across the Gray Rock."

"He never spoke of much at length, but I do recall a few chats over a late fire," said Earling, agreeing with his friend. "We were talking of futures, and pasts, and he was in a peculiar mood one night, and couldn't sleep. I think it was after he'd returned from a long trip down this way. He may have just come from you, Nob. He was restless, and sad, and spoke of many things that made no sense to me, until now."

"I remember that night, Earling. It was cold outside, and there'd been a new snowfall, and we all had a late supper in his little study."

"He told us then that he was expecting you, Borim," said Earling, turning to the new Elder. "And that he knew that Bern was coming, too."

"Speaking of Bern, what did you mean about seeing him soon enough, Nob? You spoke as though you knew something."

"Not as a fact, Borim. Just a good hunch, considering all the talks with Dralin, and knowing the way things lie. Old Nob has been around a turning or two, and can spot things as quick as the next sort who can keep his eyes open and see what he's looking at."

The old anger welled within Borim.

"I won't have Bern judged before all the facts are in. If it is true that he's the one who called the snake on us, then that is punishment enough, for he has exiled himself. There could be no more harsh penalty than that."

Nob's features softened.

"I mean no offense, Borim. These things are hard for all of us to talk of, and they aren't pleasant to think of, either. But there is the hard fact that we must follow the Law as we see it, no matter how uncomfortable it makes us, or how much we

191

would wish it were otherwise. When you begin to see it for what it is, then you'll understand a bit more, I think."

"What I'm understanding now is that until proven otherwise, Bern is in good stead with this settlement, and shall remain so. If he is guilty of any harm brought against anyone, then we shall decide what's best done."

His anger subsided suddenly, leaving him cold and empty. Bern was a problem he had not counted on, and he realized that he was most angry at himself for his disappointment in Bern, in having hoped to find a companion such as he had once felt Bern to be, in the faraway days of his cubhood. After the cloak of Elder fell to him in An Ran Bar, upon the heartbreak of his father's disappearance, Borim had been delighted by the arrival of his brother, and felt that perhaps he would at least have a friend he could trust, who was from the other days, and who would lend him the support he needed to get through the frightening and trying days that he faced. Borim's anger at his own false hopes grew, for ever making the mistake of trying to imagine who someone should be.

"I'm sorry, Nob, if I've snapped at you. It's hard for me to realize Bern is gone, and that maybe he's been the one responsible for the slayings of some of the clan. And I don't know if I want to see him again, yet you say I'll see him soon enough, which might be even worse. If he is guilty of harming the settlement, then I am the one who shall have to decide if he is to be punished, and if so, what that punishment shall be. I am coward enough to hope that I shall never have to see him again, that I can think to myself that the snake took him, along with all the rest."

"Then he can be built into whatever you want to make him, Borim. That's how that goes, I know. I have done that on occasion, to more than a few animals."

"We've all done that," said Hollen softly. "I used to do that with Kahn, when he would be gone for a particularly long time; I'd assure myself that he might have mended his ways, and started a peaceful settlement somewhere, and would soon be back to make his peace with Dralin."

Earling nodded in agreement.

"It's not easy to live with something like that, but it happens. I know none of us here are very fond of Bern, but it would be no simple thing for me, if I were to have to decide his fate, if he were to come back to us at this moment."

"You may not be far off your timing, brother," said Nob, his features unreadable.

"You keep saying that, but what do you know, Nob, that makes you say it with such conviction?"

"Because of old tales, and the nature of things. The way things are, Borim. You begin to see how things are one time, and when you come across it again, you start to know how it's going to be."

"But what is it you've seen, or what is it makes you feel the way you do?"

Nob passed a paw across his muzzle, frowning.

"When I was a cub, I saw a great, strong bear that lived in my old settlement decide that he wanted to be Elder, although that wasn't all it took. There were things you had to have, and a long time of training. But this bear wanted to be Elder, and so he set out to destroy the good name of the old Elder, and to plot, and trick, and overthrow the others' trust in their leader. It took a long while before the truth came out, and only just in time, for the settlement was on the edge of splitting apart. Of course, the bear would have been chosen as Elder for the one group who had followed him. Much as your own father, Dralin, and Kahn and Bramweld split up the old settlement of An Ran Bar. Those things happen over and again, and you begin to know when and how they will happen."

"What you're saying is that Bern is going, or was, going to pull apart the settlement, because he wants to be Elder in my place?"

Hollen replied to the cub's question.

"You have answered your own doubts, Borim. Somewhere inside you know the truth, or you would not dread seeing Bern again."

"Yet I still feel that if we could only keep him with us for a bit longer, we could win him over. He's not all bad. I know there is a decent part to him beneath all that sly surface that he puts up."

"That's well spoken, Borim," said Nob. "There are always two sides to every issue, even to those nasty things that live beyond the borders. If you stop and wonder at it, even they have sows somewhere, who perhaps raised them, and wonder about them now and again."

"I don't want to think about that," snapped Tolly. "If their sows had been of a decent sort, they'd have thrown those filthy lumps in the river as soon as they'd laid eyes on them."

"A mother sees only the beauty of her offspring, Tolly, you know that. Otherwise half of us would have ended up in a river long ago."

Nob chuckled.

"There are some who think old Nob was too mean to have a mother."

"Mother or not, it still hasn't answered my question about Bern," pursued Borim.

He paced up and down, looking away toward the distant, invisible sea.

"I haven't answered your question because there is no answer, Borim. What I know, I'll gladly share, although it's no answer. I have word that Bern was seen alive by my scouts, and that he was not hurt by the beast. He was making off in a direction that will sooner or later take him across our line of march, or if we're already in the boats, then it will lead him along the river, for that's the easiest way to travel in these parts, and that's where the food and water are to be had, so I know anyone traveling will be doing so there.

"As to seeing him soon, how could it be otherwise? There are only so many ways to reach the Roaring, and you've talked of your plans, according to Hollen, and Bern knows of me, and Tolly has said I have boats, so it is only natural to assume that Bern is going to be looking for us sooner or later, if he's still alive, and I have no doubt of that."

Borim frowned.

"I feel that he's alive, too. That's the worst of it. I also feel that he won't be alone."

The young Elder met Nob's even gaze.

"There is much to my story that applies here, my good Borim. Dralin told me much of Kahn, and the long struggle over the possession of An Ran Bar and the Horn of Bruinthor. I don't think Bern knew of that until he was in An Ran Bar with you. Kahn wouldn't have told him about that, for he wanted it for himself. Yet he knew that Bern was a means to an end, just as the old books foretold."

"Kahn didn't know his lessons as well as he should have, though," clucked Hollen. "If he had known them as they were written, he would never have sent the cub Bern to An Ran Bar, for that was the signal that spelled out the end of him."

"And Dralin and Bramweld," added Frael. "They all were a

part of the same lesson, and one couldn't exist without the other. And when Bern showed up in An Ran Bar, there was Borim, the new Elder-to-be, and it all happened so fast that there was no time to think it over or plan ahead."

"Just as there is no time now, my friends," said Nob. "I think we should set out now to meet the boats. The day is too clear, and those things have excellent eyesight, no matter what you might think of their looks. We need to be a long way from here."

At Nob's insistence, the group of leaders assigned working orders to all the members of the settlement, and divided the animals into groups of eight and ten, with instructions to keep from bunching up, so as not to be so noticeable, should any of the beasts be scouting the area.

A small party of Nob's band returned to their leader, and Borim overheard the report that the boats had been launched and were at that moment awaiting them at a ford in the river, not more than a half day's march from where they stood.

"Is it all in order?" asked Nob.

"All as well as it could be," replied the scout. "We've seen two more of those snakes within the last few hours, and they seem to be in a foul mood. They've burned down a whole section of the wood over toward Granite Pass, and I'm sure they tore up your old line camp down near Elm Run."

Nob shook his head angrily.

"I wish they hadn't done that. It was a nice spot in summer. I had some fine times there."

The scout remained silent.

The grizzled giant smashed his paws together loudly.

"It's good that I wasn't there. I know I'd have done something foolish."

"Like getting yourself roasted over a few logs and some thatch, as like as not," scolded Hollen. "We have more need of you than to help protect some shelter or other."

"It wasn't the shelter I minded," replied Nob, his dark eyes aflame. "It was one of the few places I ever found where you could hear the trees sing. They all joined in, all night long, and it was a treat to hear all their voices, some dark, some light, and some all green or blue. My old sow showed me the place, a long, long time ago."

Nob's eyes blazed again, then he lowered himself from his fighting stance, his voice softening.

"I guess there will be other places now. I'll miss Elm Run, though."

Borim started to ask Nob about the trees that sang, and wondered what sort of woods it might be that would have trees of that nature, but something in the bear's pain stopped him, and he decided it would be best to ask him another time, if he ever got the chance.

Borim had many questions to ask Nob, about the boats, and the Sea of Roaring, and his father, and Bern, and now about a wood full of trees that actually sang. He couldn't imagine whether they hummed, or really sang, in a voice like his own, or if they simply murmured like the streams playing over rocks, or snow tickling the soft air on long winter days, or squeaking underpaw as you walked.

Those questions he would have to wait to ask Nob, for the great figure of the bear seemed to shrink from the loss of the singing trees, and Borim at that moment caught sight of another movement along the farther reaches of the river, and his heart raced as he saw the smooth white form of a sail balloon against the soft breeze of the morning and carry a small bright green boat out into the center of the rapid current of the water. Borim watched as a stout young bear held the boat hard over into the wind, and slowly, so slowly he could hardly detect any movement at all, the green craft made its way beyond the current, and then picked up speed as it neared the shore where Borim stood.

The nose of the boat was run aground on a patch of grass that ran down to a rough, natural landing, and Nob strode down to greet this new arrival.

"Greetings, Sand. What news?"

"Greetings, Nob. The boats are all waiting. We've got a fair tide now, and will have tonight. It would be well if you could get to us by then. Otherwise, we may be forced to wait."

Nob studied the flow of the river before he spoke.

"We'll be there in time, Sand. You can run back and tell them we'll sail tonight at first moon. Traveling in the dark may be some job of work to keep off the rocks, but I'll stake my hide that it'll be a far sight safer than trying it in the daylight, with those snakes out after a meal."

Sand bowed low, and carefully launching his boat again into the clear flow of the river, he steered around until the sail filled once more, and the green craft picked up speed, and with a final pull of his sail, the bear set his paw to the work of getting past a patch of rocks that protruded above the white froth of water on a fall of rapids that ran for a few hundred feet, then turned once more into a deep channel, covered with bright-colored waterbugs that darted and careened across the surface. Borim was astounded at the grace of the small green boat, and the agility of the young bear who handled it so surely.

"Was that a boat like we'll travel in?" he asked, turning to Nob, his wonderment unconcealed.

Laughing, the older bear shook his head.

"That's one of our skiffs, Borim. It would take a lot of trips in boats that size to get all your settlement, and all mine, down to the Roaring."

Borim had no idea what a skiff was, but knew it was a beautiful thing to watch, just as it was to see the waterbugs darting across the surface of the deep channel in the middle of the river.

"What are your other boats like?" asked Lan, as astounded as Borim with the sight of the swift craft.

Before Nob could answer, Tolly was giving a description that had the grizzled bear chuckling.

His long-winded tirade was brought to a sudden close by a growing shadow that had begun to appear over the woods away toward where Nob's scout had said they had spotted the two beasts, and before another sentence had gotten past Tolly's mouth, the entire settlement had moved into the smaller groups they had been broken into, and hurried away toward the cover of the wood that ran alongside the river. No warning was necessary to urge them to be quiet or to hurry, and Borim, loping along at the head of the group made up of Hollen, Nob, and Tolly, looked over his shoulder once, suddenly overcome with a desire to stop and call out to the dreadful beasts that now loomed larger in the sky, hanging against the fleecy white clouds like fat, black spiders, their leathery wings beating the air with such force that it sounded to Borim's ears like a distant thunderstorm on a summer's afternoon.

He had no more time to watch, for Nob called out to him from one side.

"Keep the Horn ready, Borim! We may have to fight to reach the boats."

His heart pounding, Borim managed a nod, the terror of the day before flooding through him again. The weight of the

197

Horn was reassuring, and seemed to give him the strength to keep on, although he felt the pull of the beasts, tugging at the back of his mind, urging him to stop and surrender.

Nob called out again, this time farther from him, and he realized that he had actually slowed his pace, and was falling behind the others.

A JOURNEY TO THE SEA

A Battle at Water's Edge

In an almost breathless silence, Borim watched as the two huge winged snakes lurched heavily through the air toward him. His paws seemed rooted to the ground, and time was like honey pouring through a clear stream, golden flowing through the crystal clearness, but without weight or meaning. Far away, he heard shouts and calls, some of the voices calling his name, others nothing more than cries of terror, or the harsh, guttural calls of many voices joined in battle.

His mind reeled under a heavy cloud of sleep, only dreamless, and utterly dark, and with just a slight shiver of some unknown cold to it. He fought at it, trying to swat it away as he would a pesky fly at his honey bowl, but the more he struggled to avoid the dark confines of the cloud, the more it reached out and held him fast. At every turn that he touched it, it caught and tugged at his thoughts, at once gentle and softly urging, yet dangerous, too, demanding his surrender at risk of losing his life.

The young Elder of An Ran Bar had never faced a danger such as the beasts presented, and it seemed that two of them were more deadly than one, and that their power was doubled. All the light from the sun began to dim and be devoured by these beasts, and somewhere in Borim's mind, a voice told him that it was growing dark, and that he was tired, and should give up and sleep, deeply and soundly. He touched that void the voices created, looking over into the depths of that black pit they called sleep, and he saw instead terror and death, and vast frozen fields of ice and snow, unbroken, from the corner of the sky, all the way across the dark lines of the heavens, starless and empty, held in place by a cold sliver of moon, pinned into that heart of the shadows like a glowing silver shard.

More calls and cries dragged him from the senseless state he was falling into, and dreaming, or dreaming he dreamed, he saw the two monstrous forms of the scaled snakes hovering above some members of his settlement; then there were none, and the beasts turned away toward the river, but all the while holding him helpless there with the murmurs of the dark voices, which first wooed and cajoled, then stormed and threatened. The Horn was icy cold in his paw now, and a great temptation overwhelmed him to lay it aside and escape. That might be the easiest way, the voices told him. Hand over the Horn, it would all be over. There would be no need to worry or fret any longer, and someone else would have to make all the painful decisions, and keep all things in order and as they should be.

Borim's paw tried to open, to put the heavy burden his father had left him down, but as he struggled to release it, the small object began to hum, then grow hot, then it burst into a raging sheet of white-hot flame that seared his forepaw and jolted him down to the bottoms of his pads. It was as if the earth had suddenly risen up and slammed against him, and he sat, breathless, on the soft grass, looking around him in amazement and terror.

The Horn still pulsed in his grasp, and he saw the two vile snake forms lashing to and fro over the top of a small grove that grew nearer to the banks of the river. Their slithering forms reflected an ugly light, like sunshine through muddy water, and their great heads dipped and rose savagely, great yellow teeth bared and clacking together, snapping and tearing any unfortunate who strayed too close.

Borim tried to get his dazed senses centered, to find Hollen and Nob, and Frael, and the beavers, but all that met his ears were cries from the wounded, and all he could see in any direction were fleeing animals, all order or purpose gone, and driven by nothing but blind fear.

The two beasts swung away farther downriver, and Borim got to his feet, the spell broken. The voices still rang through his head, but their power was gone, broken by the dazzling presence of the Horn of Bruinthor, and a deeper sense of himself, somewhere far down below all things that he knew, a fire so brilliant and hot that it became as one with the flashing white flame of the Horn and the golden white heat of the sun.

It was then that Borim discovered that one of the voices he had been hearing was one that was familiar to him, which might have accounted for the fact that he had been lulled into unawareness by its smooth flow. There was the deeper, more dreadful dead tone of the one, threatening instant death if it was not obeyed; but the other was more mellow, and sounded so easy to follow, and so gentle to the ear, and appealed to the senses to lie down and sleep, and to give up the awful weight of the Horn of Bruinthor.

Borim's hackles stood on end, and he reared into his fighting stance, just as Lan had taught him to do, not so very long ago, although it seemed a hundred seasons distant at that moment in time.

Nob's figure caught the cub's eye, far away, struggling beside the river, darting back and forth beneath the horrible ugliness of the heavy form of one of the lumbering beasts, which had landed and now coiled and slithered about, clumsy, misshapen legs churning, the terrible fury of the tail lashing out in deadly circles behind it.

There were others there with Nob, mostly of An Ran Bar, but Borim saw the little green boat that Nob had called a skiff suddenly fly into the air and break into a shower of useless wood, falling all about like leaves blown from a tree by the first breath of winter. The young bear who had guided the craft so skillfully through the water disappeared into the beast's gaping great jaws, and Borim, hardly knowing what he was doing, had the Horn of Bruinthor to his lips, and a flashing white sheet of jagged flames leapt up all around him, and he was thundering toward the two beasts, his war cry rolling from him with every step he took, and a fury of anger burning his heart into a mindless rage that was all-consuming.

There was no thought as to what he would do, or how he would ever hope to overcome two such fearsome enemies, and

201

the idea never occurred to him that he had nothing to match the dreadful claws, or tail, or great jaws. The Horn called again, and the anger burned brighter, and there was nothing more for it but to throw himself into the middle of the fray, close to his newly found friend Nob and his older allies, Frael, Hollen, Earling, and Lan, whom he saw now, raised high in a hopeless defense of his friends, ears back, dashing in on the huge beast before him, although he was doing no more damage than angering the thing more.

And then there were the tiny figures of the two beavers, scurrying around in the dust of the grotesque beasts' legs, biting and nipping at the misshapen claws and being kicked roughly away, at times dangerously close to being crushed by the sheer mass of the beasts.

The voices were clamoring inside him now, one promising him a terrible doom, slow and painful, and the other cajoling him into dropping the Horn and not bothering with getting himself embroiled in a battle that was not his own. Just as Borim flung himself toward the first great beast, who turned slowly to meet him, he realized that the familiar voice was that of Bern, that it was his own brother's voice that crooned to him to stop his resistance, and to drop the Horn, and to surrender to his friends, and all would be well.

The Horn called again, its note high and wild and deafening, and Borim's mind was flooded with a white light so fierce and blinding that he could not stand to look upon it, and in a flash, a mere beat of his raging heart, he was alone on the grass by the banks of the Eagle Claw, flailing and slashing at empty air, the horrible great forms of the beasts now vanished, as had the first one the day before. However, he did not fall stunned as he had done then, and there was an odd sensation tingling through him, of the raging battle fire, and the joining of battle, then the sensation of simply being on the grass, alone, with no sign of the foe which had been before him but a short moment before.

The stench of the beast's breath and foul hide still hung heavily about, but there was no sign of the vanished thing or its partner. The voices were gone, leaving his ears ringing, and he wondered if they had ever truly been there at all.

Nob, rushing across the distance that separated them, almost bowled Borim over with his stout hug.

"You are a miracle, little brother. You should have seen the sight of your attack, coming across the meadow, your head high, blowing the Horn like the wind of doom, and a bright light like sunshine flowing all around you, and going on before like some silver river at flood tide."

Nob slapped him roughly on the back and danced around him, the battle fire not yet gone, and his great claws and fangs bared and gleaming dangerously.

"Where are the others?" asked Borim, a sudden dread tugging at him, not wanting to know the answer, if it meant that those he cared about were carried away by the mysterious beasts, who vanished at the blowing of the Horn.

"Most escaped into the woods, I think," said Nob, calming somewhat and beginning to look about, starting to reorganize his thoughts.

And as he spoke, out of the woods all about them came the members of the settlements, in pairs, and singly, first slowly, looking about in dread, as if the beasts might be back at any moment, then more surely, until at last all the group was assembled once more in front of Nob and Borim.

Hollen was shaken and bruised, and badly battered by a vicious blow from one of the beasts' tails, but was in his usual spirits, and full of advice for Frael, Lan, and Earling, who had been thrown into the top of a tree by a single swipe of a great foreclaw.

"It was as close as I ever want to get to one of those things," mumbled Lan angrily. "They're too big, and have too much reach on you."

"I would say so, Lan," snarled Earling, who was limping on a painfully bruised hindleg. "And I'm glad you've finally realized that there are some problems in life that cannot be overpowered by brute force alone."

"If these dwarf creatures can forge those things Nob says they can, then we'll see about that. Hides that can't be pierced and claws that will let you strike down even a lout as big as those things will go a long way toward evening up the score."

"If such things exist," reminded Earling. "We don't know yet if there is any way to find these dwarfs, or whether they can do all these things they say they can do."

"They can do them, right enough," assured Nob. "I've been among them long enough to know there's not much in the way of that sort of work that a dwarf can't do. They understand the workings of stone, and earth, and fire and water. I've seen a thing or two that turned my head, I can tell you square, and a lot of the things they've shown me make me wonder what we're all coming to."

"I'm wondering what we're all coming to, myself," blurted Tolly, completely covered from head to foot with the chalky white river dust that was churned up by the frantic movements of the battle a few moments before. "I'm nothing but a simple river animal, and yet twice I've been mauled and almost squashed by a monster straight out of my worst nightmares. I never asked for any of this business, and I don't know why in the name of common sense I don't gather what's left of my wits and march straight back to Green Willow."

Nob gave the tiny animal a rough cuff.

"You are magnificent, friend beaver. I've never seen such a fearless attack. I wish half my band could have seen the way you two riverfolk went after that nasty fellow. They could do well to learn from you."

"*He* might have been going after him," corrected Boomer, "but I was simply trying to get out of the way."

"That thing kept falling down over you, and I guess that kept it from reaching me," said Hollen. "I thought I was a goner more than once, and would have been, if my tiny protectors hadn't distracted that thing right at the moment it was ready to snap my head off."

Hollen turned, suddenly serious.

"Do you have any ideas, Nob, about what it is in the Horn that causes these things to disappear after they hear it?"

Nob shook a grizzled head.

"I don't know, friend. I do know that I don't think it does any more than remove them from wherever we are. I don't think it slays them, exactly, or else they'd be leaving a carcass or two about for us to gawk over, or to try to figure what to do with. And I don't know why the Horn does that, and today it caused two of those ugly fellows to find other business somewhere."

Borim studied the silent Horn in his paw, hanging quietly by the slim leather strap.

"I don't know what it is, either, but I agree with you, Nob. I don't think it slays these things. It just changes them into a different place, it seems."

The cub paused, then addressed Hollen.

"You know, when the beast voices started, I couldn't figure out why I was allowing myself to listen, until I found out that one of the voices was Bern's."

Hollen nodded tiredly.

"I heard that, too, Borim. It seems as if a familiar voice always throws us off our guard. I don't know how his voice comes to be one of those we heard from the beasts, but I know that's what I heard."

"Did you hear it, Lan?" asked Borim.

"I heard nothing," said Lan, knitting his brows to try to remember if he had heard anything at all above the boiling of his blood as he readied for battle. "Or at least if I did, I don't remember it."

"Lan wouldn't hear a thunderclap if he were thinking of something else," snorted Earling.

"How about you, Earling?"

"I can't really say what it was, or even if it was voices," said the bear, trying to answer Borim carefully.

"There was something, though, wasn't there?"

"Oh, it was something, right enough," agreed Earling.

"It may be that it's one thing for one of us, and something else again for another," said Hollen, turning over something in his mind, trying to get hold of the idea to express it. "You say you heard Bern's voice, and so did I. Yet we have Lan's word that he heard nothing, and Earling says he doesn't know, or can't put his paw to whatever it was he heard, or thought he heard."

"I see what you're getting at," growled Nob. "We hear from the beasts whatever it is that we are the most afraid of. In Borim's case, he says he heard, or thinks he heard, Bern's voice. In my case, I heard nothing but the call to give up, to surrender, and the awful sound those wings make when they're flying toward you."

"It's unnatural!" piped in Tolly. "Those things flying like some fat lump of a bird just isn't right. It goes against everything of the Law."

"Whether it goes against the Law isn't much in the way of an answer as to what it made you think of, Tolly. Did you hear anything before they attacked?"

The beaver studied Borim thoughtfully, then shook his head.

"I think I heard someone say that if I would just give up, and surrender, I'd be able to be back at my dam building tomorrow, and away from the rest of this helter-skelter life we've been leading since we left An Ran Bar."

"You'll be going back there one day, you know," said Nob, without any preface or explanation.

Tolly tried to draw the grizzled gray giant out for more details on his strange pronouncement, but Nob wouldn't budge from his silence, except to shrug.

"We all must go back, just so we can be free of whatever it is we're running away from or wanting to go back to."

"Now that's a lot of squirrelwash, if I ever heard it," blustered Boomer. "If we've come all this way to try to get away from something back there, why in the name of anything sensible would we be turning around and going back?"

"Oh, not for now," ventured Nob. "But one day."

"Then maybe when that day comes, you'll change your mind, Nob, and go back to see Dralin's settlement."

"It'll be your settlement, Borim, not Dralin's. But I have given up the desire to return that far back. When I had the news about the little forest where the trees sang, I think I went through my last wish for a place. I must find something a bit different now than merely a spot in the wood, or by the river, or the sea. I shall have to look to my own wood inside for that shelter, beyond anything a lout with a snake's tail can destroy."

"How do you know we'll be going back?" persisted Tolly. "If we have to keep dealing with the likes of those nasty fellows, we may all end up roasted to a fine turn, or disappeared like some of our lot."

"They've been disappeared is right," said Nob. "No more. They shall find their way back someday, I'm sure."

"You're full of strange ideas, friend," said Earling. "I half believe you, but I don't know why."

Nob laughed a short bark of savage amusement.

"You'll find out somewhere along the way that Nob says and believes many strange things that a lot of folk have been unable to abide, and so left my settlements wherever they were at the time, to seek out other easier, softer ways. But they have almost always come back, sometimes soon, sometimes late, but they always return."

"Is it these wild borders that cause your ideas to turn to such strange twists?" asked Earling. "And will we all be thinking like you if we stay? It seems something has already changed, for here we are talking about hearing voices in our heads that come from these hideous beasts that have beset us, and hear all sorts of wild tales about dwarf creatures, and boats, and the Sea of Roaring. I used to think I was a fairly rational animal, as animals go, but I'm beginning to doubt myself now."

"No need for that, good Earling. You've come from a long wait at An Ran Bar, where there was nothing more taxing than to worry about an occasional raider across the Gray Rock."

"That was enough worry," grumbled Earling. "And I would have thought so yet, until I came upon these nasty lumps that Borim has a way of discharging with the Horn Dralin handed down to him."

"That is but the beginning, my friend. Soon there won't be so simple an answer. I feel these things growing stronger, and taking strength from the fear of their victims. I have no clue as to who is really behind all this, but there is a guiding paw there somewhere. The attacks are never random, and seem to come at certain times, as if they were planned in advance by a general of forces plotting his strategy."

Nob looked away toward the unseen sea.

"There will be some answers for us, beyond the Roaring. I think now that perhaps the safest way for us to travel is by night, in my boats, and to get on with our tasks."

"Did your friend in the green boat escape harm?" asked Borim.

His heart was leaden with fear, and heavy with the sorrow at the memory of seeing the bright green skiff destroyed and scattered across the wood.

"Sand is a handy bear with his paws, Borim. He may remember this meeting for a long while yet, but I think he'll have another skiff built before the fine weather is gone."

A burden seemed to lift from Borim, yet there was a deeper one that ran nearer the bone, and no answer from his friends could allay the fear or ease the pain. There was but one way for him to rid himself of that shadow that lingered on in his heart, and that was to find his brother Bern and somehow to win him over to the Law, and all the joy and happiness that that way of living offered. He was sure it had been Bern's voice that he'd heard through the dark spell of the beasts, and that his brother's disappearance was tied in with this new threat, and that the trip to the sea was going to be a perilous undertaking, no matter if they walked or used the wonderful boats of Nob.

Something that Nob had said came back more strongly, and that was the statement of the fear being only that which was in the victim of the beast. They had the darkness of that fear to cloak themselves in, to lull the victims into surrender, and that mind-numbing terror was the most dreadful of all the weapons the huge flying beasts had.

And if Nob were right, as his father had suspected long

ago, that there was a power or force behind the beasts, then they would need all the strength and help they could get from the strange-sounding dwarf creatures, and every other animal alive on the face of the Lower Woods that drew breath and hoped to live a full and useful life.

He had carried the Horn only for such a short while since his father had disappeared, but already it weighed ever heavier upon him as the true meaning of his duty became plainer and the full impact of the loneliness of being Elder closed over him, and he understood the coolness his father had displayed, all that time ago when he had been but a green cub, fresh from the cave of his sow. It wasn't that he had felt too little toward Borim, but too much, and the only defense against that had been the wall of seeming indifference.

Mystery by Torchlight

Of all the things Borim had been told of the river, and the boats of Nob, and the lands that lay between the Gray Rock and the Sea of Roaring, none could match the actual sights and sounds he saw and heard, or even the faintest glimpse of uneasy stomach the first sail he took with the grizzled bear, who chided him unmercifully, and told any and all who would listen that the Elder of Bruinthor didn't have much in the way of sea legs, even if he was the bearer of the Horn.

In the first days after the last attack by the huge beasts, the settlements of An Ran Bar organized into smaller bands and chose leaders for each group, so they would not be caught unaware again.

Frael, Earling, and Lan all were elected to head up groups of animals, and assigned certain duties to be carried out in times of danger. Nob, who seemed the most experienced of all in the ways of the life of a border warrior, began to instruct the others in the tricks he had learned in his long career.

Hollen, who was too old to be given a group, stayed with Borim, as did Tolly and Boomer, after they had split up their followers into the settlements of the bears, which were now swelled by the ranks of Nob's followers. These bears never failed to fascinate Borim, for they all were of much the same stature as Nob, and all were of the same grizzled color, and spoke roughly of battles and dealings they had had along the river and down toward the sea. And they knew about boats, and could guide those marvelous things swiftly and silently across the broad silver face of the river, or turn them into the wind and let them hang motionless, white sails flapping with every breath of the wind, as they would roll onto their sides, and away they would go again, dipping and bucking against the current, forever on their way to the broad shoulder of the distant Roaring.

Bern was seldom mentioned, although all the parties of the travelers were warned to be on the lookout for any stragglers from other settlements, and especially Borim's brother, who had disappeared after the first encounter with the terrible flying snakes.

Hollen often told Borim stories from the lore books of the ancient Elders, and hinted in guarded ways that Bern was not gone, and would be back. Borim reminded the old bear that Nob had said the same things, and that he had even said that Bern would be back on the next day after the first beast attack, yet that had not been, as Borim was quick to point out.

"You did not see him," corrected Hollen. "There are two different versions of what Nob said. He did not tell you you would *see* Bern."

"I don't understand. He said Bern would be back. It's as simple as that."

"As simple as it is, there are other ways to understand it. When he said your brother was to come back, he did not say he was to come back to us."

"That makes no sense, Hollen. Where else would he go?"

"To the beasts," replied Nob, his deep voice frightening Borim, for he had not heard him approach.

"We did not see Bern that next day, but you heard him, Borim. It was Bern, right enough. And he's never far from us now, although I wouldn't want that to be common knowledge among the camp, because they've got enough to worry about without living in dread of another run-in with those snakes that fly. Dragons, some call them. I've heard them called everything from the Purge to flying snakes, but some call them dragons. I don't think the real dragons are evil, and I'm not sure where these things came from, but I do know in the ancient lore the true dragons are the guardians of the High King's realms, and have never been down in these lower regions."

"They look similar," agreed Hollen. "I've seen the pictures in the old lore masters' books of those noble beings who guard the realms between the upper and lower worlds. Only those deserving, and who can withstand the stare of the dragon, are allowed through. It's said that any thought that is not pure will send you down again to the Lower Wood for more lessons."

"You don't think those things that attacked us are any of that lot, do you?" asked Boomer, joining in the conversation.

"No, I don't," said Nob. "What I do think is that something's afoot here, and that somehow the power of those beasts has been brought to life in a lower form. They have the ability to cloud your mind, to make you surrender, to call out to them. That they do have. And they seem to be able to reach out to almost anyone, so that whoever hears the voices will surrender."

"And you think Bern was speaking through one of the beasts?" shot Borim, his brow knitted in a worried frown.

"I think what has happened is an odd thing, Borim, and not an easy one to explain. I think Bern has found out whoever it is that is behind these beasts, and that he has gone over to him."

"Do you think as Dralin did, that there is a power in back of all the strange goings-on in the Northerlands? And that it's behind these new beasts, too?" asked Hollen.

"All points to that, my friend. I have seen some strange sights these last few turnings. I've been from one end of this river to the other, and there are some things that would turn your muzzle a few shades grayer if you weren't strong enough to stand it."

"What sort of sights?" chattered Boomer, his eyes wide.

Nob turned to the small animal, smiling.

"Things bad enough to freeze you in your tracks," laughed the bear, then turned away, the smile fading. "It was this last winter we began to find traces of the new beasts, these low dragons, who copy the real ones from the Upper Wood. A party of us had been upriver on an outing, and were camped at the beginning of the ice floes, where we couldn't get the boats any farther. We'd had a late lunch, and were getting ready to shove off, when a huge shadow fell across the sun, and we all thought it must be a storm gathering, but when we looked, the sky was clear enough, except for just in front of the sun, where there was a great form, flapping away, flying toward the mountains beyond the Ribbon Hills. We couldn't make out what it was at first, and it was too far away to see plainly, but we got a long look close enough the next day, when the thing flew back, and it had a mate. They were these things that mimic in looks the dragon, but only succeed in the terror that those beasts have, without the understanding or wisdom."

"Are the dragons you speak of, these ones that guard the Upper Realms, are they friendly?" asked Borim.

Nob laughed.

"I wouldn't go so far as to call them friendly, although that's exactly what they are, if you're supposed to be there. I guess if you aren't, then they must be a bit terrifying."

"But how can these beasts that have attacked us have anything to do with these dragons you're talking about, who must be a lot different than these things?"

"We only know this, Borim. There must be some other being from the Upper Wood who is away from there for some reason, and he has brought down the power of the beasts somehow. I guess someone will find out, but it will be left up to lore masters to figure out. What we do know is that the things we are dealing with are controlled by someone, or something, and that Bern has run into it."

Borim shook his head.

"Then I've failed Dralin, and all the rest. If I lose Bern, I won't be able to re-create An Ran Bar, or go back, or any of the other things Hollen has told me of, or that the lore books say."

"Don't fret, Borim. You're to see Bern again, and I don't mean in any way other than your laying eyes on him, and to see him just as you know him. That won't be a particularly happy occasion, but yet you will be able to see him."

"These things all confuse me, Nob. Sometimes I wish I were just a simple bear like all the rest of our settlement, who could lie back and watch someone else do all the thinking and planning, and just follow orders that someone else has given."

"That's a place we've all been, my young hotpaw, yet now we're all on this end awhile, doing the thinking, and giving the orders."

"Dralin was good at this sort of thing," went on Borim. "He'd done it enough that he knew what to expect, and it was a lot easier for him. I wish he'd stayed, and that I was with him now, and he were running this. He'd know what to do."

A strange light flickered through Nob's eyes, and Borim thought he saw Hollen wink. Or was it merely a trick of the dim light of the late afternoon shadows?

"Well, I can't say that he wouldn't," said Nob. "And I don't know that he'd be doing it any differently than you are. There are some good heads among us, Hollen here being one, and I even count myself as one of the more level thinkers in this part of the wood."

"I meant no offense," blurted Borim.

"I know you didn't," teased Nob. "But you underrate your abilities, and those of us with you. Why, Tolly and Boomer are some of the most clever animals in any part of the forest, and I must even admit that Tolly, with a bit of practice, might go on to become a fair to middling boat handler."

"He might, if you ever gave him the chance," complained Tolly, now entering the group, and going to stand beside Boomer. "I'd gladly learn to poke about in one of those boats of yours if you'd ever give me permission. Those bears of yours are close-pawed when it comes to letting me take a turn at sailing."

Nob bowed low.

"My apologies, Master Tolly. We've been in a great hurry, and I regret we've had no time to enjoy the things we'd normally be able to enjoy if we were just on a pleasure cruise. I assure you, whenever we get the chance, I'll personally give you a refresher course at the helm of my own boat."

"I'll hold you to that," said Tolly, pleased with the attention the huge bear was giving him.

"I wouldn't mind a lesson or two myself," shot Boomer. "I'll need to know something in the way of self-defense."

"Tolly is a good helm tender," laughed Nob. "Except that he has a great desire to find the bottom with his boat. He's a good seeker, I fear."

Tolly fumed, but said nothing.

As they spoke, Nob's boat tugged gently at her mooring lines, in the eddy of the river. The other boats lined the small island's cove, which was straddled on both sides by rapid currents which whirled and chuckled in the growing darkness.

Nob had halted the convoy here because of the safety of the island, inaccessible by anything but boat, and because the company was all exhausted, and needed a full night's rest ashore, where the animals from the other settlements could find their sleep in a fashion they were more accustomed to, instead of on the pitching decks of the swift, sleek boats of Nob's band. This was the first night in many that the grizzled bear had allowed them to sleep on dry ground, and in the days prior, he had insisted that they continue without a halt, in order to put as much distance between themselves and the beasts as they might be able to do, by sleeping in watches and continuing their journey without interruption.

"You can believe the beasts aren't sleeping," he'd said that first night, when there were many complaints about not being able to stop to rest.

Borim had agreed with the older bear, as had Hollen, Earling, and Frael, that the best thing to do would be to go on as rapidly as possible for the coast, and that once there, perhaps the animals could catch up on their sleep in peace, when the dangers were less pressing. After talking to Nob at greater length, Borim began to realize that in all likelihood, there would be no lessening of the dangers on the coast, or anywhere else, and that he said that so as not to overly disturb the already exhausted animals that wearily paced to and fro on the decks of the boats, or stared tiredly up at him from their hard beds, made where they could find a place large enough to lie down.

Borim's head spun from all the new information he took in on each encounter with Nob, from boat building and care to the strange lore of the dragons that guarded the entrances to the Upper Wood, and whose far distant cousins now terrorized them in the lower reaches of the river that ran down to the Sea of Roaring. He knew that across that sea, according to Hollen and Nob, there was the Sea of Silence, and the Islands, where you began maybe to understand about things like the dragons and the other questions that had been heavy on his mind since Dralin had gone, and that would be a good place, to his way of thinking, for he would very much like to have some answers to some of the bothersome thoughts that refused to be put out of mind or sight until some satisfactory replies were given. And those weren't coming from Hollen or Nob, who only answered him with still more questions, or not at all.

Bern had been in his thoughts a great deal after the horrible day he had disappeared, and try as he might, he could not put his brother into the enemies' camp, as Nob had suggested, for no matter how much they might disagree, Bern was still his brother, and half brother or not, they still had the same sow, and a background of cubhoods that had taken place in the same cave. Perhaps Nob told him these things to spare him the empty grief of having Bern disappeared, which was, in a way, the worst of all, for then the terrible uncertainty always gnawed away at your acceptance, and it was like a raw wound that would not heal. There was no finality to it, and it kept on and on, eating away his peace of mind.

Hollen and Frael had spoken to him about it, as had Lan, the good and stout friend who always took the position that it was better to have lost Bern the way it had occurred than to have to discover him a traitor, which Lan was firmly convinced of.

"He was Kahn's cub, and if that were so, that is the only thing he could be, Borim. I speak to you as a friend who loves you. He'll hurt you, in the end. I know his kind."

"You're talking like he's still here, Lan."

"He is still here, to hear you go on. I can't deny that there's the blood between you, and your sow bore you both, but I feel down inside that he's trouble, Borim, like we've never imagined."

"How can you say that? You never were around him that much."

"I was around him enough to know that there is something in him that is going to see the death of a lot of us."

"Nothing will be the death of you, Lan, except maybe too much talk when you're too old to get away from someone you've offended."

"And I mean no offense to you, Borim. I have no brother, but I understand how it is you feel. I saw Dralin go through it all with Bramweld and Kahn. It was a terrible thing, and he'd often sit in front of the fire on long winter evenings and tell me of things they had done as cubs, before they had gone their separate ways."

"That's how it is with Bern," said the young Elder. "I remember things that happened, and things he took the time to teach me. I know things have changed, but I can't forget those times, either."

"Dralin couldn't forget those times, and it almost cost him his life, Borim. He went to meet Kahn, across the Gray Rock, in hopes that they'd be able to call a truce and draw the settlements back together again."

"I heard that spoken of, Lan. What happened?"

"Nothing much. Kahn had sent word to Dralin that he wanted to meet him, to talk. Dralin agreed, for he always wanted An Ran Bar to be whole again. He wanted Bramweld back in the fold, too, but he figured if Kahn came around, maybe Bramweld would come, too. Kahn was the worst, and if that was settled, then maybe all the differences could be settled."

"Don't forget to mention that Dralin was as hardheaded about his brothers as Borim is about Bern," added Earling.

"Oh, there was no question about that," said Lan. "I keep on working on Borim, hoping to change his thinking, but I remember his father, and know that's hopeless."

"There's nothing wrong with hoping for the best," said Borim. "I don't know for certain Bern is even still alive, but I do know that if he is, I'd like to try to bring him back to our camp. I can't stand the thought of just letting him go."

"Exactly what Dralin always said of Kahn. He never did accept the fact that maybe Kahn was happy where he was, doing what he was doing."

"And it all ended so oddly," went on Borim. "I mean not only did Kahn not get to get back to An Ran Bar, but Dralin had to leave. And Bramweld left Black Grove! It was like being called away in the middle of a game, and you never know how it ended."

Nob, who had been leaning against the rail watching the water slip by in the starlight, turned and spoke.

"You may always count on the deepest mysteries as being the simplest, Borim. That puzzle is as simple as the nose on your muzzle, and you'll find the answers everywhere you turn."

"How do you mean?" asked the cub.

"The problem seems so deep to you, as to its end, you say. Of Dralin, and Kahn, and Bramweld? Yet you never see the true picture! You see no answer because it is not finished. It's that simple!"

"But they're gone!" blurted Borim, the frustration growing inside him.

"They're gone from our vision, but not our knowledge," corrected Nob. "We don't know a lot of things, but there might be some among us who might tell us more than they have."

Nob paused, and his gaze singled out the beaver Boomer.

"When the time comes, I'm sure we'll get more in the way of explanations from those who have explanations to give."

Boomer blushed a shade darker, and looked away uneasily. No amount of questioning had loosened him up, although Borim had spent more than a few long night watches trying to pry some further information from the wily beaver.

"It'll do you no good to try to nose about with me, Borim,"

said the small animal. "I have taken my oath that I'd never breathe a word of anything to anyone, and on top of that, I don't know anything to breathe."

"You could start by explaining how you got out of Dralin's room without coming past us."

"Your father just had no desire to see Bern, that's all. He said there would be other times, and he wished to leave An Ran Bar with only good memories."

Borim had leapt on that opening, but could lure Boomer out no further.

"I'll tell you everything one day, Borim, when it is right. But for now, you must believe that there's a reason for my silence. I can't tell you everything yet, but I promise you shall have a full account, someday."

"All I ever get are promises," moaned Borim. "For all the information I get, I might just as well be deaf."

"You'll find your answers," replied Boomer.

And the beaver had avoided Borim whenever possible on the boat voyage, and as often as not, he would feign sleep, in order to deter any further bouts of questioning.

The animals had barely settled in for the evening on the night they harbored in the river island cove when a strange noise began to be heard over the rambling chuckle of the water through the darkness. It kept Borim from singling out Boomer again, and it had all ears searching for it to repeat itself, and all eyes peering into the gloom beyond the silver ribbon of river.

Nob had ordered all the boats ready to slip their moorings, should the need arise, and the leaders of the small groups had called their bands together, and stood by, waiting for whatever was to happen next.

After a long while, the noises became somewhat louder, and flickering lights were seen in the dense wood.

Borim thought at first it was the noise of the wind, for it reminded him of that gentle sort of snoring breeze that comes through a wood late in the evening, but then there were other sounds that made him think of rain, followed by a distant peal of thunder. Every animal's hackles stood on end, and Borim's paw tightly clutched the Horn, after having loosened the leather strap and removed the Horn from its safekeeping around his huge neck.

Nob paced silently out of the darkness to stand beside him, and after watching the strange lights flicker on and off in four or five different places along the riverbank, he suddenly raised himself upright and blew a short series of low calls on the small instrument of his own, and to Borim's astonishment, the entire river lit up as if it were broad daylight, and the banks were lined with what looked to be hundreds of stocky figures, all gaudily dressed in reds and yellows and greens, and each holding a blazing torch. The river's blackness was full of wild color now, and Nob had lowered away one of the small rowing boats stowed on deck, and was gone without saying a word.

Ellin

Borin started ashore, but had gone only a small way when Nob's great voice boomed out of the gloom above the other sounds, warning him away.

"Go back, little Elder. This is no concern of yours!"

Bewildered, he had the young bear at the oars row him yet closer, thinking he hadn't heard Nob right over the strange noise that grew yet louder.

"Beware, Borim! Go back to the boat! This is no place for you!"

Confused, yet gnawed by a burning curiosity, Borim reluctantly allowed himself to be rowed back to where Hollen and Frael stood awaiting him, flanked by the two beavers and Lan.

The bear who handled the boat laughed uneasily.

"I have not heard the Nob so angry in a long while," he said. "He only uses *that* voice in battle."

"Is it the dwarf creatures he's seeing?" asked Lan, hardly able to believe his eyes.

"Yes," replied the boat bear. "It's Ellin, or I've lost my eye."

"Ellin! But he is a friend of Dralin's," complained Borim. "I should make a friend of him."

"Not when Nob tells you to stay away. There is more going on ashore than a friendly outing, I'd wager. I've never seen that crowd of Ellin's worked up like this." He wagged his head slowly back and forth. "It's not like them at all."

"I thought Ellin had not been sighted for a while," said Frael. "Isn't this unusual? For a dwarf who has been keeping out of the way, this is pretty well a loud hello to anybody that might be abroad in these woods tonight. It's like plain daylight."

Hollen watched the proceedings across the river warily.

"They seem angry enough," he said. "And I'm like you, Frael; if they were in hiding, it's no secret about where they are now. All the beasts within a day's march will be heading this way on the run."

"What would make them this upset?" asked Borim, his brow furrowed. "They act as if they're at all-out battle."

"Maybe that's it," nodded Lan. "Maybe we've landed in the middle of a fight."

He began to take up his battle stance.

"If it's a fight, there's no one else here but us that I can see," broke in Borim.

"But look, here comes Nob back now. We'll see what's happening that has these creatures so upset."

Nob, rowing in long, measured strokes, reached the friends quickly, and leapt out of the boat to address Borim.

"They've lost a dozen of their band, and there are those among them that think it's some of our settlement gone bad. It's always a bear's lot to be blamed for anything that goes wrong in the woods."

"Why would they think it's one of us? There are plenty enough beasts to go around now. Haven't they seen these new snakes?"

"They've seen all of them," snorted Nob. "These dwarfs have been around a good long while, and I guess they know these borders as well as myself. Myabe better. I don't know how old Ellin is, but he was a name that was mentioned in tales when I was still a cub at my sow's side."

"You? Old, Nob? We didn't know you claimed a normal birth," teased Hollen, although halfheartedly.

The news from across the Eagle Claw was grim, and they had need of the friendship of these strange creatures if they were to be able to find a way to drive off, or slay, the new beasts that now began to roam freely over all the woods unchecked.

"My sow, I'm sure, would never claim me now," said Nob, smiling grimly. "But our friends there have taken it to themselves it was a bear's doings, because those are the tracks they found near where the disappearance took place, and there's no way to hide our passing, unless we use the old ways, and nobody who knows them is going to be going out trying to take a dwarf for a snack."

"Where are these tracks they found?" asked Borim, suddenly sure in his heart that he'd just heard some news, however discouraging, about Bern.

"Downstream a bit farther. They thought to ambush us all. I'm glad I was along, or there would be many of us here tonight that wouldn't be around for dawn."

Borim's brow shot up.

"You mean they were going to harm us?"

His hackles crawled, and he began to have second thoughts about these dwarf beings, and as anything misunderstood, or unknown, he began to fear them, then to get angry.

"They had best watch who they try to overwhelm!" snorted Lan. "They are awfully small to be so full of wild threats."

"They make no threats," said Nob calmly. "I told you of Alon Rab, and the pits, and they have things that can make their small size of no consequence."

"What would they be?" asked Lan, still smugly, but with second thoughts as he eyed the small figures, their shadows dancing strangely in the flickering lights of the torches.

"They have things that can slay you without ever getting near you themselves," said Nob grimly. "They have found their secrets at the bottoms of the mountains, and beneath the stones of the earth. It's said they know the underearth better than any folk, and I've seen some of their wares. It is just such things as we need to battle the snakes."

Borim's eyes were wide.

"How did they learn these things, Nob? And how is it they come to live below the sunlight?"

"Hollen could read you the lore, but it might take more time than we have now. They come to dwell below the earth for reasons that reach far back into time, when everything was new, Borim. I guess there were things made to live above and below, and in the air and water. Whatever, the dwarf clans have always done such, and prospered, at least until recently. In the last few turnings, they seem to have run onto ill times, as have we all, in one way or other. With them, it was the beasts who began to bore into their dwellings underground, and with us, they began to raid our woods and settlements. Now they've taken to the air, and I don't doubt that there may be some form of them under the Sea of Roaring, or I'll miss my mark by a long shot."

"Are they angry at your band, Nob? They seemed to be at ease enough with you."

"That's why I warned you back, Borim. There were some

there ready to slay anything, and they are a suspicious lot, and have never laid eyes on you."

"But if it's Ellin, he knows my father!"

"That's what I told him. That's the kind of thing they understand best. They're a stuffy lot, sometimes, and won't have anything to do with the new ways, or new folks. I told Ellin there was one in our camp that was the cub of an old friend. They liked Dralin immensely, and I take it your father spent quite a good deal of time traveling with them. They also seemed to know about providing a certain clan of beardom with these new weapons they have been forging belowground. Ellin said there was something big at work, and the reason he disappeared was to move their settlement and digs beyond harm's way. Yet it seems something happened as they crossed these woods on their way home yesterday. Something has found them out, so they will be moving again."

Nob paused, looking over his shoulder at the grim figures of the dwarfs outlined by the torches along the riverbank.

"They are willing to talk to you, Borim. Only you and me, though. We'll see where we get to from there."

The older bear turned an even gaze on him.

"Will you go?"

"No!" cried Lan, jumping up to grab Borim's paw. "They're trying to trick you, Borim. I'll go in your place. They don't know me from you. If it's a ploy, they won't have you! And if it's for real, then I'll repeat whatever they say. Or Nob can."

"That's a noble gesture, but unnecessary, Lan," said Nob. "And they know you, Borim, by the descriptions your father left."

"How would they know me from another bear? From Lan, or Earling, or even Frael?"

"The Horn," answered the old bear quietly. "He told them his cub would be carrying the Horn."

Borim looked down at the thing that hung safely from around his massive neck.

"Do you think the bear tracks they found are from some of our band?" asked Borim, suddenly turning to face Nob.

"I think you have discovered your own answers about that. My band is sometimes given over to a little wildness or lighthearted fun, but they don't get their thrills by slaying others."

"I think maybe it has something to do with Bern," said Borim, almost in a whisper. "I don't know how, but I feel he's somehow involved in it, just as he was involved with those lost beasts."

Nob moved around until he could see the dwarf band across the river more clearly.

"Yes, my friend, Bern has had a paw in this, as you say, and with the other beasts, and will have a paw in much more before all is said and over. But there is no need to despair, Borim, for it will all work out right in the final stroke."

A great sadness weighed heavily down on Borim's heart as he listened to Nob, and a hopelessness began to gnaw at the bright hope that dwelled within him.

"What do the dwarfs want?" he asked, his voice lifeless.

"To speak to you about the things they had talked of to Dralin."

"Let's go then. I don't want to keep them waiting beyond good bear manners."

Lan moved to stop his friend, but Borim shook his head and waved him away.

"Thank you for your loyalty, Lan. You are a true bear, and I shall not forget it. But stay and take care of Hollen, and my friends Tolly and Boomer, and the rest."

The small animals moved out of the shadow of Lan's huge frame, and grasped Borim tightly.

"We could go, Borim! They would never think anyone of our lot would have ever done them harm."

Nob laughed at the stubbornness of the two beavers.

"You may come along. I'll value your company, Tolly, for maybe you and Boomer can learn to row this skiff while you're at it."

Tolly's ears shot up.

"Can we?" he squeaked, his excitement almost causing him to bound backward.

"Of course. You'll have enough ballast to hold you to your course, between Borim and me."

The young beaver took another long look at the two huge forms of his big friends.

"Would it just be all right if we went and left the rowing to you, Nob? I don't think we should start our lessons in the middle of the night, with a load like you two."

"Well put, little brother," laughed Nob. "Then come along as my guests, and convince that thick-necked crew across the river there that we mean business, and aren't to be played with loosely."

Tolly huffed himself up a bit.

"They should know better than to banter about with a beaver," he said, lowering his voice. "And they'll find out, if they aren't careful."

"Watch out, Nob, he'll be telling you next about our great uncle Thaddeus, who once attacked a full-grown muskrat who was trying to dig up a few turnips out of his back garden."

"It was a big muskrat," insisted Tolly. "And quite nasty, on top of it. It was a wonder the beast didn't turn on him, instead of running away as he did."

"Get in the boat with you," roared Nob, waiting for Borim to settle himself, then crawling in behind.

The two small animals were seated beside Borim, one on each side, and turned anxious glances toward the far shore as Nob pushed the boat deftly into the current with his strong, even strokes on the long ash oars.

"Well, will you look at that," Tolly kept repeating.

"What?" asked Borim finally, trying to take his mind off his drumming heart, and the thoughts of Bern.

"They aren't much taller than us!" blurted Tolly, trying to stand on the gunwale of the boat, causing it to tip dangerously, and drawing a black oath from Nob.

"So they are," agreed Borim, turning carefully to study the dwarf clan more closely as they neared the far shore.

From across the river, the light and shadow had made the figures of the dwarfs loom larger than they actually were, and as the skiff slid in to a halt on the soft grass bank, a stocky form stepped down to hold the boat steady while Nob shipped his oars.

"Come ahead," said the voice, in the High Tongue, but in a voice very much different than any Borim had ever heard.

It was a deep and pleasant voice, just a range or two above what a bear sounded like, although it didn't have quite the broadness of sounds.

Boomer and Tolly scrambled out of the boat, and moved quickly to where another group of dwarfs stood farther up, their swarthy faces glowering in the fiery light of the torches. Their eyes were all an emerald green and as deep as the swift-flowing current of the river, and their noses and mouths were almost the same on every face, large and finely chiseled. Some had different-colored hair and beards, and all seemed to be dressed in shades of yellow, green, and red, with tall feathers in their forest caps that turned and moved as the dwarfs nodded and talked among themselves.

After Nob had secured the skiff, he called out to one of the figures in the crowd of dwarfs that watched their every move, waiting.

"Why have you brought the small ones, Nob? They have no business with us, and we none with them."

"They came because they are friends of Lord Borim, Ellin. They came because they are loyal and true, and because they have never met dwarfs."

"You are one of few words, Nob. I like that in you. But what of those others that travel with you? Can you vouch for all of them?"

"I can vouch for all those that are with me now. There is one that I can't speak for. It is a painful truth, and it is the Lord Borim's own half brother."

Borim, taken by the wild confusion of sights and colors and sounds, had to be prodded by Boomer.

"I see you have never been among our kind before, Borim," said Ellin, bowing low to the bear.

"No, sir, but my father told me of being with one named Ellin, when I first was new in An Ran Bar."

"I see you carry the same token of Elder. It is well. I would know that Horn anywhere, for Dralin showed it to me on more than one occasion, and bade me mark it well, for he said that one day another would come with it who would need the help of my clan's skills."

"They had never heard of any of the things you make, or forge, Ellin. Show them the nature of your work."

Nob had come to stand next to Borim.

The dwarf Ellin reached a hand over his back and pulled forth a strange object, curved and finely carved along its length. There was a cord strung between the two upturned ends, and to this string, Ellin put another stick, long and straight, and laced with feathers at one end. On the other point was an ominous-looking barb, glinting dangerously in the firelight. The dwarf drew back the cord, and as the two curved ends bent and gave, Borim watched in total amazement as Ellin released his hold on the feathered stick. A swift hiss of air sounded as the shaft sliced through the lighted darkness of the wood and buried itself in the trunk of a stout oak, a great distance away from Ellin.

Before Borim could comment on the astounding feat, Ellin had removed another shaft from behind him, and sent it crashing into the first, splitting it completely in two.

"He is the finest bowman in these parts," said Nob. "There

are many who have good reason to fear his sure eye and swift arrow."

Boomer and Tolly had crawled between Borim's great paws.

"These are the things I told you of, Borim, that the dwarf clans had found at the bottom of their delvings. They have another thing, too, which we shall have need of one day, and I suspect now that that day isn't as far off as I once might have imagined."

Nob turned to another one of the smaller stocky figures there, and held out a paw, which was filled by a strange object, thin, and shaped in a point like the arrow shaft, but with a handle, and two crosspieces right where Nob gripped it firmly in his huge paw.

"This is another thing that we shall have need of, Borim," shot the older bear, whirling on a fallen log and lopping off a row of dead limbs that snapped in brittle loud reports and flew spinning away into the shadows.

Nob struck again, and the blade hummed and sang, and a great chunk of dead wood flew up, landing at the dwarf's feet.

"These are forged in the deepest part of the dwarf digs, and are honed as sharp as our own claws, Borim, and have the strength of ten of our biggest bears. It can also cut through the thickest hide of one of those beasts that you disappeared with your Horn, and can chop down an elm in nothing more than a few whacks."

Ellin smiled an old, tired smile, which left his eyes unmoved.

"We have been having some dark times, Borim, as our friend here may have told you. Just today, we discovered that one of our wood patrols, twelve stout souls who know these parts as well as any, has disappeared, and where we found the last of their trail, we found the beginning of a trail of bear prints. They're there for all to see, and I've seen enough bear prints in my time to know what I'm looking at when I come across them. They were all over the area, and fresh."

"We think we know your rogue bear, Ellin, but we would ask that if you should find him, which I doubt, we may be allowed to deal out his punishment."

"I don't think it's only one bear," said Ellin. "There were twelve dwarfs together there, and they were all part of my oldest wood patrol that kept an eye on these borders. One of any sort of animal would hardly be a match for them."

"The kind of beast we think it may be could handle a dozen more patrols, Ellin," explained Nob. "These beasts we first saw some time back, but they have only just begun to move down this way, toward the Roaring. Borim drove them off with the Horn he carries, but they are more than a match for anyone, except those who are prepared for them, and know how to go about destroying them."

"Are these the flying snakes?" asked Ellin, although he knew the answer before Nob had time to reply.

"The same, my friend. Although you were right about finding bear tracks around the spot, for Bern, the half brother, has been taken with the power of these things, and may be gone over to them."

Hearing Nob say all these things straight out at once angered, then saddened Borim. It was one thing to admit it to himself, but another thing entirely to discuss it among total strangers, and especially strangers such as these gruff, half-sized figures of dwarfs, who looked like nothing so much as some dark-skinned animal, naked of fur except for the tops of their heads and where their muzzles would have been.

Ellin looked long at Borim, unspeaking.

"I can see you are a bear of your father's stature, Borim," he said at last. "He told me many things about An Ran Bar, and Kahn, and the long struggle that he waged to take it for his own. Now it seems as if you are to have your own Kahn, through Bern."

The dwarf shook his head, and stroked the great red beard.

"I say well met, Borim, for we all shall have our burdens to carry in this time that's coming. Nothing ever gets any easier, to my way of thinking, and this is one of the hardest tasks I've heard of since Dralin crossed water."

Boomer coughed uneasily, and tried to catch the dwarf's attention, although Ellin's mind was elsewhere. With a resounding smack, the small figure had driven the ball of his fist into the palm of his other hand, muttering darkly under his breath.

"It is no easy thing, this business," he said, regaining his composure and addressing Borim again. "And I see we shall need all the allies we can gather. It won't take much to set some of my band off and going about dealing with your clan, Borim, so we may as well get the worst of it over."

"What can I do that will convince them of our good will?" asked Borim.

"Just come along with me, and we'll mix with the lot of them, and show the Horn."

Borim looked to Nob for guidance, but saw none there. Nob

had removed himself from the talks, and was busy seeing to his boat.

Tolly and Boomer stood stiffly by his side, one close to either paw, holding tightly to him.

"Let's get this over with," said Borim thickly, unsure of his voice.

"Come along, then. We'll start with the worst of the bunch. They're the ones that gave out the rumor about bears, and got the others riled up. They'll be the ones who will give trouble, if trouble comes."

Borim marched along in the wake of Ellin, as the stocky dwarf cut a swath through the ranks of his followers until he reached a small group standing apart from the others, heavy scowls deepening the dark colors of their already brooding features. As Borim moved nearer, he was dimly aware of the weapon Ellin had used to put the feathered shaft so deeply into the oak, and the two beavers' paws fairly dug into his, but they stubbornly refused to leave his side.

"These are my friends, Borim, Boomer, and Tolly, from the animal clans of An Ran Bar. This is the cub of Dralin, who now carries the Horn of Bruinthor."

Ellin pointed to the stout dwarfish figures.

"Here are the brothers Juin, Marin, Clarin, and Dram, and then there is Leim, Ramkin, Aurel, and Glin."

The swarthy dwarfs made no move to welcome Borim or the beavers, and without being aware of what he was doing, he had unloosed the Horn from its place around his neck and laid it in the curve of his great paw, preparing to put it to his lips. As he rang out the first of the short, strident notes, he felt the tingle of air rushing by his ear, but did not clearly realize what it had been until a loud outcry from Ellin joined with the horn call, and the short figure of the dwarf had leapt quickly away, moving along with six or eight others toward the deeper shadows beyond the glittering flare of the torches.

Dwarf Craftywork

"Run!" cried Boomer, tugging wildly at his paw. "They've tried to shoot you with one of their shafts."

That had been the angry hiss of air he'd heard! It was one of the feathered arrows, with its cruel barbed tip, slipping by him so close he had felt the hot wind of its passage.

Tolly struggled along beside him, trying to keep from being trampled by the scurrying dwarfs as they rushed to and fro, calling harshly to each other and casting their torches, and the search, farther off into the outskirts of the wood.

Borim felt a paw placed firmly on his shoulder, and found Nob beside him.

"Easy, little brother. This may go either way, but I think if anything, it will turn the tide for us."

"How is getting Borim skewered going to help anything?" cried Boomer, his excitement making his voice tight and hard.

"They had thought it was a bear who had something to do with the slaying of their kin. Now they see that a bear's life has been threatened, and while he was a guest in their own camp. That's a thing a dwarf won't take lightly. You'll notice that even the sour apples Ellin had introduced you to last were some of the first to take up the fray."

"Most likely running for their lives," snorted Boomer.

"I don't think so, my little friend. Those fellows you were with there, they're a tough lot, and I've had stories of them often, and of their exploits."

Nob paused to let his words sink in.

"They are as close to heroes as you're likely to find, down in these parts."

"But Ellin himself called them troublemakers," argued Borim. "He said they were the ones that had started the story of it being bear's work that had done in their friends."

"They are heroes nevertheless. They have saved more than a few from the beasts, and given shelter to many poor souls that would have been lost without them."

"They don't seem very much the sort you'd expect to find kindness from," said Tolly. "I don't think I'd go looking to them for help."

"You would change your tune soon enough, if it were down to it. What a beaver might find helpful is not so much different than any other, and these dwarfs are used to a hard life, here on the Eagle Claw. It's not so far from the Shadow, and they've spent a long time without all the other things you might consider cheerful, or homey."

Nob frowned slightly, looking away when a greater outcry poured from a denser, more distant section of the wood. He listened for a moment longer, his thoughts far away.

"They've missed whoever, or whatever it was, by the sound of the chase."

227

In two's and three's, figures of the stocky dwarfs began returning to their camp.

"This is the most comfort any of them expect when they're aboveground," went on Nob. "I've seen the tunnels and shafts they've dug, when they have the time. It's beyond anything a simple bear could describe. But aboveground, they sleep in their cloaks, and eat when they can, and a fire is a rare treat."

"There's plenty of fire tonight," commented Tolly dryly.

"Yes, tonight there's been a big to-do, and they're angry. Just as angry as ourselves when something happens to any of our friends."

"Who do you think tried to hurt me, Nob?" asked Borim, shuddering a bit, remembering the shaft that had buried itself so easily into the stout oak.

The older bear faced Borim, looking at him evenly. The light was not good enough for the cub to read Nob's thoughts, but it seemed there was a great sadness in his eyes.

"I think maybe you know the answer to that, Borim. There are too many things that point to only one answer."

"I don't want it to be that," replied Borim truthfully.

"Nor would I," agreed Nob.

"Is it Bern?" asked Tolly, wanting it all spelled out.

Boomer elbowed his friend painfully. "It could be any number of beasts, or dwarfs, either," he insisted. "I wouldn't be so quick to jump to any conclusions."

"I agree, Boomer. But it is one thing to keep an open mind, and another to refuse to face the truth."

The beaver shook his head angrily.

"I don't like Bern any too well, and I won't say I do. But it seems to me we're all jumping the mark in thinking that anything like this has to be Bern."

"There were plenty of dwarfs that looked like they would have done us all in," agreed Tolly. "All you had to do was look at their faces."

A tiny shiver shook the beaver.

"That's true, Tolly, yet you'll find that these fellows are as quick to admit an error as any of us."

A new commotion had broken out in the woods, and Ellin's voice was heard above all the rest.

"Back! Back to the river! We'll go on with our search in the morning. We've nothing more to gain with all this thrashing around in the dark, except to maybe fire the wood, and I'm in no humor for that."

Amid confusion and loud calls on every side, the dwarfish clan began to regroup by the river, and their leader, his scowl even darker, came stalking across the clearing toward them.

"A foul-hearted thing to have happen to a guest," he grumbled. "My apologies, Borim. I'd lay down my life to protect you when you're a guest, even if you were the very worst of beasts."

Borim bowed low, the fear he'd felt having turned to anger, then dissipated by the small, sturdy dwarf's speech.

"That's an honor then, master dwarf. Well felt, and well spoken. I see the Law is followed here."

Ellin bowed low in turn.

"We have found no one to answer for this traitorous breach of manners, but we've found the trail."

Borim's heart fell, and he knew the answer before the dwarf spoke.

"There are fresh tracks that weren't there earlier. And starting right at the edge of the wood, too. Whoever our friend is, is no friend of yours, Borim. And the worst of all enemies, one of your own!"

"You found more prints of a bear?" asked Nob, although it was not so much a question as a statement.

Ellin nodded.

"And where he got the bow is answered by the trail we found earlier, where our brothers had vanished."

Nob grunted.

"Then whoever had a paw in the vanishing of the dwarf's would have had a paw in shooting at Borim. But it's lucky our assassin isn't the shot you are, Ellin."

"Can you see any other line of thought?"

The dwarf glowered, then sat down roughly in the soft grass, his gray cloak thrown back from his shoulders.

"I think I must rest on this," he declared, making a pillow for his head and shutting his eyes wearily. "I haven't slept for two days running, and it looks like there will be no rest tomorrow. I hope you'll join in with us, Nob, and you, Dralin's cub, to hunt down the assassin that's loose."

Nob coughed gently, then shook his head.

"I think we must go on, Ellin. We are due at the sea before we find our rest. You are equally welcome to join us."

The dwarf answered without opening his eyes.

"I don't think it is yet time, Nob. Not quite. There seem to be things yet undone before we meet once more and join our forces together."

"Perhaps, my friend. But I feel the time coming, and it's not too far away from us."

"Not by a long pull," agreed Ellin.

Suddenly shaking himself awake, he sat bolt upright on the damp grass bed.

"I've forgotten what was the most important thing of all," he chided himself, pinching his nose briskly.

Hopping up deftly, he strode to the band of dwarfs sitting at a small fire nearby.

"Where are the smiths, and the anvils? Bring them to me quickly."

As the dwarfs scurried away, Ellin turned to Borim.

"Come! We are going to make you safe against your friend who shoots bolts out of darkness. And you, friend Nob, who've long run these same borders with us. And for any of the rest who wish it, we can give you some safety against certain dangers."

The dwarf threw back his short jacket, and there below it was a fine coat of a fine, gauze-like metal, shimmering gently against his skin. It flexed and moved as the small creature did, and was light to the touch when Borim felt it with his huge paw.

"This was a secret that Co'in passed on to us before he left for the delvings," said Ellin. "They had found them handy things to have when they would run against the wild beasts up on those Northland borders, and they have proven to be even more handy still, here. Co'in discovered the secret long ago, and has given it to only a few."

"Will we have one?" asked Boomer.

"You shall all have them, if you wish," replied the dwarf sleepily. "The smiths will take your size, and form a fit for any who want one."

"Shall we bring the others over?" asked Nob. "Or shall your smiths come to us?"

Ellin thought carefully for a moment, tugging his beard.

"Come to us, in small numbers, a few at a time. We should be able to fit everyone before tomorrow's sunset. We'll leave the smiths at it when we go in pursuit of our errant archer."

"Will that be safe? The camp was up in arms not too long ago," said Nob.

"Safe enough for your bunch. Marin has informed me that Dralin's cub is not guilty of any trespass against our clan. And that goes for any who are with him."

The stocky dwarf smiled faintly behind the fiery red brush

of whiskers, and his eyes twinkled in a bright way that made Borim think of Dralin.

"Then we shall do as you say, Ellin. And our thanks for all you have done."

"You're welcome, Nob. I am to do yet more, someday, but we have other paths to take at the moment."

Ellin bowed to the friends, and leaving his final instructions with a group of heavy-lidded dwarfs, who stumbled sleepily as they came, he crept back to his own hard bed.

All night long, and all through the next morning and afternoon, the little creatures hammered, and shaped, and formed, working the fine, web-like metal deftly, sizing and fitting each animal, so that when each put on the protective coat, it was hardly felt at all, and it moved as freely as their own flesh.

Borim had been so amazed at the skill of the dwarfish smiths that he had to try their product in every sort of test, including having Nob shoot one of the feathered shafts at him. Nob had refused, saying he was not skilled enough at that art, but a dwarf archer had obliged him, and much to the terror of Nob, Tolly, and Boomer, had aimed and shot an arrow directly into the area of Borim's heart. They cried out, and were on the point of swift vengeance, even though they were outnumbered, when they saw that Borim was not only unharmed, but laughing, the deadly shaft broken in two before him.

"Ellin was right," he laughed, picking up the remnants of the arrow. "These are no danger if you're wearing one of these dwarf coats."

"At least, not if your archer is a dwarf," replied the dwarf who had fired the arrow.

There was the faintest undertone of hostility to the small creature's words, but Borim overlooked it, too happy with his new acquisition to have his pleasure spoiled.

Boomer, having one in a small version, turned to the cub.

"I don't think I want to try mine out like that," he chattered. "I believe it well enough, just by what I've seen."

"Almost all the others have their dwarf coats now," said Nob. "We'll be wise to think of going on where our journey was interrupted."

"Do you think Ellin meant what he said? About our meeting again?"

"I've known this hardheaded dwarf for a long time, Borim,

231

and I've discovered one thing about their kind. They don't ever say a word they don't mean."

Borim looked up from his study of the wonderful coat, with its webfine strands worked so cleverly into an exact fit of his own form.

"I hate to think of leaving Bern in a wood full of hunters like Ellin. I don't know what I'm feeling for him at this moment, but I don't think I'd like to leave him to the mercy of the dwarfs."

"There's no need to worry yourself on that count," reassured Nob. "As clever and quick as they are, they're not skilled enough to get close to these new beasts we've run into, and that, to my own way of thinking, is where Bern's gone. I don't know how it has happened, but I feel he's thrown in his lot with that bunch, or with whoever is behind it all, and no dwarf band is going to be able to get near them. That's plain, by the fact that a dozen of them were picked up and vanished yesterday, within sight of their camp."

"Does that mean they've been following us, then?"

Nob nodded slowly, choosing his words carefully.

"I think we've been followed ever since we left the last wood below the outskirts of my border. And I know that we've been spied upon since Bern has disappeared. There was no need to upset the others, or to worry anyone with a problem no one could do anything about, so I've gone on as if nothing were out of the usual."

"I've felt it, too," echoed Tolly. "Sometimes my hackles would crawl, and I'd get the wildest feeling, like I was in great danger, but I couldn't see anything, or hear anything. It was the oddest feeling."

"I know, I've had them, too," agreed Boomer. "I think the reason we didn't feel it yesterday was because we were already afraid of the dwarfs."

"And with good reason," said Nob. "They could have slain many of our settlement before we'd been able to get out of range of their arrows. Ellin said we would have those, too. But they're having to make them bigger for the likes of us, Borim. I don't think they'll need to adjust the size for the smaller animals, but for the bears, they'll have to use a bit more wood."

"He promised their archers would help us learn to shoot," said Boomer. "Which is mighty helpful, although it still seems odd, after the way they treated us at first."

"That's the way their kind behave. I've been dealing with

Ellin, and others, off and on for a long time, and I've yet to figure them out. I do know their basic goodness, though, and that if you ever befriend one, you're friends forever. It goes a bit of a way for you if your kin has known a few, too. They're very full of their kinfolks, and all those doings."

The companions were sitting at the remnants of a small fire, watching as the green boats came gracefully to and fro, bringing the others of the settlements to the dwarf smiths to be fitted for the coats that kept away arrows and the claws or teeth of beasts.

Ellin and a larger war band had gone at dawn, off in the direction where the torches had burned in the night. There had been no word since, and it was long past midday. The other dwarfs worked silently, watching ever now and again for signs of the return of their leader, but the wood was quiet, except for the soft noise their hammers made as they fashioned the hot metal into the flexible material for the protective coats. There were odd horn calls from some far-distant part of the wood that caused all the work to cease while all ears were turned to listen for further notes, but there had been none, and after long minutes of strained silence, the dwarfs had returned to their tasks, grumbling among themselves.

"Did you see Clarin this morning?" asked Nob. "He was very friendly toward you."

"I know. It was surprising, after the way they acted last night."

"That's not saying much. From all I've seen, about all a dwarf is able to do is grunt or scowl," said Borim, turning his mouth down to imitate one of the grim looks the dwarfs were forever wearing.

"Maybe you'd feel that way too, Borim, if you lived as they do, out of the sun for long periods at a time."

"Then why do they do it? Don't they ever like to have fun, or laugh?"

"I think they do, my friend. And I guess what pleases them is a mystery to our kind."

"It seems like they would move out of those holes they live in, if it made them so unhappy," added Boomer.

"If it were that easy, I'm sure they would, little friend. But could you just give up your river, and the ways you've known all your life, and go to live in the top of a tree?"

"Ugh!" spat the beaver. "We tried that. I'll leave the treetops to squirrels, thank you."

Nob laughed.

"You see? It's no easy thing to change the ways you've known all your life. These dwarfs have been going and coming across these parts for as long as the animals have, and they've always been fond of earth, and the delvings, as they call them. They know more about stone and earth and things of that nature than any other kind, or I'll miss my mark. They're very clever at making beautiful things, as you can see by their craftywork."

He indicated the muted gleam of the dwarf-wrought coat he now wore, so cleverly done and fashioned that it was hard to tell where it began and his own thick fur left off.

Borim looked down at his own.

"They know their work," he agreed. "It's almost the same color that I am."

A dwarf sitting beside the fire, within earshot of Borim, looked up from the metal he was shaping.

"We'd be able to do that, too, if we'd had more time, and not been in such a rush to do so many."

Borim laughed.

"I guess you would at that, friend. These are certainly more than just passing, though. I've never seen craftywork like this."

"Not likely to, either," snapped one of the other dwarfs, tapping a hot piece of metal with a small hammer, then holding up the piece to the sun, squinting carefully at it, checking for flaws.

"We are the armorers for Co'in and Eo'in," he went on. "They demand the very best."

"I agree with their judgment, then," said Borim, bowing low to the hearty dwarf.

Borim had begun to like and respect these independent creatures, so hard to befriend, and as distrusting as they were of strangers. There was a simple goodness to them, and a deep-seated sense of loyalty that Borim admired and respected.

The friends spent the remainder of the afternoon watching the progress of the work as the last of the settlements of the animals were fitted with the dwarf coats, and Nob spent some time showing Borim how to handle the sleek green skiff. Boomer and Tolly were delighted to see their friend so awkward with the craft, and laughed aloud when the cub missed his oar stroke and fell off balance into the bow, coming very near upending the boat. They would have all had a good swim, had not Nob caught his balance and held the boat in check with his weight. Later on, after more practice, Borim was able to move the craft back and forth with the beginning of ease, and the beavers marveled at how quickly Dralin's cub picked up the art of rowing, and the handling of boats in general.

Nob and Borim were just coming back ashore, with the sun dropping out of sight behind the distant mountains, when they spied the band of Ellin moving into the camp, their faces drawn, and their tread heavy. A gloom spread over the gathered dwarf clan, and soon enough blanketed the spirits of the animals as well. The news promised no glad tidings, and the two friends hurried to where Ellin wearily threw himself down by a fire, taking the offered mug of cold river water in greedy hands.

"We've found your traitor, Borim," he called to the cub as soon as he saw the young bear. "And we've found some other news that's not going to cheer anyone up much by hearing it."

He took a long drink before going on.

"What is it?" asked Nob. "Have you found another nest of those snakes somewhere out there?"

Ellin nodded gravely.

"And the bear tracks led straight there. That's how we found the nest, by following the bear trail."

Borim's heart beat wildly in his throat.

"We crossed the lower meadow, and doubled back over the river, and were working our way up the far side. The trail was new, and I figured we weren't far behind our friend. That's when we noticed he wasn't alone."

"What was it, Ellin? Could you tell?"

"No. But the pair of them went on into the lair, which has been dug out of the side of a hill. Those things dig well, whatever else can be said of them. They've got a whole network of caverns there, and I don't doubt that they've got them cleverly guarded as well. I'm something of an expert on anything to do with delvings, even a snake's den, and these things have a certain genius to their work, as evil as it is."

"Did you see the bear?" asked Borim, unable to contain himself any longer.

"Not once," grumbled Ellin. "But we left two sentries to watch the lair, and I don't doubt we'll have sight of him before too long."

Even as the dwarf spoke, there was a whizzing, rasping

noise that jarred Ellin to his feet, looking upward as he did so.

"It's the signal," he cried. "There!"

High over the forest top, there arched a thin trail of blue-white fire, glowing fiercely on the tip of an arrow.

"What is it?" cried Boomer.

"A signal device we came across in our delvings," said Ellin. "A simple matter, and quite harmless, really. The thing will be burned out by the time it hits the ground."

"Won't it give away the hideout of the sentries?" asked Tolly.

"No, because I told them to not signal until they were well away. Besides, they have their forest cloaks. They can be almost invisible if they have the need to hide."

"How is that?" asked Borim, constantly amazed at the clever work of these sturdy, morose creatures.

"The weaving of the cloaks is done by our womenfolk. You'd have to ask them."

"I will," promised Borim, "if I ever have the chance."

Before the dwarf could answer Borim, the sentries, winded and wide-eyed, broke into the midst of the gathered dwarf clan.

"They're coming this way, Ellin! Two of them, and the bear is with them!"

"Quickly! Positions! Get your settlements ready for a fight, Borim. We don't have much time."

The friends were in midstream, Nob at the oars, when the first of the beasts lumbered into sight, hugging the treetops, great leathery wings drooping almost to the ground, its foul breath filling the air with the promise of ruin and destruction. At the same time, Borim heard the voices begin, chiding him, urging him to surrender up the Horn of Bruinthor, and to lie down into a restful sleep, which would be long and peaceful.

Borim clutched the Horn tighter, and a paw crept up to touch the marvelous coat the dwarfs had given him. Feeling the strength of both of them, he found the will to resist the urgent, forceful voice, and as he looked over his shoulder, he saw a shower of dark shafts flying up toward the ugly outline of the beast, hovering against the darkening blue sky.

Echoes of Another Journey

After the first volley of arrows from the dwarfish archers, the beast seemed to hesitate, hanging almost in place over the companions, its great leathery wings beating a slow, drumming motion that stirred the air into hot hammers against the ear.

Borim had reached the far side of the Eagle Claw with Nob, and found that a great many others of the settlements had already arrived. Nob immediately began to set up his defenses, and his horn gave out short bursts, low and urgent, and was answered by a dozen or more calls that came from the thickets all along the banks of the river, and from both sides of the swift-flowing current.

"I've found they don't care much for the water," whispered Nob, in a harsh voice. "The one thing, as far as I've found, that they don't have a yen for."

The young Elder's eyes were wide, his paw clutching tightly the Horn his father had handed down to him.

"Save your call for last, Borim," went on Nob. "I have a feeling something here is fishy. They said there was a bear with them, so it may be something more than just an attack on the settlements."

"It may be Bern," said Borim, angry and saddened at once. "I wish I could talk to him."

"You may get your chance," shot Hollen, now beside his young student. "Look! The beasts are leaving!"

Nob frowned.

"So they are. But why?"

"You said they don't like water. Maybe they don't want to be near the river anymore."

Frael was the one to find the answer first.

"Look! There on the far side! Isn't that Bern?"

They all strained to see the tiny figure across the river.

"It is," agreed Lan. "I'd know his shape anywhere."

"He's motioning to us," added Tolly. "Or to someone."

"There are a lot of our camp still over there. See?"

Earling pointed out a gathering of bears that had now begun to come out of their cover of the trees, and to assemble themselves in front of Bern. There were a number of dwarfs in that crowd, too, who stood in silence behind the other animals.

It was some time before the gathering was quiet enough for Bern to speak, and when he did, his voice carried across the river in a new wave of strength, with no hint of the old bear at all.

"Listen well, brothers!" he snapped. "Heed me well! I have driven off the beasts, and I shall lead us all back to safety in An Ran Bar. We were fools to have left, and it is death for all those who march to the Sea of Roaring. Borim will be the death of you all, with his phony Horn."

Silent at first, one after another of the animals began to agree, nodding their approval.

Although the huge beasts were no longer in sight, Borim could still feel the tug of their power; and the voices were still active, soothing him into a mild stupor, into sleep, and rest.

Nob, shaking a grizzled head, was the first to move into action.

"It's a showdown for you, Borim. This half brother has thrown in with the beasts, and it looks like he may have quite a following."

"Those things aren't far off," shot Boomer. "I can feel them."

"So can the others," agreed Hollen. "Only it looks as if some of them have fallen under the spell."

"So has Bern," said Borim, his heart full of confused feelings.

There was anger there, but a sad forgiveness, too, for the small bear across the river, at last finding his own voice, and venting all the pent-up rage at having been second to Borim, who held the Horn, and was the heir of Dralin.

"We shall have to fight him, Borim," said Nob softly, looking down at the younger bear. "It may be that we shall even have to slay him."

"Never!" insisted Borim. "I may fight him, but it is not my paw that shall destroy him."

"I have no such ideas, Borim," said Lan. "If it comes to it, I shall do the deed gladly."

"I want no one to touch him. It shall not be that way. Is that understood?"

Borim looked evenly at each of his companions.

Lan reluctantly agreed, turning his gaze angrily away.

"It is your order, Borim, and I shall follow it. I don't agree, nor do I like it. You may mark that well."

Borim studied his friend for a moment.

"I mark it, Lan. You have taught me all I know of war and battle, and I thank you. You are a true friend."

"Your brother is playing you for a fool, Borim. He is filling the settlements with those lies of his, and you will lose many to him. You should have exiled him when he first set foot in An Ran Bar."

"It would have done no good, Lan. He would have followed us, and it would have come to this no matter what we had done."

Hollen's voice sounded older than Borim had ever heard it. The old bear's muzzle was wrinkled with a frown made up of many turnings.

"This is what Bern was to do, his part to play, and it's here. There is no one of us who could have changed it."

"I could have," growled Lan. "But there seemed to be no end of sympathy for the traitor. Now look at him."

"Hollen is right, Lan. There was no way anyone could have denied Bern his moment of glory," agreed Nob. "I've seen something like this coming for a long while, but I just didn't know how it was to play out."

A wave of cheers had broken out across the river, and some of the bears from An Ran Bar were raising their paws in salute to the small figure of Bern, who was standing on a fallen tree trunk to make himself appear larger.

And there was still the ominous leaden feeling of the beasts, lingering just out of sight.

Some of the animals from nearby moved to the water's edge and started across toward Bern.

"Where do you think you're going in those boats?" snapped Nob, who raised himself on his hindlegs and stormed forward, scattering the group that had started for the green skiffs.

They left the shore and swam through the fast-flowing river, never once turning back.

"It looks as if Ellin is having his own problems," said Frael. "There are quite a few dwarfs there, too."

"It's good we've gotten our needs seen to," said Hollen. "If Bern had come back much sooner, it would have put us in a real stew."

"We have the dwarf coats and our new weapons, though. We shall have to start using them on our own folk if we don't get the road beneath us. Bern is going to have to deal with you, Borim, sooner or later."

Nob began to see to his skiff as he spoke, and soon had stowed it neatly aboard his green and yellow boat.

"We shall have to look to it quickly, Borim. They won't be staying over there long, and Bern may call those new friends of his back on us at any time."

"There must be something else behind this," murmured Borim. "I can't believe that Bern would be able to overcome those things on his own. I feel some other paw than his guiding this whole affair."

"It's the Dark One, no doubt. They've found a new way to disrupt us, by splitting us apart. And all those fellows over there never really wanted to leave An Ran Bar, so it's easy enough to convince them they're going back. I don't know what he's promising the dwarfs, but it looks as though Bern and his new friends have found some hold over them. There's a good part of Ellin's party there now."

Bern, standing on the trunk of a fallen tree, paced back and forth, casting dark glances every now and again at Borim, and continued his speech to his new followers. The dwarfs of Ellin's party who stood before him had gone to the front of the crowd, and now and again cheered loudly and threw their bright-colored forest caps into the air.

"What has he said that has them at that pitch?" asked Earling, who was helping Nob shake out the sails and lay the sheets on deck.

"I think he just told them that they will have their old homes in the Northerlands again."

Nob stopped, looking over the bow rail at the gathering across the river.

"That would set them at it," he mused aloud. "Ellin has told me of the old delvings that were there, away in the farthest part of the snowfields. Only it wasn't snowfields then. They were evidently there from the First Turning, and I guess his kind put a powerful lot of stock in things like that."

"Like An Ran Bar," said Lan quietly. "I can see that."

"These delvings go back to the beginning, or so Ellin told me. Co'in and Eo'in had read the old books, and tried to make their new homes just like those their sires had been driven out of long before."

"What made them leave?" asked Earling.

"The same things that have made us leave our own settlements here," snorted Nob. "First a beast or two, then a dozen, then a hundred, and the next thing you know, you have everyone at it, tooth and nail, and soon the only thing left is to try to find someplace to rest and lick your wounds."

"I'm for that," agreed Hollen. "If we could only find that place soon, my traveling days would soon be over."

"Those places don't exist, my friend," said Nob, smiling oddly. "I thought, in the old days, that you could do that. I tried coming up here on these wild borders, thinking that no one would bother us here."

He laughed, but without humor.

"They didn't for a long time. Then it started all over again, first a beast, then another, then it all was around full circle."

Nob had slipped his mooring line, and let the sleek boat slide out into the current. He guided her deftly between a ledge of rocks, and steered her into the middle of the fast water. Behind him, the other boats, filled with the rest of the settlements that had chosen to stay with Borim, followed along single file, their colored sails beginning to fill.

Borim looked back over his shoulder, his mind running wild. The red, blue, and green sails bloomed on the clear face of the Eagle Claw, and the stout hulls of the swift boats cut through the water easily, driving on away from his brother, and on toward the sea.

He had not tried to confront Bern, and the thought that he would one day have to do so awakened a pain deep inside him that felt as though it were the ending of everything; and there was much more at stake now to think of, he felt, and the Horn of Bruinthor seemed to fill him with the desire to go on to the Roaring, where something else awaited him, something that was more important than any of the animals gathered together on the swift river that flowed on to the sea.

He found Nob and Hollen standing beside him.

"Did you see where Ellin went?" he asked, thinking of the dwarf again.

"I'm sure he's taken to the wood. No one knows this end of the world as well as Ellin and his band."

"What do you think Bern will do next? Go to An Ran Bar?"

"That may have been his plan all along, my friend. Kahn had had that on his mind all his life, and so his cub perhaps carries on the dream."

"But it's only a settlement," protested Borim.

"Only that," agreed Frael. "But Kahn had some mistaken notion that it was An Ran Bar that made Dralin what he was, and the reason that he carried the Horn. He had the two confused, I think. He never did understand that the physical settlement had nothing to do with the way you felt inside."

"Then what about those animals who have stayed with Bern? They came from An Ran Bar."

"And they want to go back. It is the only safety they have, they think. They belong there, it seems, for they cannot exist without those walls. They cannot allow themselves to be free."

"But I loved An Ran Bar, too! Only now I won't fight Bern for it. He'll be going back, and taking those louts that he's met with him, no doubt."

"I would imagine the Darkness has good reason to want An Ran Bar. It's a great victory for them, and it's located in a good place that is easily defended, and close to the lower plains, where they have been unable to reach before. An Ran Bar will be a new foothold into fresh territory, or I'll miss my guess. And the Dark One can boast of driving the Elder of Bruinthor from his ancient hall."

Nob's attention was taken completely by a tricky passage past a stretch of rapids, and he steered carefully for a few moments, his eyes to the sail and to the frothing water in front of him. Coming out into smoother sailing beyond, he went on.

"I don't think Bern is going to attack us outright, but I could be wrong. He has fellows who follow the Darkness now. They have other ways of attacking, by using that fear that gnaws at your mind. It is a powerful weapon to have, just as are the weapons that Ellin has made us. The fear will take away all desire to resist, and the snakes use it very well. And now the way is open to go beyond the old borders, and into new areas. Bern will be needed for a while, and kept, I would guess. And there is still you to contend with, Borim. You seem to be the most lethal threat to the Dark One now. Two times your Horn has spelled the end of the snakes, these new flying horrors that have come from the depths of the frozen wilderness to haunt the rest of the world. They know it will take a clever war to destroy you and the Horn of Bruinthor. They feel they have won the first battle, though, in having lured Bern to their side."

"Had you suspected all along?" Hollen asked. "I mean about this business? Being up here where you were surely was no accident, and being close by when we needed you."

The grizzled giant laughed.

"You have been around a few turnings, Hollen, and it's hard to fool you."

He chuckled to himself, then went on, now glancing carefully ahead, where the Eagle Claw rounded a long, sweeping bend and broadened.

"No, it was no accident that the old outlaw Nob was up in your neck of the wood. Dralin had come to see me some time ago, and we had a long while together. That's when the picture began to fall into place. He could see more to the whole affair than Kahn merely trying to take An Ran Bar from him, and knew it must have something to do with the Horn. Dralin spent many a long night up with me, trying to find more clues as to why the Horn would be so important to Kahn. We must have looked into a thousand nooks and crannies of thought, but it always came back to the fact that the Horn was dangerous to someone who was behind Kahn, and even though Dralin never sounded it except those few times, he knew that it was coming to pass that his cub would take it, and that that was the real reason for his holding it all those turnings."

"Hollen told me you're one of the Old Ones, Nob. I know that's true now."

"Hollen talks a lot of nonsense sometimes, Borim. What would he know of Old Ones?"

"He'd know plenty, and more than just about graymuzzles or tired paws," replied Hollen. "You may pass it off if you want, but the time has come that it doesn't matter who knows, Nob. We're all bound for the Roaring now, and no one is in any danger of telling someone they shouldn't. And it all seems to be pretty cut and dried, with Bern sided with our friends on the other side of the Shadow."

"What else have you told him?"

"Nothing," said the old bear. "I thought I'd talked enough already. I'm ready to do some listening myself now. High time, too, in my way of thinking."

Boomer and Tolly were at Borim's side, staring aghast at the great figure of Nob.

"You mean you took us sailing, and everything, and we didn't even know?" Boomer asked, his eyes wide.

"Of course, my little friends. That title does not make me uncaring about two chaps who like my boat and want to sail on my river."

Tolly was speechless, and kept swallowing great gulps of

air, trying to begin a sentence but unable to get any sound out but tiny squeaks.

"There's nothing so upsetting in all this," laughed Nob easily. "I've just been here a bit longer than most folk, and have a job to do, just like everyone. As soon as it's over, I'm turning in my chores for a nice quiet stretch of water beyond all this business, where I can get a little reading done, and maybe some fishing."

"Exactly my thoughts on the matter," agreed Hollen, with a laugh. "And it won't take much to convince me."

"We may still have a way to go before that," cried Earling. "There's something coming up behind us."

"Quickly, Borim, get ready! We may have need of Bruinthor's voice!"

Nob had run the boat in close to an eddy on the right side of the river, and readied an anchor. The companions watched the other boats following along in line, and one by one, they filed into the small cove Nob had found.

"Do you see it?" asked Borim, turning to address Earling.

"I can't see it," said Earling, "but I can feel it, right enough. It's almost enough to choke me."

"I can feel it, too," stuttered Boomer. "And it's getting stronger."

"The Horn, Borim," said Nob quietly, but there was urgency in his tone.

Borim unslung the Horn, and for the first time he noticed that it was glowing again, and turning a pale, fiery white. His paw shook as he put it to his lips, and a great desire swept over him to drop the Horn over the side of the boat into the deep channel of the Eagle Claw. There were the voices again, this time much more forcefully, and Bern's voice was plain and clear now, and speaking directly to him.

"You must give up this useless struggle, Borim. You can see how easily it is done for me to catch up with you. There's no escape, no hope of winning. All I want is the Horn, then you shall be free."

A fainter sound began, like the burring of crickets at dusk, and the voice went on, more compelling in its powerful sway.

"It's over, Borim. You are done! Nob is going to turn you over the side when he gets you to the Roaring, and take the Horn for himself. I am your friend. I'm trying to save you."

For a wild minute, Borim stared at the grizzled figure of Nob.

"No," he said at last. "I can't do it, Bern. You'll have to

244

wait awhile before we meet. You have An Ran Bar. That is enough."

Borim had spoken aloud, and it seemed to break the spell that had fallen over the companions. A terrific crackling noise broke over the late afternoon, and a roar of thunder struck in swift claps, one after another, and the sky filled with dark shadows that turned and writhed against the setting sun, causing the light to dim and fade.

"What is it?" cried Tolly, holding on to Boomer's paw.

"Bern, and his friends," answered Nob, his tone undisturbed.

"Are the snakes coming back?" asked Boomer.

"No, my little friend. Bern won't send them now. Borim would drive them off, too, and he doesn't have so many to spare. These are the old-fashioned beasts we have been dealing with all along. Look!"

Nob pointed to the shore, which was lined with the beast soldiers.

"What'll we do now? How will we get away?" asked Tolly, somewhat reassured by the absence of the snakes, but still glancing uneasily at the horizon, expecting to see the terrible, dark forms come winging at them at any moment.

"We will continue on with our task, my good fellow, and go on about this voyage we have to make."

And so saying, Nob steered his sleek boat once more into the swift currents of the Eagle Claw, which ran on beyond the wood and into the sea.

The others followed, and soon they were beyond the range of the beast soldiers that ran along the shoreline shouting and loosing arrows that hissed and whirred and fell harmlessly into the river behind their boats.

"We'll have to hurry," said Hollen. "They are growing stronger."

"The Purge gains power from all the rest that are won over," said Nob. "There are many new converts today, so there is all that much more strength to be turned against us."

"Do you know anything more about the Darkness, Nob?" asked Borim, shaking his mind free of the cloudy webs that threatened to choke him into submission.

"Only that it is a power from the old days, Borim, that has been around since the first. There are stories about those days, of the Great Lord, and his court, and the Renegade who would be as powerful as the One. Hollen could read you tales of that, but I'll say it simply. It's a power that's come from the

245

old days, and this Purge, or so it is named, won't stop at anything. We'd best be looking to our errand as quickly as we're able, for it may prove to be a long and weary struggle before this new dawn of the beast is over."

"What are we going to do?" asked Boomer, phrasing the question that was on everyone's mind.

"We're going across the Roaring," said Nob. "To find a dwarf."

"What for?" blurted Lan. "We've gotten what we needed from them already. We should be able to take on those flying louts now."

"We have an appointment with a certain dwarf across the Roaring, Lan. He is to form the balance that will perhaps enable us to battle the Dark One."

"What's wrong with attacking and not waiting?" persisted Lan.

"The thing that's wrong with that is that Borim might be unable to resist the next attack the Purge will make. They haven't been able to win by force, so they will resort to more subtle tricks."

"I don't believe it," snorted Earling. "What trick could those louts have that would force Borim to do anything like surrender?"

"They could offer Borim something he might want, that he is not even aware of," answered Nob, looking directly at the young Elder, piercing him with a gaze that turned Borim cold to the bone.

"Is that what comes next?" he managed at last.

"Yes," replied Nob.

Hollen looked stricken, and placed a gentle pat on Borim's paw.

Glowering fiercely, Lan swore a dark oath.

"I've always spoken my mind, Borim, and now is no different. I'd almost say give this Dark One the Horn if that would mean an end to it, but it wouldn't; so I'm staying by you, no matter, in case you start to weaken and give in."

"Lan is full of all sorts of threats," said Earling. "But I feel I must join with him in this. We can't let the Horn fall into the hands of the Darkness."

"There's no need to worry," replied Borim.

"Not yet, at any rate," corrected Nob. "But we'll cross that river when we get to it. Meanwhile, we have to reach the sea, and our meeting with the dwarf who will bring us news of the others. They were said to have once made chains that contained the old beasts, far below the earth, where they could harm no one."

Borim, deep in thought, was staring away at the river far ahead, where the water had widened into a flat mirror of light, reflecting the failing afternoon sun. He was thinking of the choice he would be faced with should the Dark One offer him Bern in exchange for the ancient Horn. He tried to reassure his friends that there was no doubt in his decision never to release the Horn of Bruinthor to anyone but the next heir in line, when the time came, but there was a dark sliver of doubt somewhere down inside his secret being, and he could not say why, but he was afraid of that part of himself which he knew was capable of betraying the Horn.

Hoping against hope, Borim turned all his thoughts to escaping beyond the reach of this Darkness called the Purge, and he turned to Nob almost desperately.

"How long before we reach the sea?" he asked.

"With this tide flooding the way it is, we could be there by moonrise tonight."

"And to cross the Roaring?"

Nob laughed suddenly.

"That might be a long while. It depends on who is on this side to keep us from sailing."

Borim frowned.

"Are there beasts there, where we're going?"

"Not to my knowledge, Borim; but there are friends of a sort that never like it when anyone takes their leave. We'll see how that goes when we get there."

Borim's attention was drawn away from his own problems when he saw a tall, black pillar of smoke drifting upward in the distance, then another, somewhere off to the left of the first.

"What is it?" cried Tolly, who'd spotted it at the same time.

"Far Reach," grunted Nob, squinting hard. "Far Reach, and the boats that Nob had left for the voyage across the Roaring!"

The huge bear clapped a paw to his tiller, and steered farther out into the strong current of the Eagle Claw, which was hurrying along at a rapid pace toward the unseen sea.

Hollen questioned Nob further, but got only grunts or nods for replies, and finally gave up and joined Borim and the others at the rail of the boat, staring away at the ribbons of

247

smoke on the distant horizon, and counting new ones that curled upward every few moments.

The clouds in the distance were as dark as Nob's brow as he scowled grimly in the direction of the fires. No one could see what was aflame, but the news, no matter what, promised no good, and the friends' thoughts grew gloomier with the oncoming night, which had already settled in over the Sea of Roaring and rushed to close over them, like the deep shadows in the clear water of the river, flowing over the shallow banks and finally turning an inky black that stole all the light.

Not long after sunset, they reached the first of the burning settlements, a small fishing village that now lay smoking and empty. Nob's party landed quickly and spread out through the smoldering ruins, searching for any survivors, or any signs of those who had set the fires.

"Was it the snakes?" asked Lan.

"The snakes and their regular friends," growled Nob angrily. "They have beaten us to the boats. There were a dozen boats here, but they are gone now."

"Look!" said Boomer, pointing along the shoreline to another blaze.

"More boats gone," replied Nob, without being asked. "They have struck a hard blow here."

"Are your boats safe, Nob?" asked Earling.

"Nob's boats won't carry those louts," shot the grizzled bear. "That's a promise that old Nob can make in good faith."

As the friends stood by the sea awaiting the return of the scouting party, Tolly suddenly cried out and began pointing wildly toward the landing where their own craft rode at anchor. There at the shore was Bern, flanked on both sides by the terrible forms of the winged snakes.

The shock was so complete that none of Borim's company even drew a bow for a moment; then there were the warning cries and signal horns that split the air with dreadful urgency.

"No, little brother! Hold them back! Let me speak!" called Bern, his voice crackling with controlled malice. "You are the Elder here, so you make the choice."

A heavy, leaden pall slowly crept over the gathered company as the terrible spell of the dragons began to be felt. The air became hard to breathe, and their eyes drooped, and the limbs of those there were like dead weights at their sides.

Nob answered before Borim could reply.

"You have wasted your time here, Bern. The lines are

drawn. You have nothing of interest to say to us. Look to your defense."

"Don't I? Come, little brother. Come with us. We shall rule An Ran Bar together, you and I. Dralin and Kahn are gone. It shall be you and I. Our forces will be invincible. No one can overcome the Purge."

With this, the two winged snakes belched green fire that threatened to engulf all there.

From the back of the assembled group by the boats, there were calls of "Bern," and some others began to filter over toward the dragons.

"Get back!" warned Nob, raised into his fighting stance.

"Come along, Borim," urged Bern smoothly. "Come along now, and I shall spare the lives of these traitors who have tried to lure you to your death. They want the Horn, Borim. They shall rule with it, once they have you out of the way. Can't you see that?"

Borim had been startled badly by the appearance of his brother, and his confusion grew as Bern went on in a soft, smooth voice. Nob reached out to touch him, but the young Elder felt himself drawn toward his half brother, almost as though something moved him against his own will to resist. He saw the eyes of the dragons smoldering gray and red as he neared, and he felt their steel minds clamping over his consciousness like unbending, cold stone.

"These traitors that are with you will take the Horn and slay you, Borim. We are here to take you with us. Our true friend awaits us!"

Bern's voice was edged with a hint of menace, and his muzzle was tightened into a smiling mask.

A strange, gentle shudder pulsed through the Horn of Bruinthor, and Borim felt himself going nearer the winged snakes, lurching in his gait as though he had been dealt a blow to his head.

"Wait!" cried Tolly and Boomer together. "Come back!"

Nob had at first moved forward to cut Borim off, but he slowly came to a halt behind Lan and Hollen, and watched the young Elder go.

"Do something!" hissed Lan, who was prepared to attack, but Nob held him in check with a look that froze him to the spot.

"There is nothing more any of us can do for him now," said the grizzled bear, his gaze following Borim's every move.

Hollen and Earling were the nearest to the young Elder, but he moved past them as if in a daze, and went on toward the terrible dark forms that stood beside Bern. As Borim walked, a tower of white flame erupted before his vision, but he could not tell for a moment if it was real or imagined; a small note of warning began to emit from the Horn, and it grew hotter to the touch.

As Borim drew next to the first of the dragons, it began to quiver and froth at its long snout, and a roll of thunder sounded over the gathering; the winged snake belched forth another cloud of smothering green fire that leapt and burned dangerously all around Borim, but the flames could not reach past the white, shimmering circle that surrounded the young Elder.

Boomer and Tolly darted forward, but were sent reeling by the blast of shrieking wind that came from the dragon's mouth.

"Come forward, Borim. Surrender to your new master! Give up the Horn of Bruinthor to its rightful owner."

Bern's voice had grown stronger, and the dragons reared up to loose another smoking blast of green fire.

Dazed and staggering as if struck by blows, Borim pitched forward and lay sprawled in front of Bern. A chorus of moans rose from the company behind him, and Nob's dark eyes flashed wildly, but he held himself and the others in check.

The Horn of Bruinthor was barely a few paces away from the grasp of Bern, and he reached forward eagerly to take it; as he bent forward, a wild howl of victory escaped him, racking his small frame, and he raised himself into a short dance above his fallen brother.

"It is I, Bern, the cub of Kahn, who has won, just as was promised. All you traitors shall pay now for your deceit and treachery!"

His eyes rolled madly in his head, and he danced about the prone form of Borim, who seemed to be stunned by the dragons and held locked by their terrible spell.

"Get up, Borim!" cried Lan, gnashing his teeth and leaping forward, his voice anguished.

Earling had fitted an arrow to the dwarf bow they had been given, but before he could loose it, a fierce blast of green fire surrounded him, setting the shaft afire and singeing the fur off his paws.

"Slay them!" shrieked Bern, bending forward to retrieve the Horn from his senseless brother.

As he touched the small object in Borim's paw, a white-hot sheet of flame flared up, engulfing the two in a river of golden fire that rose higher and higher into the darkness, turning the night into brightest day; Bern tried to withdraw, but was unable to move, and the two winged snakes shrieked and bleated in agony as they struggled to escape the scalding flames of the white river of light.

The Horn called out a long, high note that caused the animals there to cover their ears and whine, but the ugly forms of the two dragons began to vanish into the white flames that surrounded them, until they gave one last long howl of terror and vanished from sight, leaving two smoking holes in the earth where they had been.

Nob was the first to move when the sound and the river of white fire had flowed back into the mouth of the Horn of Bruinthor, leaving the two brothers in a tumbled heap beside each other.

"Hollen! Quickly! Help me!" he cried, pulling the limp body of Borim away from where the dragons had been.

The air was still foul with their stench, and a lingering fear clung to the gathering, even though the snakes themselves were nowhere to be seen. Hollen slapped at Borim's muzzle, and tried to listen to see if the young Elder still breathed.

"He's alive," snapped Nob. "He's lucky to be still among us, after that."

Lan rolled Bern over and put his ear close to the small bear's chest.

"I think Bern is through. Whatever happened, the Horn finished him."

Nob sat down heavily beside the still form of Bern.

"It is played out as it had to be. We could not have gone on without this ending. Borim had to face himself before we could cross the Roaring. It seems this poor soul filled the role of the traitor in all of us."

Hollen shook his head sadly.

"We must bury him before we go on. It is a terrible thing, but nothing more can be done now."

"Let's do it quickly and go on. We have to reach my boats before the beasts do. I don't think they will be so ready to fight now that the snakes are gone, but it is good timing for us to leave."

As he spoke, Nob directed the gathered animals in lifting the unconscious form of Borim and carrying him to the waiting skiff. Boomer and Tolly followed along on each side of their friend, each holding tight to one of Borim's paws.

Nob had carefully placed the Horn securely on Borim's great chest, where it rested, small and quiet.

"Take Bern away from here," said Nob. "We shall give him to the Sea of Roaring. I couldn't leave him here where the snakes have been."

Another party picked Bern up gently and carried him away beside his brother, and they loaded him on Earling's skiff; with no more to keep them, they cast off once more for the boats that Nob's band had concealed along the coast of the Roaring.

At a place the grizzled giant chose, the lifeless body of Bern was returned to the sea; his brother was unaware of his passing, and still lay in a deep, death-like sleep as the bright yellow boat with the blood-red sails bore on toward its destination. The ocean's calm face was unchanged by the funeral of Bern, but the hearts of those left behind were saddened and heavy.

When Borim opened his eyes for the first time, blinking in the bright sunlight, the two small beavers were still beside him.

"Well, there's a nap, if you have to know one," said Tolly lightly. "Wouldn't you know he'd pick a time to miss all the excitement."

Borim stared about blankly, then reached a frantic paw to touch the Horn, which hung safely at his side.

Nob and Hollen were there then, sitting beside him comfortably, and offering him a mug of spiced tea, which he eagerly took and finished in a swallow. The steady eyes of Nob rested on his, and the two sat silently for a long while, until Hollen finally broke in to ask if Borim wanted more tea.

"No, thank you, Hollen."

"You've had a good rest," said Nob. "There isn't any more to it than that."

"Bern?" was all Borim could manage.

"You tried, my young friend. I saw you try to bring him back to the light. He couldn't let go of his dream of power. And the Darkness had him in too strong a hold."

"I thought perhaps I might have saved him. I thought if he could touch the Horn it would bring him back to us."

"It did, in a way," said Hollen. "You may not see it now, but that is all that happened."

"And the white fire that came out of the Horn burned up

the winged snakes," put in Tolly, bubbling with excitement. "There wasn't anything left there but two black spots on the ground."

Borim shook his head.

"I didn't mean to harm him."

"We know you didn't," said Hollen gently.

"I was going to," confessed Earling. "But the snake burned the dwarf bow out of my paw."

Borim looked evenly at his friend.

"I'm glad it was not you."

"It was no one, Borim. You did everything you could have done. This was something no one could have altered. Bern made his own choice long ago."

"I know, but I hate it all the same."

The young Elder looked away over the blue, calm sea, and was silent for a time. None of the others dared to speak again, but Boomer and Tolly stayed beside Borim, each one clutching a paw tightly. They watched as the gray shroud of death and sadness played out in the young bear's eyes, ending and beginning; then toward sunset he slept again.

A day and night passed with a fair wind behind them, and they neared the place on the coast of the Roaring where Nob said his boats were waiting, along with the rest of his band. They were met on the evening of the third day by a large fleet of dark red sails that dotted the blue water like bright-colored bugs skating across a pond.

Borim had been quiet and reserved the whole time, despite the funny stories the beavers regaled him with and the constant attention of Nob and Hollen and Lan and Earling. He spent whole hours gazing away in the direction of the setting sun, but spoke only in grunts or nods.

His spirits lifted, however, as he saw the fleet put out toward them; Nob smiled beside him.

"It was one of this lot that took Dralin across, Borim. I wasn't to tell you that until later, but I think it will be forgiven me if I say so now. An old outlaw like me is always opening his mouth at the wrong time, anyway. It's almost expected of me."

Boomer looked relieved.

"I'm glad you spoke up. I've been hard put to keep silent all this time. It was almost more than a simple animal could bear."

At which point, he blushed heavily about his whiskers and shuffled his paws nervously.

253

"You mean my father is alive?" asked Borim.

"And well," added Nob. "Bramweld and Kahn are in their old wood to finish out their time. They have yet more to do there."

"Will I see Dralin?" asked Borim, cheering a bit at the thought that perhaps he would be rid of the terrible weight of the Horn.

"In due course, my young friend. There will be a place for all that."

Nob would say nothing more, but his eyes smiled mysteriously, and his brow lightened.

There was no more time to talk then, for the first of the boats from shore had met them; there was much exchanging of news and a great coming and going among old comrades in the different boats, and even Borim was caught up in the excitement of the moment; it was long after sunset had turned into full night that they watched the horizon grow reddish orange, ablaze with fires that stretched for a long way across the dark strip of land in the distance where Nob said his boats had just come from.

"It was a close thing! They barely got out in time."

Borim, his paw wrapped tightly around the Horn, thought of all the events that had occurred since that faraway day he left on his journey to cross the mountains to find his father, and he nodded to the grizzled giant who had dwelled so long on the borders.

"It seems we all got out just in time."

He, too, had left behind all his cubhood dreams, which were gone now, as was Bern; the Purge would be still battling to take An Ran Bar, yet Nob spoke of the dwarf from across the Roaring who would be with them soon, and they would free the Lower Wood of the terror of the flying snakes and all the other dark things that haunted the lives of those who dwelled there.

Borim sadly turned his thoughts away from his brother; the Sea of Roaring waited to be crossed, and there was the dwarf to find. There would be a time, he repeated to himself, for all things to come to the perfect peace he had glimpsed as a cub in Alena's cave, and heard in the stories Nob and Hollen told of the First Turning.

And knowing that deep within himself, he turned to face the fallen night with a quiet heart that was no longer full of the dark fear that had lingered there so long. That, he thought, was the first battle of the beast won, the pushing aside of the terrible black darkness that devoured the hopes and dreams of all it encountered.

He raised the Horn of Bruinthor to his lips and blew a long, sad, jubilant call, which winged forward in golden echoes and spun wildly above the deep memory of the sea and sky, lifting up the hearts of all who heard it, and filling them with the strength they would need in the long struggle ahead.